MIMADAMOS
The Eden of Choice

CHADI B. GHAITH

This is a work of fiction. Names, characters, businesses, places, and events are either the products of the author's imagination or are used in a fictitious manner. Any actual resemblance to actual persons, living or dead, or actual events is purely coincidental.

Mimadamos

For more information, please contact:
Chadi B. Ghaith
4283 Express Lane,
Suite 053-690
Sarasota, FL 34249

Cover image by:
Publishing History
First Edition, 2015

ISBN: 978-1-54395-933-8

Library of Congress Control Number: 2017942528

10 9 8 7 6 5 4 3 2 1   070117

I dedicate this novel to my father, who ignited my passion for Gnosis in early childhood; to my divinely endowed wife, Taghrid, who has lit my soul in countless ways, has always been there for me, even in the toughest moments, and often saves me from myself; and finally, to my daughters Nour and Salam and my son Einarr. You are my three precious angels.

AUTHOR'S NOTE

Oh, how we needed the sun to light our Destiny! How we needed the cycles to drive our Choice! And we would martyr ourselves to fuel the hour, not realizing we could overturn the clock by simply shining here and now.

Life is death in slow motion, and death is life fast-forwarded. What we call "real" is, in actuality, more like a reel spinning, a story projected onto the movie screen of this earthly plane. Spirit and matter are not enemies, as religious and scientific traditions would like you to believe. Matter is spirit solidified to let you dream yourself real, and spirit is matter liquidized to save you from the reel of your own dream. They are married for all eternity. That marriage was made flesh in the first man, Adam.

The beings in this egoistical world assume that "holiness" is greater than all else, and we seek its greatness beyond the Adamic threshold in the name of spirituality. We build huge, holy temples and monuments to depict Adam as small and insignificant in God's eye. We conduct wars to belittle and demean Adam, mocking him as a frail, mortal mold who conceded his power to the devil. But he is so much more than that. He is the marriage of flesh and spirit, the point—the *atom*—at which heaven and Earth converge.

Adam is like the sun, a reference point in a universe with no top or bottom, no physical end. He makes sides and directions possible. He is the miracle of the Finite born from the womb of the Infinite—the miracle of the Definite born from the Indefinite.

Humans can journey from the sun searching for greatness, but without its light, they will be left with no way to measure it. This greatness is within their reach if they don't trade what they know for what they don't know in the name of God and a promised paradise—if they don't exhaust their definite nows for indefinite tomorrows.

CHAPTER 1

ON HER WEDDING DAY, THE LADY DESTINY SAT
resplendent in her red gown and towering tantour, its flowing veil obscuring the glint emanating from the slit of her eyes and the fire within.

It was just as well, she thought, that no one—especially not the groom, still scheduled to arrive—could catch a glimpse of those eyes. If her mother and her sisters, who knew her best, had caught a flash of the need in her veiled look, they would have put it down to her need for orderliness. Destiny needed for everything to be just so at all times, perhaps even more so on this, her wedding day.

Yes, the tantour that perched regally on her head and towered higher than the horns of the mightiest beasts in the land had served her well. It would continue to do so when she walked out with the groom after the ceremony. This last requirement had been revealed to her only minutes before, as she took her seat upon the silver throne. The throne had been specially designed to match the silver of the tantour—her untrue unicorn horn.

Her groom, Fate, would soon arrive, followed all the way from Demire by his own serpentine procession. His appearance would mark the end of week-long festivities and the beginning of her new life far from the only home she had ever known.

Surely Fate and his entourage must be close by now, she thought, *no matter how circuitous their route*. Her friends had already presented her with the lengthy silver chain of cloves that started the wedding ceremony.

She had responded by attaching flowers, each of which held a silver coin. She would carry these living gifts on the journey to her new home and later attach them to the latticed gilded entrance grille of the sprawling castle in which Fate dwelled.

Everything appeared as it should be; indeed, it was the envy of every young bride. So why then was something niggling Destiny's mind? Why did a voice tell her that this was not what she wanted? And if indeed it was not, what did that say about her true intentions for her marriage?

She had all the power in the world—could turn sand into gold if she so desired—but she had refrained from using it. What was the point of using magic? It was like playing a video game in which one was granted unlimited lives regardless of performance. Instead, Destiny had agreed to play the game of reality with all its inherent rules and unpleasantness.

So, although she had the ability to think herself into any place she liked, she preferred to travel there with sunshine, good food, the company of beloved souls, and unexpected adventures along the way. For it was in the journey, not the destination, that she took the most pleasure.

A person cannot wield unlimited magic, she thought. *If one became all-powerful, one could create his own reality at will, which would make the person his own creator. But no one could stand being both the Creator and the Created in the same world, for that would engender unbearable solitude.*

Just then, the women started to ululate, pulling Destiny from her musings. The truth was, even without their celebratory wailing, she would have known that her groom was nearby; she could sense him.

It's all been preordained, she thought as she steeled herself.

A moment later, she heard his footsteps, confident and without a hint of hesitancy, approaching her silver throne. They were the steps of a warrior, of one who, unlike her, fully embodied his power. She prayed that he could protect her from the darkness that had plagued her throughout her life.

She had startled awake that morning from yet another ghoulish visitation in a dream. This one had used her groom as the villain. Destiny now drew in a deep breath and let it out, forcing herself to relax and push the dream away. This wasn't the first of such nightmares, though she hoped it would be her last. Dhumanos, Archon of all Archons, had haunted her dreams often as far back as she could remember.

Even as a preteen, she would wheedle and beg to avoid sleeping, avoid dreaming. "Mother, can I not stay up with you and Father a little longer?" Young Destiny's voice held the threat of tears.

But her mother would escort her to bed, tuck her in beside her sister, who was already asleep, and say, "Goodnight, Destiny."

As the door closed each night, dimming the light from the hall to a narrow beam, Destiny's heart would flutter a staccato beat. She would clutch the blankets, drawing them up to her ears and nose, and shiver. Eventually the hour grew late, her wide eyes grew heavy, and her sister's regular, slow breathing lulled her into slumber as well.

Her mother's smiling face greeted her dream self, leading her on a path through the garden to the small pond where fish glided beneath the ripples. "See the fish?" her mother said. "Look at the gold one! Do you want to touch it, Destiny?"

A much younger Destiny leaned across the edge of the pond toward the fish. She touched the cool water.

"Do you want to hold the fish?"

The creature swam nearer; Destiny scooped the fish from below with one hand, a trick her father had taught her. She laughed as the fish flopped, mouth gaping, slippery in her pudgy child hands.

"Kill it," Mother said.

Destiny frowned and looked to see whether Mother was serious.

"Squeeze it until it dies in your hands. It has not the rights of life that you and I have. It is just a fish. Don't be stupid, girl."

Destiny shook her head, the fish wiggling free to fall with a *plop* into the pond. As she stared at her mother, the woman's features melted into those of a woman Destiny didn't know. The strange woman sneered at Destiny, her face melting again and growing dark with hair, the teeth elongating and yellowing. The eyes glowed red, and the person grew larger than her father.

Destiny screamed, paralyzed.

Her sister kicked her under the covers, startling her from the nightmare. Destiny's heart raced, her body drenched in sweat.

"Wake up," her sister grumbled, turning over to face the other way.

Of course, it had taken some time before she realized that the star of her recurrent nightmares was Dhumanos, for the leader of the Archons never appeared in his true form but in that of someone she knew and loved. Thus, each dream would begin most benignly with the smiling face of her mother, a sister, or a close friend. Then suddenly, this trusted person would begin spouting an evil thought or encouraging Destiny toward an evil deed. Simply recognizing where the person acted out of character and the script went wrong brought the monsters and the terror into the picture but did not keep the dreams from recurring.

Dhumanos did not stop there but sought to capture Destiny's mind during her waking hours as well. As a young woman, she would imagine scenarios in which she became the hero, fixing and arranging people's lives for them as Dhumanos whispered ideas into her ear.

"You are special, my dear, a supremely talented girl. See that couple over there by the oak tree?" he had asked once. "The two arguing. Look beyond them to the girl standing nearby. See the way she swoons over the man. Now see that man down the road watching them? He has given many beautiful baubles to this woman to curry her favor; he wants to be with her more than her husband does. You could ensure that all four of them are happy. You alone can influence these two to cease their foolish attachment to such a toxic relationship and find fulfillment in others. One word from you can set in motion their rearrangement as elementally as atoms recombining to become a new molecule."

The idea that she could matchmake two new romances appealed to her; she walked closer to them and was about to say something to the couple when she stopped herself. What right had she to disassemble a marriage simply because the couple was having an argument at this moment? Destiny swallowed and pretended to look at the tree as the woman took her husband's hand and walked with him down the street. They did not appear to be angry anymore, laughing and smiling at one another. The girl standing nearby turned her attention to an old woman she was waiting for, who had just arrived. The man who wanted the woman, according to Dhumanos, left in the opposite direction, clearly not heartbroken.

Destiny became so unsure of when the impulse to put her visions in motion was from her natural talent or Dhumanos's suggestion that she suppressed it altogether. Doing so resulted in a crisis of the soul, a constant battle between the divinity of her true nature and the frailties of her human self.

Even now, on her wedding day, his presence and those of his handymen, the Archons, showed in her glazed, fiery eyes. *Please, Lord, let not their evil infiltrate my nuptial ceremony as it has my slumber.* She pinched her hands together so tightly, her nails marked the skin. *But no,* she told herself, releasing the pressure and fussing with her veil. *As Fate's bride, I will be beyond Dhumanos's reach.*

Dhumanos replied to her thoughts by laughing. "Keep telling yourself that you are stepping into a life shaped by only your decisions and those of the man you marry, my dear. We both know better." His goal was to generate and perpetuate the fear that she would somehow engage in the wrongdoing depicted in her dreams. Only finite earthly events could prove God wrong in Infinity—and what better tool than Destiny, who had already shown herself vulnerable in sleep? The fact that she was about to wed Fate only made her a more attractive prize.

Long before the wedding that would change his life and numerous others', Fate had left his birth home at the tender age of fifteen to make his own life in a rocky, mountainous area. He had searched far and wide for a place to live, finally finding the perfect place to build his home under the shade of trees, among caves, and under high rocks beside which sparkling streams flowed. There, he and his able followers set up a permanent base camp and collected the necessary materials to begin construction.

The structure, simple at first, grew into a labyrinth of rooms and courtyards to accommodate the many functions Fate conceived as he went along, for his path was even then strewn with disorder and disarray.

When the construction was finally finished many years later, the home had turned into a castle. Fate's followers spent all their time within its walls, and, as directed by their leader, they ensured that no man or woman would reach the interior unless escorted by one of them. Indeed, the halls were bound with spells to prevent intruders from making progress.

Now, for the first time since settling there, Fate left the mountainous area and traveled to the distant village of Mimadamos, a couple of days' walk using his magic bridge across the Valley of Doubt. There he and Destiny would take their vows, and after the festivities, Destiny would return with him to Demire to begin their new life.

At least, that was the plan.

CHAPTER 2

FINALLY, FATE STOOD BEFORE DESTINY, WHO looked up at her husband-to-be. She appeared timid through the fine gauze of her veil, though timidity was not part of her nature. It was a veil that only someone with her friends' skills could weave, an otherworldly creation with pictures foretold by Destiny herself of a mighty man and a small woman who would unite in marriage but not in discernible bliss. This, too, was known to her subliminally, but she would not openly admit it, even to herself.

There was no time now to dwell on this or anything else, for a large hand was approaching her veil. It grasped the delicate lower border and thrust it aside as one might a tent flap.

And then his direct gaze glittered into her startled look. He was now and would forever be a powerful man with a rare beauty. He had been described as not of the human race. Very few had the courage to look Fate full in the face, for his inner eye would reveal a person's life story all the way until death. So even while those around Fate yearned for his presence as the desert yearns for water, few would dare look him in the eye for fear of learning anything specific.

For most people, these wars took place not on a battlefield but in the mind. That was the case now as he beheld his bride and reached his strong arm toward her. "Give me your hand, righteous maiden," he said, "and step forth so that we may begin our journey together."

He knew about Destiny as he knew about all those who walked the Earth. Now, as he faced her, he also realized that she was a fine lady, one who could withstand his powerful presence. Some of this knowledge he would keep to himself. He would share with her, however, that he found her ability to look him in the eye, unshaken, extremely comforting.

Fate yearned not just for a wife in the traditional sense but a true companion, an "other" who was not him and yet was a perfect match, as best as there could be.

Destiny was that other. Fate was never so sure of this as when he looked at her lovely face and form and knew that, just like his own virile physique, it was merely a costume for this earthly plane. Theirs was a marriage of souls—genderless, timeless, formless. She was part of Fate and eternally so, but she would never be all of him. This he knew, just as he knew he must share much of his own self while holding some back.

"Yes," Fate had said more than once, "sometimes when you lose, you win!"

Was it a match rooted in heavenly math? Perhaps, but it was a love story all the same.

"Shine," Fate whispered softly to her. "Shine, my hero, my woman. Shine as I sleep to keep my seat warm."

As she stood and looked up at her soon-to-be husband, Destiny felt some measure of protection and relief. Fate reflected like a mirror all who encountered him. In Fate's presence, a weak soul or a being who knew not the power of goodness would see more of himself than of Fate. And this, as intriguing as it might be, would call forth a great fear. Fate was naturally sealed and protected by his own powers and the god that had created him. An enemy could approach him only to the extent that he could bear the sight of his own truth, and this was something even Dhumanos could not withstand.

Yes, she thought, *the Archons will be dealt with in the manner of small fry.*

* * *

One of the reasons Destiny had chosen not to walk in her full power was that she feared being isolated from those around her who did not have these abilities. Her husband, Fate, easily bore such seclusion, for he was the portal linking the human world and the Divine—ignored, feared, or despised by the former and beloved by the latter. In promising to be his wife, Destiny would stand beside him on the earthly plane; he had entrusted those powers unto her.

She knew all of this, for she knew Fate in the way she knew about herself. At the same time, it was as if she knew nothing. This was reality, with all its immediacy and malleability. All imaginary security, the fences of thoughts and visions that preceded all events, somehow dissolved in the present moment. No matter how predictive and perceptive those thoughts and visions were designed to be, reality always had a sobering effect. Its gravity would have to be lived, even though it could be foretold. In Fate's reality, everything "to become" was an "already is." There was nothing new under his sun. Yet what had to happen would have to play out. It could not be hurried or slowed; it must simply run its course.

This was the difference between knowing the path and walking the path. The mind could travel times and distances into the past and future, but something about the *now* seemed to force its mathematics no matter what.

Destiny knew this, had always known this. It was one of the reasons she had agreed to live in reality. Still, she knew she had to step slowly—yes, always slowly—or she could trip. How could one escape the laws of physics without blowing minds along the way?

Ever since Fate had entered her reality on a more conscious level, synchronicity had significantly increased in her life. At first, although she knew everything happened with cause, she thought nothing of it. But when it began happening all the time—when everything she wanted or needed, from the sublime to the ridiculous, simply turned up—she had to acknowledge that these "synchronicities" had evolved into magic.

Everything Destiny "knew" now became real, and the need to remain anchored to the ground grew along with that. Even though her mind could defy the laws of physics, it still needed those laws for any experience to hold.

Fate was the instrument of that grounding, simultaneously anchoring her to the Earth and authorizing the use of the powers she had tried for so long to subdue. He was to her like the sun to the moon. Through their union, he validated her innermost identity and the significance of the light she reflected from within. In his warming presence, Destiny's failed ego with its connections to possessions such as land and language, kinship and ties of blood, geography and terrains—whether in the plains or atop a mountain—simply fell away, revealing her genuine gifts.

About one thing Destiny remained uncertain: had Dhumanos and his dreams of evil departed? Had she barred his presence from her soul on this, her wedding day? She fervently hoped so, but if not, she prayed Fate would protect her from her own dark tendencies—the ones unleashed during her childhood.

She knew she would willingly comply with whatever her husband requested. For all her wisdom, Destiny was, left to her own devices, still an actor and a director of such stories. Thus, she believed discipline to be her destiny. She knew what she possessed within her and was keen to see it directed, as it must be, for the good of all rather than to court the darker side of humanity as she had done in the past. How she longed to live in her husband's reality, where everything had already come to such a positive end! Then she could, simply and without guilt, surrender to her true nature.

She so wanted to surrender herself to Fate, to free herself from unnecessary evils and concerns while having someone to turn to. Would she succeed? Would she grow to love him? This question plagued her in all the worldly ways it would any bride.

CHAPTER 3

DHUMANOS WAS NOT THE ONLY ONE CONTINU-
ing to cast his dream scripts of darkness on the vestigial maiden. There
were other lesser—but no less malignant—beings at work, and they
would trail the bridal couple as they journeyed toward their new life.
These beings, the Archons, hailed from the vast stretch of forest known as
the Forget Lands. It was a place of many venomous, magical, and mythical
creatures and plants.

Although the Forget Lands encircled Mimadamos, Destiny's childhood home, she had never explored them directly, with the small excep-
tion of Forget Lake, and her new husband was determined to make sure
it stayed that way. Fate knew that the forest was the jurisdiction of the
Archons; he also knew of his young bride's suffering at their hands. He
would not see her wedding day marred by the knowledge that her tor-
mentors were dwelling a stone's throw from her beloved home. Thus, he
determined that in their travels they would avoid the forest altogether.

While the Archons were certainly the instruments of Destiny's pain,
they were not its architect. That despicable distinction went to their
leader, Dhumanos.

"It is I who am God," Dhumanos was fond of proclaiming. "There is
none apart from me."

When he spoke this blasphemy, he sinned against the entirety. Yet the
Archons believed him, and he became the leader of all that was rotten

and dark and vile. The Archons' weakness came from their lack of spirit, for they were from below, while man and the divinities were from above. Like their master, the Archons stood between humanity and a transcendent god that could be reached only through knowing Fate.

Of course, Fate was aware of this and of the dark scripts the Archons had inflicted on the maiden during her girlhood. It was this evil that he now sought to shield her from.

Their first night passed in the bliss dreamed of by all newlywed couples. As the sun cast its first rays of light upon the new day, the celestial being looked upon the sleeping face of his true companion, marveling how one who was fully his creation and in total surrender to his will had also managed to occupy his attention and interest simultaneously and paradoxically. How could this be in any way other than the fact that Destiny represented the engaging passion and love involved in the power of creation itself?

Now she, too, awoke, slid her feet into jewel-encrusted red slippers, and stood still for a few seconds before following her new husband outside. They were to depart immediately.

Destiny could have swooned as they stepped into the thick of the wedding crowd. At first, there was only the sound of angels vibrating at the heavenly levels with the full-throated power of the creative larynx. Her sisters and friends swayed toward the couple, but Fate held his other arm out to defend their passage. He carved a path through the throng, which saw his heavy tread followed by her light, almost sprightly gait.

And then they were on their own, barring a small retinue. Once outside the city walls, their pace and movement changed. It was almost as though the Earth were making way, folding down under them as Space and Time seemed to collapse and the couple stepped into a dreamlike world.

It was a world that Destiny had wished for, if only because it was so far removed from the horrors she had known. As she and Fate stepped forward in unison, they were silent, contemplating the dark void of the heavens above punctuated by crystal clusters of stars.

As she looked up, Destiny felt a wave of contentment wash over her. She had always imagined herself as one of them. The notion that a star could appear eons after its death mystified but did not concern her, for she saw life and death as one and the same. Most associated her name, Destiny, with the future, but she was much more interested in being the best she could be in the present moment. What better example of that than a star shining brightly in the night sky?

Fate smiled down at his wife, knowing that he had, at least for the moment, successfully protected her from the evil lurking in that stretch of forest known as the Forget Gate. Unbeknownst to her and the rest of the wedding party, Fate had spun magic of his own by building a bridge that would allow them to bypass the Forget Lands altogether as they left Mimadamos. The bridge was created of spirits, spun with a silver thread that would both guide and support the party as they passed. Thus, as she left her homeland and traveled to Demire, Destiny would remain blissfully ignorant of the Forget Lands and the dangers that lurked there.

They continued along the path, with Fate walking alongside his bride and placing himself between her body and the chilly early spring air. Fate listened, enthralled, as Destiny identified the constellations. He knew without a doubt that he could listen to her voice forever. He knew, and she knew too, that Destiny was his soul—the Universal Soul.

There was another observing Destiny with a smile. Indeed, Dhumanos had watched the couple throughout the wedding ceremony—not with his physical eyes, for they had long since gone dark, but with his other senses. He had even "seen" the fierce glint in her eyes that day. Dhumanos thought he knew what it meant, that look. The bride, who appeared so lovely and innocent to the guests, harbored impure thoughts within her breast. And in his dark corner, Dhumanos's lips spread in a menacing grin, for he believed he could continue, despite her marriage, to engage Destiny's soul. Of course, he had not counted on Fate, for to do so would have meant knowing Fate—and in this regard, Dhumanos was truly blind.

He was unaware that Destiny's journey to the distant lands of her husband was exactly as Fate had pictured it and that she now traveled in the protective carapace of total safety. He watched, his smile turning into a frustrated snarl as she proceeded unmolested with Fate and their companions to tread upon the silver bridge of her husband's making.

CHAPTER 4

THERE WAS A STRANGE CALMNESS IN THE FORGET
Lands that night, almost as if the forest had been placed under a trance.
Fate possessed the tools to neutralize evil, and he utilized them fully,
allowing Destiny to overcome Dhumanos's works within her mind. Fate
had hoodwinked Dhumanos, who considered himself to be all-seeing, in
the manner that only Fate could. And so it came to be that the stars from
millions of light years away cast their glimmer and, like all those present
at the recent ceremony, wished them the best.

As dawn approached, Destiny thought she was a little closer to knowing the kind of man she had bound herself to. The closer they came to the
dwelling place of Fate, the more they seemed to be enveloped in a whirl of
chaos. The pole bearers knew not whether it was the tent pole or the colorful fabric of the roof that they were to uproot. It was as though they had
stepped into a forbidden world where all visuals and patterns were cast
in liquid—a place where nothing seemed to conform to a time, pattern, or
mode of operation. Everything seemed to vibrate with a force beyond the
code of their temporal species or identity.

The women waiting to receive them at the castle knew not whether
they should ululate or sing. And the very birds above them were unsure
whether to swoop down onto the hand of the tall figure of the groom
or whether to bear off the entire wedding party from the very carpet on
which they stood.

The only person who strode ahead with assured, vigorous steps, sure of the direction he had to go, was the groom. He walked as though everything around him were simultaneously being created and already relegated to the past in the way a shadow is to the real object that casts it off. He appeared to know where the chaos would ultimately deliver them and straightened out the point from which they had left off.

Destiny and Fate passed sun-filled days and cold nights on the grass and the barren Earth. They traveled across the desert, where they could see the rim of the very edge of the world. And then, when he bade Destiny look upward, she knew they were at the bottom of a hillock.

She looked up, for she thought she might have come into her own view—that her inner dark desires might find fruit there. And then Destiny saw the Astral light.

The Astral light came forth from the sun's nimbus and was drawn to all people and divine figures on Earth. The force of the sun attracted and repelled the enchanting, delightful light.

Fate halted in his long strides to talk to his bride. "The Astral light has two poles," he explained, "one positive and the other negative. The ascending serpent is positive and as eternal as the number eight." He reached for her hand. "We proceed on the ascent."

She smiled, for she was finally beginning to grasp the full import of what he had done for her, and she loved him for it. She paused to view the glint of the dying sun across the ramparts of an ancient castle that seemed embedded inside a steep, rocky mountainside, her eyes welling up at the sheer beauty of it.

The rest of the wedding party also stopped to look, a collective chill running through them as they acclimated to the new, higher vibration and the breathtaking physicality that surrounded them.

The kingdom appeared detached from any time or setting—as if a very ancient, forgotten past was reaching out to shake hands with an advanced, not-yet-encountered future. The mountain that bore the castle was an amalgamation of ageless, calcified, smooth, and slippery rock, granite, and ice, sliced through with what seemed like rapidly moving stairs.

"We call them escalators," Fate explained to his bride as she stared wide-eyed at the gliding steps. "This is my place, where I grew up to withstand the gravity of man's dreams and karmic cycles." He swept an arm toward the castle. "One day in my world is as one thousand years in yours. Here I open my eyes and close them unto a world so dependent on me yet so forgetful of who I am."

Destiny graced him with a smile for his hyperbole, knowing he did not mean Demire literally moved at a different rate from her home in Mimadamos; his perception of the future, seeing eons ahead in human history, was his divine nature.

Fate looked behind him. As though addressing that world, he said, "I know you, even though you know not me and you know not your own selves. You reach out to me like my shadow, like my past, asking for the very substance of life, yet you so elusively imagine yourself to advance away from me into some future. I see you from a place where you can never see me or yourselves. A being who rules the forest out there, built to enshroud Mimadamos in a circle, is lost in his ego, and his followers are destined to be sickened by my beauty, for they imagine me to be too great to be real. They have lost the love they had and what it takes to simply be beyond becoming, for it was not theirs to begin with. Now they envision divinity to be some beast or monster to which they must sacrifice souls and build monuments that extend into the skies like horns attempting to poke the heavenly waters."

Fate paused here a while, still looking behind him; then he turned to face forward. "This is where my wife will live with me and where my son shall be conceived. So rejoice, little bride; rejoice."

As much as she wanted to, Destiny found that her heart would not warm to the sight before her. It was as if the finality of her decision to wed Fate had suddenly hit home. She had been so focused on escaping Dhumanos that she had not realized that she would also be forfeiting Mimadamos forever.

"But I have to go home to my people when I wish!" she exclaimed.

Her husband appeared not to have heard her. He simply looked straight ahead as they stepped onto the escalators and slid up through the rocky passage.

CHAPTER 5

WHEN THEY REACHED THE ENTRANCE OF FATE'S castle, Destiny prepared to affix the flowers handed over by one of the handmaidens who had accompanied her. Each of the flowers had withstood the journey. Indeed, they appeared to have just been plucked from her garden at home. The petals of each were cleverly furled over the silver coin within. Her long, slender arms emerged from her robe to attach a flower to the wooden grille of the front gate, which could be slid downward once the wedding party had entered.

But no! Something was amiss.

The flowers slid out of the hands of the women and attached themselves of their own will to the grille in a most untidy fashion, some spilling the secret within—the silver coin—which clattered unceremoniously onto the wooden drawbridge. Destiny gasped, for she knew that the tumult of her own soul had partly contributed to this great tumult of the flowers, which would not be bound where they should.

She also knew that other factors had further intensified her unrest. A strange sort of organized yet unfathomable chaos would always dwell where her husband did. She felt a certain unease as she imagined following up after such chaos. It would require her to remain engaged in his immediate environment and called for an energy that defied the ordinary rhythm of life. It was like being near the sun and in the burning presence of Helios all the time. Could she live up to such demands? She would have to bid herself to forget about sleep or else be cast into the burning pit.

Adding to her discomfort was the awareness of an emerging way of thinking that she had believed she had long overcome. She couldn't remember the last time she had wondered about what the future held for her or had even been concerned about anything beyond the Now.

Everything about this new place seemed to incite a revolution over anything she knew for certain. As much as she had imagined this would be comforting, something about the physical manifestation of the concept—grandiose as it might have been—wasn't quite so.

It was like nothing was supposed to project any sense of time or order, yet incredibly, it would work in sequence, not unlike a machine, toward a goal that only Fate could see. Ultimately, all was expected to miraculously fall into place.

Now it was Destiny who stood still to look at her husband. Fate, however, appeared not to have noticed this small bit of mayhem as he passed through the castle gate.

Once inside the walls, he raised an arm and his burnished helmet of gold to the scores who stood within. They raised a great cheer for their king and his bride, then led them to a row of tables laden with fish, meat, fruit, and piping hot bread. There were pitchers of cool juice and wine for all to wet their throats and fill their bellies.

The sounds of merriment, of music and laughter and cheering, were so great that Destiny wondered if they could be heard all those miles away in the home she had left behind.

Despite appearances to the contrary, Fate was aware that his path seemed to be strewn with chaos, and he sought to make his wife happy as she settled into her new home. He devoted all his free time to Destiny, showing interest in everything from what they would eat to which corner of the castle library they would sit in when they read together. He consulted her on matters great and small within the kingdom rather than seeking the company and counsel of his subjects. He did everything to make her feel at home in his world and make it her own.

More than anything, Fate wished to make her an equal partner in life for the many years that lay before them, for he knew what was to come, including the child that would be born to them. Once his son arrived, he knew the mathematics would change between them, and a certain Edenic equation would surrender itself to an earthlier one.

At first, Destiny did not miss her homeland much; she was too busy settling into her new role as mistress of Demire. She found her husband to be ever kind, patient, and charming, but more than this, she found him somehow familiar.

It wasn't long before she realized that she had always looked to him for answers, even before they met. He had always been the sun of her reality, protecting her from—and anchoring her to—the physical world. In one way or another, he had always been there. Yet in many ways, she felt as she always had: that the world was not real, not a physical place.

If this is so, she thought, *then where is it? Is it "in" space? Does space even have a boundary to be within—and if it does, what is beyond that boundary? Is it on the left side of the universe or the right? Up or down? Where is it? To dream is one thing, yet to know that the dream is not "real" is another. When one wakes inside a dream, one doesn't feel like he or she has just traveled back across the physical bridge from the dream world. One understands the nature of dreaming, and life continues.*

Destiny didn't know what to make of Fate's reality now that she was so closely encircled by it. She didn't know if she was waking inside a dream to a reality or drifting inside reality to a dream.

She had always avoided seeing the world as a physical reality, for that just complicated everything. Then she would have to move beyond the laws of physics to glimpse any truth. The hard, sharp, physical realm was a manifestation of logical interaction; therefore, she had seen some immensely powerful physical forces manifest. In the mind, such forces were apparent, yet Destiny had always pondered the size of space. How far did it extend? Her mind couldn't stop expanding with the contemplation of it all. Luckily, her mind was not a physical entity or the massive expansion would have been like detonating a mega H-bomb! Yes, the explosion therein would've been mathematically inestimable; one would have just attempted to touch one's infinite aspect with one's finite aspect. Were she to touch the live wire to Earth, she would destroy the entire universe in a massive explosion!

As the days went on, these musings plagued her more and more. Whether she was walking with her husband around the grounds or going over a menu with a servant, she simply could not let it go.

It was not for lack of trying. Each day in a moment alone, she would sit quietly and close her eyes, trying to imagine there was no body. She so yearned to anchor herself back in her own self, where her body was just an extension of the mind—a way to feel and move and interact with the place so it synchronized with her imaginings.

Suddenly, she realized the paradox in what she was doing. She had always yearned for Fate to save her from her own mind, and here she was, inside the Savior's premises, returning to practice what she feared most.

Was it because she was now comfortable, so that if she fell, there would be a cushiony ground to save her?

Fate had always let her "peek" through his eyes gently, and in that, she had seen the existential paradox of the finite and the infinite—the logic and the magic. She accepted magic; she *was* magical! She was authentic and caring, and she *knew* things, but she had no real logical idea why.

It was because of this that she had instinctively and subconsciously avoided stepping into her own power, for if she did, that magic would destroy and expose this world. Everything thought to be real would have to be re-questioned. Logic was what held things apart and made them fathomable. Magic was a force that worked the other way around. Destiny realized that she wanted to keep her magic in check, but she still needed logic to live in a world of so many souls; to consider the alternative—that these souls were her own thoughts incarnated—overwhelmed her.

CHAPTER 6

AND SO IT CAME TO BE THAT, IN THE COURSE OF
Fate's ministrations and their seclusion at nighttime, Destiny found that
she would bring forth his child.

Now the story must take a turn. Fate had shared himself completely,
but what of his wife? As the day of her child's arrival approached, Destiny
felt herself slipping away from her present life in Demire and toward her
past and her homeland, Mimadamos. But why?

She had heard it said that the closer you zoomed into the central reality of an image, the less you could focus on it. It seemed as though she
could understand and embrace Fate much more from the proximity of
her home, Mimadamos, than she could in such immediate proximity. It
was like her human side was constantly clashing with the divine one with
no grey area in which to rest. It was one thing to ponder the sun at night
through the diffused light reflected by the moon and another thing to be
in the blaring presence of it in daytime.

Knowledge in Fate's realm was not about how much information one
could process but about how much information one was willing to *un*process. It was not about how much one knew but about the ability to negate
anything one thought one knew. A person could not fly with iron balls
attached to his ankle. In Fate's world, it was never about what the mirror
of possibility showed but rather about the viewer's ability to focus on the
mirror itself to see how reflective it was or how fit to be trusted.

Even though Fate did not pressure Destiny to be anything other than what she was already, the vibrations of the glittering mountains, atop which stood the glass palace and its people, had projected to her a subtle challenge that defied her history and identity. And, much as she might have liked to, she wasn't quite ready to forget who she was or where she had come from. Her people and her ways were quite distinct from what she now saw around her. How would she begin to explain herself to her husband or see herself in such a reality unless she somehow released a large portion of her earthly memory?

It was like being asked to enter heaven and then answering, "Wait, I forgot something; I'll go get it and come back." The mere fact of still having that something in mind meant that on some level, one was not prepared to be in heaven.

She and Fate could talk to each other about their immediate concerns, but could she describe those uppermost in her mind? Only a chosen few back in Mimadamos, of Destiny's own flesh and blood, knew of her inner-most secrets and fears. Even they trembled at the thought of those dream scripts. Destiny thought of her mother and sisters and longed for someone she could confide in without calculations.

She wondered if she would ever feel so at ease with her husband. He was strong and direct, his path strewn with havoc and tumult. She might have harbored some of that in herself despite their love for each other, but he would have no inkling of it.

He must not be allowed to know, thought Destiny, *not just yet.*

* * *

Fate's direct nature acknowledged only that which was spoken and seen. Being who he was, he had no cause to do otherwise. Everything he thought manifested immediately into a tangible reality. He had no need to denounce scarcity. Rather, he could just envision abundance, and it would be his. Things he did not want, therefore, simply did not exist for him.

He sensed the tumult in his wife's heart regarding his manner of being and how different it was from hers. However, because the knowl-edge would be engulfed in chaos, and he would not allow it to build to a level that would set a given pattern, he remained silent.

✳ ✳ ✳

Most of what troubled Destiny was a sense of guilt accompanied by the thought that she shouldn't feel this alienated in a world she'd assumed would be her destination and final resting place. That raised some doubts about being as special and unique as she'd always thought she was. It also revealed to her a certain egocentrism that she had secretly enjoyed, that feeling of specialness back home. It had been hidden and harnessed, perhaps, but it had been there nonetheless.

But when the burden of an immeasurable guilt threatened to descend upon her, she would escape it by telling herself that she had always been destined for this. In the dream world of their making—hers and her husband's—she could well reject what she had always imagined—or rather what had visited her mind, cast there by Dhumanos and his henchmen. In this abode with her husband, she told herself that she was far from the terror of the dream scripts.

Her visions and imagined unreality had always worked and included her marriage to this powerful being who often struck her as being too divine to be human yet too human to be God (unless God was disguised as a human). She found it difficult to accept Fate as being of this world, as she did not fully accept herself as one. Meanwhile, the fires, which were not of goodness, burned in her seemingly unseen by the outside world and by Fate.

There was, of course, one giveaway, as there had been on her wedding day. At times, her eyes would glint with a fierceness that could not set even her soul at peace. It spoke of the strife in the heavens and on Earth, of the eternal war of good against evil and of the chaste against the unchaste. The war was being acted out within her soul, and there was little she could do except bear it.

She had always known herself and her people to identify power through a certain resistance against actions and behavior. Souls such as herself and her family would taste triumph without having to resort to force and might. She could travel in her mind to the pitfalls of extreme danger and still return to a place of safety, of not needing to touch fire to know that it could burn the flesh and reduce the spirit to ash. To her, harnessing power had always been an attempt to avoid attendant behavior and actions.

The detailed elaboration and thriftiness of Fate's world seemed so different, where every thought was immediately expressed for the better or for the worse without calculation and without having to consider the many factors that could still occur, as Destiny might.

This somehow clashed with the historical side of the soul that was so conditioned to operate under give and take, punishment and reward, debt and insurance—under scarcity. Although a deep part of her was mystified and intrigued by such a dreamlike reality, it was a different paradigm. A sentence kept echoing inside her head, though she couldn't remember whether Fate had uttered it in her dreams or in reality.

"My oasis is green year-round. The more I consume of it, the more it produces. My soul: I give it all the rest in the world, and in return, it gives me all the energy in existence. In my reality, there is no saving or spending; there is no counting."

Destiny was used to ending a problem by working out the means to it, and she could somehow convey the truth about herself in loving and assured measures. When called upon, she would do so with harmony and without the slightest doubt. If her husband was unaware of much of the storm within her heart that beset her even now, she would, she told herself, find a way out.

Unfortunately, that was not how it happened. It happened in a manner that she must have seen with her inner eye, even on that morning when she had set out on the journey to her groom's home, even when she had known she would follow him wherever he led her. It would also happen in a manner that Fate, who could see the life of all beings when he looked into their eyes, could have foreseen. But if he foresaw what lay ahead for him, for his wife, and for his unborn son, it remained deep within the recesses of his subconscious. He would not acknowledge it, as was his custom.

Now Destiny, follower of portents and signs—provided they were reasonable and could be sensibly carried out by herself and those closest to her—informed her husband, "When the time of my birthing is close, it is the custom of my people that the young mother returns to her tribe and to her village for the birth itself. I would like the company of my female relatives at a time such as this, my mother and my sisters. They will provide the comfort I need, see to the safe delivery of our child and advise me well."

Fate was thunderstruck. That his wife would imagine such an undertaking was beyond what he could accept. Perhaps he had heard her wrong. "What on Earth do you mean?" he asked. "Shall I fetch you a trundle bed from your home village? Do you wish it to be carted on the strong shoulders of my brethren to be brought here to the castle from your village far away for the birthing? Shall I fetch your mother here to your side? Do you not know how fiercely I love you and love our unborn child?"

"I do not doubt your dedication, my lord," she said, looking down at her lap. "But I mean I must physically return to the home of my birth and to my family. There is nothing to fear, as I have kept the best of health during the early and middle months of my pregnancy, but now that I have grown heavier with child, I must soon depart. A two-day walk and camping between will take a toll, true, but I am strong. The baby is not due for two months yet."

If she noticed the look of incredulity that crossed his face, she gave no indication. As for Fate, he listened as he always did when his wife spoke, not just with his ears but with his whole being, and he knew now that there was more to the story—and her intentions—than she was letting on.

On the other hand, he knew better than anyone that the world rolled on as it was meant to. And, each in their own way, Fate and Destiny knew that, while she had been impregnated with Fate's seed, it would be this fruit of their union—the child—who would signal their separation.

"I cannot go with you, my love. I have obligations here," he told her slowly.

Destiny raised her chin and met his gaze. "I know. But I am a product of how I was raised, and I will follow tradition. I will go home." She excused herself and left his presence to pack her things.

Fate gazed out the window of his palace at his golden land of Demire. He had misled himself, in a manner, among the blessed roses of spirituality he thought he'd watched bloom on the cross of their significant tie-in. He had considered their union to be the perfect juxtaposition of two beings: one who loved more and another who loved better. Fate had taken upon himself the mantle of he who loved better. For love, he told himself (and wished he had expressed this to his wife) was the best doctrine available to all those who lived, human or ethereal. Did none of this account for their impending separation?

He could not help but think that her decision to leave Demire had something to do with the fury in her eye that he'd glimpsed on their wedding day. After all that had transpired between them, if this darkness was still driving her, there was nothing he could do but release her.

CHAPTER 7

DESTINY SET OUT AT DAWN THE NEXT DAY, accompanied by the one handmaiden who had followed her from her home on the day after the wedding. Fate was inconsolable upon her leaving. It was the sort of linear event he usually was impervious to, but if nothing else, Fate was a man who took his responsibilities staunchly, and his wife was in no condition to tread the path they had taken months ago by herself without his magic to shorten the journey. He would have a strong force of six men—six of the most trustworthy and strong of arm—carry her in a litter on their shoulders. The handmaiden would ride by their side on a white steed.

* * *

As Destiny departed down the rocky mountain in the same manner she had ascended it and made to cross both the barren fields and fertile valleys in scorching heat and through shaded forest, she was aware that this journey would render her a different woman from the one who had followed her husband to Demire.

Fate, in the meantime, would remain very much aware of the descending serpent in her actions to traverse the lands to return to her hometown.

Destiny was not thinking of this as she lay in repose upon the litter, watching the blood-red sun rising in the sky. Beside her, the clip-clop of the hooves of the white horse brought Destiny comfort, first because it carried the maiden accompanying her and second because each step carried them closer to home.

After a time, they paused, but how far they were into the journey Destiny did not know. Fate had let her know that the journey back home would take longer, for they no longer had the advantage of the silver bridge of spirits he had devised, which could only be activated in his immediate physical presence. They could no longer circumvent the forest that surrounded Destiny's hometown. He did not, unfortunately, know how long it might take, given the size of their party, her condition, and a host of other variables. He had wished her luck and kissed her goodbye most sweetly. And if he noticed her dry eyes at their parting, he did not let her know.

Suddenly, it was as though the sky was rent with the blood-red orb that sought to change color as it climbed high into the heavens, a searing blaze before noon. The white horse reared in astonishment, nearly unseating its rider, in recognition of the sun's astral forces. The men gently put down the cradle in which they had been carrying Destiny, then extended their arms toward the powerful one that they could see before them before they went their separate ways.

Destiny would have to return to the real world of human beings. The union of Destiny and Fate had been forecast as being blessed. They had greeted each other as they were intended. What of this goodbye then? It appeared to be purely temporal, and all concerned could only hope for the best.

Meanwhile, the sky cleared as the orb now appeared in a form of flaming, liquid gold.

"The horizontal and the vertical have converged," announced the chief of the carriers among the men who had brought Destiny this far. "It is time we went on our way."

The men bowed their heads in silence for a minute. The white horse could have been a near-celestial being, but it shook its flowing blond mane and pawed the ground in impatience. It was indeed time to move on.

The returning party took up their task and trudged on. The maid of honor, her maid, and the few manservants left to accompany her, with their task to be undertaken looked around them. They would have to assess the new ground to be covered—the ground that lay before them.

When they next stopped, it would be night, and the travelers would erect tents in which to take shelter.

What they could see was the vastness of a desert over which hung the vastness of the sky and the space beyond. The manservants would take up their task unto death if they had to, but as all looked around them, they could see that this space was nothing but eternity brought to vision.

They had their work cut out. All but the women would return at some point to the smooth and craggy rocky mountain of many-faceted precious stone and the castle that had sheltered them all their lives, to the one lord Fate, who had given them protection, but what they were looking at now was space and an eternity in disguise.

The broad curvature of the Earth, visible beyond the dunes, matched the curvature of the outer universe itself. It was where the heavens and the Earth converged. It was a point within which was encoded the very nature of man and woman and celestial beings. It told of the way they looked, and it told of the way of their permanent actions, which, in themselves, wrought other activity and effects not immediately discernible to the naked eye.

The dark forest that Fate had decided to circumvent on the way out could not now be ignored. The litter bearers and their lady, Destiny, no longer had the silver bridge to avoid the ground's realities; the magical bridge appeared only for its master, Fate. Now the forest they had to cross on their way back was dark and scary to its fullest. It seemed that there was, in their present passage, no middle ground between the heavenly magic of Fate's dwelling place and the beastly logic of the forest where hideous beings and wild trees dwelled and where rule was by the survival of the fittest.

The forest is on Earth for a reason. This thought crossed Destiny's mind like a prompt reply to a gradually formulated question. For only in a place like the forest, where everything makes so much cold, hard, physical sense, can the mind reboot.

Destiny had always thought of the universe as a "one-verse," as abstract and as random as music. An individual could take that music and turn it into a song with a beat and a chorus to sing along to, so it made sense and one could follow it. But then, with such a definition, the song then had a start and an end, and eventually, one got bored with it.

Like music, so-called reality was nothing to her but the Infinite placed within parameters, and the mind logically searched for beginnings and ends to make sense of what lay in the middle. Defining things was what made the rules of the game—a format for reality.

Destiny could not easily avoid the tendency to define the Now by way of the concern that it should be negated. Negating something required that it first be defined. Then and only then could one afford to ascend and start bending the rules gradually until they broke, which brought one to the end of the song, when the guitar solo no longer made sense—when one simply lost track of any rhythm.

Destiny feared she would always have fear—fear of losing those inner definitions—and this fear was heightened now that she felt she'd lost that subjective test of reality. It was almost as if the equation of no fear = no joy had suddenly translated Destiny's reality.

Saying one had no fear was a denial of that fear, spoken out of fear—a denial of one's humanity. Surely, one could have less fear. But that meant less joy, and so would be a time to meet the sum of all one's fears—the abyss of God.

The journey back home through the forest seemed so much darker and longer. Would Destiny be able to avoid contact with the ungodly and the demonic? The fallen creatures of the Forget Lands were drawn there because of the dark sanctity that it afforded them: the Archons and the Dhumans who counted unthinking, gross, and vile beings among them and, most importantly, those infamous gatekeepers, Space and Time.

Inhabitants of Mimadamos and the Forgetters alike took comfort in the presence of Time and Space, for each believed the duo was on their side and worked to their advantage.

For the Archons, Time and Space held a special allure. After generations of misuse, the Archons had lost their ancient powers, and they relied on Time and Space to fill the void. The Archons were convinced that Space and Time had a special connection to Destiny, and they were right. For as much as Time and Space wanted to bask in their own importance in the functioning of the universe, the truth was that it depended entirely on Destiny.

Throughout her life, Destiny had needed to stand out in her realm, much like the moon needed to light the darkness. And like the moon, which didn't realize that its light was merely a reflection of the sun, so

Destiny was ignorant of her own ego-based illusion. Were she ever to give it up, Time and Space would lose their significance. Fate had the power to make Destiny see the illusion of such a need, but since he had declined to intervene, the threat had remained dormant. For now, at least, the true danger was Destiny's transformation through her own free will, through her unborn son, Choice.

Nevertheless, the Archons knew that through Time and Space, they could keep her under watch and influence her mind. When it came to physical reality, it was unclear exactly what this connection was, but at least Time and Space were not despised by the people of Mimadamos as the rest of the Forgetters were, and the Forgetters counted on them to keep that side of the world in check for them in the same way that they counted on the Drazians to keep Demire in check.

The Drazians, too, were a minority nation that had once claimed to cross the bridge high above their dwelling place, the Valley of Doubt, which separated the Forget Lands from Demire. The bridge between the Archons' land and Demire was a tiny string so high above that few could cross without falling. The Drazians claimed that their elders—the black-robed, long-bearded five they called "the Spiritual Pentagon"—had been able to cross that bridge. Even better, they had met Fate in person, and he had delegated them to represent him in the world and speak on his behalf.

To perpetuate the myth that they were a chosen race, the Drazians secluded themselves from the world. This plan backfired, though; most people forgot about them. Those who did remember perceived the Drazians as a foolish, naive nation. True naiveté belonged to the Archons, who believed the Drazians' tall tales for the simple reason that they could not imagine a wickedness beyond their own. Knowing that most people were too frightened even to utter Fate's name or come close to Demire's borders, they never thought the Drazians would dare make up such a story. Then again, perhaps the Archons desperately wanted to believe the Drazians' claims so they might feel secure that Demire was in check, if not by them, then by someone else.

At the announcement of Fate and Destiny's engagement, Space and Time had reminded the Archons of what they'd been saying for eons. "We warned you there is a secret connection between Mimadamos and Demire."

"That deeply concerns us," one Archon said to Dhumanos. "We have done much harm to Destiny over her lifetime. We should expect a response from her side."

"If Demire is indeed supporting Mimadamos, the two might be preparing for a battle against us," said another.

Dhumanos frowned at the worry among his fellow Archons. "That is why we have worked for years to keep such a connection from forming between those two nations."

Space edged sideways and turned a smug look toward the Archons. "Nevertheless, a wedding is taking place. Fate is to take Destiny to be his bride at the next full moon."

"All the town is talking about it," Time added, bobbing up and down.

"Silver coins and flowers and all." Space fluttered his eyelashes and sighed, mocking the Archons' concern. "You should see the bridal gown and tantour being prepared for her."

"She'll look like a queen," Time said.

"Enough. Leave us," Dhumanos said, shooing the pair away. The twenty-four Archons grumbled and fretted; even Dhumanos saw this event as a serious matter.

The Drazians sought to comfort the Archons in this respect. "We have been invited to the wedding, but there is not much to worry about. For Fate, this is a passing fancy, not a permanent union."

The Archons didn't put too much stock in that. "How and when did Destiny and Fate meet?"

The Drazians conferred with each other and consulted the Spiritual Pentagon. Their answer was a vague, "Sometime in the last few months ... perhaps in her daydreams. We did not see the silver bridge in use."

"Does she still visit the Forget Lake? Did you not observe the lady Destiny there?"

Nodding, the Drazians confirmed sightings of the girl in the Forget Lands. "Yes, but she stopped coming a while ago."

"Did you not monitor her travels within Mimadamos as well?"

"We don't like to mingle with the rabble, you understand. Their beliefs are on the pedestrian side." Meaning they had not bothered to spy on the girl properly.

The Archons had many other questions, and when the Drazians' explanations fell short, the Archons decided the time had come to keep an eye on them.

Space and Time also doubted the Drazians' claims. The duo knew better; they knew that the road to Fate must pass not through fables but through Destiny herself. To Time and Space, the close proximity of the Valley of Doubt to Demire was nothing more than a geographic detail.

Now, however, as the Forest echoed Destiny's departure from Demire, it appeared that the Drazians' prediction about the temporary nature of Destiny and Fate's connection had come true.

Space and Time were not so easily convinced. They cast a spell extending Destiny's journey across the Forget Lands in the hopes that they would gain a clear perspective of what was truly going on.

Watching Destiny was nothing new for the mischievous and sometimes malevolent duo, for it was they who had paved a way for Dhumanos into her dreams and scripts. This had ended when Fate took his bride to Demire, but now that the lady was traveling alone without his protection, Space and Time reckoned they could once again access her mind and perhaps uncover the hidden knowledge the Archons so desperately desired. They peered within her mind to the loop of her thoughts as she lay within the litter.

"Why did you leave Demire?" they whispered into her thoughts.

"I'm only going home to have the baby. Mother and my sisters will be happy to see me. Mother and the aunties told me it is tradition to go home again."

"What is your real reason?"

Destiny teared up, her nose reddening as a deeper confession rose to the forefront of her mind. "I couldn't stay there forever. Looking at him was like looking into the sun. He is too perfect, too beautiful, and I ... despite what clemency he granted my soul, I still dwell in a darkness he cannot touch. I am not worthy of Demire. Of him. Can one go on with the sensation of free falling and never fear hitting the ground at some point?" Destiny slowly processed the implications and meanings of her choice to leave Fate's reality and the darkness of the Forest and lands facing her. After leaving Demire, she had not watched landmarks as they passed, subconsciously expecting not to need them on a return journey.

"Why did he not come with you if he loves you?"

"He has higher concerns than one woman's mortal frailty." She dashed her tears away, her jaw set in determination as a black thought pierced her heart. "The very fact that he let me leave shows me he doesn't care if I stay or come back."

* * *

The procession to Mimadamos moved at a tediously slow pace, every step an eternity. Destiny couldn't help but compare the magic of her journey to Demire with the sober tone of her journey back, and it made her a little frightened. Why was it taking so long, and why did she feel like she was lost? She stared at the crests and valleys along the route and found nothing familiar, which was, after all, true. It gave Destiny cause to question her personal safety. Had she ever lived in Mimadamos in such proximity to this fearful, dark area?

She was reminded of the darkness that surrounded her mind during her upbringing with the Archons controlling her mind, the nightmares, and Dhumanos's temptation to use her power unfairly, just as the Forget Lands surrounded Mimadamos. The comparison gave her courage a boost to push on, to keep moving forward. A nightmare wasn't real, after all.

As the small party cut through the wild, overgrown territory, they sensed strange creatures and fought the urge to run. These creatures never showed themselves but lurked in the trees and bushes. Watchful and wakeful, the white horse let out a loud neigh every time it sensed danger, which was quite often. At the same time, the animal seemed to sense the protective hand of his master, even now watching from his mountainous abode.

Destiny was nearing despair when they came to the last row of trees. As they emerged into the light, a deep, warm feeling of love overcame her. Smiling happily, she wondered if Fate had all along played a role in keeping safe the inhabitants of Mimadamos. Many such questions had rushed into her head during her slow progress through the forest.

The life within her stirred, possibly aware of the long separation from the life force that had created it. Perhaps the infant's emotions were evoked by his mother, torn between the man she loved and her need for order, of what must be and what must not be.

CHAPTER 8

THE NAME *MIMADAMOS* WAS DERIVED FROM THE
words *Mim Adamus*, or *the soul of Adam*, which bespoke ancient mysteries.
The name paid homage to the first man, Adam, and acknowledged that he
would always be the center of existence.

In the world outside Mimadamos, however, it was often not the divine
that mattered, but the machinations of daily life on the earthly plane.
Simultaneously, those in the great lands beyond and the surrounding
regions sought their greatness in the same way they envisioned the divine.

They sought it within and beyond the Adamic threshold and labored
to build great stone temples, presided over by priests of the highest order.
To them, the extent of substantiality was measured by how big and vast
the buildings were.

Those nations did not differ much from those who had taken up the
Forget Lands as their refuge. For that was a dark area, where laws created
by beasts were stringently enforced.

Still, they strove to preserve their own safety and continuity in these
vast monuments in the same manner as the beastly dwellers of Forget.
They understood very well that to preserve their kind of reality, they
would need to camouflage their beastliness with a semblance of law and
order, rituals and traditions, ethics and reason. And so these were manufactured, clothed in a semblance of acceptability.

* * *

Good and Evil were often misunderstood by the Forgetters. After all, the two were part of a system that sought to engage each person. Even if the system didn't win, it could engage the soul in scripts and create the noise necessary to prevent a conscious reality from manifesting. The Forgetters were drawn into this battle between manufactured Good and Evil and eventually became part of it, labeling themselves and those around them as one or the other. This was the crux of the philosophy of self-defense that inspired empires of armies, armories, and wars.

The Forgetters found themselves in holy wars of self-preservation. They didn't really want to fight; they were just doing what they were told. The Archons often influenced such wars between nations and races and religions, and then they sat on the sidelines of battle, laughing and drunk on the taste of blood wine in their mouths.

The Archons raised lost souls, Dhumans, incapable of empathy. Upon witnessing someone in trouble, Dhumans would simply say, "Oh well, that's the way of the world." Anything more would require a deep level of emotion that the offspring of Dhumanos simply didn't possess. They thought only of themselves. When they heard about spiritual matters, their eyes glazed over with boredom. They could not spare the time or effort to understand.

Their world ran on a give-in-order-to-receive paradigm. Dhumans were conditioned to sacrifice all their human values and assets, including their Now and their dignity, in return for paper currency—which was nothing but a voucher, a promise to be paid at some future time that was irrelevant to their current needs and hardships. The concept of currency had been introduced in Forget Land as a way of directing the Forgetters' focus away from the Now.

Time, which was obviously the most valuable currency, always had a way of keeping the mightiest of beasts in check. Soon this currency of deceit had the Foresters no longer wanting currency for currency's sake but to prove one was successful, victorious—to prove that one could deceive victims. It was like betting on ignorance.

The Archons had tricked the Forgetters. They thought reality was what they could touch, that nature was earth and trees. But nature was only the manifestation of consciousness playing out so that consciousness, a singular entity, could recognize its own existence. They thought history was the story of their wars and conquests. However, it was the story of consciousness viewing itself and the cycles of creation involved in this process, for the viewer, by nature, had to view something other than itself to be a viewer.

Fate, on the other hand, was pure consciousness in this *man*ifestation. He was pure energy, not as in power but as in mind, in constant awareness. He did not need to be generated; he was simply always in a state of *is*. But to be conscious, he had to be conscious of an Other apart from him. As there was no other than him, he had divided reality into Demire and Mimadamos—into Fate and Destiny—so he could view his self and, in that, recognize himself, be self-aware, conscious. And that was the Forbidden Story of which the people of Forget Land were oblivious.

The same story continued to play out repeatedly. How big was that story? How long was an hour? An hour waiting seemed much longer than an hour playing. Time was a funny thing; it was hard to pin down. Time seemed longer when you were a child and shorter as you got older. The more time you experienced, the shorter it seemed to get.

So it was, indeed, the ones who harped on and on about the ills of the world and the want for a better way who would return to ignorance, one cycle after another. Their harping bespoke of a longing, a yearning for something that was lost to them, something missing. That something was balance.

In the process, they often became what they hated, and that was the biggest problem of all.

CHAPTER 9

IT WAS NIGHTFALL BY THE TIME DESTINY AND her party got to the tall grasses and a cool cave in another hillock far from Destiny's marital home. The manservants set about washing off the heat and the sands of the desert that had settled upon them. They would also have to see to their practical day-to-day needs, prepare a meal after sundown, and set up tents for the lady Destiny and her handmaiden as well as a stable of sorts for the noble animal that had kept pace with them. As for themselves, they pitched rough cloths upon the hard ground and hoped that the canopy of leaves above their heads would provide adequate shelter.

Once the day was done and they had all partaken of simple fare, they lay upon the rough cloths to contemplate the glittering heavens. And, as reflected in the light of years before and of years to come, Fate witnessed their loyal deeds from his walled castle in the now-distant mountains. They, too, felt his protective hand.

The only one who did not know was Destiny, though the child in her belly felt his father's protection. He knew that he would always be cared for, just as he would be called to seek the one who had extended this shield over him from a time before his birth.

And so the tall grasses and the very boughs of the short trees with the wide span of leaves bent over the few who had come this way in a search for the princess's roots and her own need to infuse order. It was to be a long journey, which would take many more days and nights to conclude—a journey that would ultimately halt according to what Destiny had willed. It might not, however, have been according to the natural order of men or of the one to whom she had previously been bound.

At daybreak, the horse let out a soft neigh to awaken her rider. The manservants groaned at the thought of the task that lay ahead. Like the day before, Fate sought to divine the needs of the travelers. He would always know, always seek those he cared for most, even if they were not always aware of it. He would know through his all-seeing eye.

The travelers went their way for a great length of time. Beyond the desert lay a leafy, green, shaded grassland where they could have taken more time had it not been for the urgency of Destiny's condition. Beyond the grassland lay the land of rocks, where the stones and boulders each sported a distinct color and polish and where natural cave formations tempted them to enter. Fate had not dallied over these caves on the way out and had instructed the men similarly during their return.

When they encountered the endless Forget Lands, where they could discern neither night nor day, they had no option but to trudge on in the direction pointed out to the litter bearers by Fate. He'd also instructed them to make sure the women shielded their eyes, and Destiny donned her veil. Chaotic his ways might have been, but he had taken the time to sit down and impart this advice before they departed with the two souls he loved the most.

It was Fate alone who had seen the nature of the dangers that lurked within the Forget Lands. The travelers had to take a circuitous route, though that was made necessary by the nature of the Forget itself. They could see that their progression was being mapped in circles. Were they approaching the center? It took a day and a half, but no; they realized at the end of it that they were within a single row of trees in a great arc. They could step out.

The journey until now had appeared so much more arduous than on the way out, when Destiny had only to follow her husband. Might she never again see Mimadamos, the dearly loved, familiar terrain of her childhood? Would she ever feel a light touch of welcome, deliver a child at home—in her home with her mother and sisters, her well-wishers and friends—to see to the delivery as she had intended and as she had informed her husband in his castle home? As close as she was to despair, she still could not turn back.

It took two score days and nights before they finally arrived at Destiny's girlhood home. No one from her birth family was expecting her, and there was, therefore, no welcome back, joyous or subdued. The women who had practiced well their ululations at the time of her departure were missing.

Destiny held one hand to support her belly, grown to full size, and called and called, but there was no reply. There was no one there. Her family had simply departed—gone to where, no one was home to tell her. Destiny knew that her time had come, that she would soon go into labor. She entered the well-known, well-loved home and found it empty and dusty. No feet had walked through the halls, it appeared, in all the time she had been away—a year and more. She went toward the room where she would claim a bed at nighttime but found it locked and barred.

A few of the local folk had come forth by now, and one of them, the locksmith, came to open it for her. A kindly neighbor woman let her know that her family had moved to another land soon after her nuptials.

Destiny threw the doors wide open. It was then that she felt the pain, sudden and severe, deep in her core. The neighbor woman sagely called for the midwife. It was a long and difficult labor. In her pain, Destiny again called out for her mother and her sisters, but there was no answer. She called out for Fate.

He heard and answered telepathically, "This was what you intended. This was what you had in mind on that morning you came to inform me of our separation. I had no will in the matter, powerful as I am. This is your bed, and you must lie in it."

"How dare you?" she shouted, pain, disappointment, and hormones loosening her tongue. "You see everyone's future. You knew my family wouldn't be here for me. You knew I'd be alone. You knew, and you said nothing. I despise you!"

She wept bitter tears at her own excessive insistence, for willing what had to happen and the way it had to happen. Her husband was right— being alone at this moment was her own undertaking, and this was what she would have to live by. She had set the course of her life when she insisted upon having the child in Mimadamos. Now her litter bearers had left, and she did not know the way back in the manner that Fate did.

Besides, the child was nearly here. She would have to live by the rules she herself had created. She had no other choice.

"My beloved," Fate said to her gently, "you have set in motion a wheel of karma with its own momentum, and it will continue to spin, even now that you wish desperately to halt it."

Destiny felt on some level that all of this fell within a planned pattern. She would in time find serenity, but in the *now*, nothing could diffuse her guilt. She took note of Fate's tone of voice as he spoke to her and was calmed by it despite its bitter content. The voice would reach out to comfort her. Strangely enough, it awakened those powers in her that she had always thought were forbidden.

As harsh as the situation seemed, as she lay there enduring the labor pains with only the midwife for support, she had the thought that her gift was hers to claim. It was the first time she had realized this, and she was inspired and uplifted by it.

✳ ✳ ✳

Those who watched from the heavens would have also liked to speed the course of her labor along, but this was not to be. After half a day and night, toward the first hint of a new dawn, the midwife realized that she would have to undertake some maneuvers to facilitate the birth. She did as she had been taught. After she had painstakingly applied all the known ministrations of this civilized world, a healthy boy was born to Destiny.

Of this, too, Fate caught a glimpse from his distant home. Strong as he was, he wept at the thought that he would not be there in person to see his boy during infanthood. But he called upon all his powers and dropped the child's name into Destiny's thoughts.

She thought she could see it clearly, with figures that spoke to her and a name emblazoned in that very light across the skies. As the midwife took the boy away, washed him, and brought him back for his first feeding, his mother announced his name. It was to be Choice.

Those who watched from the heavens declared that the newborn had inherited his father's might and his mother's grace. His nature was of the divine soul like his father, but those closest to him could discern the ways of earthly dwellers, for his actions, even from the time of his birth, were infused by his mother's sense of order. Indeed, Choice bore the best qualities of both parents.

CHAPTER 10

AT ONE WEEK OLD, FATE AND DESTINY'S SON viewed the world around him with an awareness not known to most adults. Choice was already aware that he had been born of Destiny's womb and that she would extend to her child a form of anxious security. Within weeks, however, he sensed another presence, a father figure from afar that provided all the protection he would ever need. Why, then, did Choice sense that this all-powerful and benevolent force was also somehow a threat? Would this polarity between them prevent them from coming together? It was not fear—Choice's inheritance forbade that—but intellectual curiosity.

Destiny, however, was overcome by powerful emotions, mostly a longing for those she loved. She missed the family that had given birth to her. She missed her husband and the extended family she had wedded into. Was this to be her lot in life—imprisonment in impossible situations as had been foretold to her? Would she ever get back to her previous world, where everything had been taken care of? It now appeared to have been a dream; still, she sometimes imagined herself waking up one day to find her birth family by her side. To see her husband, Fate … well, that would have been a miracle.

With each day that passed, Destiny more keenly felt the absence of Fate in her life—not just as a spouse but as a spiritual compass. He knew all about the terror-filled dreams she had endured prior to their marriage.

Being the man he was, he had realized that each episode could be viewed in a positive light. Each time she awoke, he had told her, was an opportunity to strengthen her immunity to such evil. For with each dream, she would learn more about the code of evil. In turn, this would lead to the acquisition of powers that would allow her to enter other, more difficult scripts, until the evil became so extreme as to appear comical. Dhumanos's power over her would be diminished until he simply ceased to exist.

Oh, how comforting she had found those words while in Demire with her husband by her side! Now she desperately wished she could awaken into that first step of immunity. But it was not to be; as Fate had said, she would have to lie in the bed she had made for herself.

As her body gradually healed from the trauma of birth, the practicality of remaining there in her mortal home asserted itself. She had decided she would not return to Demire—not if Fate didn't come to collect her himself and escort his family back to his shining palace. She told herself that the reason lay in the harrowing journey she had endured on the way home, in not wanting to repeat that with an infant at her breast. Nor even with a small child two years hence.

She sensed Fate's concurrence with that conclusion. His agreement salved a measure of her guilt, but she knew the road ahead – raising the boy on her own – would be difficult.

Now in the moments between sleep and awakening and amid the pain of having to endure the lonesome path she had chosen for herself, Destiny saw traces of Dhumanos's influence. With a shock, she realized that she was looking at the ancient Devil's war, not just against her but against humanity. She saw his war in the illnesses as well as the diseases of the flesh and the mind that afflicted all. She saw it in her home of Mimadamos; she had even sensed it in the manservants who had carried her this far before leaving without a goodbye.

One morning, she awoke with a gasp after seeing in a dream the images of an ancient script from a time long before her birth.

Fate stood on a mountaintop. "Good people of Earth, I ask that you take an oath accepting Destiny as my representative. She will be a delegate to the mission of life, to the enactment of laws decreeing right and wrong. You may look to her as your spiritual compass."

The people, however, had greeted the request with their heads bowed and faces turned away. In the vision, Destiny was privy to hushed discussions, especially among the Drazians.

"He wants us to listen to this powerless creature of his?" one asked. "What is this?"

"And a woman, too," said another with a sour face.

"What guarantee have we that this Destiny will not lead us astray?" spoke a third. "Fate is solid and true, decided for us, a path laid out. But Destiny is cloudy, hidden, guesswork. I don't like it."

"It's as if he expects us to decide our future for ourselves," another complained. "How can we shape society and our young without absolutes? How can we keep everyone in line?"

Destiny grew cold listening to them discuss manipulation and control. She hadn't known this evil ran through her people and the Drazians.

Finally, the leader spoke up, addressing Fate. "My lord," he said, "We can accept no one less than you as our guide and master."

Fury filled her husband's eyes when the verdict was delivered, when the people said that they would not receive orders from her, but he said and did nothing. Destiny was his soul. But free will was sacrosanct, and he could not interfere with it in any way.

Destiny flung an arm across her eyes and slowly replayed the script in her mind. For the first time, she realized two things, the first being the act of love it had taken for Fate to return to Mimadamos for her. How hard it must have been for him to travel through the Forget Lands among those whose stubborn denial of Adam's significance had inspired empires and realms of escapism. Her other realization was how interconnected their worlds were—Fate's in the land of ice and crystal mountain and rock and hers here in Mimadamos surrounded by a dense, tangled land of separation, where fearful creatures were known to dwell even now.

Why did Fate, who could end the world and crush those stubborn heads in seconds, have to comply? In the next instant, it dawned upon her that everything—even the current path of her family and the few townsfolk left in Mimadamos—made sense. Everything had to play out in its own time.

Even in the face of this truth, the doubts began to multiply in her head. Had the instrument of ego come into play here to be used against Fate as the Devil had used it against Adam? Dhumanos had seen to the expulsion of the firstborn of humankind. He had seen to his banishment. In the same manner, there might be similar attempts against her golden child, her Choice, begotten and brought into this world outside the land of dreams, according to rules set by herself and Fate and no other.

She had set the order, and she would have to be very careful if she were to keep the child destined for much greatness—for the blood of his father flowed through him. His human life must not be devalued. Destiny promised that she would extend to this child every form of security that she could summon. And yet from deep inside her, Dhumanos, who had taken root, smiled to himself.

She considered again her decision to leave Fate and bring up the child on her own. Would he ever meet his father, given that Fate had shown no inclination to return to Mimadamos? And if he did come, what then? Would she surrender her son to Fate? Of course, Destiny already knew the answer to that, for her choice could not change the fact that eventually everyone met Fate.

Even as she mulled over all this, a mosquito flew near her face, and she heard that deep, dearly loved voice of the greatest of men. "See this mosquito?" Fate whispered in her ear. "It clears a trajectory that has to be. The Law of life, of good and evil, of the great war to uphold that which is right, can yet be as vulnerable as that fragile creature and as intricate. For nothing as mighty as the forces of good or as tiny as this mosquito can ever escape its mathematics."

Destiny leapt back, startled even now that he could reach her from such a distance. She walked over to the sink to splash cold water on her face. Lifting her head, her eyes pierced into the mirror and she gasped, for instead of reflecting light and wisdom and even her own image as it might have been then, the mirror chose to look deep into the future. She skipped centuries, some five millennia and more. She found that she was looking at an old-new land. She was looking at one of the countries of the Levant, bordered on the west by the ancient sea.

She could see all within this antediluvian city, which was the oldest in the world and home to the wisdom of the ancients and the birthplace of progress. But Dhumanos had been at work here as well, overturning the sagacity and understanding of the Phoenicians and Babylonians.

The mirror then reflected the long, pale face of Dhumanos as he appeared in this land—as one who either did not understand or refused to understand that he was like a handicapped child alone in the world, yet causing a storm of evil all around, devouring his own people and causing millions to flee to conditions that were worse still. She saw the terror and sadness on the faces of men, women, and children. Yet these people were in the very image of Adam, as was her husband and newborn son. Would there be no recourse for these people?

She looked back at the face of the one who did not comprehend, the face that refused to bear empathy or sympathy, the chief who sought to impale his own people. The land would, in the distant future, be called Syria.

Destiny turned away from the reflection, deeply saddened. As she did, she again heard the voice of Fate in her ears. "I am who I am, molded of honor and disgrace. No matter what is said and done, I will claim my Time and Space."

She then saw the face of the first man, Adam. He was saying that he was all men, yet he could not claim to possess any kind of greatness. He instead referred to himself as simply "the median."

As Destiny pondered these things, she had no way of knowing that the infant Choice, asleep in his woven rush crib, already knew more than most could hope to realize in a lifetime. For he had been born of greatness and had been familiar since his inception with the concept of numerical codes and the role they played in weaving the spiritual and physical planes. This knowledge was as much a part of his DNA as any physical trait.

As she meditated, the spirit of Demire—the feasts and the community, the people's obeisance to Fate—suddenly made sense to her. What she had mistaken to be chaos was a beautiful, quite logical dance.

"When a dark thought strikes," Fate whispered in her ear, "you must never attempt to combat it with another. Instead, you must use the dimension of space and time to put a beginning and an end to it, diffuse its mystery, and subject it to history."

It was these words that encouraged Destiny to open the door, literally and figuratively, to a new era in her life.

CHAPTER 11

IT WAS A BRIGHT, SUNNY MORNING WHEN Destiny answered a knock at the door and saw a man of about sixty or so standing there. His name was History, he said, and he had only just arrived in Mimadamos. He was looking for work.

Destiny took one look at his kind face and his head wrapped in a high turban and decided Fate might have sent him to watch over her and her son in those critical times.

She invited History inside and rang for tea. As they sat there, he spoke of the gardens he had cultivated over his many years. Destiny was impressed by his obvious knowledge of horticulture, but her interest was really piqued when he spoke of the many families who, while under his care, escaped a variety of ills that might have occurred had he not been there. Everything History said seemed to fit with the notion that he had been sent by her husband.

This time, she resolved to pay heed to Fate's voice. He had promised to rid Dhumanos from her soul, and who was to say History was not an instrument in that regard? Accordingly, she told the man that she would consider his kind offer.

History's arrival seemed to come at the perfect time. Through Fate, she had learned that fear and guilt were negative energies that often resulted in blocking the flow of meaning. What a relief that was! Whereas she had always refrained from using her powers, concerned that it might be her ego ordering her to do so, she now felt quite justified in doing so on behalf of her son. She would create a perfect world for Choice, and if doing so required the use of magic, so be it.

The infant sensed this change in his mother and took it as a powerful affirmation to do what was right. Unlike his mother, who had to come to this realization through the soul-wrenching consequences of her own decisions, Choice innately, if subconsciously, understood that he was a union of the human and spiritual and that this would be the only way that he (or anyone else) could render Dhumanos powerless. He knew this as one knows that the union of two numbers is an equation with a predictable outcome.

✳ ✳ ✳

Destiny also fell to doing what she did best—looking through to what must come and doing something about it. It did not matter that she had chosen to tread the path alone for herself and for her son. It did matter that the decision had been hers and hers alone. Would she have made the decision to leave Demire had she known that her birth family would not be at Mimadamos? She did not know, but it didn't matter. She had made that decision and would have to follow the story to its logical conclusion. When other forces asked to be considered, they would have to do so without upsetting or informing Destiny, for whereas in the past she had accepted the present moment as it came, she would now immediately look through to see what a move or a change meant for Choice.

Even as she pondered the bigger picture her decision had created, she went about the day-to-day business of mothering. She dressed the infant in robes of spun gold, as if she somehow knew that his favorite color was a golden yellow, and she fed him only the healthiest and tastiest foods.

She also began to formulate some ideas about what would be best for the child in the long term. First, because he had been born into a family unlike any other, she must not let him feel different. Meanwhile, she would allow him to benefit from the beauty and freedom of his environment. She wished it, and his father would have wished for it. That meant she didn't want to bring him up in this unlived-in, dusty, and discarded house.

Destiny had sadly learned that her parents and sisters had moved to the Valley of Doubt after her wedding, hoping that the proximity to the edge of Demire would place them closer to her new home. Sadness soon turned to anger that her family had fallen for the wicked tricks of the Drazians after all her family had known about them. It was a setback like that of someone who had graduated from college and then failed a secondary school quiz.

Later on, her experience with Fate and how he let her go to explore the mathematics of her choice gave her strength to do the same with her family: let them explore the mathematics of their choice. She never bothered contacting them, nor did she want them in her new life with Choice. This was their karma, she believed, and they must live it.

* * *

The furnishings Destiny had loved as a child had been removed, marks on the floor and walls showing where they had stood. An old bookshelf that had not been stable enough to move remained, empty of all but a few outdated titles that perhaps no one had wanted to pack. She had been lucky to find one bed still in the house, an old, squeaky frame and tired mattress barely adequate for rest. The scent of her sisters lingered in the fabric, a comfort on nights when she felt lonely.

Destiny shed a tear as she thought of how it had been during her childhood and youth. There had been many people living here—her parents and her sisters. They had laughed and played in these rooms, but the rooms remembered nothing.

She had grown up and moved away. Never again would this be the happy place where she had spent her childhood. Her longing for her mother's cooking, her father's laughter, the shrieks, giggles, and gossip of her sisters would remain unfulfilled, even were she to seek them at their new home. The realization hit her that she could never go home again.

She stroked the old door that squeaked when opened, smiled at the window that had always stuck, and laughed at the pantry her mother had cursed as being too small. Perhaps her mother had a larger one now.

This empty house had been Destiny's happy place. It was also where the scripts of Dhumanos had visited her at nighttime. This was where the Archons had reached out for her, where she had shrunk as far as she could from their touch. The nightmares entwined with the ghosts of happier times dragged at her soul, draining energy she needed to give to her baby.

She might be able to live in the old house for now, provided she could design and build a beautiful new home for the boy here in Mimadamos, where the soul of Adam had wandered. The new home need not be a palace, like Fate's home in Demire and the too-large temples built to intimidate man. But it did need to be aesthetically pleasing. It would have a garden. There should be plants and trees, pets, and birds free to fly the skies. That would be what a young boy, Choice, would look for. It would stimulate his imagination and love of experimentation.

It would not be dissimilar to the best garden of all, the garden at the start of humanity and akin to heaven itself, the Garden of Eden. In thinking this, she realized that there was something Edenic about Mimadamos itself, situated as it was in the middle of the Forget Land, the fallen world, like a pupil surrounded by an iris or like the resting eye of an ever-blowing hurricane.

On present-day maps, Mimadamos fell in the Mediterranean region—in the Lebanon of ancient times. It was also the land of the Phoenicians, of the phoenix that rises from the ashes time and again to fly to a new beginning. Destiny was about to start another life for herself. She was in the land of the phoenix, about to build a Garden of Eden for her son.

Like Adam and Eve, Fate and Destiny had been joined in their minds long before the nuptial ceremony, and their connection did not end with her leaving Demire. Their union justified the desires of good people and continued to serve a greater good after their separation. It did so through their son.

It was a testament to her understanding of this that Destiny resolved to build for the boy a home like no other and attach to it a garden as a reminder of the world's first garden, untouched by contrived mimicry of what might or might not be best. She resolved that the home and the garden would be prepared for Choice to ensure his evolving mind and his happiness.

Destiny planned everything, from the smallest precious stones set in the roof of their home to resemble stars to a single, large cast-iron front door that featured the center of the universe, the sun. Destiny resolved that the outside world would never touch her son in the manner Dhumanos and his helpers had touched her.

She planned every inch of the garden as well, from the paths along which they would take lengthy walks to stimulate his enquiring mind about plants, shrubs, and flowers to where the grass would be laid out to resemble a rolling green carpet.

As she went about her plans with gusto, she was unaware of the presence of the boy's father, Fate. For just as Dhumanos had put the words in her mouth for her to leave Demire, that same dark force was still working to ensure their continued separation. It was Dhumanos who filled her mind with chatter, blotting out any sense that her husband was watching over them. As a bonus for Dhumanos, resentment grew in Destiny's heart when she did not hear from Fate. It was bad enough that he did not care about her, she would mutter aloud, but to abandon his child was unforgiveable. Her negativity fed Dhumanos's lust for causing trouble.

But for Dhumanos, it was not enough to keep Destiny from returning to her husband in Demire, for this separation was merely physical and, therefore, meaningless in the scheme of things. It was not even enough to foster her ill will toward Fate. Dhumanos's plan was on a much grander scale, and he thought gravely about how to achieve it.

The opening came when he learned of the home Destiny wished to create for Choice. He quickly sent his Archons to look for a man who would suit his purposes.

CHAPTER 12

DESTINY WAS BLISSFULLY UNAWARE OF THIS AS she went about creating the home for her son, first engaging the best architect to create the design, then the finest artisans to build the structure. She marveled that she felt justified in using her powers for Choice's sake. It was as though Choice brought with him the license for Destiny to make peace with who she was and what she could do and permission to finally accept her gift as part of herself and not relate it to a strict sense of duty or mission. She sought perfection in both the home and the garden. She visited the site every day as the work progressed slowly but to her exact specifications.

Long before the building began, Destiny knew where she wished to install every stairway and hall. The house was to have the look of a cottage but the size of a mansion; its vast garden would spread over acres. Starting the day of her wedding, Destiny had never promised to be pure, from her towering tantour worn to remind all about the horn of the animal that would not survive to her piercing eyes and her need for order. All were in harmony with the episodes of her past. And so, with a blend of good and a sprinkling of the long-ago fire, she progressed in her duties.

As the house developed and began to grow into a great mansion, Destiny continued to see to Choice's studies and other daily needs. As he advanced through childhood, people spread the word everywhere about the child's good looks and sensibilities. This came as no surprise, of course, for everyone knew that he'd been selected from the highest gene pool.

Knowing how others perceived her son, Destiny couldn't help but wonder if Fate knew it too. Could her all-powerful husband see her now, see their son? Could he see their cottage now growing into a mansion? For there were rooms for every type of activity and for times of repose. At the topmost floor would be their private quarters, bedrooms, each reached by its own stairway leading from the more public hallways on the ground. The house would exist in reality the same way it had existed conceptually in her mind. Since Destiny imagined nothing without thinking through every detail of the operation, she spent hours envisioning the construction of their home as well.

It came to be that elements would be transported from faraway places through levitation to fit in place, just as in the flashes she saw. As for the workers who labored to build the site, their remuneration was not enormous but commensurate with the project they were undertaking—a home intended to generate comfort to those who dwelled within. But it was the garden on which Destiny was most focused, for she wanted it to be the finest in the land. Her meticulous planning aside, she intended for the plants themselves to come up naturally. However, even though Destiny had grown used to planning and working on her own, she realized that she would have to find someone to see to the daily cultivation of the garden and, perhaps, provide some sort of protection for her and her son.

She sent word of her need to the people, and soon several men sought to meet with her about the position. Even as she met with them and found a few to her liking, History returned to her mind and, with him, the thought that he might have been somehow sent by Fate. It made the man stand out from the rest. Upon their first meeting some months ago, History had mentioned that he had built many gardens and had specialized in managing and guarding homes and properties.

Destiny attempted through her inner eye to gauge his experience but turned away when the vision that greeted her was none other than the devil in the Garden of Eden itself. She told herself that she was seeing things, confused by the whisperings of Fate and her own musings about the consequences of her decisions. She told herself that she had to sort, in her head, the truth from that which could never be. And so she told

History she accepted his offer to oversee the garden and manage the security of her new home.

She soon found that the newly appointed gardener had been truthful about his expertise. He could collect supplies of the most exotic flowers that not only bloomed according to their season and by day, but also by night, and he tended them with the utmost care and skill. She was quite impressed with what she saw, but there was something unsettling behind his friendly countenance that she could not decipher.

But even as she questioned History's motives, she questioned her own. She well remembered the fire within that she had experienced on her wedding day and had hoped that none could discern through the layer of her veil covering her eyes. Had the awful vision of History, of this seemingly innocent man before her, sprung from the same darkness?

If only she trusted herself! Had she had more clarity, Destiny might have realized that this elderly man, History, had come on a mission from the beasts and vagrants of the forest. For he was in fact, "His Story," the story of the greatest evil of all: Dhumanos.

History had been prepared for his role by Space and Time, who had known that his path would cross with Destiny's. They were also working at the behest of the Archons and, by extension, Dhumanos's. The Archons did not heed the Drazians' scenario of Fate and Destiny's connection; they knew what they had done to Destiny and had always expected revenge from her.

When Space and Time discovered that she was carrying Fate's child, they were surprised. Like everyone else, they had never imagined Fate to be a real person. He had always entered the myths and fantasies of men as a god.

Bringing the news straight to the Archons, Space and Time said, "We heard that Destiny is pregnant with Fate's child."

Dhumanos looked startled. "What? Is he even human enough to beget children?"

Another Archon wrung his hands. "Has it not been prophesized that our demise will be at the hands of a child?"

Dhumanos ordered Space and Time, "Summon the Drazian Pentagon for me now. They should know what's going on."

The five Drazian men known as the Spiritual Pentagon were transported to the Forget Lands by Space and Time.

"What's going on?" Dhumanos asked one of the five, looming over him. "We heard that Destiny is pregnant with Fate's child; haven't you confirmed that their marriage is temporary—a fling—between angels and humans?"

"Haven't you always claimed that Fate is not even human?" another Archon added.

The Drazian bowed obsequiously. "Yes, but this could be false news. She must be bearing the child of another, and for this reason, Fate demanded she leave his premises."

The Archons were not fully convinced, especially as they pondered Space and Time's reaction to the Drazians' story. So they demanded of Space and Time, "We need to know more. We need a spy. Find us someone Destiny can trust—someone smart or indispensable to her household."

Space and Time wondered what more fitting end it would be for the Archons than at the hands of Fate's offspring. They decided on History. The monitoring of Choice must be of the highest priority.

CHAPTER 13

AS A TODDLER, CHOICE WENT OCCASIONALLY
with his mother to the construction site, but he did not live in the home until he was five years of age—and a precocious five-year-old he was! Honest and fair, he was also—even among children—extraordinarily inquisitive, relentlessly seeking knowledge about that which caught his eye.

The child felt that this home and this garden had to be the most perfect in the world. He also thought he had the most beautiful, intelligent, and loving mother. What Choice couldn't understand was why such an incredible woman had no man by her side.

Similarly, he wondered why he had no father to see to the training upon which he would embark as he grew, no one to oversee and to hone his skills of study and physical prowess or to supervise his introduction to the world. He had no father whose thoughts and actions he could emulate. This was the biggest mystery in his life, and one he felt he would eventually do something about. Conversely, if a father hadn't been mentioned in his first five years, there must be a reason, and he would not force the issue.

Instead, Choice waited. Meanwhile, he soaked up the multifaceted knowledge his mother imparted to him. He especially loved to read and write, and he was delighted when, on one birthday, Destiny threw open the doors to a room on which the construction workers, designers, and office workers had been laboring. She presented to him his very own personal library, filled with over a thousand of the best manuscripts and texts amassed from every corner of the civilized world.

Choice also began lessons with a private tutor, and a whole new world opened to him. Here were history and the arts. Here was everything known to man and discussions about what the future could hold. Choice could ask about anything and everything—everything, that is, except the question uppermost in his mind about the one person he would have liked to have there with him and his mother.

As the boy continued to advance in learnedness, his reputation for intelligence and beauty spread further throughout the land.

"There goes Destiny's boy. Such a smart little fellow."

"Smart as a whip, that one. Why, just the other day, he explained to me why we make carts and wagons in the dimensions we do, the physics of load bearing. I'd never thought about that before."

"The librarian is hard pressed to find books the boy hasn't read yet."

"And so polite—everything is 'Yes, sir,' 'No, ma'am,' and 'How are you today?' And do you know—I'm sure the boy means it and is actually interested?"

"He's still so young. I can only imagine how much more he will learn and what he can bring to our community when he's grown up."

And as he became increasingly familiar with his new home and a garden that was still in the process of being set out, Choice got to know the gardener and their security-in-charge. Choice began to talk to History about all the matters uppermost in his mind, including those he could not discuss with his mother and his tutor.

This suited History perfectly, for besides keeping an eye on Destiny and her child, he was expected to make regular reports to make sure she was not planning a rebellion against Dhumanos for all the harm he had caused her over the years.

History was also supposed to report any indication that she might decide to reunite with her husband, the king among men, Fate. History had been asked to make sure of this for a reason. Of the many tools at his disposal, Dhumanos favored using separation between people—husband and wife or parent and child—to facilitate his nefarious activities.

In this, he had two other brutes to assist him. Space and Time were well acquainted with the people of Mimadamos and the Forget Lands alike, and they had gained this acquaintance by creating a façade of neutrality, portraying themselves as gatekeepers with no agenda of their own. Of course, there was nothing further from the truth.

Even as they worked on behalf of the Archons, however, Space and Time always felt a strange connection to Destiny, a love–hate relationship of sorts. They liked the part they understood about her and grew weary of that which they couldn't understand—the part of her that linked her to Fate. However, if they could have only seen things in perspective, they would have realized that the Archons did not truly respect them or their physical laws; they wanted only to gain power over them.

Only Dhumanos was wily and crafty enough to realize that, without the support of Space and Time, which could happen if they collapsed, he would be crucified and exposed for being what he was. He would be exposed for being nothing, zero. Accordingly, he had indicated to History that when the elder arrived in Destiny's home and garden, he was to make sure the boy did not get the chance to decipher their secrets and manipulative doings, for that would undermine everything.

History, however, did not approve of Time and Space—he thought they somehow preserved a balance that was simply unhealthy. History liked to unravel things! He liked happenings and events. He catered more to the Archons' appetite for scripts and roles with their dramatic beginnings and ends.

All the same, he knew he had been cursed when Dhumanos had pressed him into service. In the meantime, he tried to carve out a pleasant existence for himself in Destiny's garden.

And so, History was being truthful when he said to Destiny, "Yes, great lady, I will be able to take upon myself the responsibility of laying out the type of garden of which you speak. I can take upon myself the safety of your life and your son's."

No matter how he felt, History did not have a choice in the matter; he must do Dhumanos's bidding. He would have to carry on as he was, as a figure no one could fully recognize, as a person who did his task but chose to be reflected in a diffused light.

History did not dwell overmuch on these matters, for his greatest concern was preserving his own role in the goings on in the world. He wanted his own fingerprints upon the story, and this he sought to accomplish by separating Destiny from Choice and, in the process, inciting Choice to rebel against all he had learned from his mother.

What better way, History thought, *to cultivate a desire within the boy to one day strike out on his own?* History imagined Choice lost in the Forget Lands. *Perhaps*, he thought, a small smile fluttering across his lips, *the boy will find such a different lifestyle most alluring and, therefore, will be much more vulnerable to the Archons.* Like the Devil, who under the guise of knowledge had sought to tempt Eve and pierce Adam's soul, History used his learnedness to hide his evil and crush Destiny and Fate through their only son.

The one thing History did not count on, however, was that the whole of this story had long been unfurled in Fate's mind. Had History known of Fate's vision for his son, he might very well have stopped Choice from leaving Mimadamos.

Choice, meanwhile, knew nothing of the machinations of the adults around him, just as they did not know what the boy yearned for most. Now ten years old, his wish to be with his father drove Choice into the realms of wild imagination. *Could it be*, he asked himself, *that my father is a king who does not know of my existence?*

When his father became aware, Choice told himself, he would call for his son and give his throne to one who would be known as the seat of knowledge. Or maybe his father was a simple, law-abiding man renowned for his skill in his chosen discipline. Maybe his mother had left his father because she had found his lifestyle too modest to suit her tastes. And what if his father was skilled in one of the sports or was a brilliant military strategist able to win mighty battles—even entire wars—based on his maneuvers?

CHAPTER 14

AN UNFILLED NEED CAN LEAD TO BITTERNESS, desperation, and even depravity, or it can drive one to reach new intellectual and spiritual heights. For Choice, it was the latter, and when he was old enough, he channeled his curiosity about his father into exploring the cycles of nature.

Each day, after completing his lessons, Choice would escape to his own special garden, the one his mother intended him to have. It was presided over by a strange but mighty elder. There was much to be learned here. There were water bodies and fountains. Fish of every hue swam in the tanks. Natural streams flowed from mountain snow and fed the fountains, where water danced upward and then fell gracefully back to Earth with a quiet, gurgling tone.

Grass grew in short tufts between the flagstones, and flowers bloomed according to the season of the year. Fruit trees grew so tall they had to be climbed if they were to give up their offerings. Only the cypresses were still short, as they had not had that many years on this Earth.

In his library, Choice had gained some knowledge about the trees and their fruit, the birds, and the tame animals that roamed, the grass, and all the natural vegetation that abounded here. Some information he had dug out of his creative imagination. But most of it, he had gotten by simply asking the gardener.

This gardener was to be found either working or taking his leisure around the garden and guarding those that dwelled in the big house. He had been around ever since Choice could remember, yet it was only now, as the boy neared adolescence, that he had begun to talk to the old man. Choice would ask History when the seeds he was sowing would become plants and when the fig trees would bear fruit he could pluck. He even asked what the flowing waters of the mountains bore down in their rush and why only the feathers on the grey partridge's underbelly were striped in black. The gardener's skills with flora and fauna knew no bounds and neither, it seemed, did his knowledge.

Slowly at first, the man who had made the garden his own began to talk to Choice about the many wonders of the earthly world. He spoke about the Fertile Crescent and the origins of civilization. He spoke about the faiths associated with this fertile land and the Garden of Eden. But here History paused as he remembered those to whom he had vowed allegiance.

"You will travel from the Forget Lands to Mimadamos," Dhumanos had ordered. "I want you to keep an eye on Destiny and her child. That girl has a long history with us. We almost had her on our side until Fate stepped in and wooed her away from me. Let us say our persuasion was less than strictly truthful, and she may find herself with leisure time to foment rebellion in retaliation."

"Against yourself, Excellency?" History asked.

Dhumanos grunted. "Precisely. I want you to undermine her authority with her people any way you can. Introduce questions such as, 'Who is Choice's real father, and why did Fate let her go so easily?' Things like that. Also report any indication that she is renewing relations with Fate or preparing to return to Demire. I would much rather keep those two entities separated, for together they could tip the balance away from our stable rule."

"Not one for family togetherness?"

"No. An individual can be led if he is separated from his fellows, you see. Brother from brother, husband from wife, parent from child. I want you to find a way to mentor the boy and steer his thoughts away from the discovery of our plans for maintaining power and control."

History had bowed. "As you say, my lord."

As he spoke to Choice of the first man, he stressed Adam's wrongdoings but not those of the evil one who had driven him to the deeds that led to his expulsion from the Garden.

History, who was never sure whether he should strive to do Dhumanos's bidding or his own, had hit a lucky streak, for History had found Choice to be trusting rather than threatening as he had earlier envisioned. Dhumanos would be pleased with his efforts, earning History a valued place in that alternative seat of power.

Space and Time hovered nearby as History reported his progress to the Archons. "I have been teaching the boy directly. He is a sponge for information, and the more I differ from what his tutor tells him, the thirstier he becomes. Redirecting him is quite simple. His mother keeps him so sheltered that any information from outside of her carries more weight."

The Archons murmured approval and offered suggestions of what to "teach" the boy. Dhumanos wore a bemused expression at their outlandish ideas, each more shocking than the last. History was more interested in Dhumanos's opinion, as his word would lead to advancement.

History raised a hand to be recognized again. "Excellency, I have focused our discourse on small concepts and pieces of, you'll forgive me, history the boy can relate to. While he is intelligent, he is only a decade along in life."

Space shook his head, knocking himself sideways, where he floated nearby. "Do not underestimate the child of Fate and what he can do."

Time nodded, bobbing beside his brother.

One of the Archons replied, "It is not confirmed that he's the child of Fate."

Time said to the Archon, "Do you honestly buy into the tales of the Drazians? You know well enough the real reason Destiny left Demire ... as if it was not me and Space who played with her mind and planted the thoughts of separation in her head."

Dhumanos raised his eyebrows, challenging History to refute this.

"No matter that Choice is Fate's son," History said smugly, staring down Space and Time. "He is also just a curious little boy who is easily handled. I'll open wide the distance between Choice and his mother, I assure you."

"Yes, yes," the Archons said. "The wider the gap, the better."

"Be sure the cracks begin with greying right and wrong," Dhumanos suggested. "Children are literal. It worked with his mother."

History bowed. "As you wish, Excellency."

Thus, whenever Choice asked History questions about the ancients, he promptly replied, hiding his eagerness under a quiet reserve. Just as he patiently sowed the seeds in the garden and waited for the plants to bloom, he spoke of the sins of Adam in a way that twisted right and wrong. Then he waited for the lies to blossom in the boy's mind.

As it so happened, History's smugness was justified, for Choice had begun to find such lore infinitely more interesting to follow than his schoolroom lessons or those of his mother. Choice turned to History to be the mentor—and perhaps father figure—he had despaired of finding.

There was something about History that appealed to the boy and went even beyond knowledge. He had a way of projecting a world beyond his words—a world with wild laws, quite unlike the well-organized, nurturing design he had sought in this garden commissioned by Destiny. History introduced Choice's awakening intellect not only to a linear way of thinking but also to a definition of freedom vastly different from the one his mother had taught him. Destiny had intentionally created a maze-like, circular world in which one's destination was not important; the focus was Now.

To History, however, freedom was more about an uncertain future than any present moment, no matter how precious. Everything about which History spoke pointed to a linear path, where every action would have a consequence that could not necessarily be guessed at the onset. It wasn't long before Choice was spending less time in contentment with what was and more time wondering about what was yet to come. He found he could imagine a specific goal or destination and pursue it in a different way. It was in much the same manner that he could heal the sick, by touching them and visualizing their energy shifting, picturing their very cells moving into alignment with nature.

Whereas Destiny had taught him to overcome the implications of his name—just as she had overcome hers—History was now directing him toward it. *Imagine,* thought Choice, *a future that no one could have foreseen could be mine for the asking, and I alone will decide how to go about it!*

History was also giving Choice other, more practical kinds of information, for History was indeed a learned man and imparted lessons that were true in many forms. He told Choice that this was where civilization had first found fruit, and he showed the boy the methods of irrigation that would yield the sweetest. He taught him how to grow the tallest stalks of corn and how to rear animals respectfully so that they knew only love and harmony.

Wherever he looked, Choice saw the physical manifestation of History's words, for indeed the fruits in the garden were the sweetest imaginable, the corn grew a foot taller than Choice's reach, and the animals that wandered their garden were peaceable and loved humans. History also showed the boy how to make soap and perfume from the herbs that grew in the garden, which he then presented to his mother.

For all the knowledge History gave the boy, however, he took much from him withal. As he gradually chipped away at the moral code instilled in Choice by his mother, History's perspective of his own assignment in Mimadamos began to change. Now, besides achieving Dhumanos's goal, he began to relish the influence he had over the boy for its own sake. It was a thrilling realization.

Yet even History may have underestimated Choice's insatiable hunger for knowledge. For all the boy asked of the wizened gardener and valued every kernel he received, Choice turned to his tutor and his mother as well.

Now the tutor was also a very knowledgeable man.

Choice asked him, "What is the nature of the universe?"

"The universe has no top or bottom and no physical end," the tutor answered. "Their mathematical progression leads to the fact that the linear is an illusion."

"Does that mean that creation can spread out in all directions?" the boy asked.

"Yes," said this tutor, only too happy to explain the concept of the expanding universe to his young charge. "Adam is the sun that makes sides and direction possible. It is the miracle of the finite born from the womb of the infinite, as in the immaculate conception. It is the miracle of the definite born from the indefinite."

"But Adam was a man, wasn't he? And he lived in the Garden of Eden. Mother says the garden outside is like the Garden of Eden, but how does she know?"

"And why not?" his tutor replied. "If time and space were dissolved, the Garden of Eden would not be far from the place of your mother's birth."

The tutor paused, stroking his beard. "Eden is more like a moment than a physical place: it existed in the minds of the two prime aspects, Adam and Eve. They were two voices in one mind, and when they joined, they birthed a self-awareness neither could have achieved alone. It was a symbolic tale of the mind collapsing into One and, in that, nothing."

Choice squirmed in his seat.

"Adam was born on this Earth in time for Armageddon; in fact, it was because of him that it happened at all. Armageddon, which the world envisioned to be a great battle that would end history, simply means 'awakening.' Adam awakened, and as he did, his mind created the Kingdom, a new reality. The evil ones had once experienced the Kingdom, yet they tripped out on its magic and thereafter were known as Fallen Angels. The good ones, the chosen, came forth to Earth to brighten the darkness of what resulted from the Fall.

"This was where things took a turn. The Garden of Eden story became linear, as we mortals think in linear terms, and we struggled to find a beginning, just as science does. Of course, we struggled, as there can be no beginning! Think on this, boy. Tell me how the story became linear."

Choice thought, remembering the tale. "Adam and Eve had Cain and Abel, Cain killed Abel, and then Cain had children."

"Ah, but who did he marry? One of his sisters?" The tutor shook his head. "There must have been other people in the world. We know from breeding stock animals that fresh blood is needed to keep the herd healthy. How could the whole of humanity have descended from only two people? No, there were others. Therefore, Adam and Eve are symbolic of the beginning of our spiritual family, of our beliefs."

The tutor most often spoke about humanity's essential and immutable nature. "Who we truly are," he said, "depends not on the circumstances of one's life—or many lives—but on their character."

As Choice viewed all knowledge as a gift, he was grateful for his tutor's explanation; however, in comparing him to History, he also realized that his tutor believed that knowledge itself had more to do with the ability to conceptualize things than to experience them.

"One need not touch fire," the man was fond of saying, "to know what it means to burn." The pedagogue sat in a scholarly posture, one hand to either side of his chest hanging onto the fabric of his robe as he explained. "An intelligent, living soul should travel and explore in his mind. He can do this not for the sake of reaching that destination but only to learn how to appreciate the present moment—the Here and Now.

"Everything fades, Choice, whether it be joyful or painful. You have lived many lives, but you will never fully remember them. This tells us that history is not important; it's but one moment in the life of the gods."

"So how come," Choice pointed out respectfully, "I get flashes that I know are not from this life but are no less real than those of my own childhood?"

The tutor was silent for a moment, so amazed was he by the boy's precociousness. "Yes, of course," he said finally, "but the historical you is not the highlight of who you are. In fact, you might as well have been another person. That person did not think the way you do now; he or she was a limited version of yourself."

The tutor placed a hand on Choice's shoulder. "We transform and evolve throughout our lives—that is a given. Just keep your mind focused on the Now without looking for 'signs' about what's coming in the future. Signs are not the language of the enlightened soul, my boy, but of the psyche. They cater to the ego, which is always trying to hoard memories of a past or imaginations of a future to anchor itself due to the fear of dissolution."

The tutor chuckled. "'I am this, and I am that.' 'I remember this, and I foresee myself as that.' In the end, those thoughts about who you are and who you will become will frame you and imprison you inside the walls of the ego. You will become their hostage. It is the purée of all your experiences over all your lives that make up your overall character, son, and character cannot be overestimated."

"You're right," said Choice, "but the one thing I do know is that no matter how many lives you live, you are always the same person. That never changes. You might look different and have a different lifestyle, but you are fundamentally the same. After all, the soul is eternal, isn't it?"

The tutor nodded. "Yes, Choice, but my point is this: while I know that reincarnation is a fact, I also believe it is almost irrelevant. You cannot hold on to memories. The only benefit of reincarnation is living over and over as if it's all new again. The 'real you' that you speak of is still always in the Now, not in the future or the past."

Choice listened to every word, but while he could not dispute what his tutor was telling him or deny that the man had the best of intentions, he also felt himself being pulled in an entirely different direction. All this talk about the Now seemed to go against everything the other man—the one with an even greater influence over Choice—had taught him. Each time he and History spoke, Choice was getting closer to when he would touch that fire.

In general, Choice agreed that it was better to let go … but sometimes there were things one's mind could not help wondering about. He wondered a lot about his father. What did he look like? Why was he not here? What would it have been like if he was? There were many questions.

The boy stomped his feet with pent-up frustration he had not even been aware of. "This place is not real! It's almost like a dream! You know, when you dream, you sometimes play along with it for a while, even though nothing looks right. You try to carry on as normal."

"Yes," said his tutor, "things can often seem this way, but, Choice, this place *is* home. Now see what you see and enjoy what you see, but the minute it's over, move on without looking back or ahead. If what you saw is important, it will find its right place and time to resurface gently within the natural flow of the Now."

The tutor sighed. "I know you're curious about what lies outside. I know you think your father is out there somewhere—but trust me, this place was made for you. It was made to embrace you with love, to hug and protect you. You don't know what the world outside is like. It's a sneaky place with a culture built on fear, blame, desire, and reward. The world's inhabitants are never satisfied with the Now, always stepping over it, back and forth, from a past they regret losing to a future they desire having, forever hungry, like beasts, unhappy and unsatisfied."

Choice just nodded as if in agreement, but he was really thinking again how much the tutor's view differed from that of History. To History, knowledge was worthless without experience, a perspective that Choice could not help but feel was more attractive.

Thinking the matter settled, the tutor returned to another topic, a favorite for both of them. He spoke of the sun as a reference point in endless space. "One could," he explained, "travel away from the sun in linear directions, searching for extreme greatness, but since the universe is endless and circular, it would be difficult to know the midpoint unless one took that to be the sun.

"Of course," he added, "the sun here is a metaphor for the Spirit as the traveler is for the Soul. Directions and extremities can only be defined by the light of the sun."

Choice dutifully listened and replied in all the right places, but he was still thinking about the two quite different paths presented by his two quite different male role models. He decided he needed another viewpoint altogether.

That evening after the tutor had departed, he sought his mother and asked her, "Will I ever find a great man, a father figure?"

CHAPTER 15

SINCE THE DAY CHOICE WAS BORN, DESTINY HAD
wondered when her son would ask about his father and had wondered
how she would answer. How many times over the years had she questioned her own decision to leave Demire and the boy's father? As any parent would, she offered an answer for the highest good of the child, even if
she had not always conducted herself as such.

"You ask if you will *ever* meet your father," she said. "First, my dearest
Choice, you must understand that everything is on a schedule. It has never
been about 'the definite' that the ignorant waste their lives running in circles to touch, armed by a love–hate, desire–fear philosophy. No, son, it has
always been about the *possible*—all that's possible in infinity. At times, the
seeming emptiness of infinity resembles spiritual hunger, but when we
try to measure its space, count its time, or embark on a linear journey to
discover its boundaries, we exhaust hope along the way."

She saw that her son was about to interrupt and put up a hand to stop
him. "We all have to make our own way, experience all that is laid out for
us. When we fall, we panic and cling. We feel we must do things, that we
must control something when, in truth, existence has no floor. Son, this
world is a like a Möbius strip, a living illusion in which we kick and fight
as we attempt to define ourselves. We often go through the linear journey
that we see as progressing into what shall become, when, in fact, it only
regresses into what already 'is.'"

She took Choice's hand. "I have been learning for many years now to overcome acting out of desire or fear, to let go of attempting to control, and now everything is clearing. No one will ever change this world; it works fine the way it is—well, when you know what it is. You must let this go. Desire only generates fear; it holds you back. This place is a phase. So I tell you, we will get to a better place when the time is right."

Destiny was silent after that, trying to gauge whether she had reached Choice, but his face was unreadable. She gently pulled him by the hand and guided him outside to the garden.

"Beloved Son, don't trade what you know for what you don't in the name of greatness and a promised paradise that might hold the man you seek. Remember, son, this home and this garden have been designed to help you grow into all that you need now. I have seen to it that you need not seek anything beyond this enclosure. Don't exhaust your definite present for an indefinite future."

She then spoke to him about the ego and the many difficulties it can cause when one gives it too much heed. Her words were much the same as what the tutor had said earlier. In fact, most of what she said echoed that kindly man's sentiments.

What Choice did not know was that in speaking of ego and the fear it inspired, Destiny was really speaking of herself, for she still grieved for herself and the evil burden of dream scripts. She had lost much of her fear when she returned to Mimadamos, but she had found in its place a new enemy: control. She was trying to control her mind so that she could understand what she was waking up to. Finally, she realized that she needed to understand just enough to let it all go.

"It's a bit like standing on a high cliff, tied by an anchoring rope and telling yourself that all will be well," she explained. "You understand the rig, you saw the last man go, so you know all will be fine. You must understand that. But then you jump—you just let go and enjoy the sensation. You can't put logic to it.

"Trying to get a grip and let go is a bit stupid, really, so I guess you can divide it into 'learn,' then 'jump.' So you see, knowing is one thing, and being is another." Then, not wanting to continue this maudlin topic, she centered her next analogy on music. "What is music, really, if not mathematical cycles? The first cycle is the beat, a simple repetitive cycle, and then you need a theme. But the theme gets boring, so you must extend and vary it. Then you need a resolution to the theme, an answer, an antidote, a polarity shift, and that is the chorus. So you flip from the verse—the theme—to the chorus. You must keep looping back to connect the cycle, or the music becomes abstract. When you vary the main theme, it always helps to keep subtly suggesting the theme, or you get lost."

Choice looked at his mother, startled. Did she realize that he had grown weary of Mimadamos? That he was yearning for change? He wondered for a moment whether the tutor had repeated to her his comment about this place being a dream. Did she realize how frustrating it was that all he needed was a simple and clear answer about his father and the man's whereabouts, but all he got was more philosophy?

He understood that music, like life, was born of cycles and symmetry. He was also aware of the great mystery music presented, for no one knew why it resonated with the soul or why a type of music resonated with one person and not another. When constructing a tune, it was easy for him to see that not all notes fit together! He could spot a bum not a mile off and could have without any musical training at all. Life was the same, his mother had taught him; it also required balance and harmony.

So he spoke up. "When I started learning to play music, I first had to learn where all the notes were and how to play them. Some notes, Mother, I feel are missing in my life or from the instrument you manufactured for me. I always feel like I am being forced to play a wide tune in your head with limited notes, and it's like sometimes you're asking me for a miracle. Like you secretly expect me to crash into the chorus or verse without even an intro. Do you see what I'm getting at, Mother?"

When she heard this, Destiny's eyes filled with tears, for this she had not anticipated, and it broke her heart. She folded her son into a hug so he wouldn't see, but he already knew.

✳ ✳ ✳

Choice barely slept that night, so full his mind was with all that his mother and tutor had said. It was not that he disagreed with them about the nature of life or the ego or linear-versus-circular time. He understood every analogy and thought them all excellent. Still, he sought the truth about the man who had never been there to guide him.

The next afternoon after his lessons were over, he went outside and, under an unending sky, took his query to the gardener. He found History squatting beside a shrub laden with ripened strawberries.

"Do you live by the code?" Choice asked him after a perfunctory greeting. And History smiled, for although Choice was different from other children in so many ways, he shared their impatience.

"Yes, I do," he said and saw the interest in the boy's widened eyes. "As a gardener who cares for all that grows from within the Earth, I have to rely on both my own skills and the seasons. I must take care of the land so the waters will flow and nourish the soil from below; otherwise, a seed will not come to life. I must trim the shrubs and trees to clear the way for new growth, and I must make sure everything that grows receives water and food. Occasionally, I must transplant and remove weeds. A gardener must live by his garden and be happy doing so. He must love all that grows there, and that requires action."

Choice listened to it all as he would a soft, mesmerizing melody. How different History made the code seem from his mother! When Destiny spoke of the seasons, it was as if she considered them projections of the soul with no roots in the natural world.

Indeed, to History, the code meant the power to change things and not to dismiss change as a mere illusion. He saw the look on the boy's face and smiled, for he saw that Choice was beginning to see it this way too.

CHAPTER 16

FROM HER BEDROOM WINDOWS, DESTINY watched the elderly man leading Choice around the garden, pointing out a flourishing shrub or picking a succulent fruit and presenting it to the boy.

She smiled at the sight, but she still had the inkling that something lurked inside History, that he played a totally different symphony. She sensed a darkness in his nature that he kept a tight clamp on. But as she had done often enough over the years, she pushed the thought from her mind.

Choice needed a role model, so she did not overmuch oppose Choice's spending time with the gardener, especially given the boy's recent inquiry about his father. *Besides*, Destiny told herself, *how harmful could History be?* He was just an old man with exceptional agricultural skills and perhaps a few quirks. Should she judge him simply because he had traveled to Mimadamos from some other land?

She decided to simply appreciate History for what he could do rather than what she had sensed and was not sure about. Destiny had known the workers in Mimadamos to talk much and achieve little. She generously thought of her townsfolk as being open-hearted yet lacking the knowledge and expertise of someone like History, who could design and bring a garden to life. She told herself, *History has not only excelled at the job for which I hired him, but he has also proven to be a companion to my son.*

Meanwhile, out in the open garden and in the schoolroom, Choice hung onto every pearl of wisdom he received. Soon he realized that History spoke of a great many things, but he rarely spoke of himself.

"Do you have a family, History?" he finally asked one day as they feasted on blueberries and peaches. "Any children?"

History paused for a moment, almost as if it were an unusual question. "Sure I do, Choice, but why do you ask?"

Choice shifted his weight uncomfortably. "But if you do, why are you always here, looking after Mother and me and guarding our home?" He gestured to the thriving flora and fauna around them. "Always working in our beautiful garden?"

History paused again, and Choice could see that he was thinking, formulating his answer. *What*, the boy wondered, *could be so complicated?*

Finally, History spoke. "You see, Choice, I am of humankind but perhaps a little more, for I honor life in all its forms. These plants and trees, the flowers and grass bring out my instinct to nurture and reveal. *They* are my children, and I toil because I want to see them change and grow and evolve into something higher, as any parent does with a child."

History looked almost sad as he shook his head. "Unfortunately, they can grow only so much, even if the cypresses grow for a few hundred years and the firs taller. They cannot see distant hills and seas as I have ... as you might still."

It was now Choice's turn to be still and silent. Even as History moved on to a tutorial about the best way to fertilize the blueberry plants, Choice could not stop thinking of what the old man had said. Not about the plants being his children but that other tantalizing tidbit: the suggestion that Choice might one day leave Mimadamos and see the world. But what of all his mother had told him, that everything he needed was right here? Could he go elsewhere to seek his destiny on his own? Was it possible to listen to that tiny voice of rebellion rather than stifle it? Destiny had always subtly discouraged mention of the world outside Mimadamos, but Choice was starting to think that was just her own overprotectiveness, a mother's refusal to acknowledge that her son was growing up.

As any child who aspires to do something of which his parent will disapprove, he knew he had to tread lightly. Destiny had always taken an interest in his education, but these days, she seemed to meet more often with his tutor, as if trying to gauge more than his aptitude for math, science, and computer studies.

When she looked at her son, it was with the same directness as always, yet now he noticed a slight furrowing of her brow. Perhaps the pupil had asked the tutor one too many questions and this had gotten back to Destiny. Of course, there was no way to know, but he was sure that life's one true freedom—that gained from knowledge—would be gained from History. And perhaps it might also lie outside their walls.

For now, he decided, the best way forward was to guard his words, especially around his tutor. When he was indoors, he spent much of his time in his room, quietly contemplating, or in the library, soaking up information not covered in his lessons. He had noticed recently that his sessions with the tutor were now limited to the study room. Was this his mother's doing? Was she worried that the many volumes would further stoke his curiosity?

It didn't matter. For as anyone knows, the best way to interest a child in something is to restrict access to it. The less forthcoming his tutor and his mother were, the more Choice became convinced that a different reality awaited him outside the confines of his home and his garden—outside Mimadamos altogether. It was a scary yet thrilling thought, but Choice would not rebel for rebellion's sake. He would not seriously consider leaving unless he was confident that it would be a true path to discovery. But who was he seeking to discover—himself or his father?

If he were being honest with himself, Choice knew the two were the same. He couldn't seem to shake the feeling he'd had since early childhood: that his father was somehow looking out for him and his mother. It was almost as if Choice needed to see himself through his father's eyes as much as he needed to meet the man himself.

Just as Choice's mind was being opened by curiosity, Destiny was allowing hers to be closed by fear. Her suffering at the hands of Dhumanos, coupled with her separation from Fate, had constructed barriers in her perception and blinded her to everything but the overwhelming need to keep her son safe. Although Fate was still her husband in name, their lack of communication since her departure led Destiny to believe that she—and Choice, for that matter—were to him a closed chapter.

Just as well, she thought, *that Choice knows nothing of his father.*

It had been unsettling enough that her son was growing up with only one parent and no friends his own age. The least she could do was create a home environment that nurtured him, body, mind, and soul. Now she realized that she'd been hoping it would be enough to quell any longings he had for the outside world.

Of course, Destiny was aware of her son's curiosity about that world, but she was unsure of its extent. Was it merely academic, or was he truly yearning to go beyond the walls of Mimadamos? She, who once could glean all, now barely knew her own son's intentions. As alarming as this was, she refused to give in to her fears and risk allowing Dhumanos's poison back into her mind and possibly her life with Choice.

Instead, like any mother with limited knowledge of her child's mind, she used the tools at her disposal. She gave Choice's tutor strict parameters for his lessons, even telling him to confine them to the study room. The one thing she did not restrict was access to the garden and the odd but kindly old man who tended it. But it was in trying to keep her son safe that she pushed him into the arms of danger.

* * *

Destiny knew how happy Choice was in History's company, but she was wrong about the reason. While the boy indeed loved learning about the flora and fauna of the garden, what he loved most about History was the way the old man encouraged him to find his own answers. Sometimes it seemed that History knew of Choice's questions even before Choice did!

One day, Choice sought the old man and found him seated under the shade of a young pomegranate bush, from the boughs of which hung miniature fruit. As always, History seemed to have been expecting him, and Choice understood that when he gestured for the boy to sit beside him, it was also an invitation to give voice to whatever he was pondering.

"History," he said, "my tutor spoke today about Adamic history—something you yourself have alluded to in the past. But it remains a mystery to me and, I suspect, to my tutor as well. Can you tell me more?"

History plucked a fruit from the bough and handed it to the boy. "What did the tutor tell you?"

"Well, he said that God has projected His great mystery onto Adamic history. What this means, in mathematical terms, is that the high and the low meet on the matrix zero-one. 'Look around,' he told me, 'everything you see and do not see, from thoughts to objects to events to space and time itself, are all scripted by this simple code, zero-one!' He said that the particularity of those objects and events—what makes history—isn't important. What is important is the perspective of the mind that projects them into being."

History's lips twitched, then curled into a smile that Choice had never seen before. It was a smile without humor. "In time, my son, once you discover new spaces and events, you will discover the importance of details and how making history is what men live for—and what they die for, too."

"But when?" Choice asked impatiently. "*When* in time?"

History did not hesitate. "The most expensive currency in time is time itself, something that cannot be saved or spent." He continued to say that Mimadamos was deemed to be timeless, that there was no measure of time for Choice. "To claim your role in history, to have people remember your name, you must first discover the world."

He paused for a moment to weigh his words. "This place is too sterile. You take your shoes off when you go in, put coasters under your cups when you drink, and spread covers on the sofa before you lie on it. As soon as something is dirty, someone is there to clean it up. They want everything to stay pristine in here. They want to keep the soil outside, but the only way to do that is not to use anything, not to live.

"I have learned to embrace the messiness of life. That's why I like gardens more than walls." He smiled again. "There was once a very clean Garden called 'Eden' that didn't last very long. I wonder what the future will bring—for me, for you, for those you see around."

CHAPTER 17

IF HISTORY WAS AT ALL CONCERNED ABOUT
whether Choice would return, he didn't have long to wait before he had
his answer. When Choice approached him later that day, History was
elated. His work at Mimadamos had been even more rewarding than he'd
expected. Now, after learning of Choice's innocence and Destiny's naive
trust in him, he thought he could do Dhumanos a bigger favor than keeping the mother and boy in check—and gain further prominence for himself—by sending Choice forth into the Forget Lands and into the hands of
the Archons. The more History thought about it, the more intoxicating the
idea appeared. In this present state, he could easily get Choice to step into
the shoes of a rebel.

History's imagination rose to higher and higher peaks. Why, he could
get Choice not just to peek over the walls of the compound but to move
out of Mimadamos altogether! He could see to it that Choice went to the
Forget Lands and lost himself there. Perhaps he would be enticed by
Dhumanos's lifestyle and by that of Forget's longtime dwellers, such as
Space and Time.

History had to control himself from rubbing his hands in glee. Why,
Choice might even be pursued by and relegated to nothingness by
Dhumanos in the same manner as humanity's firstborn, one who was
close to being divine. For History was well aware of Choice's parentage,

even if the boy was not. To History, the winning side was clear, and he was going to be on it.

However, the boy was not there yet, so History continued using the art of subtlety, introducing bits of the outer world as he would with any lesson, knowing he was dangling the proverbial carrot in front of the boy's face. He told him about a world that operated on currency, where things like clothing, food, lodging, and travel were exchanged for gold and silver.

Choice said nothing, but his wide eyes indicated his interest, for he had never heard of such a thing. In Mimadamos, where everyone relied on the old barter system, clothing and food *were* the currency.

"In this world," History continued, "time is a hot commodity—people compete for it! Everyone wants to experience the most in the least amount of time. Currency is a way to organize, institutionalize, and measure that competition."

These concepts of time and competition intrigued Choice. In the naturally growing maze in the garden, he could lose himself to solitude in a passage where time seemed nonexistent. He did not need to ponder the fact of aging and its implications just yet. Destiny had created a world truly detached from any reference to time, a world where there was no need to hurry to advance on any linear path and no room for the one closest to her to practice any form of choice.

"My boy," said History, "you cannot find what you seek without using the yardstick of space and time. That currency comes from the term *current*, and it speaks the language of dreaming in a way that is relative to the times, relative to history."

The old man watched as the confusion faded from Choice's face as the boy said, "I know now what you mean by your own name. I know now that History indicates a story of some sort, *his* story. But who can *he* be?"

History laughed. "You will soon learn to maximize your presence in space and time to receive the best future that currency could promise and provide in return."

He watched as Choice's brow furrowed again and realized that he would have to explain himself better.

"But where is the meaning in this picture?" Choice asked. "Where is the element of life that connects the now with the future?" Choice paused to formulate his words. "You work now to save a currency that does not relate to your present—disconnected as you explain this currency that you speak of in the timelessness that you describe. It is like working on a great monument that you will never see finished in this lifetime in return for a promise to build a small house by the river. How can you relate your future to your present?"

As History pondered Choice's question, he might have reached up to scratch his head had he not been wearing his tightly wound headdress. It made him appear to be a wise, experienced man. He only smiled and shook his head, his long, flowing white beard gently undulating in the shade under the sweet-smelling pomegranate flowers and fruit. One red pod had burst and leaked onto the green grass at his feet. But in shaking his head, History had shifted his cap slightly, giving Choice a glimpse of his elongated ears and low forehead.

This man is full of mysteries, Choice thought, wondering what else was hidden beneath the cap. What physical deformities, what secrets of the universe? All he needed to do to get these secrets was to continue his visits to the garden. But after that, what? Could he pass the walls of Mimadamos, leaving behind his beloved mother and the beautiful world she had so carefully built and nurtured through the years?

Over the next few months, Choice weighed the cost of his freedom, during which the cypresses grew visibly taller and the fig tree spread its branches everywhere, though the pomegranate bush remained as it was.

Each day when the garden beckoned, Choice would step outside, tread the carefully laid paths under clouds and clear skies, and clamber over the large, smooth boulders to get to the spot where he knew History waited for him.

As they continued their discussions on the nature of life, Choice became increasingly aware that History was waiting not for further questions from his ward but for a sign. History was waiting for him to take action of some sort.

Inside the house, Destiny was aware of the same thing. She had watched with growing anxiety the way her son escaped into the dream garden as soon as his tutor had completed the day's lessons, which she had carefully selected for her son's growing imagination and his intellect. Destiny had always thought that out there under the vast expanse of green leaves and blue sky, her son was receiving lessons of another kind. Now she began to worry about the nature of those lessons.

On the other hand, History had provided them with security for so long. She believed that security had something to do with a powerful soul high in his castle in the glittering mountains of ice and rock. In that, she was right.

Destiny had also begun to accept the unshakable truth—her son had been born to souls who communed with the Divine. Freedom was his birthright, and she could not take it from him any more than Fate's elders had done when, as a young man, he had chosen to wander with his followers into those glittering, glasslike mountains and build for himself a world in the remote area near the village of Demire.

Slowly, very slowly, Destiny began to shake her feelings of anxiety and replace them with respect for what was best for her son and respect for what he sought. It would be up to the youth to seek his own destiny. Simultaneously, she knew he would always be cared for and that she need not fear for his safety if he were to seek his freedom. She was so engrossed in this logic that she forgot to consider the same factors for herself.

✳ ✳ ✳

In the meantime, Choice continued his multi-pronged quest for knowledge. Just as often, it was History who began the inquiry, usually by throwing out some mysterious comment, then waiting for the boy to take the bait. Choice always did.

"Time is akin to emitting," the old gardener said one evening when Choice came to find him after dinner, "which in turn is a live action." He handed the boy a ripe peach and waited for his answer.

"Is time, if emitted, not a dead unit of value?" Choice asked.

"Well," said History patiently. "Time is a code that you cannot stop or reverse; you can only imitate its value through script currency."

But Choice was in no mood for mysteries that evening. He wished to know what History meant by script currency.

"Script currency can be said to be dream paper," the old man explained, "paper that allows you to dream big and beyond the little dreams of men who just want food and shelter."

This answer still made little sense to Choice, for he had not, in his day-to-day life or in his mathematical lessons, encountered the meaning of currency and certainly not the need for it.

History closed his eyes briefly and felt his mind suddenly flooded with words, thoughts, and perceptions. He knew they were not his own. He was being telepathically prompted by Dhumanos from his underground lair in the Forget Lands.

"Who am I," History said slowly, "to think that I can be more giving than Time itself, to reject the offerings of script currency?"

History knew Dhumanos was referring to Time, of the Time and Space duo. Nevertheless, he wanted to hear Choice's analysis, for the boy had willed him, as much as Dhumanos, to make this statement.

By claiming he had won a battle against Fate's delegate, Destiny, Dhumanos had convinced himself that he had defeated God. He fabricated lies and inserted them into the translation of the sacred doctrines, thinking that by altering the translation, he could alter the core—the meaning being translated. This was a pure fantasy that he became trapped inside.

Of course, such a construct could deceive people only for a limited time, History thought. The truth always had a way of becoming known, though sometimes it was bruised and battered. Besides, this was not any ordinary truth, but it was the biggest reality controlling the whole universe. There was no way Dhumanos could alter the course of fate. Even Space and Time, whom Dhumanos believed to be his loyal servants, would in the end be the agents of his own crucifixion, not of his body, but of his ego.

CHAPTER 18

IT WOULD TAKE ANOTHER COUPLE OF MONTHS
and many more conversations with History before Choice finally voiced
his longing for freedom. When he spoke to the tutor about his wish to
savor the big world, to meet and interact with the souls, great and small,
who lived there, and to explore currency, Choice was met with a blank
stare. That was because the tutor himself was of Mimadamos and was
limited to matters of philosophy and academia. He had never even pondered the concept of currency, and he certainly never entertained the idea
of traveling outside the walls of Mimadamos.

On her way to her daily meeting with the tutor, Destiny overheard
what Choice had said. Although she knew this had been coming, her heart
raced in her chest, and she had to take a second to calm herself. A hundred thoughts raced through her mind in that moment as she weighed
the approaches she might take. Should she forbid him to leave and risk
losing his affection forever? Should she act as if she were unaffected by
his decision? Both options were equally gut-wrenching. In the end, she
decided the only thing to do was what she had always done when it came
to her son: impart information and pray that he would choose for his highest good.

When the lesson was over, she asked the tutor to kindly take his leave
so that she could speak to her son. "I know you are curious about the
concept of currency," she told Choice, "and I will tell you in the simplest

terms: currency was introduced to direct the Forgetters' vision away from the Now."

If Destiny thought this would suffice, she was mistaken. Choice's head tilted slightly to the right, a silent indication that he wanted a more complex explanation.

"The true base currency," she continued, "is food, then shelter, then tools, and then conveniences, but before it all gets too complex, it's much simpler to see it in terms of survival than in the way you're now curious about."

Choice looked at her. "Trade?"

"Yes, trade. I give you apples, and you give me potatoes. When I have more food than I need, I will trade for a blanket or even a horse or a plough. *Trade* is also called *barter*, and this is the system we use here in Mimadamos to exchange goods and services within our community. Elsewhere, they use a specific item, sometimes precious metals or jewels, as currency for trading. Each item of trade has value. However, as we progress, things get complicated.

"Say I make iron tools, and the tools are so good that everyone wants them. I can't make enough, so I need help. I get together with other blacksmiths, and we all work together, because we can make more tools together than we can individually. We then employ a furnace keeper; we each give a percentage of our earnings to pay him, which is worth it, because that leaves us more time to make the actual tools that bring in the currency.

"The furnace keeper does not make tools; his 'job' is to help the blacksmiths make more tools. When he made tools himself, he had to get raw iron once a month, which was a three-day trip. Now he must employ a worker to haul iron, but he does not make tools. Hauling iron on its own will not bring currency, unless, of course, the man works and trades to buy his own horse and cart and then buys the iron and resells it to the blacksmith. That's when they must figure out the cost of the iron in relation to the tools and in terms of how much food or other items he can buy. He also must figure how long the tool will last."

Destiny paused to see if her son was following. "Here's where it gets messy. The man who hauls the iron knows all the variables. He knows how much the tool is worth and how much it takes to make one. He realizes his earning potential. In all fairness, it takes a lot of time and effort to make a tool, and therefore, the higher percentage of the profit should go to the toolmaker. But the hauler has other ideas; he wants more. Without him, the toolmaker can't make tools. The toolmaker pays the hauler's higher price but then saves his currency and buys his own horse and cart.

"The hauler is now out of business, so he secretly attacks the new worker's horse and cart and smashes it up." Destiny considered stopping there when she saw her son's eyes widen in horror. Choice had never heard of such cruelty before. She then remembered that this was knowledge her son had requested. If he didn't get if from her, he would get it elsewhere. She placed a hand on his shoulder and softened her tone.

"He then offers the toolmaker iron at an even higher price. The toolmaker pays for a while and then buys a new horse and cart and pays security guards to protect it. Of course, due to these costs, he is forced to expand his business to make more profit to pay for all the overhead.

"All goes well for a while, but then someone else develops a better tool, which comes on the market backed and funded by—guess who—the hauler! And the cycle continues. They call it *supply and demand*. What is the price of water to a man dying of thirst? He would give you all he owned for one small drink. Trade can be exploited in the same way that everything can be exploited. It's like, 'Hey, I have more apples than I can eat; you pick what you like and let me take some of your oranges.' So the guy turns up with a huge carriage and picks them all!

"Now they introduce a word into the equation: *competition*! They say competition keeps prices down. The fact is that the main destabilizing variable is man and his greed. And this is why God told man to live in peace, to help one another, because when man becomes secular, the competition will not end until everyone is out!

"You have no idea, my son! Behind all the sophistication of the promised world you're dying to explore, there are two Stone Age men going at each other with stone axes over who gets to use the water hole. The axes are now sophisticated weapons, bigger and better for sure, but it's the same old thing."

Choice was shocked into silence at what he heard. He had never heard his mother talk this way before. Even more mind-boggling was that he'd never known she knew this much about the outside world. It was both disconcerting and exciting. He finally felt free to voice his wish to be on his own and explore that world for himself.

Destiny said nothing but looked at her son with a love and a sadness so profound that a wave of guilt washed over Choice.

However, even as he downplayed his desire, she knew in her inmost heart that his time had come, just as she had known when the time had come for her to leave Demire. Back then, all she could think of was her need to return to the organization that only a linear motif could provide. Only now, on the verge of losing her son, did she truly begin to understand how her husband had felt at that moment. She would have to allow Choice to walk his own path just as Fate had allowed her to walk hers. Destiny was trying so hard to quell the swirl of emotions circling her mind that she was unaware of the Archons' influence over them and the words she spoke to her son.

Emboldened by the knowledge that his mother would not stand in his way, Choice, who had skirted the topic of departure with History, now told him directly. It was time, Choice explained, for him to depart this carefully crafted dream world that had arisen from the depths of his mother's imaginings, a world that had both nurtured his intellect and kept him sheltered from the outside world. All he knew of this world he had gleaned from his trips to the library, but it had been enough to convince him that there were people and places out there who would fill the gap left in his life by his father's absence.

After Destiny headed back to the house, Choice sought History and found him pruning a magnificent purple shrub. Nearly bursting with excitement, he asked the question that had barely left his thoughts since he decided to leave Mimadamos: would his old friend help him find his way once he left the safety of these walls?

History turned his face toward his chest, burying it in the swathe of his white beard. For a long moment, he sat perfectly still on his seat like a great stone man carved onto a ceremonial perch. Then just when Choice began to despair, History spoke, his voice as deep as the rumble of thunder that now sounded from the rain clouds above them.

"Yes, young one," he finally said. "I will accompany you."

History had succeeded in what he had pledged to Dhumanos. Why, then, did he feel so unsure? It could be that History had a premonition of what was to come. Then again, if History had known of Fate's vision behind Choice entering the Forget Lands, the old man might have stopped him from leaving.

But being the weasel that History was, he had imagined that Choice would easily be lost amidst the tall forest trees that belted the thousands of acres around Forget's central area. Perhaps he would be enticed by a whole different lifestyle and become a hostage of Dhumanos, a permanent insurance policy against rebellion from Destiny.

Once History had promised his assistance, Choice felt great joy in his heart, and a wave of peace descended upon him. As he stood to return to the house for the evening meal, he thanked the old man.

"Can we set out tomorrow morning?" Choice asked. "I would like to spend one more night in my own bed."

In reply, History nodded but said that he had one condition. "We must be out of the gates of these serene surroundings before the first rays of the rising sun."

That night, the boy knelt by the side of his bed and prayed to the great unknown God of the world and of all things living. "Please, Lord, allow me divine guidance and assistance in making the right decisions as I take my first steps toward becoming the man I wish to be."

CHAPTER 19

THE GRAVEL PATH OUTSIDE THE GREAT GATES OF
Mimadamos appeared to wind away into the distance. Choice trod lightly
but quickly, the light bundle stuffed with a few of his belongings flung
over his shoulder. To his surprise, History kept pace with him, old as he
was. Choice had long marveled at the man's stamina as he toiled endlessly
in the garden, but this was something altogether different.

As they traveled, History also helped Choice cast aside all doubts—and
guilt—about leaving Mimadamos. Now as he and History chatted com-
fortably, Choice wondered whether the old man was his answered prayer.

The gravel before them was lit by silvery moonlight, for true to
History's words, the first rays of the new day had still not fallen upon
the Earth. The boy and man spoke to each other in hushed tones, both
unwilling, it would appear, to break the quiet of the departing night. They
had long ago fallen into easy camaraderie during their discussion every
evening in Mimadamos. Choice could bring up any matter, large or small,
and know that the two of them could speak of it with mutual respect
and, if not complete understanding, then at least the promise of it. Gone
were the days when the youth felt awkward about talking about his personal quest, when he would have to search for the words to formulate his
thoughts and queries. This day, when he was leaving the home where he
had come to live as a child, would be a new dawn in many ways.

"History, I cannot express this sense of freedom and elation," he said. "A sense of the boundless Earth and the skies above … it shakes me to the depths of my being like nothing I have ever felt before. This, even though I've had to leave behind my beautiful, thoughtful, and considerate mother and the marvelous home she has given me!"

Choice sidelined the thought of leaving as he recalled the tearful moment that he and his mother had shared before he left. The guilt rose in him again for a moment, then dissipated. He squinted at his mentor, trying to read his expression in the darkness.

"You know," said Choice, "you might have something to do with how good I feel. Is it because you are striding beside me, extending your assurance of safe passage as you had earlier assured us—mother and me—of a safe abode?"

History did not answer right away; he just smiled into his beard. He had done this on a few other occasions, and it seemed to indicate to Choice that he was loathe to say what was on his mind.

"It is for you to discover the source of your feeling, young master," he said finally, "but I must tell you that my role in your passage to freedom is at the behest of another; it is *his* bidding I do here today. Now I was not supposed to give you this information, but I can tell you that this is the result of your wishes. You and you alone have brought this plan to fruition. Even now, you can feel it in your bones, your need to escape the confines of your 'safe' home." History paused, as if still weighing his next words. "Given my commitments, I should be neutral to your choice, yet my years in your home have made complete neutrality impossible. All the same, you should know that this is not my story, not really."

When History saw the excitement and surprise flash across the boy's face, he tucked his face into his beard once again, for he had little doubt what the look was about. Finally, he had done what he was meant to do; he had set Choice on the path to separation from his mother as Dhumanos had requested. But he had done it in his own way, and he had taken it further, pointing the boy in the direction where a great evil lurked, where he might even come to bodily harm.

Yet even at the completion of his task—a task that had required years of meticulous planning and flawless execution—History found himself feeling incomplete. For unbeknownst to Dhumanos and his henchmen, Space and Time, History had a moral code all his own. He had been forced to overlook that code from the day he'd been sent to Mimadamos to answer the call for a garden designer, nurturer, and family protector. The code had remained buried under all the careful conversations and manipulations, and it was the source of his dissatisfaction now.

Striding beside History, Choice tried to control the conflicting emotions welling inside him. He had been looking for reassurance from History about embarking on this adventurous escapade; however, what he had gotten was a riddle. While this was not the first riddle he had received from his mentor, it was the first that whispered of Choice's dearest wish. His trust in History was absolute. When the old man said that it was for Choice to discern the nature of his feelings, Choice took this as a sign of respect for the boy's autonomy, not an attempt to duck responsibility for leading him from home. This was not what History was most excited about but the confession that History had acted at the direction of another. Could that other be the one Choice himself had longed to know for so long?

Choice thought again about his need for History's support, and suddenly, the words of his mother flashed through his mind: "When something goes wrong, as it often does, it is better to suffer the bitter taste of your own judgment and your own choice rather than to rejoice in the reflected sweetness of someone else's decision."

For years, she had articulated this sentiment in one way or another, but never had it seemed so relevant to his circumstances. As much as he wanted encouragement from History, the man he most respected, he had also been raised by a strong-willed mother to accept only that which had been fully initiated by his own will, might, and strength. He had been right in seeking to break away, he thought, and he could feel the confidence surge within him. It assured him that his endeavor, whether right or wrong, would be validated.

From the corner of his eye, he could see a glimmer; then, the first ray of sunshine struck his path. It was a good place to stop and mull over matters. *Then again,* Choice told himself, *why bother?* He was sure of what lay ahead. Another ray appeared to dance beside him, and he laughed. "Thank you for being here with me, O Giver of Light!"

He turned to share his mirth with History, only to realize with a start that History was nowhere to be found. The man who had spoken to him at length about whether this step should be taken, who had supported his decision and sent him safely on his path, had simply vanished!

For a few moments, Choice stood there, looking around in astonishment. He knew that he could not have stepped away from home had it not been for History. The man had made him feel so safe and secure on his journey out of the gate and beyond the high walls of their home. Now the sun was spilling here and there, but there was no one else about. Had something happened to History, or had his friend simply abandoned him?

The birds in the trees were astir, as they tended to be this time of the morning. A cool breeze was blowing along the path in the direction that he had been walking in, shivering the leaves of the trees around him. The trees held their boughs aloft. Were they calling to him, telling him where he must go?

He looked around again, realizing that he still felt as he had when he and History had started along the path. History had told him that this journey was of his own doing, so why shouldn't Choice feel as elated and as confident as when his mentor was standing beside him? The fact that the old man had left him on his own was a vote of confidence.

A great distance ahead, there appeared to be a cluster of trees. History had spoken of a tall forest tree belt that surrounded and protected the Forget Lands. *Perhaps*, he thought, *my proximity to Forget had something to do with the reason History left.*

Could this be the dark forest with trees taller than those in the garden at home, the one he had heard of as a boy, the place where children ought not go? *It is worth investigating,* thought Choice, who believed he had long ago left childhood behind. He was fifteen now, old enough to walk his own karmic path and be held accountable for the choices he made. So, as he set out toward the cluster, he felt that he was on the right track.

A few minutes later, he found himself passing through a portal, a wide gap between the trees. The path he'd been walking had quite abruptly ended, but Choice continued, telling himself there was nothing to fear. Yet he could not deny that the place was forbidding with its tall trees that grew untouched and wild. Suddenly, he wished he had his companion and mentor to guide him. History must have returned to his beloved garden at Mimadamos—or had he? The way the old man had departed without a whisper, Choice wondered if History—or that life in Mimadamos—had even been real.

CHAPTER 20

FOR A MOMENT, CHOICE IMAGINED THAT HISTORY might have existed only to counsel him and smooth his exit from Mimadamos. He guiltily pushed the thought from his mind. The world, after all, did not have to revolve around him, though his mother had raised him to think so. History was a real man, with a story beyond the limited chapter of escorting a boy out of Mimadamos. Shouldn't History, like any man, have his own significance? Had he no one to tell it? Choice wondered, for it seemed his mentor had no people of his own.

It struck Choice that he had never considered these things, never thought of his mentor outside his own need for his counsel. Perhaps this was why he had now arrived in this dark forest, where nothing moved and nothing guided him in any direction. Perhaps this was where his ego had led him.

Choice looked up past the treetops and watched the white clouds moving across patches of blue sky. There were no birds singing in those trees, no sound at all but the rustle of leaves. He looked again at the group of trees closest to him. Their boughs twisted and turned this way and that, hemming him in. This was a forest without direction, without any signs of life save his, and without any of the organized systems his mother was so fond of and had built into every aspect of their lives.

He thought back to the trees and vegetation of the vast garden at home and to the great house his mother kept in good order. He had known nothing 'til now of the wild nature that existed outside its walls. He was noticing more and more the lack of order, for there was not the slightest semblance of paths, nothing in the forest that seemed to point in any direction. Yet it seemed as though this unruly growth of trees had a purpose. This realization of things yet to be discovered invigorated Choice and challenged his senses. Everything surrounding him seemed to be an adventure beckoning him.

Choice thought back to the many conversations he'd had with his tutor and mentor about this place. History had said, "The forest is a place of wild growth with an abundance of greenery and animal life. A moody jungle filled with both things to eat and things to eat you. Therein lies the challenge for the adventurous and brave, for a man willing to seek himself and his place in this world on a physical plane and, thereby, learn about himself on a spiritual level." He had eyed his young friend and added, "A youth safe at home with his mother may not be the right sort to seek fulfilment there."

Excited by this idea, Choice had sought his tutor's opinion about exploring the forest.

"The forest beyond Mimadamos hides darkness that needs not challenge the person wise enough to avoid it," his tutor had said. "While facing both fear and difficult tasks causes one to grow, and through failure comes learning, there is no need to reinvent the wheel, as they say, and there is great wisdom in learning from the mistakes of others. No, the dark forest is best avoided. Why travel its paths when everything you need is here?"

As Choice continued to look around, he noticed that the untamed wilderness had a curious uniformity about it, an abundance that seemed to suppress the uniqueness of things. It was like an ecological storehouse that reduced each object's significance and made it less likely to impart knowledge. These trees and his wandering here could not be representative of anything or lead anywhere, he felt. This whole place and his journey here could have been a play of senseless numbers.

The trees were thick and tall with countless large leaves big enough to shelter an infant. But he had encountered no one. Not even birds sought to nest in the mighty twists and turns of the thick boughs. What was this place where dwelt no other forms of life? This may have been a garden, but it was as far from the garden at his home as he could fathom.

Choice dropped to his knees to view the thickly forested ground and saw that nothing crawled along this natural floor, at least not just now. What about the chipmunks that scurried up the fig trees and gnawed at the succulent bark in the garden at home? There were none here, but there was a bizarrely twisted tree—its trunk must have twirled when it was young and pliable. It reminded him of the spiral staircases at home, but when he attempted to clamber up one of the trees, it led nowhere.

Could this forest have grown in a great spiral, the lack of paths and its great circular trees part of a larger, chaotic plan that spiraled to a pinpoint? And if so, what would the iris of the great eye represent? It would have to be the place of his birth—Mimadamos, which was aware of this great forest but denied its existence. For how else could he have known so little of such a vast area of unchecked wilderness relatively close to home?

He had to admit that he was surprised at what he saw around him. Until yesterday, Choice had encountered only that which was in place, that which had been planned, organized, operationalized, and used accordingly. But when he examined his feelings a little more, he realized that the surprise was mild and held not a hint of fear. In fact, he was not sure he'd recognize the feeling; his mother had always protected him, had always feared on his behalf so that he would not have to.

Just as he had seen fear in Destiny's eyes, he had also seen it on the face of his tutor, who had often grown silent at Choice's more disturbing queries, or at least those for which the man had no answer.

Choice also remembered the day he encountered a lizard in the flower garden and watched it pluck off a small bee supping at nectar with the tip of its tongue. For one instant before the insect disappeared into the belly of the reptile, Choice could sense the panic in the tiny bee. That was fear, and for the first time, Choice wondered if the emotion had its usefulness. Should he be fearful now? Would the forest turn out to be a fearful place? Could he examine this forest carefully and without impediment if he knew the signs of danger?

No, he decided. He would find out in the way he had intended when he had planned to leave home. He felt no fear and could do without it.

He could not do without food, however, and he wondered if any was about. In all the excitement of discovery, he hadn't given nourishment much thought, and now he was starving. He didn't have to wander long before he realized that the forest was quite bountiful—and in a most unusual way. There were low-hanging grapes on one bough, cranberries on another, and his favorite—blueberries—on another. How could one shrub sport so many kinds of fruit, and all of them luscious and ripe? The only answer was that he'd found himself in a tumultuous riot of another type of nature. If Destiny had made her garden as close to Eden as possible, what then was this overgrown forest? And could it be home to various kinds of beings—good or perhaps not so good, even evil?

Occasionally, the undergrowth and even the tree boughs rustled as though they bore the temporary weight of a living being. But when he looked in their direction, he could see nothing and no one. If there was life here, it was as though the other was aware of his presence but had chosen not to reveal itself. One thing was sure, though. This was a living forest. Whether the life was all plants and vegetation or whether it was fortunate to share its bounty with other kinds of biodiversity, only time would tell.

CHAPTER 21

MUCH OF THE FOREST'S ALLURE, CHOICE CON-
ceded, was how different it was from the meticulously planned and
lovingly tended garden at home. The trees looked as though they had
stood there in chaotic communication for hundreds—no, thousands—of
years. From what he could fathom, some of the trees might have fossil-
ized and turned into rock, indicating millions of years. The Forbidding
Forest seemed more like a wall separating the land of Mimadamos from
the Forget Lands. It might not have permitted life from outside to advance
and savor its sweet fruit and shaded leaves until he had come upon it.

It struck him anew how easily he had gained access to this place, as if
a portal had invited him in. Was it by accident, or had it been prearranged
by History or some third party? That had yet to be revealed; however,
Choice intuitively knew that he couldn't have advanced this far without
some form of hidden permission, for the forest was both forbidding and
forbidden. Even as it called to him to investigate further, Choice began
to doubt the role of History and whether it was preplanned or as sponta-
neous and natural as it had previously seemed.

However he had gotten here, something was telling him that there
was more to this place than could be learned in books or even seen by
the naked eye. If the environment could indeed communicate with man,
it was doing so now. Why, even the trees, holding up their leaves as a
canopy, appeared to be urging him to make this forest his abode. It wasn't

that he did not appreciate the perfection his mother had created for him in Mimadamos, but he could not deny that in this thickset forest, the mighty forces of nature itself were tempting him like a siren's call from afar.

He now came upon a burst of color. Here were flowers he had never thought possible. There was night-blooming jasmine in the daytime and in all colors and bright tropical hibiscus to outdo them.

He decided that he could rest here a while. Something had directed him toward this sea of flowers in the forest. The something or someone was sending out a strong message, one he would not overlook.

And then he knew. There was not a force from without that had sent his footsteps toward the tropical flowers, a sweet temptation to offset the rational order of his childhood home and garden. Indeed, that was what had brought him into this beautiful, tumultuous jungle. He could only hope that he was not imagining what he now beheld before him, for it seemed like a dream.

Once again, the thought crossed his mind that the decision to go was not completely his own. Someone had sent him forth from Mimadamos, and something here was bidding him to stay and investigate. The some-one at home had been History, but what of the something that was draw-ing him farther here in the tangle of trees and branches, giving a hint of how colorful life could be if he would but stop and look and let it speak?

He had hoped at the outset that this place, this forest, would lead to another kind of home, albeit quite different than the one he had known. "But what can you assure me?" he asked this unknown entity. "How would I sustain myself? How would I shelter myself, and what would I do to pass the time?"

He waited a while, but there was no one clear answer. It was as though a multitude of voices were speaking to him. He heard the deep voice of a man, who told him that he was needed here as the frontrunner of a great battle still to come. Then he heard a harsh voice saying he had played into the evil one's clutches. In between, there were lesser voices, some shrill, some soft, all drawing him farther in.

Even as he listened, he looked up again to see the light filtering through the leaves. It had to be noon or close to it—time to move on. His discovery had driven him to this place, and he would have to stay and decipher all the messages streaming through in the same way that the sun was beaming forth its rays.

As he began walking farther into the forest, Choice glanced again at the dazzling orb he could see through a network of light and shade. The words fell into his mind, "Behold the sun, the highest symbol of giving. Behold the rays of the sun! Does the sun present its rays to light a world into the presence of man and his environment, or does it simply shine for itself, for what it is?"

At that instant, the sun was so strong that he thought of having to run back to the shelter of the giant trees. Instead, he stopped and raised his face, then his arms, paying tribute to the great, life-giving orb.

Choice paused to think about the nature of the sun, of its rays and light. Sunlight could see through the history and geography of the world and its people. It could filter through their anatomy and influence their psychology. It could bring forth what it wished anyone to see. And then as he watched the particulate dots of light that continued to dance in their wave formation, he thought he could make out a frail figure, partly obliterated by the shafts of luminescence that danced in straight lines in front of it. For a second, he thought it might have been his mentor History, for the two shared a certain artisanal quality, but History wasn't as old and was not the slightest bit stooped, as this figure appeared to be.

Still, Choice was hopeful as he stared for a long moment at the figure who appeared to have been beamed into existence by the sun. "Who are you?" he asked finally.

"Boy, I am the Demiurge," the figure said. "I have been responsible for the fashioning and maintenance of the physical universe and the element of light that you were contemplating today in such depth. These are aspects of knowledge, some of which you have always held within yourself since birth and some of which you have been eager to learn from the books in your library and from your tutor."

Choice just stood and stared at the figure in surprise. Could this Demiurge be the same emblem of the Gnostics that he had learned about in his lessons in spirituality? Choice knew that the Demiurge was not a person; so how, then, could he dwell in this forest?

As if reading Choice's thoughts, the Demiurge looked him in the eye and shook its head *no*. It would have the boy feel that it was somewhere between an inner projection and an outer reality, a visual explanation of the nature of sunlight as it converges with the light of vision. It was as if both the Demiurge itself and the material from which it had fashioned the universe had always been there, for the universe was uncreated and eternal.

It might be the Creator, or it might be a figment of Choice's imagination. Either way, by its very presence, it seemed to be warning the youth against the material universe. Could it be referring to the comfort of Choice's life until the day before? This time, when Choice asked it to clarify, the luminous figure nodded *yes*.

Choice looked around him in wonderment. So this was it! This pure, natural forest, which was alternately threatening and tempting, would have him enter still farther. This, then, was a non-material interest. Still, he thought it might fashion a dwelling place.

As Choice continued to gaze at the figure, he realized that he had just received a lesson simply because he had been in the right place at the right time. Had he not entered the forest on this day, he might not have encountered this phenomenon. He wondered if his decision to leave home would deliver him from the constraints of earthly existence and usher him into the supramundane place of freedom he had dreamed of.

At that, the wrinkles of the figure's ancient face lifted into a smile. Now it was the fire it held within its own being that showed through, for this was a spirit that was eternal.

Choice looked upward again at the streaming particles of life, grateful for his luck on this portentous day. He was confident that he had received blessings of one who was Divine. He thanked the stars and the very sun above and turned back to the eternal wisdom that had chosen to visit him. But when he looked back at the figure, it was gone, just like his mentor. It was as if they had never been. Once again, Choice realized that he would have to find the answers on his own.

CHAPTER 22

AS HE CONTEMPLATED THE RECENTLY DEPARTED
figure, Choice recalled the spiritual truths his tutor had imparted. Some
months ago, he'd hinted that Gnosis was the forbidden religion of the
mind, which would not be given a place in any man. "The mind," he had
explained, "cannot be truly activated, save in grey situations where right
and wrong are not clear cut.

"For there is no clear-cut right and wrong, my son, despite what the
feebleminded want you to believe. There is only ignorance and knowledge.
Knowledge is like the sun, and ignorance is the endless space around it. It
stretches in all directions, and the farther you get from the sun, the more
you lose any sense of direction or have any idea of your own whereabouts.
This is ignorance, my son, to be lost to the point that you forget what it's
like to be guided."

Choice couldn't help but see the correlation between the tutor's words
and the lands he now found himself in: the Forget Lands. And what of the
many moods of this forest, the signs of emotional turmoil he was receiving
even now, as he mulled over all that he had come to know? For the trees
and flowers and shrubs were continuing to communicate, to speak to him.
They might have been communicating about themselves, and they were
definitely communicating about him, telling him to go forth and discover
more, as he must, while cautioning him about the unknown.

It wasn't just nature's bounty that he was listening to, either; there were also hints of the same voices he had heard earlier. Were any of those voices human? Some certainly sounded so, while others emitted strange, guttural noises he'd never heard before. One thing was sure: they were all clamoring for his attention. He wondered for a moment if he should try to get away, for what they were saying brought him close to a feeling of alarm. Were these the sounds of Hades, of beings that went about daily tasks but were devoid of a soul?

Beneath the cacophony, Choice could distinguish more refined voices that spoke of a secret link between the heavenly and the earthly in an unending pattern of simplicity. Even now they were revealing the timeless code that bound the two seemingly separate worlds in a logic of its own. If that link existed, could there not be another, viler link between the earthly and the labyrinthine Hades? Choice bent his head, his mind in awe. This journey, only recently begun, had afforded him lessons unlike any other. He had been tutored in this great forest about matters he had not known existed.

If this much knowledge had flowed into him during one day, what more awaited in his next steps? He walked farther into the depths of the forest and came upon a great tree, the gnarled roots of which had turned clockwise on itself to present a most comfortable seat. He sat upon it and leaned against the trunk. The bark felt as smooth as the face of a rock that had split open to provide shelter for men.

Suddenly, a wave of sleepiness came over Choice. It was not unpleasant but more like the tiredness one feels after a day of frolicking in the sun and surf. He could snooze here a while; after all, what else did he have to do on this day other than find sustenance and shelter? Food was not a problem, for even farther into the forest, he'd found the same abundance of fruits, edible flowers, leaves, roots, and shoots. But what about a place to sleep tonight? Would the forest provide that as well?

Then again, he thought as he snuggled his back against the smooth tree trunk once more, *this might do nicely*. His body was comfortable and his mind at ease; in fact, after this great day, with all he had learned and experienced, he would love to surrender his destiny for all time to this forest.

Yet as at home as he felt, Choice was still aware that he was *not* home. Deep inside, he knew that staying in the forest meant never seeing his mother, the most beauteous and most thoughtful of all mothers and all women. It was a terrible thought, even if, as he suspected, it was his destiny to come here.

He wondered again to what extent History had pushed and influenced him. Could his escape to his future be a retreat to the past? Could he be on a circular journey, only to realize that the parameters of destiny limited his choices?

He loved his mother too much to think of his decision to leave Mimadamos as an escape from her and her carefully designed environment. It was, rather, a journey during which the boy expected to discover a great deal, as he was doing even now. A wave of homesickness washed over him, followed immediately by the thought that this was irrational. How could it be, if the decision to leave had been his? Why was he overthinking what had taken place right after it had happened? Who was he to judge it to be good or bad?

Even at this young age, Choice intuitively knew that such obsessing led to circular reasoning, and that was never productive. If he could not get by without Destiny, he would at least have to stay with his decision. Too much pondering along these lines would only hold him back, and he would end up being a loser, he knew. It would be worse than being the youth who was planning to step out back there in Mimadamos. It would be a confirmation that he had lost his way back and had no destination. He had no way of knowing that he was working this out in his mind much the way his mother had after leaving Fate's home in Demire.

As the angles of light shifted with the passing hours, Choice remained seated at the base of the tree and marveled at the great activity of his mind even as his body lay in repose. This forest might not have had any physical paths for him to traverse, but he was discovering more and many paths through which to channel the equations of his mind. At last, he was beginning to grasp why his mother had a maze installed in their garden: she had wanted to convey that there was no one path to the truth. There lay many paths, and they were all drawn beforehand by an inner map. Heaven and Earth, too, he realized, could be immeasurable.

His mind raced on and could sing and dance its way through all the paradoxes that presented themselves to him now and at any one instant. Being alive itself could be an equation that would not be activated without paradoxes. He had certainly entered that grey area his tutor had discussed, a place where there was no apparent clear-cut right and wrong.

Grey, he now understood, awakened the mind; it was the logical bridge between poles and paradoxes and gave rise to the autonomy of thought and direction. He tried to imagine the reason why God had chosen to create the first man, Adam. Had He done so just to fully control Adam like some machine programmed to undertake tasks with complete neutrality, or had He expected more from him? Would He want His creation also to be a creator, even bypassing Him to create something new? Then, of course, there was the risk that Adam would turn from God to exercise his own godhood and write his own history.

History ... Choice again conjured up the old man in his mind's eye. His thoughts raced back to that morning, to History as he had stepped away and probably returned to his greatly loved garden and his task of taking care of all that lived there. History had simply let go without a murmur. It suddenly occurred to Choice that, for all their time together, he knew very little about the man himself. Moreover, they had never discussed God, and Choice wondered whether History even believed in an entity that upheld the order of the world and the universe, the singular, unified Creator of the dimensions. History had alluded to a master, though, so who could that be?

It suddenly struck Choice as odd that, for all the times he'd been so enamored with what History had to say and for how eagerly he had waited for his lessons to end so that he could run to the garden and speak with his mentor, ultimately their discussions had not touched on anything of real value.

No matter, he thought now, snuggling against the tree, *for I have all the time to investigate such matters in this place.*

It was dark now, and his belly was full, so he did not have to move from his seat of comfort at the base of the tall tree with its branches spreading upward and outward. He craned his neck as before to look up at the dark sky through the leaves above.

Though he had seen only the Demiurge, Choice sensed the presence of a multitude of beings—the same who had been speaking to him before. But as for any of the order of atoms and molecules being real, Choice did not know for sure, in the same way that he could no longer say with finality whether his home in Mimadamos had been real.

For an instant, he thought he had another vision of the Demiurge. He thanked him for making this day possible, and then he nodded off to sleep.

CHAPTER 23

CHOICE DREAMED THAT HE WAS HIS MOTHER, seeing through her eyes, standing by the Forget Lake, the famous body of water separating Mimadamos from Demire, located in the narrowest area of the Forget Lands. It was nighttime, and the moonlight lit Destiny's reflection as she gazed into the lake's murky depths.

A beautiful reflection stared up at her from the surface, a more perfect version of her face. It called up to her, "Join me, sister. Come into the water."

"But I cannot swim," Destiny said, searching her memory to recall if that was true, suddenly unsure.

The reflection beckoned. "Come in! Indulge and baptize yourself within the depths."

A voice within her cried out, "No! Stay where you are, for down there in the water world you have created is something deep, heavy, and contaminating."

The woman in the water, who was she and yet not she, smirked and mocked her. "You might sink to the bottom and drown, or you might rise to the top on your rolls of buoyant motherhood fat." The woman leaned toward her, the image expanding to reflect Destiny looking closer into the surface. "Or you can continue to stand there safe but forever haunted by the possibility of 'what if,' doomed to a life not fully lived."

The third option, she found most disturbing of all. Destiny felt drawn inexorably toward the water. But why was this so? She, who had always been her own person, was now enveloped in the grip of a malevolent impetus as she imagined plunging into the depths.

As though some force pushed her or made up her mind for her, she stepped into the water and waded in above her ankles, knees, waist, and shoulders. Soon her feet ceased feeling the silty bottom, and she waved her arms to keep her nose and mouth clear. Icy fingers massaged her scalp as her head dipped below the gentle waves.

The water closed over her head, and she sank to the bottom with a force that pushed the air from her lungs. Even as she held her breath to keep the fluid from rushing into her nose and mouth, she could not stop the thoughts from rushing into her mind. She realized that she was no longer Destiny. She had left her physical self. The one known as Destiny had transmigrated into the body of her son as he slept in a dark forest under the protection of a tree. Destiny was encased in the being of Choice. Her will to cast herself into the lake had grown from her will to see and experience what Choice was seeing and experiencing at this time. It was the need to reach out for him and her own yearning for a freedom that had been unfulfilled.

At that moment, curled under his tree, Choice felt an incredible lightness of being. In his dream, he, too, had plunged into the deepest water, but it had been of his own will. Unlike his mother, Choice was at home in the water. He had known how to swim and float from infancy. Joy surged within him, and it was Choice who floated up in the water with an inexplicable exhilaration. Not even heaven (as the faithful villagers in Mimadamos described it) could have made him more joyful as he came up for air.

Then, even as Choice floated joyously on the surface, he could see his mother, who had been transformed into him only minutes ago, still standing at the edge of the lake. It seemed that she was paying heed to that inner voice to take care. In the next instant, his joy evaporated, and he froze, for he saw that Destiny was being set upon by an untold horror – misshapen creatures hunched a few feet away, gearing up to attack. He watched helplessly as they began throwing stones at her without thought, their only intention to harm. Just when he thought it couldn't get worse, they called her names—awful words he never heard before but instinctively knew were utterly vile.

"Whore!" one creature shrieked, savoring the word as one would a salty treat.

Choice flinched at the sound, wondering whether he could get to the spot where she stood, but he couldn't move. The savages closed in on his mother and tore at her clothes. For what seemed like hours, they viciously attacked her in every way possible. Finally, they left her bruised and beaten at the side of the lake. Again, Choice tried to move toward her but found that he couldn't leave the water.

Destiny groaned, and he saw that her stomach was starting to expand. Not believing his eyes, Choice blinked several times. To his horror, he saw his mother's stomach split open and a multitude of half-human, half-savage offspring crawl out.

Suddenly, Choice found that he could move. As quickly as he could, he waded toward the shore and climbed out, but before he could reach his mother, the creatures, sensing a threat, turned to him. Choice gasped when he saw that every one of the creatures looked exactly like him! As they raced toward him, he instinctively backed up to the edge of the lake, debating how he could best protect himself but coming up empty. Then he noticed something curious—the beasts appeared to be fearful of the water. Their steps slowed, and their faces scrunched anxiously. They looked like doubtful thoughts wearing human flesh. Choice stepped into the water, eliciting a series of angry grunts. They looked like Choice, yet they lacked the courage to jump in as he had.

Choice's victory meant little to him, because he still couldn't protect his mother. This, he realized, was what the beasts wanted: for him to suffer through his mother's suffering. They wanted to mock his love for her.

Choice had to do something, but what? His mind raced for a moment before he remembered that he was in a dream. He couldn't move on a bodily level, but perhaps he could alter the events some other way using his mind. He willed himself to the beginning of the dream when he'd seen Destiny standing by the lakeshore and contemplating whether to go in.

In the original dream, Destiny had thrown herself into the lake and had been transformed into him. That was when he had come to consciousness and his being had taken over. Could he reimagine an alternate course? At first, it seemed so unlikely that Choice began to panic. But then he took several deep breaths and reminded himself that these horrors, no matter how vivid, were not real. He could control them.

What, then, was real? Choice willed himself to turn away from the mayhem imposed by a pack of humanoid animals on the shore. He thought he could shake it off and come out of the first dream. But when he did, another thought arose in him. Choice had realized by now that the Forget Forest had much to communicate, much to reveal. Now he realized that in the vast forest dwelled many secrets he had yet to know about.

He'd no sooner had the thought when he felt his inner self detaching from his physical body and lifting high in the air. Choice could see himself still lying on the forest floor at the base of the tree. He was having an out-of-body experience, looking at himself from above. He could see the treetops, see his treetop and the place where he reposed against the polished bark.

Destiny was not here in body or in spirit; nor was anyone else. Could he continue this journey and flit through the branches of the sleeping trees as a bird might, even in the daytime? Again in his mind he wandered through the forest, savoring its sights in the dark through the mists of dreams, each more pleasant than the last.

But Choice was still a youth. At some time in the aftermath of the nightmare, he had yet another newfound sensation. He had always had the security at home of knowing that his mother would be nearby, that she was there when he needed her. Now that this was out of the question, he began to miss his mother dreadfully.

Like most children, he had always thought of Destiny as simply his mother, solely there to comfort and guide him. The dream, as awful as it was, had taught him that she was much more than that. Though she had never complained to him about anything, Choice could sense a great pain, a torment that nothing could quell. He sensed for the first time that she, too, had a story, a struggle that she had hidden from him. Now he began to suspect that this struggle had something to do with the Forget Lands, that it was the reason for the scary stories he'd been told as a boy.

Despite this, Choice had the resiliency of a child—one whose mother had taught him that he was capable of anything. So when he awoke the next morning, he allowed the light of day to dispel the horrors of the night before. He could see that the sun had long ago begun its climb and was beaming its rays between the middle branches of the trees.

He stretched lazily and realized that he was no longer leaning against the bark of the tree but was lying on the plush carpet of green grass. A blanket of moss covered him, and another was cushioning it. Who had cared for him in the second sleep?

He wanted to find out, but first he needed sustenance. He glanced around, then moved toward another tree, where he drank the tea off the strong middle vein of a bramble leaf. Beside it was one of those trees that sported many types of fruit. As he munched on cherries, he heard, from the branches above, the warbling of a vireo. Yesterday, the forest had bidden Choice to enter, and today, a bird was singing seemingly just for him. He wondered if he should go forth once more or stay in his very comfortable place of repose, which seemed to have been built around him, enfolding him in its arms as he slept.

Even as he pondered whether or not to stay in his temporary abode, he thought again of Destiny and the grief he sensed within her, the pain she could never explain to her son. From there, his thoughts ran to the unknown image of a father, a man strong enough to let his mother go. The thoughts behind the images were clamoring for his attention, and he was given an inkling of why and how his parents had come together in the first place and why they had separated—or had they?

Clearly, Destiny thought they had. She had seen fit to build a house and a garden designed to last a lifetime and more—for Choice and his descendants and their descendants – without any involvement of his father. But what of her husband? Did he feel the same way? The answer was negative. Of this, Choice was as sure as he had been of his mother's grief the night before.

He was suddenly struck with the realization that his father had known about their lives all along—including the house Destiny had designed for their son. Perhaps he had even been with them from day to day! It was what Choice had fervently wished for all along from the time he had been born into consciousness. His heart racing, Choice wondered if Fate could see him now.

The answer was a thunderous "Yes!" that resounded inside the mind of Choice.

Was his father the one who had bidden him to enter the Forget Lands and sent the vision of the Demiurge to inform him on the first day of his travels?

The answer, this time, came in the form of a rustling of leaves and a happy warbling song from the sole bird.

It's like a drug, thought Choice, *this ability to ask a question and have the answer neatly delivered into the mind. How am I receiving all these answers?*

"Through mind-reading and transference," he was told.

His excitement growing, Choice asked, "Has my father read my mind before?"

"Yes, but you were still a child then and were not aware of such transference, at least not on a conscious level."

Choice heard a man's deep chuckle, but the Demiurge had more to communicate. This time, Choice only heard the voice without seeing the image he had seen before.

"He can do this only with you. Yes, he can tune in to your perception, feelings, and afflictions, as well as your day-to-day experiences. He has mastered the transmission of information from one person to another without using any of your known sensory channels or physical interactions."

In that moment, Choice knew that his father had to be living somewhere close to the Forget Lands. That must be why this forest appealed to him in every way, giving him sustenance and safety, and why he had set forth in his dreams last night. Anxiously awaiting the next transmission, Choice put out a feeler in case this forest was indeed the abode of his father.

"But why have you not revealed yourself, Father?" Choice had been here for some time now. Was the forest that keen to keep his father in hiding and not reveal his presence or his identity? And if it was, how could it stop his father from making himself known? "Surely a man powerful enough to know his son through transference cannot be stopped by anything, can he? Not even a forest."

Choice asked the environment around him once more, "Why should I have such a thought? For if my father is not a man, what is he? Can he be of the divine?"

But this time, he received no answer at all.

His confusion seemed to be mirrored everywhere in the chaos of the forest. There were vines but no vipers, twisted boughs that could have been stairways spiraling to nowhere, and flowers that bloomed whether it was day or night. A forest that appeared 'til now to have no presence other than his own. But what of those others—not all of them human—that he could sense? Could those awful creatures he had seen so clearly in his dream, those who had set upon his mother, be real? And what of the result of their attack, those creatures who looked exactly like him but lacked a soul? Choice's flesh crawled, and he did not wish to know any more. The silence that had met his last query directed at the great unknown was an answer itself.

Choice could not simply shut off his mind and ignore all that was going on around him. What was the nature that dominated this forest and made it possible for a nightmarish dream to be transformed into reality? Was Choice simply at the start of a great adventure that would lead to the parent he had missed sorely since birth?

With that thought, Choice's somber mood lifted, and he became energized once again. He now had a notion of the horrors that might greet him here, and he was prepared. He was alone in this place, and with every step, he would have to consult his inner senses to make sure he was going in the right direction.

After walking for some time, Choice realized that he was once again famished. He'd no sooner had the thought than he spotted a shrub full of blueberries and cherries. As he plopped down under it and began to pick the fruit, he wondered what it would have been like to grow up in this place. How would things have been with the forest as his home if Destiny had provided the food from these boughs and from this soil? How would it have been if all knowledge in the library could have been stored instead in these natural surroundings? It was a delicious dream, but he tried to shake it off, telling himself that there was no point in speculating on what could have been. He had adventures to embark on.

CHAPTER 24

CHOICE WAS RIPPED FROM HIS MUSINGS BY THE sudden rustling of leaves followed by the distinctive sound of a twig cracking. There was movement afoot. Could it be another person—or persons? His eyes darted to and fro; he looked all around him for who or what it might be.

They were nearly upon him now. He heard, then saw one light set of feet running in great haste. At first, he could not see anything else through the thick shrubbery; then a girl came into view—a damsel fleeing from something or someone. Choice heard her plaintive cry for help and then the heavy footsteps of men running after her.

Without thinking, Choice assumed a crouching position, facing the direction from which they would come. He had no idea who this girl was, only that he had to protect her. When he saw her fear-filled face, it reminded him of the nightmare—watching in helpless horror as a woman was set upon by evil creatures. He was also struck by the girl's beauty, for she had the face of an angel. He had seen only one other face with such sensitivity, such beauty, and that was his mother, Destiny.

As the girl ran past him, Choice stepped out from under the shrub. Their eyes locked, and she slowed down as if realizing that she would now be safe, that Choice would protect her. She stood there for a moment, hands on her knees, gasping for air.

Choice drew himself to his full height, trying to look as imposing as he possibly could at his youthful age. It worked. Two men burst through the trees at breakneck speed, only to come to an abrupt halt a few feet from where Choice stood. They were bigger and far stronger than he, yet the two were clearly intimidated.

Choice did not give this much thought, however, for his only priority was the girl. This was new to him, the feeling that he must protect someone; everyone had always protected him. The only other time had been during the nightmare, when the beasts had set upon his mother. He had not been able to save Destiny then, but he would save this girl. This determination gave him courage to do what he must.

Choice was utterly shocked when the two brutes turned and began to run back in the direction from which they had come, cursing and yelling as they went. The direction ... As he watched them, Choice realized that the men had not just run away aimlessly but with purpose, almost as if they were going to report what they had just witnessed to some party more important than themselves. Choice didn't know where they were going or to whom they were reporting, but he promised himself that he would find out.

What disturbed Choice even more was what he had heard the two of them yelling. What was this cursing all about? They had not cursed him as he faced them in the stance of the protector but of all people, History! What possible reason could these two ruffians have to utter his mentor's name—and with such vitriol?

Even more curious than the expletives was something Choice had heard as the two ran away. "We knew this man was crazy!" the one snarled. "It's one thing to trust him and another to send him on a mission that our whole destiny depends on! He wasn't meant to direct the boy here! That was never part of the plan."

"How will we explain this to Dhumanos?" the other cried.

Dhumanos? Who is that? Does this all have to do with History? Choice wondered. This cemented what had begun as a suspicion about History. Had History sent him here to face the dangers lurking in this overgrown forest, knowing Choice could never make it through safely?

A still worse suspicion entered his mind. Could History have wanted to have his way with Destiny and wished Choice out of the way? Had

Destiny been held all this time in Mimadamos in compliance to a certain threat or in fear of a power who had ordered her so?

Even as fear raced frantically through his mind, Choice could still hear the hoarse voices of the two men: "What will happen to our rank and reputation now? Why did History go to such lengths? Why did he let the boy out of Mimadamos?" He strained to listen to the last of this, for their voices were fading away.

It still made no sense to Choice. Behind him, the girl waited, trembling in fear of what could have been.

"What's your name?" he asked her.

"Hope," she said.

✳ ✳ ✳

Time and Space ran through the forest in retreat; they were not used to seeing such conviction in the Forget Lands. The laws of this place had not been founded upon usurpation; however, over the years, it had become so. Its children were the fruit of force and rape, and they carried with them some latent memory of the instant they were begotten. They would also represent a certain doubt akin to that which haunted Destiny in that dream before she threw herself into the pond and surrendered to whatever awaited her.

That moment of doubt seemed to be encoded in those born in the forest. These Forget dwellers greatly feared the unknown, a power they did not understand but could sense. Perhaps this fear had inspired and given rise to the law of the heartless; whatever the case, they had accepted it, kowtowed to it, and allowed it to become part of their fabric.

Space and Time detected in Choice a great power that combined goodness with might. It defied claims by the Archons that such foolishness had no place on Earth. Choice's power was such that it could only reflect an unknown code to them, or perhaps it came from the privileged bearing within him. He was made, quite literally, of different stuff.

Space and Time were programmed to prolong the faulty dream setting of the Forget Lands, to allow the Archons' scripts to flourish and expand, and to prevent an awakening that would collapse dimensions and bring back the messed-up creation to its Creator. This boy, Time and Space realized, could put a wrench in those plans, for what flowed from his eyes was the same ferocity seen in the gaze of his father, Fate, whenever *he* was disturbed by a wrong.

"We must find that rapscallion History," Time insisted as they ran.

Space scowled at the trees in their path. "Indubitably."

CHAPTER 25

IN TRUTH, SPACE AND TIME HAD ALWAYS PRE-
sented themselves as the wise among the Forgetters due to their strong
position with Dhumanos and their unique ability to enter Mimadamos
without revealing their true nature. Of course, no one in Mimadamos
knew that they had secretly given their allegiance to the Archons. Truth
be told, they had done Mimadamos a favor, for in trying to impress the
Archons, they had prevented many of the attacks they'd planned to level
at the village. In promising the Archons more power at the right space
and time, Space and Time had managed to keep the hellions' appetite for
destruction in check.

In the meantime, they enjoyed the confused energy of the forest while
imposing laws and restrictions on others through bullying, cajoling, or a
combination of the two. Thus, Time and Space continued to straddle the
worlds of Mimadamos and the Forget Lands. They had both been invited
to Mimadamos on Destiny's wedding day and had watched from afar
the many celebrations, even though they couldn't catch a glimpse of Fate
himself. They, too, had seen the glint of fire in Destiny's eyes, and they'd
suffered pangs of jealousy at what they'd seen—the love and trust that
the lady Destiny had extended to her husband. To them, she had always
seemed untouchable, out of their league, and they resented her attachment to another.

Whatever goodwill they had for Mimadamos, it did not extend to Hope. Whenever they saw that fragile maiden, they chased her down like a lion chases its prey. They could never catch her, though. Hope always managed to give them the slip one way or another. This last time, it had been Choice who stood in their way, an unexpected event for which they blamed History.

History shivered in the cave's dank, damp darkness. He closed his eyes, trying to project himself back among the sun-drenched plants of his garden at Mimadamos, but when he opened his eyes again, he was still tied to a rough-hewn chair in the inky blackness.

After the debacle with Hope, History had been summoned to the Forget Lands, where Space and Time had promptly dragged him to this cave, tied him up, and interrogated him. The two brutes now stood beside him, trying to keep their fury in check long enough to get information about the boy.

"I know nothing, no more!" History rasped, struggling against the cords binding his hands and feet. "I really don't know why I encouraged Choice to make a choice!" He shook his head. "You see, if there's one thing I realized while in Mimadamos, it is that this so-called reality we're living in is unreal. It's regressive, not progressive. It revolves in a descriptive mode to explain what already is, never informatively to discover what shall become. I felt so useless in such a reality. I wanted to prove myself real. It's as if the alleged ending our masters fear has already happened long before the beginning or as if the ending and the beginning meet at the reverse ends of a circle. We're only here to witness and understand it."

Space and Time popped their eyes wide open as they heard the man speak. It was as if his words came close to demystifying their significance as well. Armageddon was not an event waiting to happen. The ending had preceded the beginning, and people were here on Earth only to comprehend its machinations, like a star that had died millions of years ago but could still be seen in the night sky. Space and Time had the power to deceive the mind, to trick it into believing that what had already happened was yet to happen.

Such was Dhumanos's need for Space and Time. Those two, however, knew the truth: that Armageddon was only a figment of the Archons' imagination and that the real big event had already taken place. This was why they viewed the Forget Lands as a hell or a judgment field that they had to find a way to endure. So they played games with Hope, chasing after her here and there. They practiced tricks on the Forgetters and made them dependent on paper currency.

"What is this gibberish, old man?" Space asked. "Have you gone crazy? Has Destiny bewitched you? Have your years in that garden turned you soft?"

They kicked and punched him, but he just smiled and blurted, "Armageddon!" Noting the enraged faces of Time and Space, he added, "Torture me as you wish; end me if you want. The time for secrets is gone. For fifteen years, I've tried to warn you about Mimadamos. I sent you messages, but you were too busy waging your wars of greed to listen!"

"This is all our fault," Time muttered.

"Yes," agreed Space, "we never should have sent this nut on such a delicate mission."

History smirked. "You sent me there to keep Destiny in check, because you feared her vengeance, but you had no idea how divine vengeance works. This is not a game, and I don't have a PhD in Godhood. Our end is near. I can't describe it, and you can't even get ready for it. It's not the size of it that shakes me; it's the deceptive simplicity! It's written on the helpless faces of the Forgetters, and it's personal, for Fate will come neither like the mighty dinosaur you imagine nor like the helpless Messiah you mock! He will not come to fight you from somewhere outside; he will come from within like a thief on a moonless night. Just pray you maintain your sanity or withstand the power of his presence.

"You ask if Destiny bewitched me? I don't know if *bewitch* is the right word, but she has affected me. You two are right about one thing," he spat at them with disdain, "I am not the same History you knew or sent on a mission back then.

"I myself do not know yet how and why I let Choice out into the Forest. For the first time ever, I am sure of nothing, not even my own actions and my reasons for doing them. I fear it wasn't the real me but a high or drugged version of me—or perhaps I was but a mere tool in hands bigger than I can imagine.

"I fear my spell has been broken, and I have no significance in the timeless world to come—or perhaps in the world that has always existed without us knowing of it. I pray only that I preserve enough sanity to recollect who I once was."

History smirked again, enjoying the fear he saw on the faces of Time and Space. "None of this matters, you see, because from Fate's point of view, this all has already happened. We were all 'history' long before we ever were conscious enough to realize it. We're here in space and time to comprehend our sentence, not to alter it, as a prisoner singing in his cell could never alter the reality of his imprisonment."

History paused, wondering how he had ever gotten mixed up with these two fools. Then he shrugged and said, "Damned if you do, and damned if you don't."

CHAPTER 26

HOPE WAS A DRAZIAN. SHE BELONGED TO THEIR ruling class. A happy child, she simply accepted her station as normal, but as she got older, she began to realize that something wasn't right. Hope was also interested in Fate. Like many other young Drazians, she consulted the Spiritual Pentagon, a group of five long-bearded Drazians who claimed to have direct contact with him. She asked them every question that came to mind but found their answers sorely lacking. Eventually she perceived them as little more than con artists selling spirituality in exchange for the financial support of their followers.

Their goal was not to lead their people toward material and spiritual abundance but to foster dependency; otherwise, so many would not be living in such despair. When she heard that History also offered spiritual instruction, Hope abandoned the Spiritual Pentagon altogether. Later, to her family's dismay, Hope started speaking against those of her class and exposing their lies to anyone who would listen, but the people of Mimadamos remained largely in the dark.

Hope's efforts had not gone completely unnoticed. Not only had she succeeded in spreading awareness among other honest Drazians, but Fate himself had also taken a keen interest in her.

"Hope," he said, rousing her from deep sleep into a dream they could share.

Hope blinked, holding her dream hand in front of her dream eyes to block his brilliant shine, which was like the sun. "The Drazians claim to know you," she said, "yet they have never described your likeness."

Fate laughed. "I do not believe I could describe them as individuals either." He dimmed his brightness until she lowered her hand, and then he sat nearby. The landscape morphed around him in the dream to resemble a cool, green forest filled with birdsong.

"This is lovely," she said, looking around.

Fate shrugged. "This is only a construct in your dream. You are the one to control this with your spiritual energy, not I." He lifted a flower from a nearby plant. "This is your memory of a flower, not an actual flower, for example." He turned it this way and that and smelled its fragrance. "You remember it in great detail, evidently."

"It's one of my favorites."

"And you are one of my favorites. I want to thank you for seeking the truth and not allowing yourself to be constrained by the rules of the world that bred you."

She narrowed her eyes at him and got right to her point. "Is it true that a person must tithe and guard his or her actions to a narrow path and give only to the causes the Spiritual Pentagon deems worthy?"

"I would never," he told her, "promote an agenda to gain followers. The same power I have is inside every person; they just have to tap into it."

Fate taught Hope the delicate balance between spirit and matter, helped her establish this balance in her own life, and rescued her from a hollow future based on lies.

Disgusted by the Spiritual Pentagon's cheap tactics, Hope decided to live among the Forgetters in the hopes of spreading the truth to them. In time, many other Drazians began following her, their numbers growing daily until nearly one-third of their people had pledged their allegiance in varying degrees of candidness.

Although many Drazians believed in Hope, there were many unscrupulous Drazians who hated her just as passionately. The leaders of the Drazians spoke to the Archons about her. "How dare she defy us and rebel against our traditions? More than once, we have complained to you about letting her live in the Forget Lands. Hope is hatching a plan to overthrow the Forget Lands and the Valley of Doubt. The longer you ignore the problem, the more likely it becomes that she will succeed."

The Archons answered, "We will check up on the girl." After the Drazians retreated from their presence, the Archons spoke among themselves.

"What can one tiny human girl do against our legion of loyal followers?"

"We have good reason to doubt the credibility of the Drazians. After all, who wouldn't be suspicious of those who claim not only to have met Fate but also to have the authority to speak on his behalf?"

"According to them, he made them his personal representatives in distant lands. It all seems rather far-fetched."

But the Archons had continued to indulge the Drazians with every complaint on the off chance that they were telling the truth.

"Fate has not ousted them from the Valley of Doubt. Maybe he does have some affinity for them."

"On the other hand, we have it from several sources that the Drazians are liars. Remember that Time and Space shared with us some of the Drazians' rumors about Destiny's marriage to Fate—rumors everyone knew to be false."

"My lord," the Archons said to Dhumanos, "the Drazians are making noise about some girl named Hope who pickets their worship services and spreads spurious rumors about their spiritual leadership and connection to Fate. We do not know whether to believe them."

Dhumanos made a face in thought. "It is time to figure out the Drazians once and for all. Fetch me Time and Space."

When the twins arrived, he ordered them to catch Hope. She would tell him what he needed to know—or else.

* * *

To Space and Time, the forest and their role in it were much clearer. They had convinced every living being in the forest that they could earn their exit into better, more sophisticated areas of the Forget Lands if only they would hoard and pay obeisance in the form of the currency.

The forest Forgetters continued to strive hard, complying with the rules and restrictions set down by Space and Time in anticipation of a reward that would never come. However, the harder they worked, the more difficult attaining their prize became. It gave Time and Space the chance to apply restrictions and cut off everyone else from the free living that the environment of the forest could otherwise have afforded. They became officious, granting permits and creating obstacles in the creatures' affairs.

Only Hope defied this order, roaming freely in the forest in a circular mode that reminded Space and Time of their original neutrality to all sides and their ultimate decision to shirk that duty. They could not tolerate Hope exposing their tyrannical ways and openly living in contradiction to them. They could not tolerate such freedom of physical movement in the girl; however, they grossly misunderstood her nature and, therefore, underestimated her threat to them.

Hope had the ability to elevate her mind from the obstacles of space and time, meaning she could rise above the frustration of waiting for desired things to manifest in the physical realm. She did this by shining a bright Now, projected from the inside out, through the light of which events and circumstances were seen positively from all directions.

It was when crisis loomed that Hope stepped most fully into her power by channeling new creative possibilities. For with great need came an unusually wide range of ideas as well as such positive emotions as happiness, joy, courage, and empowerment. Detached as she was from her surroundings, she still always seemed to muster some reason to live for tomorrow—a goal—yet without the need to define that goal or touch that tomorrow. To Hope, it was not about tomorrow or the goal itself as much as it was about a certain way of seeing things that energized her mind and body in the Now.

It caused Space and Time no end of frustration that Hope had managed to live within the Forget premises on her own terms in the way she wished without fearing constant harassment by the Forgetters. That meant that she had chosen to ignore their presence, their currency, and their linear philosophy even while she remained aware of them. In any case, she had never taken their threats seriously until the day they caught her unaware. Unfortunately for Time and Space, the boy with the fiery eyes had sent the two of them running.

This fact they could not reconcile themselves to. Space and Time worked to promote a setting for scripts—like the mind chatter Dhumanos put upon Destiny—to take place. Even though they never liked to stick their noses in actual scripts like History, they understood these scripts were necessary for the survival of their significance. Scripts were nothing but a circular code put into a linear illusion, which was Space and Time's domain. Hope's moves in the Forget Lands were contrary to any linear logic; she was immune to scripts.

Hope's presence in the forest indirectly gave them a constant meaning and mission. Their objective had been to capture her to unravel her mystery and report to the Archons news that could silence their worries of the unknown. Whenever they caught a glimpse of the girl, they would follow her footsteps and try to track her whereabouts and her pattern of movement. Yet she remained far out of their reach. There was something about Hope that was simply forbidden to them. Of course, that kept them fixated on her.

The mystery only deepened after their unsuccessful interrogation of History. Could it be that it was not History but Destiny herself who was responsible for sending her son forth to face Dhumanos? Could this be the revenge they had always feared from her?

CHAPTER 27

IT HAD HAPPENED A LONG TIME AGO – SO LONG
ago that few of the Forgetters even knew about it. In the ancient sacred
books, it was referred to as "Destiny and the prostitution of the soul."
While in the Archons' captivity, she had suffered a humiliation that no
other soul on Earth could have borne. This was a secret chapter in Destiny's
life, one that no one knew of and one she was loath to think about, even
in times of solitude.

Destiny had been born to a wealthy yet reserved family and spent
most of her youth as an only child. Many years later, her parents added
two girls to their family, and all of them lived in a remote area near
Mimadamos, which was separated from the Valley of Doubt by a lake that
fell within the Forget Lands.

Not so far away lived the Drazians, and while their proximity to
Mimadamos influenced their spiritual façade, their allegiance was to the
Archons. In a pious disguise, they deceived the villagers of Mimadamos
by pretending to be the delegates of Fate on earth, assuming sacredness,
holiness, and divinity mainly through performing pretentious rituals that
they had coined themselves. Each time they lured one of the villagers
to the Forget premises, they were generously rewarded by Dhumanos.
How were they able to do this? They warned the people of Mimadamos
against exposure to the sacred scriptures, saying that this knowledge, if
not filtered through the pentagon's guidance, could burn their souls and

do them more harm than good. The Drazian spiritual leaders painted an image of spirituality that was too hard to attain without direct allegiance to them personally and was, therefore, unbearably discouraging. This prepared the villagers to be ready to depart into a world that spoke more to their souls' needs and desires.

The ancient scriptures spoke of the works of the Drazians known as the Letters of Deceit, which were worse than those of any Archon who had ever stepped on this Earth. This was because they had led the souls of the righteous astray, spoken lies about Fate, and pretended that their impossible laws were inspired by him and mandated under his supervision and guidance.

Destiny's family was among the very few people of Mimadamos who knew what the Drazians were really about. Thus, they interacted minimally with their surroundings while trying their best to spread authentic knowledge to those in whose essence they sensed promise.

As a very young child, before she had been joined by her sisters, Destiny was known to be a beautiful girl. She spent her days in solitude in her room, most of the time with no one to behold or appreciate her capabilities and her beauty.

Since her youth, Destiny had believed in true love. Moreover, she was haunted by a yearning to surrender to the one true love, once he had been found. She believed that every living being was entitled to eternal love such as this and that her one and only love would be waiting for her. She believed that he would show up in due time to make himself known.

Destiny was merely six years old when she was first visited by Dhumanos. He gifted her with a mirror that would change the way Destiny grew up. Through that mirror, she began to ponder her beauty daily. Destiny envisioned eyes of imaginary beholders verifying this beauty that she thought she alone possessed. Destiny grew vain. She imagined such suitors would make themselves known to her, because they would always praise her looks.

Of course, Dhumanos had a purpose behind the gift. The Archons were experts at tampering with the quality of mirrors and mastering the deceptive powers of translation. This was the sole method through which they deceived millions of souls, and even Dhumanos followed this rule in every way.

He had sensed that Destiny had been granted great powers at birth, and he had taken note of the source of those special gifts. They had been granted to her by a powerful source of light, which was the god of the sun. The god king dwelt in the forbidden land, the land of Demire, which was known never to harbor sleep; nor did it ever undergo darkness. He was known as Fate.

Now Dhumanos took care to snoop around and to discover that access to the land of light was forbidden to him and his fellow Archons. This was so because Dhumanos and the Archons had been born from the depths of darkness, and no one knew if they would survive the white light that streamed from the land of the sun. If they were exposed to such powerful light, they might simply ignite and incinerate until they turned to ash.

Destiny was their only hope—the only way they could wreak their evil and affect the laws of the land of the sun god. Through her, Dhumanos thought he could get access to Fate and his power without confronting him directly. Destiny could be compared to a moon that reflected the sun softly in the darkness, diffusing its light and projecting it in a manner that would not threaten the Archons' reality in any way.

Dhumanos had to think mournfully about how to get through to Destiny—how to seduce that moon to see and claim its own beauty and acknowledge the role of darkness in highlighting it. He could see that she would be very close to the all-powerful, all-mighty Fate in the future. She was the key for Dhumanos to get through to the king of the land of bright light, to Fate.

Finally, he devised a plan. "I want you all to contrive scripts to prolong the night and prevent the dawn of that sunrise when the moon surrenders its diffused light to the sun and the two become one."

The Archons exchanged blank looks.

Dhumanos sighed at their lack of poetry. "We cannot allow Destiny to meet or become involved with Fate just yet. We must delay this."

The Archons huddled and discussed ideas, finally arriving at a plan. One said, "We shall engage Destiny with dream scripts that will keep her entangled in darkness and prolong the dark night of the soul. It will prevent any hope of an awakening that could bring her into a state of atonement with Fate."

"Fate alone can bring that about," said another.

"He will not want her by the time we're finished," said a third.

Thus, they sought to defile Destiny's innocence and stain her pure image in the eyes of the man who would become her husband. They produced dark memories tinted with desire. That was the light of remembrance she had held within her eyes on her wedding day when her groom had come to fetch her to his home in Demire.

Dhumanos had planted in Destiny's mind the notion that she desired to be deceived by him and that she desired to give birth to a multitude who would admire her and populate the world in darkness. The Forgetters' spiritual birth came from the womb of Destiny's desire to be deceived by Dhumanos. The Archons were thereby lifted from darkness one at a time by keeping her company as Dhumanos took advantage of Destiny's innocent yearning for her true love. The wanton creatures passed her spiritually from one to another, each hammering a nail through her being. Fooled by each to believe that he was the one she had been waiting for, Destiny was seduced by their need to survive and her role as the unique giver who could fulfill that need.

Young and optimistic, Destiny could not see the evil in their scheme until it was too late. Some made use of her by force, while others did so by seducing her with a gift like Dhumanos's mirror. The process was not physical; it was spiritual, happening only through a dreamlike experience. No matter: they left real bruises on her soul. She quickly lost the inner glow of childhood. By the time she realized where she stood in the eyes of the Great Father, she felt extreme sorrow and guilt. She believed it was too late to repent or to retrieve the innocence of her youthful soul, never realizing that the only sin was losing hope in the Father's mercy.

The Archons impregnated her mind with images of how they viewed her so that she had to turn away from her image altogether. Destiny felt humiliated. The offspring of her spiritual intercourse with them was humanlike beasts called Dhuman Adamics, or Doubtful Thoughts in human form. They formed an entire nation to the extent that the deformed nation of thoughts made the Forget Lands their dwelling place.

Like Dhumanos and the Archons, little light filtered through the tall forest trees where they dwelt and projected their laws unto the lands of sophistication beyond the forest belt. In the vast Forget Lands of Sophistication that stretched way beyond the forest premises, they constructed tall buildings and monuments to resemble the tall trees of the forest in the same spirit of fear and resistance to light.

The Dhuman Adamics, also called the Fragments of Eve, were a race known to diminish everything they touched. They set rules on the planet. They decided what would be worn and thought. If they saw something different, someone trying to express himself or herself, something shining, they would try to kill it. They didn't want anyone to shine, because it reminded them of how drab they were. They liked the dark.

These were the creatures whose offspring controlled all the domains in the sophisticated world; they couldn't shine, so they tried to give themselves glory by inference. They didn't even know who or what they were or why they did the things they did. They lived eternally in the dark, grabbing, controlling, exploiting, and strangling the very world that sustained them. Like cancer cells, they accumulated, expanding disproportionately within the body sustaining them.

They originated from a sick and feeble race—mute and blind, lackluster and unthinking. They turned to violence at every opportunity to express themselves. Their tribe would meander among the foliage and the trees in chaotic trails, with a mind only to their own needs. When seen, they were found to push each other with brutish effort.

Any one of the Dhumans made it known that he would try to subdue the other. Any one of the Dhumans would wish only to enforce his own presence. And so, the Dhuman Adamics came to be known as the beasts of the Forget Lands in the way they behaved and competed. For, in truth, it was competition for either light or darkness. The evil laws of Forget prevailed, and there were no rules in place to tame their carnal nature.

Destiny felt a great, shameful responsibility for the Nation of Thoughts that had come into embodiment through her primeval actions. Eve was to blame for the fall, and Destiny held this karma from that ancient time. It led to her fleeing her home near Mimadamos for many full moons to the Forget area by the lake across from the Valley of Doubt. She had fled there in a futile effort to evade her sins or, perhaps, to face what she considered the reality she deserved, for Destiny was driven by the feeling that she deserved to dwell in the same darkness where the beasts derived from her actions lived.

By now, Destiny was feeble of mind and spirit. She was downcast and desolate, for she had entered a nightmare without being able to find the one true love she had so staunchly believed in, the one good man she had desired.

One night, a new presence came into the void created by her feelings. Fate was looking down from his high perch when he saw a beautiful maiden alone, and he projected his presence to her. She appeared to be watched by dangerous humanlike beasts, who peered from behind the broad tree trunks.

They watched and they leered and they might have been waiting for another opportune moment to strike at her. The lady was in danger; yet in her deep remorse, she was hardly aware of anything related to her physical surroundings. Worse, the maiden was sobbing. Fate, the all-knowing, could see that she wept bitter tears because of all that had befallen her. She wept to vent her suffering and disgrace. He heard her loudly repent of her prostitution. Fate could also hear her sad flute-like sighs as they echoed amidst the guttural sounds made by the creatures of the forest, the Archons and the Dhuman Adamics.

Fate was surprised to find himself at a loss as to how to console such a beauteous lady who had committed no other wrong other than the extent to which she judged herself. As he continued to look upon her, Destiny began to call upon the Great Father so that he might help her. Fate wondered whether he, being close to all souls divine, should make himself known.

"Save me, Lord, Thou long awaited," she wailed as she beat her chest. "What I did, I did out of love and longing for You. Behold, I will render an account to Thee and submit to Thy justice, for I have abandoned my house and birth family and fled my maiden's quarters. Restore me to Thyself again."

In truth, Destiny was calling for her one true love to make himself known. When Fate saw her in such a state, he wished he could do something for her, for he counted her worthy of his mercy. As he now told himself, many were the afflictions that had come upon her because she had abandoned herself and that most precious possession of all: her soul. Fate decided to reveal his presence.

And so, Fate materialized before Destiny and said in measured tones, "Come, thou promised bride." His thunderous voice broke the silence. "I shall remove your prostitution from your existence, and I shall remove your adultery from between your breasts. I shall render you as innocent as the day you were born."

Chadi B. Ghaith

When Destiny perceived her situation and the extent that it was apparent, she wept. At the same time, she was surprised at the empathy this man expressed and his awareness of all that she'd experienced. Did she reveal herself to humans to such an extent? If others were not aware of how she felt, how did this man, who seemed to be above men, have knowledge of all this? Destiny did not have a great deal of time to dwell on this, as she felt the change he immediately made possible.

Destiny felt cleansed of the internal pollution that had been pressing upon her all this time. She felt a great rush of cleansing in the same way that garments dirty with ink are put into water and turned about until the ink is loosened and removed.

Then she heard the voice of the greatest among men, he who stood before her, whisper in her ear. "I am the firstborn who speaks thy Father's tongue. You are renewed to be a bride, and I shall be your bridegroom."

The maiden Destiny was engulfed in a great, peaceful joy. She had sinned, it was true, but forgiveness had been wished for her. This man's miraculous presence had cast off her sins. She did not fully recollect this then, but it was as if his voice was coming from inside her, as if her entire life was made of noise conspiring to hide this one true moment. It was as if she was back in the time when earth was created and she had been a little girl who knew nothing of the ways of the world.

Meeting Fate changed Destiny's entire perspective. She returned home to the bosom of her family, from whom she had separated herself because of her own self-imposed punishment. She returned from the lake cleansed and full of hope. She filled her home with sweet-smelling flowers and perfume she had gleaned from the flowers of the lake.

Destiny and Fate had every reason to "live happily ever after" in his mountainous abode at the edge of the world, but the evil script of Dhumanos had sought her even there and eventually planted the thought that led to her leaving Demire. Her departure was an error, for with that action, she'd also left her present to return to her past, to what should have been history, to her birth family, where none had expected her to return, so they had moved on. Destiny, thus, was lured back in a sense by the Archons, who would have willed her to do harm once more and to yield to their ways.

Space and Time were among the very few who knew Destiny's secret from the time before she was wed to Fate. They were the most original embodied thoughts born of her spiritual womb, which facilitated the birth of all scripts. They had successfully contrived to have her returned to a spot within their ambit, though they had also cleverly contrived to make her think it had been her own idea, much the way History would later make Choice believe that the decision to leave Mimadamos was his alone. It would be some time before Destiny would be forced to give herself back into their hands and their ways, they thought.

They had once believed the same about Hope. However, Hope never submitted to them, not because she was stronger than Destiny but because this evil was beyond her ability to withstand. Hope's role was to reverse the magic on the magicians and engage them instead of allowing them to engage her. She had been directly tutored by none other than Fate himself.

Space and Time could not let go of the notion that Destiny, not History, had sent Choice into the Forget Lands to exact revenge. If the youth was her instrument, what form would that punishment take? Until they found out, they would live in dread of Choice and what he could do to them.

CHAPTER 28

AFTER CHOICE SAVED HOPE FROM THE WOULD-BE
evildoers and it became apparent that the two attackers were not returning, a silence once again fell over the forest. Hope stood there, her arms
wrapped around herself, until her trembling subsided. All the while, her
eyes never left Choice. She was amazed that he had appeared when all
had seemed lost.

"Thank you," she said.

"You're welcome," he said automatically, with the manners taught by
his mother. "Did you know those men?"

Hope nodded, retying her hair, as some had come loose around her
face. "Their names are Space and Time. They've tried to catch me before."

He'd heard of Space and Time in whispers spoken by the villagers
back home. They were the gatekeepers who served both Mimadamos and
the Forget Lands. But then why were they chasing Hope? He could not
imagine, but it was as though their lives depended on possessing her.

"How did you do that?" she asked. "How did you send Space and
Time running? Do you have the powers of the Great One in you? You
must, for that is the only life that they fear."

Choice did not know how to answer, for their retreat had shocked
him as well. He could not get their words out of his mind. *Why did History
have to let me out? My mother would have kept me by her side!* Since coming to this forest, so much information had been delivered to his mind

as effortlessly and instantaneously as an email sent to one's inbox. Yet now that he needed to know something, the information was hidden from him. Choice ground his teeth in irritation. How dare these two ruffians want to decide what could be? And what, if anything, did this have to do with Hope?

He stood still, mulling over the sudden happenings in the previously quiet forest. It was hard to believe that he had entered this place only the day before yet had experienced so much. His first impression had been that the forest was devoid of other people. Then came the visit from the Demiurge. But even the Demiurge, Choice reminded himself, was neither man nor beast but of the divine. Could the maiden Hope also be made of antimatter, formed through rays of sunlight? But as he took in her exquisite, very human form, he knew that was not the case.

The girl, it appeared, had a need to remain busy, perhaps to ward off the lingering fear of the earlier incident. She went toward what must be a safer and more serene corner of the forest.

She stopped and turned, noticing he had not followed. "Come with me."

Choice fell in step with Hope as she marched up the trail. He had been an only child, and his life in Mimadamos had afforded him little opportunity to interact with other children. It had made him a bit of a loner, but now, after being in this forest for two whole days, he could do with some company, especially one so lovely. Besides, it would help to figure out who was who and what was what.

This could be another adventure, he thought, *an adventure within an adventure.*

Choice stood straight as he walked, his very being tingling with joy, and his youth radiating another kind of consciousness. The first adventure had brought him to this point. Now he turned again to the natural beauty of the forest, to the sun's rays as they reflected on Hope's fresh face and auburn hair.

He also realized, in that very instant, that he was being studied by many sets of inquisitive eyes. There were deer and squirrels, bluebirds on low branches, and the towering falcon up high. The very life of the forest was taking stock of this newcomer in their midst. The dynamics of this environment were shifting, bringing in the new, eager to cast off the devilish and old. The thought uppermost in the minds of all creatures great and small was the great war to come.

They knew, as the world had always known, that this war would be upon them eventually. Someday there would be a war to flush the world of evil and renew the light of angels, of good women such as Hope. The Great Father looked at his few people scattered here in the forest, and he looked, too, upon the son of Fate, as he would take a stand in the war. He would do well to be a warrior on the winning side, though no one knew what that winning side would be.

Even as Choice felt eyes upon him, he continued to gaze upon Hope, asking himself why Space and Time would be chasing one such as this pretty maiden. He wondered if it had to do with some intangible quality shared by Hope and Destiny, for Hope reminded Choice of his mother.

Destiny had always pointed out to him the need for the here and now. Hope also had some of that quality—Choice could see that, and it appeared that the two rogues could see it, too. After all, the chase had occurred on this very day, and Choice had the good fortune to be here now to ensure that Hope was saved from them. He could feel this synchronicity flowing through them.

Choice also felt that this was why the forest had been his destination the day before. Suddenly, the nature of the forest and his reason for being here made more sense. To Choice, the forest felt more like Hope than the duo who had chased her. In fact, it appeared that the forest was prompting him to surrender any sense of space and time, which he found curious, considering that History had described it so differently. How far astray had his mentor been leading him?

Choice had goals as well, and since he had been raised to live in the Now, he understood that the only way in which his present hopefulness was different from optimism was that the former included practical pathways to an improved future that related to who he already was, not who he would like to become. With Hope by his side, he was now twice as determined to focus attention on the wisdom and significance behind his presence in the Forget Lands, drawing on tacit knowledge of how to reach any goal he had in mind, even if it was the simple goal of gathering sustenance for the day. Meanwhile, he could not shake the feeling that the world—and his place in it—was about to change.

CHAPTER 29

CHOICE AND HOPE SPENT THE DAY WANDERING
the forest and discussing their innermost feelings on the nature of life. It
was as if the very forest was validating their presence and purpose there.
They were serenaded by a great many birds who seemed to want to attend
to them. As they trod, the grass sprouted beneath their feet. The shackles
of Space and Time fell away, leaving these creatures to their own bidding.
Now they could march to another tune, and since all things in nature
were also ordered by the Great Father and would rather follow Fate, the
lesser birds, animals, and plant life were finally able to give in to their true,
sweet-natured sensibilities.

As they stopped to pick berries here and vibrant blooms there, Choice
realized that Hope reminded him of the teachings of his mother, of the
importance of the Now. But unlike his mother, Hope had fought for her
freedom instead of succumbing to her inner doubt and others' bullying.
Of course, Choice, who'd had no contact with any other woman, young or
different or not different, had little to compare Hope to. Still, he was sure
that Hope was the one to follow, the one with whom he would most like
to spend his time.

* * *

To Hope's surprise, it was the same for her—she who had frolicked
through the forest like a sprite, unattached to anyone. She, who had

convinced herself that she could live and wander alone here, could now feel the beat of her own heart. She could sense the blood rush to her face in the presence of this young man. It was both the most joyful and the most disconcerting experience of her life.

Could her attachment to Choice pose a threat to her independence? She had always been sure that her power lay in her personal moral code and her independent nature as well as her ability to detach from the outcome of a desired goal. Like Choice, she was not used to feeling beholden to another.

Choice, meanwhile, was talking to Hope about all sorts of matters. He wanted to know more about Space and Time and why they were following her. She debated whether or not she wanted to answer him now. To do so, she would have to describe the nature of this forest where she dwelled. She would have to explain its many living hierarchies, the good and the bad, and these were things she felt she should keep to herself.

Hope held her nose proudly in the air, hoping that what she said would come across as trifling but also hoping Choice would recognize the gravity. "I have long decided what is worthy of my attention and what is not. I considered Space and Time to be the latter until the day you arrived and saved me. I'm rather dismayed that you're giving value to discussions about those two old characters. That wasn't the first time they've been a bother."

"What of the higher power they referred to?" asked Choice.

"Who knows?" Hope knew but did not wish to air her knowledge about what passed in the forest, for she considered it all transitory. What was happening at any given time might not be so in the future.

Still, she was pleasantly surprised by how very safe and secure she felt with Choice; it was surprising, because until this day, she had never realized that she had anything to be kept safe from. It was perhaps how Destiny had felt during the year she had spent with Fate and his people in the mountain stronghold above Demire. Hope felt that her personal path was, for the first time, converging with another's; it was also the first time in her young life that Hope had found herself dreaming of a future linear Now.

She cast a shy, sidelong glance at the boy now, taking in every detail of his profile. While she might have been completely unaware of her own pleasing looks, she had always been able to appreciate other manifestations of beauty, regardless of their form. Prime among these was the sun, for she considered light to be the most beautiful revelation of God.

"I love the sun," she said. "Each morning I rise long before it does. I complete my duties and await the first sighting of a single dart of light. My focus on that first sighting every morning is followed by the ascendance of the brilliant red orb to the position it seeks in the sky. I then raise my arms high above my head like this." She demonstrated. "It's my way of expressing devotion to the giver of light. To me, the day would not be complete without this simple rite.

"I believe that, if you can spare time during the day to look at the sunrise, you will chase away wrongdoings for days to come. It certainly worked today." She gave Choice a teasing glance.

"I'll have to try that," he said shyly.

✳ ✳ ✳

The Earth's creatures could learn so much from the sun, especially about abundance. The sun gave without accounting or projecting an image of loss and without taking away from itself. It gave generously without thought of what it would get in return. If only humanity could adopt this stance! It would no longer have the need to hoard objects or food or to conceal wealth for fear that it would disappear. It was this sort of knowledge that Time and Space wanted to bury and the reason that they were so eager to rid the Forget Lands of Hope's influence. She was the only person other than Destiny who had ever come close to circumventing their plans.

Time and Space had been incensed when they learned that Destiny's sprawling compound ignored the very laws they imposed on the forest. Clearly she had returned from Demire with a wealth of knowledge gleaned from her time with Fate, and she had put that knowledge to use while raising his son. Choice was growing up in a manner Fate would consider worthy of him.

Seeking to undermine Destiny's plans for Choice, Space and Time had enlisted History's help. They asked him to grow many tall trees in the garden of Destiny's home in Mimadamos to make it more akin in nature to the Forget Forest.

Using security as an excuse, History had tried to pitch the tree idea to Destiny, explaining that tall trees could act as a fence. However, Destiny, as protective as she was, didn't welcome the idea. The woman who had left her family as a young girl to live on her own by the Forget lake, never considered security and protection to be elements related to physical factors, and the last thing she wanted was for her son to grow up inside a fortress. She instructed History to scatter trees in a random fashion and mix tall with short ones so that no area was ever blocked from sunlight.

Time and Space would have to find another way to drive a wedge between mother and son. They had not, however, considered Fate's plans for the boy.

CHAPTER 30

FOR ALL HIS PRESENT CONFUSION AND UNCER-
tainty, History had played a key role in convincing the forest creatures of
the rules and regulations set down by Space and Time. He could remember a time before he had been ordered to present himself at Destiny's door,
a time when he had served as tutor to a young girl in the forest. That girl's
name was Hope.

Hope had been living on her own, spreading a new gospel to the people of the Forget lands. She had sought History as a spiritual instructor of
renown, yet she seemed to be a repository of all knowledge connected to
spirituality, a child who could tell him what was what and who was which
at times when he himself would not be sure. Much in the way Choice
later asked him questions about the meaning of life, History utilized every
opportunity to ask Hope questions about the world of the Great Father,
about divinity itself. When it came to Hope, the tutor became the student.

"I never worry about where my next meal is coming from," Hope told
him one day. "When I am hungry, I am thankful for what is before me at
that moment. Sometimes this is in the generosity of others sharing with
me. Sometimes it is the bounty of the forest. When at times I go hungry,
I am grateful for the reminder that we can't always have what we want
if we have not worked for it. Wanting what I cannot or do not have is a
waste of energy."

"What if several days pass without that magic meal falling from the sky?" History challenged.

"You would be surprised by how creative one can be when great need arises," said Hope. "That goes for more than just food—anything of material want or need. The Drazians would have us believe that tithing to the Spiritual Pentagon puts in a good word with the powers that be and that those who do not tithe will suffer and go without. I have found the opposite to be true out here."

History said, "Man always asks, 'What is my fate? What will I become? What will happen to me?'"

Hope shook her head. "Truth lies in what we do today. Right now. What we become is a factor of how we spend our time and energy *now*. If you were to ask in spring, 'How large will my crop be at harvest?' I would say to you, 'How much seed are you planting today?' If you asked the same question midsummer, I would say to you, 'How much water and fertilizer have you given your crop today?' The future is built on today followed by another today and another. The future comes in time. What you get in the future is what you put in today. Now. And in each 'now' that follows."

History had the ability to see and the grace to appreciate that Hope could set her own rules and live by them, unlike his other students, most of whom had been brought within the grasp of Space and Time.

It was he, History, who had informed the brutish duo, "You should keep an eye on Hope. She might be one who will always remain outside your grasp."

Space had rolled his eyes, his body spinning in a gentle circle.

Time had looked bored. "Why?"

"Because she's the hardest to convince," History replied. "Because her nature is quite divergent from that of all other forest creatures, human or higher."

Space and Time believed that their evil ways would always reign. "Hope has no allegiances," Space reasoned out loud. "How can one small girl possibly threaten our control over the Forgetters?"

"The idea is preposterous!" Time affirmed.

The Archons, however, took the matter much more seriously. "Keep tabs on Hope," they demanded of Space and Time.

Space and Time never truly saw her as a problem, however, until she encountered Choice. It was the two of them joining hands—literally and figuratively—that changed everything and created a world-class headache for Space and Time.

Dhumanos was enraged. "How can you not control one small human girl?"

Space and Time shifted the blame. Space said, "History failed his mission to keep Destiny and Choice in check. Choice is the linchpin of the equation."

Time added, "But for History's failure, we believe Hope would have been inconsequential."

Even this was a misunderstanding, for the duo did not understand Fate's overarching role over the whole affair.

* * *

Even as Dhumanos and his minions plotted against them, Hope and Choice were, for the moment, left to ramble through the great circular forest that separated Mimadamos from the Forget Lands. Both youths catered to a law quite different from that dictated by Dhumanos through Space and Time. This was the law of universal good and doing good. It had begun at the beginning of existence and at the cradle of time. It had always been and would always be. It was the law that determined the rhythm and order of the universe. It had run through every living being since the beginning of the Earth and every moment of their lives. It had provided the forefathers and foremothers of all humans with every life experience.

Neither Space nor Time could affect this law, but they were completely oblivious to this fact. Given the powers they possessed to separate lands, people, and events, they thought that they could bend a law of nature, which they could but sense, to their own whims and purposes.

They were also completely unaware of the Law of Interaction that was forming their life experience. All players—Choice and Hope included—were somewhat more aware that this all-powerful law was working through their hearts and thoughts. They had called the Law of Interaction into action.

In truth, Choice had been witnessing the law in action his whole life – in the garden his mother had designed and History had tended. It was as if the plants had felt the love the old man had given them and had responded in kind, flourishing as History and Destiny had intended. History had felt it despite his mission, and Choice knew it, too, in every cell of his existence.

On this day of their exploration, Hope and Choice came upon a lake in which swam a mother duck and four of her offspring. As they approached with their hands intertwined, a white bird and a blue one brought forth a flower ring of bluebells. They turned to each other in amazement.

Choice said, "We are different from the other people of this Earth, but we are meant for each other."

Choice and Hope appeared to be as one. The very trees now bent their heads to form an arbor, and the small animals of the forest, hidden until now out of fear of Space and Time and their dictates, came forth to celebrate the forces of attraction and love. The deer came and the rabbits and squirrels. All had a grand feast at this union of the two beings, Choice and Hope. What would life hold for them?

One person knew—and that was Hope. She knew that she loved Choice, but she would not subjugate herself to enter into a union with him. Instead, Hope, regardless of where her daytime adventures with Choice led her, chose to continue living as she had previously, in a leafy bower that was her special place in the forest. In a way, this was more revolutionary than what Destiny had done when she declared to Fate that she wanted to bear her child away from him. Meanwhile, Choice continued to seek shelter at nighttime in the many places the generous Forest offered.

Space and Time could not figure it out. Why, they wondered, had Hope not thought of Choice as a pursuer in the manner that she had judged Space and Time to be? Why had she let herself fall for Choice? Why hadn't his presence violated Hope's code of conduct, the dictates of which required her to remain independent and unattached like Space and Time? Did Hope have an agenda they did not know about, an uprising planned for all those currently under Space and Time's control? And had History, who had known Hope as a girl, conspired against them by sending Choice to meet her? If not by some plan, how had this fiercely independent soul become attached to Choice so quickly?

For all their pondering, Space and Time knew even less than they imagined. Although they were twins, they never felt the sort of connection the young ones were experiencing and the power that this connection engendered. Now as Space and Time ruminated and worried in their dark, shadowy home, they couldn't help but remember that occasion long ago when another young couple had acted in contradiction to their plan.

"I never intended for Destiny to marry Fate and go off with him, did you?" Space asked.

"Why, no, brother," said Time. "In fact, we've done everything in our power to keep her feeling unworthy of him."

"Still, Destiny married him and left for Demire."

"She returned, of course." Time chuckled.

They put their heads together. Finally, Time said, "A thorough review of Hope's history is needed if we're going to come up with a successful strategy."

The brutish duo had gloated many hours about this over the years, but now Space wondered, "Is history repeating itself? Will Hope and Choice make a different decision?"

CHAPTER 31

THOUGH THEY WERE DRAZIANS, HOPE'S CLAN
had migrated from areas under Drazian control and into the Forget Lands,
particularly the forest areas around the Great Forget Lake, close to the
Mimadamos border. They preferred to dwell amongst the Dhumans, they
said, who were at least honest about their evil as opposed to the Drazian
spiritual leaders, who employed false spirituality to deceive the weak.
Their façade of modesty hid a deep egoism—one that brought them to
mock and belittle the significance of Destiny and Fate's will for her to be
his delegate. They built an entire philosophy around a fear of Fate and
used it to scare his people into submitting to their ways.

The strong among them, however, knew that Hope was authentically
connected to Fate and that being around her was to live without fear. They
noticed the direction in her steps and her trance as she trod where Fate's
voice bade her. In noticing this, they realized that there was much to be
learned from following in her footsteps.

* * *

Of all the flora and fauna that Hope and Choice had seen, this bush
had to be the most exotic, with multicolored leaves and the fattest, sweet-
est-looking berries.

"It's amazing!" Hope exclaimed, her eyes alight. Her favorite aspect
of the forest was that it never ceased to surprise her.

She released Choice's hand and wandered closer to the large bush. She closed her eyes and inhaled its scent deeply. When she opened them again, she found herself walking along a path of ice and rock. She should have felt cold, she supposed, but she didn't. Nor did she feel fear. She didn't even realize that she'd traversed not just geography but time. All that mattered was that she keep moving to where she'd been called by Fate.

Before Hope could reach the timeless premises where Fate was known to dwell—the glittering mountains of ice and rock—she had to traverse the dangerous path connecting the Forget Lands with Demire above the steep Valley of Doubt. Hope would have to cross a narrow path on a wooden-slatted bridge that moved with each step and threatened to topple those who traversed it into an abyss below. She would have to get across, Hope could see, for this wooden, ropelike path would deliver her from the mountaintop where she had paused. It was a bridge that connected two mountaintops. Hope would have to get to the other side, as the voice of Fate had bidden her.

A few of the dwellers in the Valley of Doubt saw Hope crossing the bridge to Demire, so they followed her. They had always wanted to meet Fate and see what lay beyond in Demire but had lacked the courage. Now that they saw Hope crossing, they felt safer following her. They followed her, astute in their belief that Hope's destination would reveal much knowledge. It was the path of the great light, they were convinced.

They followed as their hearts and heads considered they should, slowly measuring every step. The peak from which they would have to step onto the bridge and the next mountaintop, dazzling as a multifaceted diamond, was extremely high, and none wished to drop into the abyss below. They could see that there was danger, but nothing that they could not surmount.

Hope trudged straight ahead, undaunted and barefoot, free of fear. She had set an example, and the others followed. Was the secret, powerful force of Fate helping her along? If anyone had asked, she would without thought have replied in the affirmative. As she crossed over the valley that marked the outer zone of the forest on the way to Demire, she witnessed the Land of Doubt below. It almost seemed as if it belonged to the kingdom of Fate, yet it could be seen on the way back from Demire as though falling under the Forget Lands. There was much amiss here.

Hope could internally hear the cries of those in the valley's abyss. Those rebel Forgetters had once tried the very same path she was walking, only to fall. When there appeared to be no way out, they simply settled there. The cries Hope heard were followed by an image of the people crying. They were in bondage, their shackles not metallic links but their own misery.

Who were these people? She wondered, and the voice of Fate came to her mind.

"In this place of nonlinear time," he told her, "where the past, present, and future are one, you, dear Hope, are witnessing the origins of the people known in your world as the Drazians. For it was they who once attempted to reach my home in Demire to earn special favor among the Archons. They had placed their faith in an egomaniacal man named Drazio, from whom they got their name.

"The people in the abyss below you are not all damned. Some are from the Chosen, yet their goodness is still dormant. They have been made to believe that the path to me is one of great sacrifice and negligence of worldly affairs—so much so that they have been crippled, neither able to live on Earth and enjoy being human nor to reach the heavens to be rewarded as angels. They are simply losers from all sides."

The members of Hope's clan who were following her, witnessing what lay below in the Drazian premises from pain and suffering all in the name of being good enough for Fate, formed strong opinions about him. They decided that he was some sort of merciless dictator. Whether Fate was watching from his high castle and agreed with what was going on or whether he was watching and disagreed, he had let it all happen nonetheless. No matter which way they viewed it, it just didn't seem right for him to allow those people to suffer and be enslaved in such a manner.

"Fate must be heartless," they said, "if he can witness the plight of these people and not be moved."

"Fate might not be the person Hope has believed him to be," said others as they crossed the Valley of Doubt.

The only one who did not seem to have been affected was Hope, for she made greater haste, and her energy appeared to increase as she trod in the direction she had been called. She still strode with single-minded purpose, convinced that the great voice she had heard in the past and again now had a greater purpose to reveal. She paid little attention to the scenes she saw from above, and she would not heed her followers from behind who attempted to warn her of what could be awaiting her from unexpected dangers if she continued on her path towards Demire.

Was Hope completely without feeling toward the plight of the enslaved below? It seemed so, for not only had she appeared to be in a trance at the start of her journey, but now she also felt as though she had entered a dream setting. Besides, Hope had refused to judge Fate even as the cries of the damned continued. As she carried on across the narrow path on the precarious bridge, she could sense the many eyes turned toward her and the questions of those wondering what was driving her.

The enchained nation looked up toward the narrow bridge that the travelers would cross and were stepping on even at that time with Hope in the lead. These eyes, however, were without hope. To them, watching those engaged only in their own bidding was like watching something forbidden, even obscene. A great cry arose from them and was met with an answering cry from those on the bridge, those who wondered if Hope might now be striding toward the destruction of all.

Suddenly, a thunderous voice penetrated the air. "In honor of you, my dear Hope, and to celebrate your presence on my premises, I shall free all these men and women from captivity."

The scene below erupted into chaos and confusion as the enslaved revolted against the Spiritual Pentagon. Those on the bridge were filled with joy as they considered what might have been and the surety of what lay before them. They no longer dared to look down, for they were still not a hundred percent sure of the great promise that had rent the air. And so they hurried on until they reached the other side and heard a different cry altogether—a collective cry of joy.

Now when Hope and her followers cast their glance downward, they could see that all were being freed. Moreover, the horrible mountain that isolated the valley from the Forget Lands was split in half, making a path toward the still-unseen forest. It was a clean, clear path that signaled the direction for those in the Valley of Doubt to leave the place of their bondage.

The freed souls wasted no time as they rushed toward the magical path. They were fleeing in joy, no matter that they were returning to the beastly land of the Archons. Somehow, it was as though confronting and understanding Fate was a state liberating beyond the mathematics of paths, regardless of whether it dictated going forward to heaven or backward to hell—for there was no hell worse than living in the grey area of doubt.

They ran without thought. Only later did the slaves of the past think they should have thanked someone for the miracle. Still later, they knew that the one to thank, the one the thunderous voice of Fate had referred to, was Hope. Now, though Hope had reserved her judgment this far, she knew the larger percentage of slaves had been some of the worst and most fallen on Earth. These people, who'd toiled without recourse until now, must have come here seeking something.

A thought struck Hope. They'd probably heeded Space and Time and their promise of a better world outside the Forget Lands. They must have approached Demire with the wrong purpose. These poor, unthinking souls had considered the journey to be a promised release to a better life, to salvation!

Their biggest error was that they had never stopped to consider Fate beyond their enslavement to a cause. Even worse, in falsely claiming to be his representatives, they had cast Fate in a bad light to the world. Fate had been portrayed as a merciless god who was hard to reach or please. The Drazians, in drawing attention to their own plight, had undermined his power and importance: the great good that was Fate.

What would happen to these beings who had known only this enslavement and had toiled solely to fulfil their egoistic desires and savior complexes? Hope pondered this for a moment. Then the thought came to her that their freedom from chains would be the beginning of their real punishment and suffering, their karmic payback. They would not, she knew, be well received back in the Forget Lands, for their weakness and lies would be exposed. They would be pursued according to the laws of the Forget Lands, which meant the cycle of terror might continue but this time more on a physical scale than spiritual.

Finally, Hope reached the end of the ropelike bridge. As she and her followers stepped into Demire, she was hit with Fate's powerful presence. Would she finally see him?

The voice of thunder arose again. "Stop!" it bade her. "You can no longer step ahead, at least not all of you. I address your followers, dear Hope. Only you, my beloved, can approach."

As Hope advanced a few steps, she, who was always bold and direct, felt a tremor of trepidation. She looked in the direction of that voice but could see no one. Then her attention was drawn to the unusual lay of the land ahead of her. It was like a surreal landscape, littered with old, used objects and what appeared to be colossal mechanical instruments.

Some seemed self-powered. Others were pneumatic giants made of iron and steel that might have ushered in an advanced civilization that once existed. All were here to be researched and tested, as if the place were a lab for the eons. There were a great many old and new together, some of which would be put to much use and others that would be useless, but none of which Hope could understand.

Hope approached alone as she had been asked, and as she trudged through miles of this strange land, she began to identify a complex order to the placement and nature of these objects. All were arranged in a pyramidal model, with those for general use at the bottom. At last she reached the finest of objects that could be powered by the light of the sun, their complex filaments arranged in a trembling web for use by humanity. As she looked upon these things, it was no longer clear to Hope whether Fate communicated telepathically via spiritual means or advanced technology. It really didn't matter, because either way, it was nothing short of magic. She had come to learn that matter was nothing but spirit solidified to allow humans to dream their selves real and spirit was matter liquidized at the end of the dream cycle to save humanity from the reel of their dream.

At the far end stood a mighty man. She had never set eyes on this towering figure before but knew instantly who he might be, for he could call to Hope in that mightiest of voices, and she felt no fear. All the same, Hope approached him slowly until she was close to where Fate stood waiting. She stopped and looked around at the strangely ordered mechanical, useful artifacts that she had passed and that had taken all this time to study. To her bewilderment, everything seen from afar now appeared in perfect, astounding order.

Up close, Hope could see that huge objects were arranged so that they were aligned to each other as in a colossal jigsaw, the least useful to the most sophisticated. She studied it meticulously; this order was miraculous. It was as though a giant ruler had placed them, as if some giant hand had been strong enough to pick up each item and place it where it thought it should be.

She addressed Fate. "O beloved eye of time and cause of all causes, why do you allow the eyes of man to misjudge you? You can have control over all if you wish. Yet you allow them to judge you as a being who is ruthless and chaotic, when in truth, you can appear to men as you wish them to think of you. I say this because, Fate, you are the keeper of order, and you are the gentlest and most loving in the universe in the way that I and others near you can see."

"Let them misjudge," Fate replied, "based on what their soul's vision allows them to see. Better that than to judge correctly based on what they can't see. Their only hope for seeing is Destiny, my delegate whom they rejected, and Destiny shall rule their sight or lack of it whether they like it or not.

"Hope, I ask you to let them fathom their truth-in-finality at their own pace for their own sake. What you call 'truth' is more about your ability to see than about what you finally see. What they call 'truth' is but a shield."

It took her some time to mull over what Fate was saying. She had the opportunity to come this far and hear firsthand his observations about what could be right and wrong with the great world out there. But by then, Hope had floated off, as is common with mortal men and women, so she might be in a dream world.

I should try, she told herself, *to return to the reality of my days and nights in the forest.*

Hope thought to rouse herself from the dream. In the next instant, she found herself back in the forest on the very path she had previously trod with her partner as they circled through the great forest. But Hope could no longer see Choice; nor could she see her followers, who had accompanied her to where Fate had beckoned. She could, however, feel the warmth of Fate's voice shielding her like the sun, his eyes watching over her safety and security, his hands cushioning the earth underneath her bare feet.

And in that moment, Hope changed. She who had always been a free spirit was now even more free and bold in all she chose to do. Just like Destiny, who on the day she had given birth to Choice had felt a certain liberty in using her magical powers to her advantage, Hope now for the first time felt the liberty to adopt a linear direction without feeling any threat to her circular independence. At the same time, she would never be completely sure whether the world she had visited had been real or a dream.

From the darkness of their cave, Time and Space shrank in fear, for the Forget Foresters had told them of Hope's visit to the lands beyond the Valley of Doubt. They knew not what she and Fate had spoken of, but they did hear the shocking news of the Drazians' lies, the claims of not just meeting Fate but also representing him.

CHAPTER 32

HOPE DIDN'T KNOW HOW MUCH TIME HAD
passed, but when she next opened her eyes, the first thing she saw was
Choice. He had been joined by a faithful few gathered in a clearing to hear
what she had to say. Some had been with her on the journey to Demire,
and she now approached them seeking answers. When she asked if they
recalled coming along, a few immediately answered in the affirmative.
They were aware of what had transpired when Hope had left them on the
edge of the mountain of ice, glass, and crystals, called forward alone by a
powerful voice and venturing into what appeared to be a dreamlike fog.

They had even heard Hope speak and the voice commune with her
before they found themselves back in the forest premises, aware yet not
aware, unable to cast off the tiniest detail of that incredible journey.

"Hope," they cried out, "there is much we must ask of you."

"Yes—you are our link, our guide, our interpreter—"

"The messiah!" someone else called out.

"—the deity through which the Great One has chosen to commune
with humanity to make his ways known."

Hope listened to their elevation of her rebellion. With dignity, careful
to respect their fragile trust, she climbed on a fallen tree trunk to address
all from on high. The people whispered and shushed each other, many
sitting on the ground before the trunk to allow others to see.

Somberly she spoke. "I ask of you strict and uncompromising unity, for the Great Father is both Transcendent and Imminent. He is above all attributes, yet He is present like you and me. We, you and I, are the anointed, the saviors or liberators of a group of lesser beings within and outside the forest. The ones you saw yoked below the bridge have been put to drudgery because of their lack of belief in the Great One and the fact that they have seen fit to pay heed to the utterances of the false would-be messiahs, the Spiritual Pentagon, those secret followers of Dhumanos."

The villagers erupted into "hear-hears" and other exhortations of agreement. They, too, had abandoned their belief in the Spiritual Pentagon to follow Hope into the forest.

When they settled again, Hope spoke of the universal mind, the universal soul, and the word whose story and interaction as real persons— namely Fate, Destiny, and Choice—represented the blueprint of the Heavenly Kingdom and the road to the emancipation of the soul.

"This trinity is reflected inside each of the Chosen ones," she said. "For each of the Chosen is an eternal embodied ray of the universal sun, a manifestation of an eternal thought of Fate."

The crowd murmured. Choice looked thoughtful, his arms crossed in front of him, his eyes focused near her feet. She wanted to pull him aside and speak with him privately about this but was obliged to speak first with this gathering.

She continued. "On the other end of the spectrum are those false ones whose behavior is not acceptable, those who embody the thoughts of Dhumanos. They have acquired their human likeness from Destiny, yet having not been exposed to the great light of the spirit known as Fate, they are destined to be like blind actors inside a script they cannot control. Still, no matter how many games Dhumanos plays in the hope of making evil a reality, he can do nothing except serve Fate, albeit unconsciously.

"Thus, in Fate's reality, there is no real tension between good and evil. There is a kind of balance that calms evil, tames its beastly nature, and puts it into the indirect servitude of the good. Dhumanos has no access to Fate's reality; he can only play games within Destiny's realm.

"In Fate's reality, there is no need for an evil entity. Good undoes itself, and the action of trying to become whole creates the hole. It is a constant cycle that loops back on itself; the beginning is the end. It is one journey that seems to come from evil into good as good triumphs. That is how it felt—or had felt – until the fall."

∗ ∗ ∗

That was Fate's reality. On Earth, it was a different story. Here there were seasons to consider: dark, harsh winters that could kill off the ill-prepared, followed by the rebirth of spring and the glory of summer, then back to the melancholy of fall and the threat of another winter. There was a duality, good and bad, rather than just what was.

There was much other confusion as well. People equated heaven with joy, but that was not so, for heaven equaled truth. That was the problem with the religious-minded: they were forever in denial of the physical world that was their lesson plan. A priest would sit in his holy temple and pray in the time of an earthquake, "Please, God, I have been good. Spare me this cup, and I will be even better."

Such blind faith and denial of the true meaning of evil! For, yes, there were evildoers who could surely be blamed by those they had wronged; however, there was no absolute darkness, because darkness was measured by light and could not lose such relativity. Thus, Dhumanos's relationship to Destiny had a meaning beyond his evil scripts: she was his only hope, his only connection to Fate, the source of light.

Similarly, Space and Time's connection to Hope was beyond their evil schemes. Their attraction was their hunger for survival. Even as they waged this war, even when it seemed they were winning the hearts and souls of those they enslaved, these evils did not understand one truth: there was no devil who could withstand the presence of Fate. Even if they did know this, they would not have understood the reason for their inevitable defeat. They could not fight the core; there was nothing to fight. No one could fight the truth. No one could bravely attack and be killed in the attempt. And, oh, how one might wish for death! Well, until one was drawn so deep that there was no future, no next moment. How could anything ever change? How could anyone die?

CHAPTER 33

CHOICE DEEPLY WISHED THAT HE HAD BEEN
with Hope on her journey to Demire As he sought the edge of the trees
from where Hope had gone on that journey, Choice had a sense of déjà-vu,
for he now felt that all he saw around him he had always known. Had
his life before this been real? Had it really happened? Beyond the forest
was the edge of a steep cliff. Choice stood there a long time, savoring the
stretch of sky before he looked down. He would have loved to taste the
freedom of a jump, except that he was mortal and could not fly. But what if
he did take the leap? The thought sent shivers down his body. As he stood
there trying to shake off the impulse, he noticed something else floating
before his eyes.

Choice had sighted a single cotton fluff that had burst its pod. The puff
was moving level with his eyes and at a close distance. He kept his eyes
fixed on it as it drifted. It was a bit windy, and there were other leaves and
flowers and produce of this environment blowing about, but this flower
was somehow different. The fluff of cotton drew his attention.

It blew around his face and finally came to rest on his toe. If Choice
had not followed it as it drifted around, he would not have been aware
of this little fluff on his toe; it was that light. But now he bent down and
picked it up between his fingers.

As he did, Choice froze, for he had heard a voice like distant thunder,
the voice Hope and her clan had heard on their journey. Choice could

guess who that voice belonged to, for he heard it clearly. He could not miss the meaning of the words: "I will come into your life, my son!"

The words hit him full blast, for they not only signified what he had waited for all his life but also confirmed that all his instincts had been correct. He would meet his father, if not today then tomorrow. His father's words also confirmed that what Choice had felt—that his life had been unreal until now—was not incorrect.

It was as though all Choice had ever known or experienced was a script preparing him for the moment he woke inside the dream. He was trying to keep it together, and it took every ounce of strength to get himself away from that cliff. His feet felt heavy, as if tied to iron balls. He wasn't sure if he was dreaming or awake. He didn't feel safe, so he looked for a reference point to anchor him into some reality. And there she was: Hope, standing not too far from him.

It took a while until everything felt normal again. As Choice stepped back, he approached Hope and tried to confirm that he was not dreaming by touching her face gently. He presented the cotton flower to her. She smiled and accepted the token.

Choice's mind, however, was processing a flow of meaning like never before. He started to understand how everything worked, but the rush of concepts was a bit confusing. It was like spontaneously understanding something and, in that avoidance of the learning process, having no way of explaining it.

As fast as his understanding came, it went. He'd had it; it was on the tip of his understanding, and then it seemed to have vanished. Oh, how frustrating this was! Choice realized that he had always made the mistake of thinking that there was his world on one hand and his father's world on the other. The reality was that nothing could be random. Both their worlds had never diverged to re-converge. It felt like everything was complete, like everything—even his reunion with his father—had already happened.

The thought challenged the wisdom behind his decision to leave Mimadamos on a linear journey in pursuit of his father. An even bigger, more challenging thought came to mind: *Did I not have a choice in leaving, either? Is there anything accidental or random in life? If not, it's like waking up in a dream only to discover you are the dreamer and the dream at once.* It felt like being buried alive with reality being his coffin. It felt like his journey in the forest was a regressive one, whose only purpose was to describe the wisdom behind what already was and not what was to come; it was as if the Forest was a detailed explanation of Mimadamos as opposed to being a field of discovery that could lead Choice to reunite with his father.

So there he was, clinging to every drop of reason he could muster to prove to himself that his life had been real, that his decision to leave Mimadamos was real, that the Forest was real, and that his choices so far had been real. The only calming proof to him was Hope's eyes, which vibrated with an energy that could not but escort the viewer into the certainty of the Now.

Choice began to feel more grounded. "That is real, isn't it?" he said. "Hope, you are real, aren't you?"

What Choice realized in this brief dawning was too vast to fit into words. Before he had heard Fate's voice, he had felt his mind expand toward the infinite to the point that he was no longer aware of his physical presence, as there was no feedback loop of recognition. And then it was almost as if his mind was forced to split into viewer and viewscreen aspects like the first division of a fertilized egg! Even then, there was still no other than the Now consciousness, no memory of anything that was, no reference to anything that would become, like nothing to be experienced. He existed, but nothing was happening, so it was a real short circuit. *I am, I am, I am. ... What am I?*

Suddenly, Choice could feel his mind splitting into many aspects and interacting with itself to reveal nuances. It was like playing himself at chess. The aspects had to vary and even contradict themselves to stir the still waters, to test creation, to solve the differences, and ultimately to facilitate manifestation. The mind, he realized, had to separate itself into aspects to *be*.

It also had to forget parts of itself to allow the backward journey of remembrance to present itself a forward journey toward discovery. It couldn't go anywhere. It was already All, everywhere. Thus, it had to forget and remember what always was, separating into viewer and viewscreen in the mind to create the feedback loop of thought and many soul aspects so the game could be played experientially. It also had to control and direct itself without realizing or remembering the whole. If all aspects knew they were One, nothing could manifest.

Choice experienced this logic, and it felt suffocating. It had the effect of making him godlike and threatened to cause his ego to explode into countless pieces. It was as if Fate was testing him to see whether he possessed enough power to withstand his presence and the amount of light that was projected by such a presence.

The cycles he felt were never ending. The moment felt like an eternity. Choice wished he could somehow avoid the equation and vanish into nothingness. However, he'd had this epiphany, and he could not un-have it.

As Choice struggled to understand, his chain of thoughts brought him closer to the concept of Fate and why Fate—the mightiest of all—needed Destiny and, perhaps most importantly, why Fate didn't interfere, at least not directly, to change the course of events.

Fate, he realized, was of the time keeper; he was a finite representation of how the entire system worked. It was Fate who rose and fell cyclically like sleeping and waking or the change of the seasons.

Therefore, one soul mind had to try to see God, eat the fruit of the knowledge of good and evil, and fall. When seen this way, perhaps history and religion did make sense. When Adam fell, the world fell. When Adam rose and remembered God, the world stabilized, and harmony and magic returned.

CHAPTER 34

CHOICE REALIZED THAT THE WHOLE CONCEPT
of the Kingdom was a return to the fantasy that dreams are made of. No
death, no pain, anything one could imagine was possible. In the sacred
books and villagers' tales it was heaven! His mind so wanted to cling to
his life memories, to preserve the logic.

"Reality is not a logical concept," Hope told him. "People forget that
reality equals magic. Some try so hard here to see the whole in a logical
way and expect a fierce battle to end history; they've been here too long.
The return is to the magic. It's the magic that will eventually end cycles as
it ended Atlantis, because humans will indeed go too far, see too much."

Glumly, Choice said, "And when that happens, the kingdom will fall.
Adam's mind will fall apart, and he will become a figment of his own
imagination. He will lose cohesion, and he will fall."

"The cycle will start over. Adam will realize fully that he is One. The
kingdom is closer to Fate, the core, the center truth. As one approaches it,
time does not pass! The farther away one is from Fate, the more space and
time have room to play their tricks on the mind."

This made perfect sense to Choice, and he could now understand
Hope's immunity to Space and Time. However, this was already too much
for Choice to ponder, and night was approaching. He tried to relax. He
tried to explain to Hope what he was thinking and feeling, but words were
inadequate to portray the images he was trying to express.

"Shhh," Hope said, smiling as she placed her finger across his lips.

She could relate to Choice's confusion, because it reminded her of the day she had visited Fate and found herself back in the Forest unable to explain if what she had experienced was real or a creation of her brain. It sounded odd, but as she had seen herself thrown back amidst the Forest that day, she had tried to fall asleep so that she could awaken back in the reality she so missed. It had somehow made sense at the time.

Hope now could detect the fingerprints of Fate in Choice's situation. She was certain that Choice and Fate were strongly connected, and the thought comforted her, because it authenticated her trust in Choice. That was something she had never done before—trusted a soul in the Forest. She knew that anyone connected to Fate in any way had a divine, ascended origin.

Choice lay his head on Hope's lap. She placed her palm on his forehead, shut his eyes with her fingertips, and caressed his hair as if she could ease his thoughts and prompt him to sleep.

As Choice drifted off to sleep, the information started streaming at him again so fast it was as if he was remembering, not learning. The physical world was not real, and the great suffering of the Chosen Ones in it could be eased only by such softening truth. Otherwise, his mother Destiny could not have survived the worst of scripts that a human had ever been subjected to. Images of horrors visited upon his mother flashed past his mind's eye, a repeat of the nightmare he'd had of being Destiny drowning in the lake.

There was no real physicality to anything; it was the logical and linear mind that made it appear so. However, the closer one got to Fate, the clearer the view of God and the infinite became. Those who were alive inside Fate's vision—the Chosen ones—would fall into the arms of Fate, who would catch and cushion them. Those who were not would have their ego inflate and drive them into a path of self-destruction.

Drazians, Forgetters, and the two men who had chased Hope crossed Choice's mind. The forest melded into the garden back home in Mimadamos and expanded to encompass what Choice assumed was the original Garden of Eden.

Fate could bend the laws of physics simply because the world reflected his mind. Therefore, Fate would intrinsically destroy all evil as one awakened, but this awakening depended on the individual. Fate would not do anything to speed this awakening, for that would trample on free will. A sudden heartache erupted in Choice's chest at an image of his mother leaving what felt like home, carried on a litter, and followed by a white horse. He had an empty sense that she would not be returning and that everything precious had gone with her.

That was why Fate did not, could not, force Destiny to stay. Fate's voice rumbled through Choice's head, "It had to be her choice. You were her Choice."

Choice then found himself staring at a house lit in the darkness with sounds of music and cheers coming from it. He walked toward the house and knocked on the door. A man wearing a goat mask answered.

Choice asked him, "What's going on? What's this music? What are you celebrating?"

The man replied, "It's a celebration of the return of the Kingdom to its rightful owners."

"But why are you wearing scary masks? Do you think it's funny to look evil?"

The man replied, "Evil is exactly what you just said. It's funny. The physical world is an illusion created by Fate, and we are all thoughts dancing inside his mind. This very ground you stand on is located inside his mind. We take on a shape and form only so that dreaming can be possible."

"Wake up dreamer!"

Choice suddenly saw himself inside what seemed like a lecture taking place under an apple tree. All students were seated on the ground listening to a man in a green gown pointing his forefinger at an eye-shaped map hanging on one of the tree branches. Mimadamos, the man explained, lay inside the part of Fate's mind connected to his heart, and the Forget Lands protected that part, like an iris protected a pupil on all sides. "All Forgetters are prompted to remain occupied in their vision into Demire and what lies outside those lands, when the real secret lies inside Mimadamos in its core."

"I am the only reality," thundered Fate's voice inside Choice's mind, "and what happens at any given time anywhere only describes what's happening inside my mind momentarily."

Choice pondered over that concept for a moment. "I am inside your mind how? Do you mean you think about me?"

"No, son," the man in green said, speaking again for Fate. "He means you are one of his thoughts. What you perceive as the physical world is a construct within his mind, given a form so that he may observe the interactions of different aspects of himself to make sense of it all.

"Your mother's journey back to Mimadamos represents his choice to empower the live part of him over the dead one. Your conception and birth represent this choice put into action. You came to this Forest for a reason. It's not a journey of discovery; rather, it's the journey of returning the lost Kingdom to its rightful owners, conquering the Forget Lands, and overthrowing its leadership through the logic they can understand. It's a translation of Fate's choice to prevail over his own dark thoughts that Dhumanos and his offspring represent inside his mind—thoughts that have threatened to doubt and deny his ability to choose in defiance of the Great Father's gift for him, which is this very ability."

Choice could never have imagined that this was the purpose behind his journey. History had painted a different logic behind his departure. He had made the Forest seem like a grand opportunity for him to fulfill his linear dreams and visions.

"But how could the world be real?" Choice spoke to himself in his sleep. "Fate can't even be in space, as space has no boundary to be within; it never made sense." Choice could see not only the other side of the forbidden simplicity of this revelation but also how negativity could easily sneak into the picture if the dreamer for a moment switched from being a lucid eye witnessing the dream to an active limb struggling to be real inside it.

Choice was escorted into the mind of Dhumanos, inside Fate's mind. "Nothing is real? Did I never go anywhere?" Choice asked himself. "Did I never do anything?"

Choice felt a snake wrapping around him. As he struggled to breathe, he spiraled down, losing all his options, feeling that he had no choice but to admit that he was nothing more than the helpless victim of the sickest cosmic practical joke.

"You are nothing." He heard a damp voice saying, "You are no one. You have never been seen by anyone; you've never been loved by anyone or even spat upon. You are damned, eternally damned."

* * *

Thus, the sound of his own mind became Choice's greatest enemy. It was an agony he had never felt before, and it was his greatest teacher. It taught him that false hope caused pain and that trying to reconstruct a reality always failed.

As a microcosmic fractal, he shifted continually from the finite waking state to the infinite sleep state, the manifest observed to the un-manifest unobservable. From one to zero! It was a never ending pulse.

Ommmmmmmmm. He heard this pulse, like a drone reduced to a static *hissss*: the sound of the snake, the long tale/tail with the poison at the head that consumed him whole. But then it was as if time froze in a giant endless now, and there was no next moment to exit into. He got stuck and felt so very tired. He became disoriented, and there were no external reference points, so his mind spun, and he wanted to be sick, but then he didn't have a body. There was no relative difference between the imagined puke and his gut.

Oh, what bliss it would be to hurl. If there were puke and a gut, he had space, and time was tied to space, so he could build a whole universe out of puke! The concept of food was real, and that meant the planet was real. But he couldn't puke; he had no physical form, so he couldn't alleviate his sickness and disorientation. He felt like garbage. He could be a hero due to such endurance, but who would ever know?

Unsung, unseen, unloved, pointless piece of crap! He felt dirty with no way to get clean. In trying to remember the moments to prove he was real, he thought of an earthly memory—when he had met a person who loved him so much!

Oh, please, no one loves me! How conceited do I have to be to invent such a lie? There is no one else but me.

He could feel sorry for himself and cry, but what was the point? He'd be like a kid who fell over and then looked to see if anyone saw him before deciding whether to cry.

Inside Dhumanos's mind, there was simply no hope! Choice was undone.

✳ ✳ ✳

Choice then heard the voice of Fate, like thunder shattering the deafening silence of Dhumanos's mind. "Choice … Choice …"

As Choice responded, he opened his eyes to see Hope uttering his name. Apparently, Fate had called him through Hope to wake up, as a sign this world was proof that there was a reality to celebrate even inside the dream.

Choice was so glad to hear Fate's voice vibrating through Hope's lips. The whole episode condensed into the feeling that Fate had simply thrown and caught him as a father does to his baby son. For a second, the child feels unsafe and unhandled. Then his father catches him. Incredible!

He felt so warm and loved, the way he must have felt in his mother's womb. Destiny, his mother, came to mind, and tears rippled through his eyes and leaked onto his cheeks. For the first time, he felt Destiny as pure, magical warmth detached from any reason, logic, or philosophical explanation. For the first time, he could just feel her warmth and love—which seemed to condense eons' worth of thoughts.

It was paradoxical to Choice that the minute he felt Fate's presence, he immediately felt Destiny's. It was as if they were one and always had been, and their historical and geographical separation was an illusion. History came to mind, flashing into Choice's consciousness that aura of loneliness that History projected. True, he was always busy, and he was good at what he did, but it was like a gardener good at decorating a cemetery. Apparently, to History, Destiny was a victim, a woman buried alive, and that aura had influenced Choice into feeling some emptiness.

But now that he thought about it, his mother had never made him feel that way. She never made him feel that Fate was not present. She never acted like a woman separated or a sad, helpless widow. Choice could see clearly now the pitfall of Dhumanos and the reason behind his bitter vengeance, for the devil simply couldn't handle being unreal.

✳ ✳ ✳

Dhumanos and the Archons had no connection with that part of Fate's mind that anchored reality. They could not handle the fact that they were never invited to Fate's reality. Nor could they fathom the connection between Fate and Destiny. Dhumanos loathed being a mere eyewitness enjoying the scene without allowing his numeric presence to take over. Thus, he protested creation through creation. He entered the dream to be real, only to deny the reality of the dreamer. He believed that he could somehow seek exit from Fate's mind using the physical dimension as a weapon to prove Fate unreal. That was an absurdity, for what was matter but spirit solidified to allow one to dream a reality into presence? And what was spirit but matter liquidized to save the eye from the entanglements of such reality as it caved in upon it?

Dhumanos's elusive journey to exit Fate's mind was, in fact, Fate's journey to purge his mind of Dhumanos. In other words, Dhumanos's plan could never escape the mathematics of Fate's plan, nor could his vision see beyond Fate's light. Using Space and Time as tools, he built empires on tedious physical laws and traditions, hoping to claim his spot in Fate's reality and in doing so, become real himself.

His conspiracy had targeted Destiny, since she was Fate's reference point for the reality he chose in his mind. His scheme was to separate the two physically using his agents, Time and Space, while capturing Hope inside the Forget Lands and forcing her to submit to Time and Space's logic.

Dhumanos viewed the Forest between Demire and Mimadamos as an agency of separation that decreased the chances of Fate and Destiny reuniting. He thought History's presence at the gates of Mimadamos could prolong his story and freeze Fate's Choice to bridge his world and Destiny's. He constructed Forest's laws based on a schism between mind and soul, desire and reason, using the fear of punishment and the desire for reward as methods to break any possible balance between desire and reason or a possible link between the two kingdoms.

The Foresters were trained to think like animals, chaotically reacting to kill anything different from them, to fear physically, and only to desire physical rewards. The most ambitious among them, the Drazians, tried to elevate their minds to higher concepts to cross to Demire, but they failed, because they hadn't been true witnesses to Fate and Destiny's wedding. They weren't invited to that magical day to fathom the logic behind magic or comprehend the nature of such love. In fact, that day they understood the meaning of falling from that bridge, and they never felt that fall's dark side more than that day, when they didn't know what to report to the Archons or how to falsely devise a scenario that explained the wedding or the nature of Fate's connection to Destiny. All they could do was describe it as a fling and belittle Destiny's importance.

Meanwhile, Dhumanos constructed systems aimed to deny Fate's significance and belittle his importance. The Drazians were the agents that served Dhumanos most in this respect. But he was made to believe that they had crossed into Fate's land and were keeping things in check. What he had lately discovered was that they had fallen off that bridge and into chains, and all they had ever promised was lies. He was thus awaiting their return to the Forget Lands to inflict upon them the worst punishment imaginable.

CHAPTER 35

CHOICE REMEMBERED A TIME IN HIS CHILDHOOD
when he had climbed a tall tree and could not climb any farther. He was
about to give up. If he did, he'd fall at least four yards and hurt himself,
yet he had no strength to advance anymore. He remembered History's
voice from below shouting, "Come on, climb! Move on!"

Until then, he'd thought he was alone and unobserved. Once he realized that he was being watched, somehow he climbed. Once he couldn't
afford being a loser in someone's eyes, he simply did what he had to do,
or he'd risk losing himself.

Everything in that dream was telling Choice that "me," the finite person he believed he was, was not real. The world was not real. Then suddenly Fate came flooding into his reality and swept him up. He felt like a
baby held by his father for the first time. He knew he was supported but
simply couldn't see what or who exactly was supporting him. He knew it
was Fate. How did he know? It didn't seem as though he was processing
or discovering that knowledge. It felt as if he was simply allowing it back
into his memory, recollecting it. It was all dawning upon him—what he
was and how he existed. He sobbed and sobbed in his dream until he
woke to find his eyes wet with actual tears.

"Nothing is linear," Choice reckoned. "We might seem to grow from
A to B, but A *is* B. We always are, but to have a linear experience, we forget and then remember. That's why, when you wake, you seem to learn

so much in such a short time. That's not possible, as learning takes time. When you wake, you remember what you are, what you know. It's like waking from a really intense dream or nightmare. It takes a moment to remember reality, but you do."

Fate revealed to Choice so many things without actually revealing himself. In the reality of Choice's story, Fate had not yet appeared, and there was still this scene that had to be lived: Choice meeting his father. True, he was tested many times, as if Fate were toying with him to see how strong he'd become, though *testing* wasn't the right word, because it was Choice who needed to realize his own strength. Fate already knew.

Choice knew too much to feel at ease with where he was and what was about to happen, yet too little to feel confident and capable in facing that challenge. "Time reels in on you," Choice told Hope. "The life you thought was real melts like a dream in the morning. The past was nothing more than a distraction to the fact that you always exist 'now.' The fall of Adam, you see, was Adam trying to be as God, trying to be infinite, and in that he fell. He became singular; he was all that existed. I am completely alone from this perspective. I always have been."

Hope replied calmly yet with the tone of someone who had been slapped by a different sort of fact. She had grown weary with her independent nature, and Choice's presence made her forget herself or perhaps make peace with otherness.

"What's new?" she said. "I have always felt this way in those lands. My whole life has prepared me to confront this truth you're uttering. I did not meet you, Choice; you were invited into my world. You do not represent company to me; you are merely a beautiful thought inside my mind that I kept inviting long enough to now see its face and hear its voice. The sickening part is that you try to argue against this solitary truth. You grasp at straws with thoughts such as, 'I remember my life. It must have been real. I remember when I fell from that tree or walked across that road and the children laughed at me, so there are Others. Then I sink as I remember I made up the scene and played all the parts.' You con yourself. You try to pretend that you weren't all alone forever! So many nows I seem to have lived, a stream of nows. It makes it seem as if I am linear, but in Fate's reality, everything coexists 'Now.'

"It's not so hard to believe when you think about it. Who doesn't exist now? No one exists in the past: that now is gone. No one exists in the future: that now is yet to come. You only ever exist now. You carry your now with you. In Fate's reality, it's one big, fat now with nothing missing, so time and space don't count. The now isn't split; it isn't frames that pass in front of your lens. Eternity isn't a very long time. Infinity isn't a really big thing, because it has no size. Anything with size is defined and, in that, is finite. Infinity is nothing, *no thing*. It can't be quantified.

"Eternity is no time, the lack of linear time. You simply 'are,' and the real killer comes when you become infinite—well, as close as you can get. There is no next moment, so how can you ever leave? For something to change, you need a next moment: 'time.' When there is no future, there is no hope; you really are damned! Infinity and eternity could be hell to someone who's inside Fate's mind yet can never know that or succeed in remaining in the center of his vision. He becomes a Forgetter! Pure and simple hell!"

That thought used to sadden Hope in some hidden way, perhaps adding to her loneliness in that Forest, until Fate whispered to her and invited her to his premises. His voice was more real than reality to her ears—so much so that she was willing to leave herself behind and be nothing but an ear listening forever. She felt that Fate had promised her a gift that day—which was her birthday—beyond freeing the Drazians in her honor. Now it hit her that the gift was Choice himself, for ever since she had met him, she had totally forgotten about Space and Time and, most importantly, her loneliness.

CHAPTER 36

"LET US PROCEED," CHOICE SAID TO HOPE. "LET us visit the regions below."

Choice's words echoed in the ear of every Chosen soul that dwelt on Earth, and everyone in the house of Fate rejoiced that the boy was one of them. They were of a single mind, and once Choice made the decision to claim his role, they charged him with a power he had never felt before. It was as it was always meant to be; all that had been needed was for Choice to exercise his will. Nothing could be hurried or slowed inside the mind of Fate. Everything had to play out as it should when all the conditions for it were met and all laws were respected.

In truth, Choice had been willing this ever since the revelation. He had willed it by way of avenging his mother for what she had been subjected to on the lakeshore that night. He had willed it for the sake of Hope, for her trials and tribulations with Space and Time. Yet not all the conditions had been met. It was only when Choice came to understand that the Forget Lands and its people fell inside his father's mind that he realized that it would be Fate's decision conveyed through him. Fate had the power to crush them in the blink of an eye if he wanted to, but there was more to power than force. Love had to enter the picture somehow, and so did free will.

Destiny, too, could have avenged herself, but she understood, perhaps on a subconscious level, that those beastly offspring were part of a reality she had to preserve. Even though she had been called a whore by those Archons—because of the innocence usurped from her—she never sought to exact punishment. These offspring had grown from her temptation to see her reflection in that lake. They came into being in an empty glory, and because they were not directly seeded by Fate, they ended in destruction.

Choice had always been able to channel Fate's power; however, this ability had lain dormant. Now it was fully activated. He also had the power to visit any earthly dwelling from among the Agents of Awakening who were captured and imprisoned inside the Forest in chains.

He projected a presence there, and the Archons, with the begotten powers of the Forget Lands, were shaken to the core when they saw the likeness of Fate flash across the boy's face. Choice did not reveal the love coming from him, for he did not want to sway people with emotion but with the simple, eternal Truth. What was revealed instead was strange enough to a nation that had dwelled so long in darkness. It sent ripples of fear and confusion through the entire region. Still, there were those who realized that a wondrous thing was happening, and they felt hopeful, perhaps for the first time ever. As for the ruling Archons, the committee of the twenty-four, they reacted by bringing about physical torture on every soul who pledged allegiance to Choice.

"They're trying to kill me," said Choice, who felt the pain of the afflicted, "not knowing that I am he who grants death its form and meaning."

The Archons were more confused than ever. They suspected Fate had entered the Forget Lands and was approaching their core dwelling place; however, since they didn't know who Fate was, they mistook Choice's presence for his. They didn't realize that Fate was speaking *through* his son. The Drazian Spiritual Pentagon and their followers were summoned to present their view of what was happening and their plan to retain control of the region, but they, too, were at a loss. This failure only infuriated the Archons, who sent them into underground captivity. There in the caves below the forest, these long-bearded, once highly-esteemed beings who had long reveled in their superior intellect faced a hell of their own making. They would spend all eternity doubting their understanding, replaying different scenarios of what could have, would have, and should have been if they had only made different choices. It was the worst kind of destiny for men who valued the head above the heart.

That was when the voice of Dhumanos was heard. "I am the God of the Fatherless, and there is no father above me."

Choice laughed joyfully as he listened to the empty words. But even as he asked, "And who, then, is Fate?" the entire spiritless group among the Drazians, who had falsely claimed that they had seen Fate and his dwelling and spoke on his behalf, continued to laugh and mock Choice's words.

In doing so, they were completely removed from the majesty of Fate's consciousness and again aligned with the worst imaginable destiny. For them, this destiny was an eternity of lack, a sense that there was never enough of anything.

And there came about a disturbance around Space and Time as news of History's death surfaced. The old man had been found lying lifeless in the garden he so dearly loved; apparently, he had suffered a heart attack while tending to his latest project, a strawberry–orange hybrid. Space and Time knew the truth. History had been charged with separating Choice from his mother. But his creative solution—encouraging Choice to depart Mimadamos—had served only to reunite Choice with his father! For this, History had been judged harshly by Dhumanos and the committee, who conveniently forgot that they had once championed this approach. Space and Time had no love for History, but they felt his loss keenly, for it signaled the crumbling of the paradigm that held them in such high esteem. Without History to help define them, what was their relevance?

Choice also heard of History's demise. Once not too long ago, the boy would have been shocked and saddened by this news. Now the information simply washed through him for some reason he couldn't fully fathom.

"Space and Time knew me beforehand," he said to the gathered Drazian doubters, "because of Hope. They sensed Hope's connection to me and thought that by capturing and killing her, they could hurt me. The ground underneath Hope folded, and she found herself enchained amidst a circle of Archons. I did not succumb to them as they planned. Hope's destiny is not in their hands to decide. She is so anchored to the Now that nothing can ever happen in her world uninvited. Hope's presence inside the Forget Lands is to preserve balance and prevent them from self-destruction. She has kept Space and Time busy and, in doing so, divided their attention and diffused the darkness of their schemes.

"I was not afflicted at all. For those who were punished, I was inside them, receiving the punches on their behalf. And those who appeared to die did so only in appearance."

This idea was met with derision among the crowd. Many shifted on their feet and whispered to their neighbors, but no one left. In fact, others stopped their travels to listen.

"I removed the shame from myself," Choice continued, "and I did not become fainthearted in the face of what happened to my mother at their hands. Yes, I was about to succumb to fear, and I did suffer in witnessing the scene, but in the end, their violence resulted in their own demise."

Choice's voice strengthened as he warmed up to his point. "In torturing Hope, they tortured what was left of hope inside them. In thinking they could kill me, they killed what was left of choice for them. In mocking Fate, they mocked the final thread of reason they needed to face their eternal punishment. Dhumanos, their father, sensed his ending, even amidst their sadistic mockery of everything good and holy. All the while, I was laughing at their ignorance."

It was then that the Drazians all heard the voice of Fate come through Choice's mouth. "Come forth, Children," he thundered. "You will see me from every side without hatred. Those who see me will be seen, and those who do not put me to shame will not be put to shame either. If you are not afraid before me, you will pass every gate in my mind, and you shall return to dwell in my heart, in Mimadamos, without fear. You will be perfected in the third glory. I am the alpha and the omega, the first and the last, the beginning and the end. I am above death and crucifixion, and fooled is he who believes I was ever crucified. He asked for me, he who never found me, and he found me, he who never asked, for the secret of asking lies in the heart and not the mind. Evil was crucified long before History's death. It was crucified on the cross of Space and Time in the very moment of their birth. The two are forever oblivious to the implications of their presence and absent from the meaning of their names."

The stunned crowd muttered and looked for support from each other. These words and ideas contradicted what they had been brought up to believe.

Then Choice spoke again, addressing the Chosen: "You will become victorious in everything – in war and battles, jealous division, and wrath.

For in our love, we are innocent, pure, and good, since we are preserved in the Eden of my father's mind, where the sun of his vision never sleeps."

Choice watched as first one Drazian, then those around him raised their hands to the sky, eyes closed, worshipping the idea that glory was so easy to find. Accepting Fate as their lord was not a difficult transition; dividing them from the Archons would be harder.

"The Archons do not understand the ineffable union of Fate and Destiny," he told them. "They do not realize that it was a wedding of truth and a repose of incorruption in a spirit of truth in every mind and a perfect light in an unnamable mystery. With this lack of understanding, they instead created an imitation of freedom and purity, a façade to hide their doctrine of fear, their slavery to worldly cares.

"Fate guards only he who is from him without word and constraint, since he is united with his will—he who belongs only to the Ennoia of the Fatherhood—to make it perfect and ineffable through the living water, to be with him mutually in wisdom, not only in the word of hearing but in deed and the fulfilled word."

A tingle ran through Choice's senses as his Father took him over as a vessel for his Word.

"I accomplish everything through the Good One," Fate continued, "for this is the union of the truth, that the Chosen ones should have no adversary. But anyone who brings division is hostile to them all and will learn no wisdom at all, because he brings division and is not a friend. He who lives in the harmony and friendship of brotherly love naturally and not artificially, completely not partially, this person is truly the desire of the Father. He is the universal one and perfect love."

A man spoke up from the front of the Drazians. "Your words counter those of Dhumanos. 'I am God,' he has said, 'and there is none greater than I. I alone am the Father, the Lord, and there is no other beside me. I am a jealous God, who brings the sins of the fathers upon their children for three and four generations.' Who are we to counter the words of such a powerful entity? We feel his influence and must believe."

"As if he had become stronger than Fate and Destiny!" Choice laughed, having his own voice returned. "Though he might appear like a god at times, given the way he messes with reality on this earthly place, his is but an empty glory. Oh, those who do not see, you do not see your blindness. You did not follow him in knowing obedience but proceeded under a misapprehension, as the blind are always senseless slaves of law and earthly fear."

A murmur of mixed anger and fear ran through the crowd that by now stretched down the street.

Choice stepped forward and announced, "I am Choice, the Son of Fate and Destiny, the one from you who is among you. I am despised for your sake so that you yourselves might forget the difference. And do not become female, lest you give birth to evil and its brothers: jealousy and division, anger and wrath, fear and a divided heart, and empty, non-existent desire.

"I am an ineffable mystery to you, oh perfect and incorruptible ones, because of the incorruptible and perfect mystery and the ineffable one. You do not know it, because the fleshly cloud overshadows you, but I alone am the son of Destiny. I have been in the bosom of the father Fate from the beginning in the place of the sons of the truth and the Greatness. Rest, then, with me, my fellow spirits and my brothers, forever."

All eyes turned to the boy just as Hope came to stand by his side. The two joined hands, looking out at all the faces, seeing hope in some and denial in others. In some they saw that questioning look that said they were wondering if this was indeed real.

CHAPTER 37

DESTINY GENTLY RAN HER HAND ALONG THE silken sheet, marveling at how one place could inspire two completely contradictory emotions. But as she sat smiling in the exact spot where she had given birth to her son Choice, she was also reminded of another choice, the one she had made to leave her dearest husband Fate and return to the ancestral home of her birth family. It had been no less painful for its seeming inevitability, yet Destiny had never experienced the anguish of timelessness as acutely as she did now.

She had been waiting for her son, or at least news about him, but nothing came her way. She found herself trapped at a single point. Mere seconds stretched into centuries, as often happens when waiting is combined with a high degree of longing. Her life was not moving in any direction but remained so still and so stagnant that it invited the lurking danger of death.

Confined within her abandoned family home, Destiny had made peace with her fate. She could not live in the beautiful dwelling she had built for her son. Yet there dwelled inside her a hope of being reunited with her Choice.

It was at one such lonely moment when she heard a knock on her door. It was a woman, clearly once beautiful but now haggard and worn. Thinking that the woman was selling something, Destiny was about to turn her away when the woman said, "I come with news of your lost family."

Destiny's heart quickened, but she hid her excitement just in case the woman was somehow trying to deceive her. "Come inside," she said with a wave of her hand, "and have something to eat."

The woman nodded and followed Destiny into the dining area, watching as Destiny laid out a light meal. The woman ate with gusto, barely looking up from her plate until the food was nearly gone. Then she finally said, "Choice has claimed power in the Forget Lands."

When Destiny heard those words, she could not keep the proud smile from her face. She had always known that Choice, given his parentage, was destined for greatness, yet like any mother, she'd had her concerns. The woman's comment had assuaged them somewhat, even if they did not ease the aching of her heart.

There were two ways of looking at Choice's departure. The first was that Choice was like any other young man who had struck out on his own, but she knew this was the easy way out. The other more likely explanation was that she had allowed her weaknesses to overcome her and invite that snake History to slither into her son's life and lead him astray. She vacillated between these theories depending on her state of mind, but in her heart, she knew the latter to be true.

There was also a third option, one she rarely entertained, that what had happened was nothing more than Fate's plan. She could sense his fingerprints all over the place, leaving their mark on the past, present, and future. She knew nothing escaped him; she also knew the price of meddling with his designs.

* * *

Miles away in the Forget Lands, the situation was full of chaos. The death of History had left a void in the Forgetters' minds and had begun to erode the very fabric of their society. That society was premised on apocalyptic thinking—namely, that the end was in sight and that they alone had the power to hold everything together. They had used History to advance this philosophy and to control everything and everyone around them. For a long time, it had worked, but they had not counted on Choice. Choice and Hope had reminded the Forgetters that divinity lived within them, and that they alone had power over their future. Even now as their empire crumbled around them, the Archons could not face reality: that as History himself had predicted, his own death would signal Armageddon.

Twenty-four Archons had met to formulate a plan. Despite their efforts, the situation continued to spiral out of control.

"Summon Time and Space," their leader said finally.

It was a last resort. Time and Space had never been faithful to anyone except each other, and even that loyalty had not been truly tested. Up to this point, they had worked in concert, so when they received the message to go to the shady forest of the Forget Lands, they decided to go and hear what the Archons had to say. Of course, Time and Space had plans of their own, but that would be kept between the two of them.

They arrived early at the meeting place—or rather above it in the wild, twisted branches of a tree. Within a few minutes, they saw the figures arrive—large, looming figures just as gnarled as the tree they clung to. Time and Space counted the figures, then glanced at each other when they realized that all twenty-four Archons had gathered below, their hulking, cloaked figures reeking of nastiness and cynicism. It was a horrifying scene.

"Are you ready?" Time asked.

Space nodded reluctantly. With a swift swish of wind, both stood in the group's center.

"Where have you two been?" one of the Archons growled.

"Why, waiting for your summons, of course," Time replied, adopting an obsequious tone that never failed to fool the Archons. Although they took great pleasure in using Time and Space to their own ends, they never stopped to consider the fact that Time and Space were always everywhere. If they had, they'd have to question who *really* had the power.

"We wish to speak of your work on behalf of Dhumanos," one Archon said, his voice a loathsome, screeching sound in the dark forest.

"We have done many things for him," Time and Space said in unison, glancing at Dhumanos. "Of what event do you speak?"

This annoyed the Archons enormously, for they were sure that Time and Space knew precisely what they were talking about.

"We are referring," one of the Archons said through clenched teeth, "to the portal you made that allowed him access to Destiny's mind."

"What of it?" Space asked.

"We need you to give him that access again. There is much chaos in the world. We need answers, and Destiny's mind is a great place to find them."

"Whatever you wish," said Space. He paused for a beat before adding, "I warn you, though, we may not be able to make it happen this time."

Time nodded in agreement.

The Archons looked at them in confusion. "What do you mean?"

"We mean," Time said slowly as if talking to a child, "that we may not succeed at constructing a bridge between your world and her mind."

"And why would that be?" the Archons snapped, their frustration growing.

"You do realize," Time said, "that Destiny is no longer the young, innocent maiden she was when she married Fate. Back then it was easy to manipulate her. Everything was new and romantic to her, and there was space in her subconscious, which we filled with vice and spite. It was temporary, of course, for her true nature is like an unborn child's, pure and covered under three layers of protection. But now Lady Destiny is completely different; she thinks and evaluates everything. She has faced pain and fought it. She has emerged from it scarred but stronger."

Space added that Choice was partly the reason for Destiny's increased fortitude. "It has something to do with becoming a mother," he said.

The Archons were silent for a moment before Dhumanos said, "Nevertheless, we would like you to break that barrier and manipulate her again."

Time and Space exchanged a glance, each aware of the other's disdain for the Archons. "Whatever you say," they chorused. Then they left the Forget Lands.

As soon as they were away from the Archons, Time and Space discussed the matter.

Time shook his head. "We have done damage to Destiny at their behest before, but even we have our limits."

"Do those fools not understand that causing Destiny's demise would threaten our existence?"

"Destiny was at her best when she took Fate's love and showered it on others."

That need was so strong, in fact, that it had driven her down into a dark world of duality and imperfection so unlike her own.

"Destiny birthed us to give this dimension a physical presence," Space said. "Without her, our fate will be sealed as well."

"For all their cunning, the Archons do not know this; they do not realize that we are as vital to the Universe as the four elements are to Mother Earth."

Space scoffed. "Even if the Archons knew, it wouldn't matter. They think they are flying spirits separate from this physical plane. Little do they know that, like all beings, the destruction of the Universe means their destruction as well."

Time and Space thought about all the wrongs they had done to Destiny. Her presence, which projected warmth and love, always eased Space and Time's minds away from the dark truth. They knew Dhumanos's efforts would prove useless in the end, which was why they suffered when he forced them to harm Destiny. They understood that they were harming the only sunshine in their dark world. The only thread of logic that prevented those two from ever emerging from their deep sense of despair was the fact that they never knew Fate. Destiny's birth preceded their birth. Thus, any personal knowledge of Fate could come only through her.

"I still feel poorly about our treatment of her," Time said. "After all, aren't we the ones who influenced her to leave her beloved Fate all those years ago? Was it not we who persuaded History to separate her from her son?"

"Yes. No matter how many times we wanted to turn her life into a scene from Hades, I still adore her. She is the reason we exist. Try as I might, I can't change my innermost feelings for her."

"You know," Time said thoughtfully, "there was too much power in the eyes of that young boy. When he stood like a shield for Hope, he looked rather like a prince valiantly defending his kingdom."

"Yes, I know," Space replied, recalling how Choice had defended Hope when Time and Space had chased her through the forest.

"I fear that something is about to happen," Time said, "and this time it's going to fall outside the Archons' plan—and our control."

Space nodded. "We've caused a lifetime of trouble for Destiny without much thought to the consequences, but now I feel like we're playing with fire."

"I have always felt a timeless sense of warmth around Destiny. What about you?"

Space nodded.

"What if," Time continued, "we were to move somewhere near her, not to do the Archons' dirty work but for our own destiny this time—to preserve our reality—our sanity? We could always take refuge at the outskirts of Mimadamos."

Time knew very well what History's death really meant: the end of the world's trajectory. Since then, Time and Space had felt as if they had plunged powerless into a new reality. Now it suddenly occurred to Time that this could be a blessing in disguise, an opportunity to create a new world. He found the thought surprisingly appealing; he wanted to start the world over again from scratch. This time he wanted to make the right choices.

Of all Time's regrets, Hope was his greatest. He had first met her in History's class and had been immediately struck by her innocence and courage. A favorite topic in the class had been how the impure loved to target the pure, so it was ironic that in their last encounter, Time and Space had chased Hope around the Forget Lands. They had no intention of causing any physical harm. In fact, deep down they admired her, for she greatly reminded them of Destiny and was the embodiment of a virtue they only claimed to have: neutrality. After all, Hope was originally a Drazian, yet she dwelled in the Forget Lands and roamed it in a circular fashion, keeping an equal distance from all places and times.

Even now they had a strong desire to trace her footsteps, observe the wise ways that had kept her from falling into the pits of the Forget mentality. She was the epitome of innocence, yet she had the wisdom and strength to move around the maze of tricks and traps without once questioning her reality. Oh, what Time and Space would do to possess such astuteness!

Time and Space were so engrossed in their conversation, they did not realize the presence of another being around them. Just behind the trees, two Archons keenly observed them.

"How dare you think of defying orders from Dhumanos!" one of them growled, startling the two.

"You sneaky devils!" the other spat.

Time and Space took in the brutal visages of the Archons, then glanced at each other. *We don't have to stand for this,* each was thinking. *We could just get out of here.*

Time and Space could levitate. They could project the aura of a satellite dish. They could be anywhere, anytime; they could appear or disappear at will. Yet they didn't. They never abused their power this way. Somehow they knew that this was one line they must not cross lest all sense of law and order fall away.

As they stood there, trying to think of another way to handle the situation, the Archons attacked.

CHAPTER 38

TIME LOOKED AROUND THE DANK CAVE, HIS LIPS
twisting into a humorless grin. This, he realized, was where History had
been taken after the Archons had discovered that he had led Choice to the
Forget Lands. While he appreciated the irony of history repeating itself,
Space, who was claustrophobic, was thinking only of how they could
escape their confinement. He was glad to see twenty-four of the ugliest
faces in the world appear in the cave to begin the interrogation.

"Two of our most trusted Archons have caught you planning your
traitorous departure," their leader snarled, his voice echoing through the
cave. "Do you deny it?"

"No," they answered together.

Time and Space had always worked in synchrony. It had been the
secret of their survival since time immemorial. If not for that, their inca-
pacity to move beyond the concept of linearity would have rendered
them obsolete.

Few souls dwelling in the Forget Lands had the courage to offend
the mighty Archons. Time and Space, however, felt they had nothing to
lose. They were completely convinced that the Forget Lands and its inhabitants were ultimately doomed, so why curry favor with Archons or even
Dhumanos? There was no point.

Yet one thing haunted Time. History had once said that in the eyes
of Fate, everything had already happened. Time tried to ward off these

thoughts by telling himself that History was crazy, but he knew that often those who were mad spoke a greater truth than the sane.

Even as they admitted their betrayal, someone shrieked. It was one of the Archons who was notorious for panicking easily. "This is the beginning of dreadful times for our noble race! We must crush these dreadful seeds of conspiracy lest they sprout and infiltrate our pure gardens with their weeds!"

Space immediately shook with fear, but Time did not betray any emotion. He knew that emotions were like currency, and the only way to destroy currency was to dilute its value. Instead, he waited to hear what the other Archons had to say.

"Time and Space," they said after a moment, "we ask you to perform this last service and reveal the complexities of Destiny's mind to us. We want you to give us access to every corner of her brain. Following the successful completion of this task, we will set you free."

Time knew that there must be something more to this offer but waited patiently.

Space could not contain himself any longer. "And what if we say no?" he shouted.

The Archons laughed as if they had been waiting for this outburst. "Failure to comply," one of them said, "will result in the revelation of your true nature to the world. The world includes Mimadamos, of course."

Time's mouth stretched into a grim line. So there it was. Despite their base natures, the Archons were not fools; in fact, they were quite perceptive. They had sensed that Time and Space were planning to run away. They had also sensed their protectiveness over Destiny. Most importantly, they had realized that Time and Space could not afford to be exposed to her or the other people of Mimadamos.

Space's mouth opened as if to say something else, but Time silenced him with a look.

"But Destiny is currently at her weakest," Time reasoned. "What could you hope to gain by accessing her brain now?" Even as he asked this, he knew the answer.

"She may be weak in your eyes," the lead Archon said, laughing softly, "but as long as she has a connection with Fate, she has value. Even History, failure that he was, acknowledged that Destiny had power over him. The source of such power could be only Fate; therefore, when we have access to her brain, we will have access to him." He laughed again, an evil sound. "We are aiming to catch a glimpse of the sun reflected by the moon. There is a connection between Fate's soul and Destiny's—their separation has not changed that. It would be a pity not to take advantage of a great situation like this."

A shiver ran through Time as he understood the plan. He glanced at Space and saw that his companion was about to faint – whether from fear or claustrophobia, he did not know.

"If we are to be of any use to you, you must free us immediately," Time said as he jerked his head toward Space, "especially him."

The Archons did so grudgingly. As Time and Space rubbed their wrists where the shackles had been, a look passed between them. Neither wanted to do the Archons' bidding, not only because of the damage it would do to Destiny, but also because the threat of being exposed to the world had robbed Time and Space of their free will. Unfortunately, they saw no other way.

Finally, they bowed to the Archon of Archons; it was a gesture of submission signifying that a deal had been struck.

CHAPTER 39

TIME AND SPACE HAD NOT BEEN ALWAYS ON THE
Archons' side. The truth was, even when they had proclaimed their allegiance to the Archons, there were moments when they went by their
instincts. Now perched on a tree branch, Time was visiting such a memory
on the movie screen of his mind.

It was Destiny's birthday. She was not yet six years old. Dhumanos
had not bestowed the mirror upon her to corrupt her mind, and she was
still as innocent as a rosebud. There had been a large, lavish party attended
by all in Mimadamos, but what Time remembered most was a very old yet
very beautiful woman whom everyone called Mother Earth. She moved
gracefully around the party, enlivening everyone she encountered. When
Destiny cut the cake, everyone asked Mother Earth to bless the party with
a few pearls of wisdom. She smiled and gave a heartwarming speech that
Time still recalled in its entirety.

After some kind words about Destiny's beauty and intelligence,
Mother Earth had said something that Time could not in that moment
fathom, but which now made perfect sense as he settled on the tree branch
on the darkest night of the coldest month.

She had said, "It is true that different beings require distinct com-
positions for their sustenance. Yet it is also true that most of these are
made of the same elements with only a slight variation in proportions.
Therefore, instead of investing our energies into finding what is different

between us, why do we not focus on our similarities, like the elements? If there were enough of them, everyone could use them according to their needs. It is important to achieve a balance for vitality. Forget about the positives and negatives, and instead try to achieve the zero state, the ultimate neutrality!"

"Neutrality is what we need above all else right now," Time told his brother, bobbing in his up-and-down way.

Space nodded. "We have stretched the delicate balance of the universe to the extreme left. In doing so, we have done much damage to Destiny."

"We must right things now, or things could turn ugly," Time said. "If we manipulate Destiny further, you and I will be threatening our own existence."

"If we cease to exist, or even if we lose our memory, the whole of humanity will lose its memory as well."

"Memory is a beautiful thing; it allows humans to relive happy moments or avoid repeating negative ones."

"Yet memory is also functional, for it gives human and Archon alike a reference point from which to operate on this earthly plane." Space shook his head sadly, shifting himself to the side. "We have already lost History; without memory, I fear the fabric of the universe will be destroyed."

Indeed, for Time, forgetting Destiny was the worst possible scenario, even worse than breaking her mind for the sake of the Archons. If he defied them, he risked Destiny learning of his and Space's role in separating her from her husband and son.

His eyes were moist as he looked up. He could not see any silver lining of a moon between the entangled branches of wild trees.

Space was resting on a lower branch of the same tree. Although he was not happy about the arrangement either, to him it seemed more of an inconvenience than a tragedy. *As usual,* he mused, *Time was being overly dramatic.* Space could almost hear his partner in crime fretting a few feet above him. Finally, he heard the obnoxious sound of Time's snoring.

The names of Time and Space had always been inextricably linked—people never spoke of one without the other. Yet the truth of the matter was that Space was much more dependent on Time than the other way around. Time had defined Space. Before Time's arrival, Space had no identity, and he was lost in the land of Forgetters. Every creature used him and benefited from his presence, but he had no idea of his worth. It was only his beloved friend Time who gave him a direction. Time had such a positive effect on Space that the same man whose thoughts used to be scattered all over the place had now discovered four separate ways to sort his views. There were times when he would produce at least four distinct but equally brilliant solutions to the same problem. He attributed all his brilliance to Time's presence in his life.

Time knew very well how Space felt about him. In the beginning of their friendship, Time had felt superior, but soon he'd realized Space's significance. Time had no existence without Space, either. Besides, they'd lived together for so long, neither could function without the other. It was a truly symbiotic relationship. The difference in their behavior was only because of the dissimilarity in their natures. While Space liked the feeling of belonging, Time had a habit of simply passing by. He was fast and did not like inhibitions, which were the manifestations of long attachments. However, he knew that he was stuck with Space. Similarly, he felt a strong connection with Destiny. Both were vital to his survival.

Time and Space both knew that they were supposed to be together. As long as they enjoyed each other's company, they had no issue with their fate. In fact, it was not only their fate but also their destiny. Each possessed exactly the right amount of strength that the other needed. They empowered each other, joining forces to build the last bridge, which would give the Archons access to Destiny's thoughts.

CHAPTER 40

THE SUN HAD NOT YET RISEN, BUT DESTINY WAS
already up and moving about. She had covered herself with a large shawl
on which an ancient spirit had drawn intricate patterns. She knew nothing
about those spirits, nor did she understand the purpose of the shapes on
the fabric. All she knew was that Fate had given it to her, and every time
she wrapped it around herself, it was as if he was still there protecting and
comforting her.

She slipped from the bedroom, her footsteps light and quick toward
her destination. Choice had left her long ago, but this was the first time
she'd felt a need to visit the paradise she'd built for him. She didn't dwell
on this strange, sudden desire; she was blinded by love for her son and
driven by the thought that it was a signal from him. He must be awaiting
her in his old home!

The faster Destiny moved, the more tired she felt, but she ignored
it and kept on. Just as she was nearing her destination, she was gripped
by an old, familiar feeling that mired her feet and made her shiver with
terror. It was the same sensation she had felt in those awful dreams that
had plagued her. She almost turned back to the safety of her house, but
Choice's face danced in front of her eyes. Was it another sign that he was
waiting for her? She thought it must be.

No one can touch my mind, she thought, trying to shake off the ominous
feeling, *no one but Fate*. She was not the young, foolish, and vain girl she

once had been but the wife of the mighty Fate and mother of the King of the Forget Lands! That would never change no matter how much time had passed since she'd seen her beloveds. *It's just excitement,* she told herself. *It has nothing to do with dreams.*

It was not as if the battles of her soul had ended completely, but the nature of the fighting had changed. It was not about good and evil anymore but about choosing pain or happiness. She had spent too much time reveling in her grief; indeed, the only moments of true happiness she felt were when the majestic voice of Fate filled her being or when his presence found a way into her soul. She still had no idea of the situation outside Mimadamos, but she now chose to believe that everything was going the way it should. She would often find solace in her memories of Fate and the way he remained optimistic in every situation—but then, he knew everything already. What if, she wondered during the darker moments, Fate's right was her wrong?

Entangled in such conflicts, she was surprised to find herself at the gates of her paradise. She stood there for some time, tossing the lingering doubts around her mind, then pulled open the gate. At first glance, the place appeared as lovely as she remembered, but as her eyes grew accustomed to the darkness, she saw that the memories of her son had clouded her perception.

The once exquisite plants lining the path to the house had long been strangled by weeds. The once magnificent house now looked haunted and uninviting. Still, Destiny felt no fear of entering; she had planned the house to its last detail and had infused love into every brick.

What disturbed her most was the dreadful condition of her garden. What onlookers used to call paradise now more closely resembled hell. All the beautiful life had died, and the only life forms that had managed to thrive were thorny bushes and venomous plants. Destiny made a mental note to have the place cleaned. There was a small voice at the back of her mind telling her to retreat, but she refused to give in to it—not when there was a chance she might see her son again. She took a deep breath and stepped inside.

The moment she crossed the threshold that separated her paradise from the rest of the world, a high-pitched, horrific shriek escaped her, and she fainted. When she opened her eyes again, she blinked a few times, not sure if what she was seeing was real. She seemed to be lying in the labyrinth garden of her house. It did not feel like her dream but more like a part of a stranger's nightmare. Even though the strange situation baffled her utterly and all her senses were questioning the reality of this place, she was aware of one truth: she needed to reach the apple tree.

As often happens when someone realizes that they need to do a particular thing, they make all efforts as if their life depended on it. Destiny was convinced that the apple tree would somehow give her the salvation she sought. With this conviction, she started making her way through the maze, only to realize a few minutes later that she was moving in circles.

Those few minutes felt to her like eons. She was thirsty and tired. Her hair was disheveled, and she had no idea where her shawl was. She couldn't remember removing it. There were many other things she couldn't remember, but she had the vague sense that the shawl was more important.

She tried to push the garment from her mind and ignore the growing fatigue. It was as if with each step, the energy was being drained from her limbs. Each time she fell, it was harder to get back up.

Hovering high above the garden, their faces twisted with fury and pain, Time and Space watched Destiny stumble to the ground once again. Nearby they could clearly see the twenty-four hideous Archons pressing the poor girl's mind with all their energy. As much as they loathed what was happening, Time and Space could do nothing except grit their teeth.

Oblivious to this, Destiny struggled to her feet and looked around her. She had no idea how to escape this maze, but she had a vague sense that it had somehow transformed into some other place. With a sudden jolt, she realized that it was the Forget Lands. How could this be? She had no way of knowing that she was still standing in the ruins of her paradise; the Archons had merely projected the image of the Forget Lands there. It was the perfect place to hunt her, for they knew it well.

A desperate sadness suddenly gripped Destiny. She was, she realized, the loneliest person in the world. She had nobody in her life, and nobody had ever been there for her. Hopelessness threatened to consume her. She felt as if someone were asking her to be a queen over a kingdom, but there was no person to rule. They wanted her to be the queen of an empty island.

She wanted to wake up and end this dreadful nightmare, but no matter how hard she tried, she couldn't break free. In a last desperate moment, she called out the names of Fate and Choice, and immediately their smiling faces emerged inside her head.

"I want to reach the apple tree," she said and pointed in a random direction.

She felt something stir inside her. Then her middle and index fingers moved on their own, pointing and jerking forward. Destiny stared at them for a minute before she realized that they were showing her which way to go.

Slowly at first, she allowed her fingers to guide her. She followed them deeper and deeper into the garden until, finally, she saw the apple tree. Her heart leapt, and she moved toward it, her hand outstretched. Before she could reach it, a strong wave of exhaustion swept over her. She felt as if she had been traveling across the desert of eternity for centuries. Her feet could not support her anymore. With her last ounce of energy, she flung herself beside the apple tree, and that's when she realized that the Archons were waiting for her there.

CHAPTER 41

TO THIS POINT, THE ARCHONS' PLAN TO TOY WITH
Destiny's mind had been successful. She felt like a piece of fruit squeezed
in the hand of a mighty giant until the last drop of juice had been wrung
from her. Through her half-open eyes, she saw the twenty-four Archons.
They were standing in a tight circle around her, chanting something as
they prepared to perform some other dastardly deed. She knew that she
should be afraid, but she was simply too tired. Her eyes got heavier and
heavier until they finally closed altogether.

She awoke sometime later to the sounds of the Archons singing. It was
more chant than song, hateful in nature, and a slow, deliberate monotone.
"Mimadamos, Franco, Herodos," they said repeatedly, "Mimadamos,
Franco, Herodos …"

Destiny didn't know the significance of the words or why the Archons
were chanting them, but she could not deny the strange effect they had
on her. It felt as if they were flowing through her veins, making her limbs
weak, and rendering her head heavier than ever before. She tried as hard
as she could to fight it, but she slipped into a trance.

She found herself looking out over a breathtaking, snow-covered
vista. "It's all yours," a voice whispered, and she smiled.

She was queen of this land and ruler of all who lived here. Who
needed that other world so full of pain? It was so peaceful here, so quiet.

In fact, it was as silent as a tomb. Where was everyone? She walked for a bit but saw no one, just a vast, white space.

She opened her mouth to call for someone, but no sound came out. Placing a hand to her throat, she tried again and heard nothing. What was wrong with her voice? And why was she alone here? Now the vast space felt as if it was closing in on her. She was trapped, and no one even knew she was here! As panic threatened to take over, she forced herself to focus on her son's face, like a beacon.

In that moment, Destiny realized that the Archons were trying to break into her mind, and she began to fight back. As they watched her eyelids fluttering violently, the Archons realized something as well. If not for their heinous tricks, they could never in a million years have bested Destiny; they would have been no match for her enormous strength. Most importantly, they finally understood that she, not Fate, was the source of her power. Even Time and Space, still witnessing the scene from above, were shocked by what they saw.

The forest filled with light from two vastly different sources. One, a single grey beam, came from the feeble minds of the Archons. The second light, however, was coming from Destiny's mind. It was white light tinged red. The two energies intertwined, battling for control. Then just when Destiny's force had nearly shrunk the Archons into nothingness, the moment passed. All her forces shattered into the atmosphere. She had surrendered.

The small ring of a dozen Archons found free access to every corner of her magnificent brain. The war of minds had been waged and won, and now the victors were ready to collect their bounty. They closed their eyes, and scenes from Destiny's life started playing. It was not an enjoyable experience, for they had to endure her heartache as well. They were indeed shocked by this, for although they had corrupted her mind before, they had never experienced the bitter taste of their work in Destiny's mouth. However, there was not much time to reflect on it.

Time and Space knew very well the reason behind the pain. The bridge they had cemented was losing strength. Time knew that this might end with their death or, at the very least, their memory loss. He had never imagined that the last thing he saw would be Destiny, writhing in agony.

As the images of Destiny's life flashed before their eyes, the Archons began to understand her true significance to Fate.

"Fate's existence is beyond our reach," one announced to his brethren. "Destiny is his only connection to our world. In fact, his only interest in the world is Destiny."

"She is the center of his earthly connection."

"He is like the sun, whose only purpose is to bestow light on the moon. The fact that its rays are beneficial for all is just a bonus."

"We could simply kill her," one suggested. "In doing so, we will cut the eternal connection between Fate and Destiny and restrict Fate's power over our world."

Yet something gave them pause.

The process of life was dynamic, and anything that failed to move ultimately ended in nothingness. There was always a war between two opposing forces facilitating the movement of any system. However, reaching equilibrium was desirable, and the system must not tilt toward any single direction. The battles of relative good and evil had never ceased to exist. Both sides had won and lost, but there had never been an ultimate victory for either. This was what had kept the system going. The moment one side claimed its victory, there would be no need for the universe; it would die on its own in an apoptotic event.

Although the Archons were not consciously aware of this, the thought of harming Destiny conjured up another, more disturbing vision in their minds. They saw the world destroyed and themselves experiencing the sort of torture they never could inflict on their greatest enemy. As heinous as these images were, the wave of confusion that followed was even worse. The Archons could contemplate anything—even their own destruction—with cold-blooded calm, but confusion sent them into a full-throated panic.

Each of the Archons had his own ideas about how to deal with this.

"We must plant more false images."

"We should retreat and consult Dhumanos."

"The contrast of living in Demire opposed to the rest of her life is the problem—let us blend that out."

"No! We must reduce the shadow of our meddling, so she never knows that we were here."

"To do that, we must delve further into Destiny's mind. Those memories are far behind her current life as wife and mother."

While they appeared to be working in lockstep, beneath the surface, there were different motivations.

One thought, *We must find more information from Destiny.*

Another thought, *The girl must die.*

The result was chaotic and uncontrollable, with Destiny's sanity and even her life hanging in the balance. So preoccupied were they with their evil plan that the Archons didn't give much thought to Time and Space. It was only by chance that one of them glanced at the sky and saw those two powerful, deceitful spirits crying out in torment.

CHAPTER 42

WHATEVER WAS HAPPENING TO DESTINY, TIME and Space seemed to experience it with twice the intensity. As the Archons looked to the sky, they saw Time and Space making strange, jerky movements and howling as if their brains were being ripped apart. The Archons squinted at each other, genuinely puzzled; none of them had any idea why Destiny's pain was affecting them so much. Destiny knew, though, and since the Archons were still connected to her through energy flow, they were about to get their answer.

It came to them in another rush of images from Destiny's life. The first showed her as a newborn in an ancient time and setting that seemed altogether foreign to them. At first, the Archons could not understand the purpose of the image, but then they saw two beams of light emerge from the newborn's mind. They were two separate beams and moved at perpendicular planes to each other, yet they had something in common. It came as a shock to the Archons when they realized that those beams were the humble beginnings of those great spirits Space and Time.

There were other images showing Destiny giving power to Time and Space through her mind. When she was young, they were her imaginary friends. Although she thought she needed them for her survival, the opposite was true. Indeed, her powers had shaped Space and Time's reality. If not for her, Fate would not have allowed them to thrive.

There was a flash, and the Archons saw another image. It showed Fate standing on the highest mountain in Demire. One look at his posture revealed that he was far above the trivial happenings of their world. Suddenly, the image focused on his eyes, and the Archons saw, in the golden lenses of the godly figure, the truth of all truths. The only person Fate cared about was Destiny. Her well-being and that of their world were inextricably linked.

The Archons were horrified. "Our entire universe exists only because it is kept alive in Fate's memory through Destiny! If she chose to forget us even for a second, our entire world would be jeopardized."

Before their very eyes flashed the image of their world being sucked into a black hole.

One Archon said cynically, "I would understand if she had done it all for power or even pure vanity, but love?"

Another one muttered, "I've never heard of any theory more absurd than love. How could she advocate the very same thing that has caused so much degradation to her soul?"

To accept love as a practical concept of cause and effect was completely beyond their capacity. Nevertheless, love and only love had motivated Destiny to create these thoughts. It was indeed love that had made her fall for the Archons, too. They remembered her foolish thoughts, and they were even more confused.

The first Archon then continued, "*Tch*. Love. At best it is an abstract construct designed to bond a couple long enough to reproduce and raise the young to independence."

"Look how well that worked out for Destiny—Fate left her to birth and raise their son alone," the second replied sarcastically.

Even now, after learning the truth, they still mocked love. And why wouldn't they? The Archons had never experienced the feeling. They had spent all their lives under the curse of darkness; all the people and spirits that had ever touched them were full of wickedness. Evil was their reference point and their source of power, and they wielded it in all matters. To the Archons, Love was simply incapable of conquering evil.

Now faced with the reality that love alone was the reason for their survival, the Archons did the only thing they could: they sought some magical explanation to refute love's power.

One Archon stepped up and spoke in an optimistic tone. "Remember how the Drazians mocked the union of Fate and Destiny? They were sure Destiny would once again be abandoned and love would fall. And they were right!"

This thought gave the Archons immense relief.

On its heels came another, more frightening thought, this time voiced by one of the most skeptical among the committee of the twenty-four Archons. "What would Fate do if he learned that we broke into the mind of his most beloved?"

Dhumanos, feeling an escalating sense of panic among the Archons to the latest remark, spoke in a calming tone foreign to his usual way of speaking. "On the other hand, what has he done to stop us? No lightning bolt has struck us down, no consequence at all."

Emboldened by this realization, they decided to penetrate even further into Destiny's brain. The Archons were nothing if not greedy.

When they saw the Archons gesturing for them, Time and Space looked at each other and sighed. Clearly the Archons were not done with them—or Destiny—yet.

"I don't feel sane anymore," Time said, clutching his head and drifting upward.

Space nodded, edging sideways. "I wonder what torture they will inflict on us next."

"Well, I won't accept their demands anymore," Time replied, and Space could see by the set of his jaw that he meant it.

"What is our role in the story?" the Archons demanded as Time and Space approached.

Time and Space just shrugged.

"Well, if you don't give us the answer, we will get it from her." The Archons then ordered them to construct a bridge even deeper inside Destiny's brain.

Time and Space looked around, and their eyes fell on poor Destiny. She was lying on the muddy ground. They could not see her face clearly, for it was half-covered with her hair. They pitied her, even as their bodies were aching with severe pain.

Time thought for several minutes before answering. "If we try to force our way into her mind any further, irreversible damage will happen, not just to her but to our world as well."

The Archons were torn. Time had just confirmed what they already suspected, yet they still wanted to manipulate Destiny. One of the Archons opened his mouth, but before he could say anything, Space started talking.

"To go into her mind again would be suicide. You may not care what happens to us, but you would be signing your death warrants. If you had been paying attention to any of the happenings inside her head, you would have understood this."

The Archons looked at each other, their confusion lifting at last. No matter how they hated to admit it, it was time to back away from Destiny or face the most serious consequences. Finally, they turned back to Time and Space and nodded.

Space and Time exchanged a look of silent celebration. The Archons would leave now, they were sure of it, and not harm the poor woman any longer.

A moment later, the Archons turned to go, all but one. Dhumanos, the Archon of Archons, was much more disturbed by the goings-on of the past several hours than he'd let on. He had always considered himself the ultimate source of power, and the reality gleaned from Destiny's mind did not make him happy. Now as he stood over her, his eyes fixed on the helpless figure, his anger mounted. He wanted her to know how much damage she had done to them.

Unexpectedly, he plucked an apple from a tree and tossed it hard at her head. He wanted to slap her with the same reality with which her mental images had slapped him. To him, Destiny was not only the reason for their survival but also the inevitable cause of their destruction.

Just as the apple struck her, she woke, for the Archons were leaving her brain. She felt extremely weak. For a minute, she had the vague impression of Space and Time crying beside her, but when she looked around, she was alone.

CHAPTER 43

THE WIND BLEW GENTLY THROUGH THE FORGET
Lands, caressing leaves on the trees and rustling the tall grasses, with no
idea that it would soon be fouled by a dark, all-too-familiar presence.
Sure enough, the wind turned a sooty black as the party of twenty-four
Archons entered its space. Now stagnant and rather stale-smelling, the
wind slowed to a crawl. Such was the effect of the Archons on the elements of nature.

A moment later, the sounds of the Archons filled the Forget undergrounds; all of them were talking simultaneously, so nobody could make
out what the others were saying. This continued for several minutes before
the air was rent with Archons' twisting and crying out in pain.

"No doubt our duty is to spread chaos in the universe," came the
voice of Dhumanos, "but that does not mean that we should do the same
amongst ourselves." He withdrew the negative energy he had been zap-
ping them with. "To deal with the enemy, we must be united."

Now trying to catch their breath, the Archons merely nodded
in agreement.

"The situation is grave," he added, "and difficult to navigate. Our
world is the brainchild of Destiny. We need not only her survival but also
her deep interest in us to keep us alive."

The Archons looked at each other, eyebrows raised. Of course, Dhumanos knew what had transpired when they invaded the woman's brain. He knew everything.

"Considering this reality, I fear we made a mistake when we separated her from Fate. We may be her creations, but the fact remains that she is only the means. The true source of energy is Fate. If she's not with him, there is always the chance that he might forget about her. This will lead to the destruction of our world as well."

One of the Archons took a step forward. In the Forget Lands, the gesture meant he wanted to say something. It was especially used when talking to a person of great stature.

Dhumanos narrowed his eyes at the Archon, then nodded his approval.

"I respectfully disagree," the Archon began tentatively. Immediately, the tension in the air thickened, as it always did when there was a chance Dhumanos might be angered.

Dumanos just nodded again at the Archon. "Go on."

"I do not think it was a bad idea to separate Fate and Destiny. Remember, her life in Demire was comfortable—luxurious even. There was a high risk of her forgetting us, which would have proven equally disastrous for us."

His words set the rest of the Archons chattering again until they felt the second blast of energy from Dhumanos. They gave a collective shriek, then fell silent.

"He is right," Dhumanos finally announced. "Both must remember us, Destiny directly and Fate through Destiny. It is necessary for our survival that Destiny does not slip from Fate's mind. What do you counsel?" He directed this question to Sonamrud, the Archon standing to his right.

Sonamrud was known for his profound wisdom and clarity of mind. As the most intelligent of his kind, Sonamrud's chief duty was editing scripts that the rest of the Archons wrote. As this duty required not just skill but supreme wickedness, Sonamrud excelled at it, for his wickedness knew no bounds. There was nothing he enjoyed more than directing it at Destiny.

To the Archons, the more cunning a person was, the more he was respected. In this regard, it was no different than many other societies around the world. Sonamrud knew this firsthand, given his status, and he often used it to play upon the guilt of the minds he was trying to manipulate. This had been particularly effective with Destiny, for she, like so many others, often saw her sins as minor compared to others'. And Sonamrud used every opportunity—and the Archons' evil scripts—to remind her of all she had done wrong.

"For Destiny to remember us," he said now, "it is necessary that she dwell on her guilt. Here is the challenge we face: ever since becoming a wife and mother, she has grown strong. Most importantly, her conscience is clear, because she has been purified."

Several of the Archons opened their mouths to reply but were stopped by a warning look from Dhumanos.

"As long as she is free of remorse," Sonamrud continued, "it may not be easy for us to influence her. The only way I can devise is to restore those earlier shameful memories that Fate purged from her all those years ago."

This suggestion brought snorts of approval from his comrades, but before they could say more, Sonamrud held up a hand to silence them. "This is not as easy as it sounds, so don't celebrate yet. We have another problem. Choice has proclaimed dominion over our land and is moving toward Demire, the land of his father, as we speak."

Another Archon said zealously, "We will generate great scripts in minimal time."

Sonamrud's lips split into a condescending smile. "It is not about the scripts, you fool. A complex procedure is required to make her forget all about that occasion. Unfortunately, none of us has the ability to do it."

The celebratory mood abruptly evaporated. Sonamrud was right, of course; only Fate had the ability to erase harmful memories from Destiny's mind. He had done it that time she went to the lake seeking to punish herself for the promiscuity she had indulged in before her marriage. For although she had not engaged in physical transgressions, she had allowed her mind to be invaded. It was almost worse. It was only after being purged of these memories that she had agreed to become Fate's bride.

"But," Sonamrud said, and everyone looked up once again, "it can be done. All we need is to persuade our little friends, Time and Space."

A loud, foul laughter escaped Dhumanos, echoed by the Archons. This was indeed the ultimate solution to all his problems.

* * *

Miles away from the polluted air of the Forget Lands, Time and Space were resting on the apple tree in Destiny's garden. Although they had no idea of the plan being hatched by the Archons, Time's instinct told him that something bad was about to happen. That feeling was confirmed a few moments later, when they received their summons.

CHAPTER 44

TIME AND SPACE FOUND THEMSELVES ONCE again standing in the company of the Archons. Time had half a mind to ignore the call, but he knew better, for this time it was Dhumanos he would be defying. Besides, where would he and Space go? They weren't well received in Mimadamos or among the Drazians. Although they had tried more than once to gain people's trust, Time and Space were viewed suspiciously. It was one of the reasons the two had lost their neutrality to the Archons.

A long time ago, when they were not quite as experienced and wise, Time and Space had attended a funeral in Mimadamos. The two had sincerely wanted to prevent the evils lurking in the forest of the Forget Lands from attacking Mimadamos, but they had soon realized that the very people they were trying to protect were not interested in their help. In fact, the people kept Time and Space at a distance.

Wounded and disillusioned, Time and Space slowly began accepting the Archons' propositions. Sure, they still had the appearance of neutrality, but it had become merely an illusion. Any feelings of guilt soon melted away, for Time and Space found they were much more at ease with these dark souls than with the so-called good people who had made them feel unwanted.

Time had said to Space several times, "All men are the same no matter where you go."

Space couldn't disagree, for that did appear to be the case whether they were in the Forget Lands, Mimadamos, or even Demire. Lately, for reasons not entirely known to them, Time and Space had begun to have a change of heart, especially when it came to Destiny. They could not exactly tell this to Dhumanos; he did not understand the concept of compassion let alone entertain it. As for the other Archons, they had broken their promise of setting Time and Space free without another thought.

"Well, well," said the Archon of Archons, "good to have you two back in our company so soon."

Time and Space said nothing, just kept their eyes on the ground.

"From the way you were shrieking at our last encounter, we thought we might never see you again."

A wave of snickers spread over the other Archons as they remembered the pair's agony by the apple tree.

"Does this mean that you are breaking the oath you made to us?" Time asked somberly.

Dhumanos just smiled, revealing a mouth of yellow teeth. His followers laughed in agreement.

"What do you want this time?" asked Space.

"It is very simple," Dhumanos said, "and the best way to approach the matter at hand."

Time rolled his eyes. "All your tasks are supposedly simple, but that is never the case."

"We need you to restore Destiny's memories—those Fate purged from her mind that night beside the lake. She should not remember how he removed all the signs of prostitution from her and sent her home pure."

Time and Space looked at each other, their hearts welling with sadness. They desperately wanted to refuse Dhumanos but knew they couldn't suffer the consequences. Besides, if they were gone, Dhumanos and the Archons would find some other way to hurt Destiny.

"Why do you want to do that?" asked Space.

Time did not say anything, but he already had an idea of what Dhumanos was up to. He was right.

"It is quite simple. We want to possess her as we did in the past. We want to control her every movement." Dhumanos's tone was even more chilling because it was so matter of fact.

"What good would it do?" asked Space.

Again Time knew the answer, but there was something else in the conversation that had grabbed his attention.

"We are working for our survival and, most likely, yours as well," said Dhumanos. "The only way to do that is to keep Destiny busy in our scripts."

Space was about to ask another question when Time finally spoke up. "You are fools!" he shouted, startling the others and turning Dhumanos's face red with anger. "Why do you not realize that hurting or destroying Destiny will threaten your existence? We all depend on her well-being for our survival. Therefore, instead of trying to control her, let her be free. This would allow her to give more love, and *that* is the source of her energy."

"Fate," Dhumanos corrected coldly, "is the source of all energy, and love is nothing but weakness. Now you will do exactly what I have asked you to do, or you will face the consequences, which, as I'm sure you are quite aware, will be severe."

Seeing Space about to ask what those consequences were, Time reached over and clamped a hand firmly on his shoulder. He knew they would have to do Dhumanos's bidding. What did the details matter?

Space hung his head as the two left the council of the Archons and headed into the forest of the Forget Lands to perform their duty.

As soon as they were out of earshot, Sonamrud, who had been observing Time closely throughout the meeting, stepped out of the shadows. "He was right, you know," he told the rest of the Archons, "but of course, he does not know about the rest of the plan."

"What do you mean, the rest of the plan?" they asked. It was not the first time Sonamrud had said something that had stumped them, but they had been following the conversation very carefully and could not believe that they had missed anything.

"Destiny and Choice have always had an exceptionally strong bond, even for a mother and son. I am willing to bet that the connection still exists despite their physical separation. If she is happy and strong, so is her son, so it makes sense that anything we do to damage her would deprive Choice of energy as well. I would even go so far as to say that if we torture her soul enough and show her illusions, we can trap Choice and control him as well."

The Archons smiled as the realization hit them. Even Dhumanos was pleased; always cunning and manipulative, Sonamrud had truly out-done himself.

CHAPTER 45

WHAT IS THE IMPORTANCE OF LIGHT WITHOUT darkness? Is it not the night that makes the white of the moon shine? What are angels without demons, and who would value the blessings of health with no sickness in the world? The alternating shades of a single color impart beauty to it.

Like the moon, Destiny needed the darkness to retain her significance. Perhaps, as some speculated, it was the reason for her so-called love for the Forgetters: she felt her importance only relative to her creations. Fate was a different kind of light. He had that touch of divinity that does not require duality to define itself. He was the sun that shone even if there was no universe to bring into light. He shone so brightly, he illuminated everything around him indifferently.

The Archons had learned these things in Destiny's mind. They knew that her soul was thirsty for admiration and attention. It was apparent through her actions as well. They all remembered quite well how she had accepted the gift of the mirror—oh, how easily she had fallen for that trick! Conversely, Fate's light was too pure and strong. Sure, Destiny could reflect a portion of it, but if she ever tried to absorb it all, she would only be burned. Indeed, Destiny had often felt she was in danger of being swallowed by Fate; it was the reason she'd returned to Mimadamos for the birth of her child. She wanted to be seen for her own light, her own grandeur.

This desire to shine her light on the world was, ironically, the dark side of Destiny. Her vanity was her downfall. Although she had overcome these desires, the Archons knew that they were still there, hidden somewhere inside her. Reawakening them was the only way to conquer her.

It took Destiny many rotations of the world, spent in complete solitude, to understand herself. Until now, Destiny had believed that her defense of the imperfect creation that resulted from her interaction with the Archons was a matter of vanity. Yet after reflecting on her behavior, she found a ray of hope. For the first time, she understood that it was not solely a matter of her desire to shine in a less-than-perfect world in need of her light but also her deep admiration for Fate and all that he represented. She wanted to have a world where she could practice what Fate had done for her. For this reason, she was granted this world so that she could be a savior for the Forgetters just as Fate had been for her throughout her life.

The Archons knew nothing of this, of course. Although they had looked inside her brain, their perception of what they found there was limited by their own dark, hateful natures. It cast a veil of negative energy over everything, including Destiny's desire and innocent love for Fate.

The Archons did sense that Destiny had come a long way from her old naïve self. She no longer needed to create her own separate world to experience true love, for now she knew that Fate was her one true love, and his world was her one true reality. If she ever attempted to join him again, all their work would have been for naught. However, the moment she let her reality melt into Fate's, the dream world of the Forgetters would end.

Destiny, however, now understood that caring for a world prevailed upon by darkness—and at the risk of her salvation—was not a wise and worthy pursuit. She finally recognized the importance of a soil rich with the fertility of love. There was no point in expecting the barren lands of hatred to turn green with the foliage of love and happiness. She removed the weeds of vanity and the temptations of loving any creature less than herself from her foremost concerns.

For the Archons, the only way to ensure that Destiny never reunited with Fate was to use their son. Choice was Destiny's weakness. Like Time and Space, he embodied her earthly memory and was, therefore, the Archons' ultimate weapon.

So far, that weapon had worked like magic. Despite all her progress, the waters of Destiny's life were never so murky. As hard as it had been to be separated from Fate, at least it had been her decision. But to have Choice taken from her as well? It was beyond imagining.

The situation was also becoming bleaker for the Forgetters. The death of History and the subsequent influx of Drazians had thrown the area into chaos, a situation exacerbated by the withdrawal of Time and Space. With no sense of the past, the Forgetters could not get a handle on the present, let alone prepare for their future. The resulting uncertainty left jobs scarce and currency nearly worthless. Forgetters from every walk of life were struggling just to survive.

Far away in his home in Demire, Fate could sense what was transpiring in the Forget Lands, just as he sensed everything in the world. There was one difference: for the first time in the history of time, it mattered to him. Indeed, it was the only thing that mattered to him in all the dimensions and universes across his vision. It mattered to him because it involved the one person that constituted the universe, time, space, and reality to him: Destiny.

CHAPTER 46

THE DRAZIANS HUDDLED MISERABLY IN THE
deepest pits of the Forget Lands. After snatching the last vestiges of their
identity, Dhumanos had damned them to rot in that hellish place and
quickly forgot them. Now, however, Sonamrud realized that they could
be of use to the Archons and asked Dhumanos to set them free. Had anyone else asked, Dhumanos would have tortured him just for the fun of
it. It was only because he respected Sonamrud's diabolical mind that he
finally agreed.

Oblivious to the bigger picture, the Drazians raced out of the pits,
unable to believe their good fortune. Before long, they realized that
Dhumanos's mercy came at a very steep price. They were to be in perpet-
ual service to him, performing any number of loathsome tasks. Their main
job was to travel outside the Forget Lands and bring news that would aid
the Archons' mission.

After several fruitless trips, the Drazians were exhausted and frustrated; they even wondered whether Dhumanos had them running around
just to torture them. Then one moonless night, the Drazians arrived in the
Forget Lands with a great secret that, until then, had been known only to
Fate and elements of nature that were indifferent to its consequences.

They found Dhumanos sitting on his throne, regaling the Archons
with his various talents of cunning and deceit. Only Sonamrud seemed
distracted—staring into space as if he already knew something strange

was about to happen—but as he often did this, nobody paid him any mind. Dhumanos had just gotten to the goriest part of the story when the long-bearded chief of the Drazian Pentagon stepped forward and said that he had news to report—indisputable news, as he had gotten it by torturing the ancient oak tree and the oldest living owl.

"Dhumanos, King of Hell most honored," said the Alpha Drazian, head bowed, "we have called upon you to share important news."

Dhumanos did not even bother to favor him with a glance, just gestured for him to continue.

"We feared this news would incur your wrath upon the universe, but after talking among ourselves, we have decided it is necessary for you to know it."

"What would really incur my wrath," snapped Dhumanos, "is your continuous teasing and lack of any worthwhile news."

A shiver of fear ran through the Drazians.

When the Alpha Drazian finally spoke again, it was with a trembling voice. "The wisest and oldest of elements have informed us, after much persuasion, of course, that there is a rather enchanting connection between the three magical people, Fate, Destiny, and Choice."

He stopped to breathe, but before he could resume, Dhumanos shouted, "They are related. We all know that! There was no need to extract that information from the old and wise."

All the Archons laughed at this, all except Sonamrud.

"It is not just the relationship, my king," said the Alpha Drazian. "The three have a spiritual connection much stronger than you could imagine."

It looked as if Dhumanos was about to say something before the Alpha added, "Their connection could prove to be the means of destruction for our world."

All the Archons straightened at this, and Sonamrud looked even graver than usual, for he had an idea of what was coming.

"We know this," Dhumanos roared. "You'd better have something more than this, Drazian."

Clearly, the time for preamble was over. The Drazian nodded quickly. "Fate, Destiny, and Choice form a magical trinity. They contain strange energies deep inside themselves. If they were to collide, in that moment this world would end, and a new world would replace it." The Alpha

Drazian paused, then added, "Both the ancient tree and the wise bird confirmed this."

He paused again as if waiting for Dhumanos to scream or torture him, but when he looked over, the evil king was staring at him in rapt attention.

"According to the wise owl," the Drazian continued, "their union would result in a triangle-like prism, which would direct a strong beam of light into our world. The Forget Lands are nothing but the product of a dream. This light would wake everyone, especially the dreamer. All our reality would be forced into oblivion in the unconscious chambers of Fate's mind."

A collective gasp went up from the Archons before the crowd fell silent. Finally, Sonamrud asked the Drazian, "Can you tell us any further details?"

"What do you want to know?" the Alpha asked coldly. He did not trust Sonamrud, because he had devised the punishment for the Drazians after they had failed to explain Fate's voice speaking to them through the atmosphere. The fact that he had also orchestrated their release made no difference.

"I want to know how what you've just told us is possible," Sonamrud said. "How would that beam of light work, and would we have any kind of existence in the new world at all?"

"Well, as far as we know, the light resulting from the union of the three would be so strong, it would penetrate anything, even the darkest of souls. The great intensity of the light would obliterate anything in its way. As for your survival, it looks unlikely. Even if you did survive, your memory and appearance would be so altered, you wouldn't recognize yourself."

Everybody shivered at the thought.

"We'd be like wood thrown into the fire—transformed," Sonamrud remarked.

"What could be worse than losing our identity?" Dhumanos wondered aloud.

"Being wiped altogether from the surface of the Earth," said another Archon.

"The three must never meet," said another. "Trapping Choice in the Valley of Doubt would prevent that."

He was met with several grunts of agreement, but Sonamrud shook his head. "Have all of you forgotten how Fate filled the forest with his presence that night? The way his voice flowed through Choice? This does not happen unless the entity being channeled has prior knowledge of the conduit. Physical distance does not mean much in the face of that kind of connection."

"Okay," Dhumanos said, "so what do you suggest?"

"I think the core of their connection must be identified and attacked. There must be something that could be used for this purpose." Sonamrud was quiet for a moment, and then a cunning smile danced on his lips. "There is another thing," he added.

"What is that?" asked Dhumanos.

"The medium we've been using to mesmerize the Forgetters by manifesting their negative side may not be required anymore."

Everyone looked at Sonamrud in surprise. "Are you serious?"

He nodded.

Miles away, a shiver went through Time and Space. Although they were nowhere near the meeting place, they still understood that somebody was talking about them.

CHAPTER 47

IF THE LIGHT OF THE SUN TOUCHED A SURFACE directly, what would be the result? The surface would burn. But if a filter were used, that same light would warm and illuminate. Fate's light was like the light of the sun, and the only filter that worked was Destiny. Destiny was the only one who could look into Fate's eyes—stand his enormous power—and remain unharmed. But what of Choice? What was his role?

This question had plagued him ever since he was a young boy being tutored by History. These lessons had always made him think of his father, whom he desperately wanted to meet. For some strange reason, he had always felt he should do that on his own without his mother. He yearned to know Fate, not just the image he had pieced together from his mother's brief stories. But there was another component Choice did not understand; like his mother's vanity, it was his own dark side that made him want to bask in his father's undivided attention.

Destiny knew this feeling all too well, for she also loved when Fate beheld her with single-minded adoration. So while she had been wounded by her son's abrupt departure from Mimadamos, she was not completely ignorant of the reason. Although weakened by time and distance, the mental connection between Destiny and Fate still existed, and she sensed that he had played some subtle role in their son's decision to leave. Of course, Choice didn't know this, for as always, Fate was careful to respect free will. As for why he had influenced Choice to leave, Destiny trusted that whatever Fate's reason, it was for her benefit and the benefit of humanity.

In the months after he left Mimadamos, Choice convinced himself that he had forgotten all about the house his mother had made for him. He was no longer interested in the Garden of Eden. He wished only to leave it and his loving mother behind. It was only after he had been in the Forget Lands for a while that he realized that this was impossible. He could not stop comparing the place with Mimadamos, and his mother's hold on him was strong and not easily forgotten. Even when their physical bodies were many miles apart, each could sense when the other was in distress.

The night Destiny jumped into the deep waters of the lake but failed to float back to the top, Choice had done it for her. He was her free will, the part of her that she had found in Demire. It was the main reason for her return to Mimadamos—she had wanted to own this part of herself and exercise it without constraint. This, however, had come at a very steep price. It was only after her son was born that Destiny witnessed true free will in action.

Unlike her, Choice had the ability to transform his thoughts into action without guilt and desire. He was free will personified, but he had no idea that he owed this to his mother. Fate provided the light, but in its direct glare, Choice would have found it nearly impossible to explore his individuality. In fact, he may not have even recognized the point at which his father ended and he began. Destiny was the filter, sending that diffused light to Choice. In doing so, she took all the responsibility and hesitancy upon herself, thus freeing him to choose with an unencumbered heart.

＊＊＊

Destiny sat on a silk-covered divan by a large picture window. Outside, the trees were in full bloom, and the birds were chirping melodiously. She barely noticed for all the thoughts swarming in her head. She was still unsure about what had happened in the Garden in the pre-dawn hours. All she knew was that she had gone—or more accurately, had been lured—there to be close to Choice and had lost consciousness several times along the way. She did have a vague sensation of evil surrounding her, but she could not seem to recall specifics.

Suddenly, an old, familiar desire gripped Destiny. She remembered the time Fate had purged her thoughts by the lake and recalled how she'd returned to Mimadamos feeling light yet filled with a desire for life and living it from the heart. She realized with some surprise that she had passed that spirit to her son Choice. He had inherited her love for complete freedom and could practice it oblivious to the price of doubt, guilt, and self-inflicted punishments that she endured.

Her thoughts shifted again. Without warning, her brain started replaying memories of how she had once been responsible for the creation of an imperfect world—the result of her impure interaction with the Archons. With a shock, she realized that she still harbored a deep desire to be this world's savior. She wanted to see and feel her own love reflected to her, if only through those semi-human Forgetters and the rather base ways they expressed their needs. It was a strange yearning, but she could not help it. No matter how much she tried, there seemed to be no way for her to undo her past; what's more, part of her didn't even want to.

She knew her intentions were good, and she held out hope that something good could come of it. But then she remembered the fruitless years of waiting and thought, *What's the use?* The wickedness of Dhumanos encircled this little world of hers too deeply and entirely for anything good to penetrate it. Besides, the Forgetters' concept of love sprouted from feelings like ego, envy, pity, need, and desire.

Still, Destiny could not give up on the Forget world. It was true that the Archons were creatures of darkness, as they did not have the divinity of Fate inside them. Their love had a self-destructive quality, and they had no way to understand the divine concept of love. However, Fate's light, as diffused through Destiny, had entered their world as well. It was apparent that none of her possessions was free of Fate's presence. Although they were two different people, Destiny and Fate each shared a tinge of the other's existence.

CHAPTER 48

THE DARK, MURKY WATER OF THE LAKE IN THE
Forget Lands was home to several creatures, each more hideous than the
next. None was more despicable than the enormous beast lurking in its
depths. Whereas the other creatures fed on each other or on rotting plant
life, this beast fed on fear. When well-fed, it swelled to unimaginable girth,
but the most it had ever swelled was when Destiny had been near the lake.

Now the fiend was the size of a large balloon, and it was hungry.
Surrounding the lake were twenty-four Archons, and while they certainly
had concerns, they had not risen to the level of fear. As they began their
meeting, vile creatures in the lake strained their ears, chuckling every time
they heard some evil tidbit. But then came the one they had been waiting for.

"We all know very well about the difficult challenge before us,"
Dhumanos said. "But to ensure our survival, we have no other choice."
The Archons nodded eagerly, trying to hide their fear.

Dhumanos was not fooled and gave them a scathing look. "Sonamrud
the wise has done many calculations and drawn a few conclusions as well.
It is based on this information that we made the following decisions."

Sonamrud cleared his throat. Then, as was his custom, he gave a brief
history of their dark world before reciting his recent poem. As was their
custom, the Archons only pretended to listen.

Finally, he came to the point. "There are many things to be considered and even more to be done," he said vaguely, as he always did when he wanted others to feel inferior. "Our first concern is, of course, Choice, for he is nearly impossible to manipulate, and he moves toward his goals without hesitation. He is most unlike his mother in this matter."

Time and Space sat on the branches of the elm beside the lake, their long limbs hanging listlessly. They knew that Sonamrud must have some task in mind for them, and they knew that whatever it was would be dreadful. It wasn't a moment later when Sonamrud turned his gaze toward them.

"Here we go," Time whispered in Space's ear.

"Do you realize that they could all just die if we stopped helping them?" Space replied, and they chuckled.

Sonamrud continued, oblivious to their whispering. "We need you to go to Choice and stop him from moving toward Demire." He narrowed his eyes. "This is something only you two can do."

This was the last thing they wanted, yet Time and Space nodded anyway. What choice did they have? It was getting so Time and Space couldn't remember the last time they had any control over their lives.

Far below them in the dark, fetid depths of the lake, the monster began to expand.

✳ ✳ ✳

At the same moment, Choice was also resting on a high branch of an ancient tree. Like the sunlight beating down on the Forget Lands, so was his heart burning with the anticipation of finally meeting his father. The feeling was mixed with sadness, for although he was excited about going to Demire, he still missed his mother terribly. In his loneliest moments, he found himself wishing that he could return to Mimadamos, but it was simply not an option. Choice was capable of many things, but moving backward was not one of them.

During his stay in the Forget Lands, he had learned many things, things he certainly wouldn't have learned had he remained under the care and protection of his mother—or any of his teachers, for that matter. He could hear their stories and read their books, but there was only one true teacher, and that was life.

His eyes were just beginning to droop when he heard familiar voices nearby. For a moment, he was tempted to get up and see who they were, but he was just so sleepy. His eyes were closing once again when he realized that the voices were becoming louder, growing closer. He looked down and saw two men standing right under the tree.

The first thing that struck him was that they did not look as if they belonged anywhere near the Forget Lands. They were physically fit and wore odd but fashionable hooded robes and dresses of fine silver fabric, but it was more than that. Baffled, Choice studied them a moment longer. Finally, it occurred to him: they weren't cloaked in the misery worn by the local inhabitants. He cocked his head to the side to listen and was surprised to hear his name spoken.

"Poor Choice has never seen or even talked to his father," one was saying.

How do they know this? Choice wondered.

"His mother hasn't been fair to him," the other added.

The first man nodded. "No wonder he's going to blow her up."

Blow her up? What are they talking about?

"I would, too, if my mother did what his did."

The two grunted in agreement.

Choice couldn't take it anymore. He left his place on the tree branch. In one swift movement, he was standing right in front of the startled strangers.

As usual, Choice was direct, for he knew no other way. "What were you talking about?"

The men stood in shocked silence for a moment. Then one said, "It's all right, kid. We understand why you're doing it. Destiny deserves to perish."

The man had an unfamiliar accent, but Choice barely noticed, so shocked was he by the words. "Why do you say that? I love my mother very much, and I don't want anything to happen to her. I would certainly never plan to harm her!"

"It's nothing. We were just talking nonsense," the man replied.

The other nodded so fast, Choice was afraid his head would separate from his neck any moment. If the two were thinking that answer would satisfy Choice, they were sorely mistaken.

"We are foreigners here," the first man said, "come all the way from Demire."

Choice's heart leapt. Demire! The land of Fate! They must know his father; perhaps they even knew why Destiny had left him. In the meantime, he needed his other question answered.

"My mother," he said, "has the pomp of a queen and the grace of an angel. Now I want to know why you spoke of her with so much disdain."

"We are sure that your mother is a lovely lady," one of the men said cautiously, "but even the best people make mistakes sometimes."

Before Choice could say anything, the other man said, "Your mother, however, keeps making the same mistake time and again."

"Sir, I must insist that you explain yourself," Choice said, his voice containing a rare note of anger.

"Before she married Fate, she made herself *available* to the Archons." The man's lips pulled back in disgust as he said *available*. "The very land you're standing on and plan to destroy is actually her creation. Through her intention and attention, she created the Forget Lands."

"You know what that means," the other man added conspiratorially. "The moment this land is destroyed, so she will be."

Choice was trying to digest this information when the men made the most shocking claim of all: that Destiny had left Fate without any reason other than that she wanted to.

"Don't misunderstand us," the first man said. "It's a good thing you're going to do." He glanced at his companion, who nodded for emphasis. "Awakening the world is necessary for all of us. Your mother may not survive, but sacrifice is often necessary for the greater good."

How dare they speak of his mother's fate so casually! Choice was seething but kept his expression neutral, hoping he could get more information from them. Then, as he opened his mouth to ask a question, the two men disappeared! Choice spun several times, certain his eyes were playing tricks on him, but the two were nowhere to be found. Finally, he moved on in the same direction he'd been traveling before he had paused to rest. A few times, he thought he heard laughter, but no one was around.

High above on the thick branch of a tree, the two men looked on with mirth.

"Haven't had that much fun in a long time!" said the first man as he pulled back his hood.

"Yes," the other agreed, shrugging out of his robe. "The way he went looking for us, it was priceless!"

The two looked at each other and burst into another round of laughter. They were none other than Time and Space.

* * *

After the two men disappeared, Choice wandered aimlessly for a bit, his mind racing with questions. He tried to tell himself that he didn't even know whether they were telling the truth, but it was upsetting nonetheless. How badly he wished he could ask his mother! He hadn't walked long before he realized that he was even more desperate to meet his father. It was then that he once again turned toward Demire.

He heard the voices just as he was crossing a wide but shallow stream. He turned and again saw two people, standing just out of sight behind a large tree. He was about to step onto dry land when he distinctly heard the word *Mimadamos*.

"Have you heard the news?" one of them asked. He had a deep voice.

"Indeed, I have," said the other, "but I didn't have to. I knew it was coming."

"Of course, you always know these things."

"It wasn't that hard to figure out," his friend replied with false modesty. "But let's face it, the Archons have been growing restless for a long time now."

Choice's heart sank. The Archons had done something in Mimadamos, and it could not possibly be good. The conversation that followed confirmed his fears.

"I bet you only know half the story," the man continued.

The other man said nothing, so Choice figured he must have gestured for the other to go on.

"Not only have the Archons invaded the land of Mimadamos, but I have heard they also captured Destiny!"

"This is awful!" the man with the deep voice exclaimed, sounding genuinely upset. "I was always rather fond of her—such a strong woman."

"Well, I think she deserves it," said the other man. "These are the fruits of her ancient wrongdoings run amuck." He harrumphed loudly. "We'll see how strong she is without the help of her husband and son."

Choice could hardly breathe, and his eyes were wide. There was no way he could leave his mother alone now. With one last glance in the direction of Demire, he turned back in the direction he had come. He was needed back in Mimadamos, and that was where he would go.

CHAPTER 49

AFTER MEETING THE FIRST TWO MEN, CHOICE'S
body had moved slowly while his mind raced. The opposite was true after
he overhead the second two men talking behind the tree. His footsteps
were light and quick, and his mind focused on one thought: concern for
his mother. It never occurred to him to sneak up to the tree and see their
faces. If he had, he would have been surprised to see two Drazians standing there—the same Drazians ordered by the Archons to spread the rumor
that Destiny was in danger. They knew that Choice would never abandon
his mother, even if it meant giving up the dream of finally meeting Fate.

The Drazians were known throughout the land for their extreme
cunning; however, like any other race, there were many good, honest
Drazians as well. They were well aware of their people's reputation, and
they knew it was deserved. Drazians were always putting on airs that
they were spiritual people when, really, all they did was make people turn
from teachings.

Nothing was worse than claiming to have met and collaborated with
Fate while living in the Valley of Doubt. *Who would find out?* the Drazians
reasoned. After all, only failed people traveled the narrow stretch of land
separating Demire from the Forget Lands. But as always, the truth had
eventually come out, and the good Drazians had been punished with
the bad.

After years of living with the shame, they had decided that enough was enough. It was time the innocent people of Mimadamos were told about the fraud being perpetrated on them. This was no easy task, for the rotten Drazians had used their trickery to gain power.

Of course, others in Mimadamos had been seduced by the Spiritual Pentagon. Destiny's family was among them. Lured by the promise of enlightenment—and the chance to be closer to Destiny—they had gone to live among the Drazians in the Valley of Doubt. They did not find the answers they sought, but they did lose the wealth and social position they had strived so hard for. Still other citizens of Mimadamos chose a darker path and even helped the Archons carry out their heinous plans.

Meanwhile, an underground movement had developed to eventually overthrow the Drazians and their cohorts, and the face of their struggle was none other than Hope. Time and Space enjoyed chasing Hope so much, they forgot the real purpose behind it. By the time they got serious about their mission, Choice stepped in and defended her.

Hope would later be captured by the Archons, but by that time, they were too preoccupied with Destiny and Mimadamos to investigate the Drazians. Eventually, the Archons decided it made sense to entrust Hope to the Drazians for the time being. No harm was to come to her, the Archons said. She was just supposed to be confined so that she couldn't cause any trouble. To the Drazians' great delight, the Archons also handed them the reins of the Forget Lands for a short while as they busied themselves in the Forget Undergrounds contriving schemes to prevent the Trinity from ever uniting. Finally, the Drazians would have the power they so longed for!

However, their eagerness to rule the Forgetters exposed the Spiritual Pentagon as the power-hungry despots they were rather than the spiritual beings they pretended to be. The Drazians who had followed them now pledged their allegiance to Hope, which only placed her in graver danger.

When Choice realized the gravity of Hope's situation, he took every precaution to make sure she would be safe while he was in Mimadamos. He summoned the Warriors of the Awakening—mostly Drazians who had either seen the truth in Hope's word or lost faith in the Spiritual Pentagon—and infused them with the presence of Fate. He knew that his father's energy would make them stronger warriors. It would increase their chances of survival and Hope's as well.

Still, Choice might have been afraid to leave Hope had he not known of her direct connection with his father. She had told him of her dreams, and as he had similarly experienced the presence of his father, he knew Fate did not have to be physically present to convey his messages. Yet as he prepared to head back to Mimadamos, he was still anxious about leaving her behind.

CHAPTER 50

IT HAD TAKEN MUCH TIME AND EFFORT, BUT Sonamrud had finally created the perfect script for the dangerous scenario facing him and his brethren. True, his fellow Archons had come up with intelligent ideas, but he'd had to do much work to make sure the plan was flawless. It was true that he was the mastermind behind every strategy that the Archons had ever used. Nature had bestowed this gift on him. He was also aware that, given his strengths, he could easily overthrow Dhumanos. Nineteen out of the twenty-four Archons respected him more than their evil leader, and the others, while weak, could probably be turned as well. The question remained: was he ready to start a rebellion? Sonamrud was a wise man, probably the wisest in these lands except for Fate and the Demiurge, but he was just a man nonetheless.

Someday, perhaps, he had often thought after submitting every script, *I will try my hand at ruling the kingdom, but now is not the time.*

And so, Sonamrud had designed the final plan for dealing with Destiny. Without a second's delay, Dhumanos had approved of it, for he knew that Sonamrud was meticulous in all things. This would be no different. Somewhere in the back of his mind, Sonamrud knew that they needed Destiny to remain alive, just as a vampire needed blood. They could easily forget everything, but this one truth had somehow remained with them. Therefore, in crafting the new chapters of the story, he had incorporated events to keep the Archons' fire under check for at least some time.

His work complete, Sonamrud lay down for a well-deserved nap. The last image he saw through his half-closed eyes before drifting into the world of dreams was Time arguing about something. It did not bother him, for it was expected. He knew about so many things before they occurred, it sometimes bored him. His lips curling into a devious smile, he fell into a deep sleep.

While Sonamrud's dreams were peaceful, Destiny's were anything but. In fact, her nightmares had grown so vivid and terrifying, she dreaded the hours of sleep. This resulted not only in many sleepless nights but also in anxiety during her waking hours. She walked through her days in a nearly catatonic state; she often forgot things and could be found staring blankly out the window. For the life of her, she could not understand the purpose of such dreams now after so many years of a chaste life. It was only when she started seeing the faces of the Archons in those dreams that she truly began to panic.

It was her seventh sleepless night when Space and Time visited her. Dreading another nightmare, she resisted going to bed as long as she could. Finally, she could take it no longer. The moment she touched her bed's soft, silken sheets, her eyelids began to droop; seconds later, she fell into a deep, dreamless sleep, courtesy of Time and Space.

They had gone there to do the Archons' bidding, but when they saw the dark rings around her beautiful eyes, they took pity on her. *What would be the harm,* they told themselves, *in letting her catch a few hours' rest before filling her mind with lies?* After a few minutes of weighing the pros and cons, they had cast a spell of peaceful sleep over her.

For a long time, they just watched over her, taking great satisfaction in the way her lips slightly parted in repose and her thick, luxuriant hair fanned out against the pillows. The wind blowing from outside was cold, and Time closed the window. The lights in the room were still on, but Time and Space dared not switch them off for fear they would alert Destiny to their presence. The peaceful scene made them loathe themselves all the more for hurting this lovely soul once again—as if they had not done enough damage already!

Before they knew it, half the night had passed. Time and Space glanced sadly at each other, then removed their spell.

Five minutes later, Destiny slowly opened her eyes. She felt better than she had in some time, and it was then that she realized that she'd had no nightmares that night. She wanted to believe that they had passed, never to return, but she felt that this was not the case.

A knock on the door startled her. Who would be knocking on her door at this hour? She sighed, thinking it must be a servant reporting one household emergency or another, and she called for the visitor to come in. The door opened, and Destiny was shocked when not one but two men entered her room. She was even more surprised when she realized that they were Space and Time. They were in the same physical forms they always took in Mimadamos.

She sat up in bed, eyeing them with a mixture of relief and suspicion. Certainly the two had helped her out of a few tight spots. However, she also had the feeling that they had orchestrated or at least been involved in other unpleasant things that had befallen her.

They bowed in greeting before launching into their typical preamble about how her beauty and wisdom were an inspiration to all. As always, they went on a bit longer than necessary, which only made them seem disingenuous. Still, Destiny found it impossible to remain completely unaffected by the beautiful words. Finally, they broached the purpose for their visit.

"Dearest Destiny," Time began, "it is with the utmost grief that we bring you this news, but given the circumstances, we could put it off no longer."

Destiny said nothing, just continued to look at them. For a moment, she wondered if this was yet another dream.

"Sweet Destiny, do you remember the Drazians?" Space asked.

"How could I forget those beasts?" she snapped. "They were the cause of my disgrace." A shudder went through her, and Time and Space knew that, for a moment, she was reliving the memories of her departure from Demire and recalling how the Drazians had spread rumors about her being Fate's fling whom he eventually got bored with.

When she looked up again, her eyes were full of rage. Although Time and Space knew it was not directed at them, they flushed red in the face. It was their own guilt and fear of being found out. If she knew about their role in separating her from her husband, she would hate them even more than she did the Drazians—and this, Time and Space could not bear.

"Of course," Time said when he could steady his voice, "that's why this is so difficult to say. Those scoundrels are spreading rumors about you again." He paused for a moment. "And these rumors have reached the ears of your son as well."

Destiny's first reaction was joy. If Time and Space mentioned him, it must mean that Choice was safe. A second later, her hand flew to her mouth in horror when the full import of their words hit her.

Summoning her courage, she asked, "What type of rumors?"

"Well, for starters, they've told Choice and anybody who would listen about the *mistakes* of your childhood."

"You mean my past experiences," she went quiet for a moment, "with the Archons."

Time and Space looked at the ground, both wanting to drown themselves in the deepest of seas. They knew that it was their doing that had put Destiny in this state today.

"Yes, about that and Fate," they said in unison.

"What about him?" Destiny asked, her heart quickening.

"They told Choice that Fate gave you a choice between a peaceful life with him and the chaotic life of your past, and you chose the latter. You abandoned his idyllic home in Demire and instead decided to raise your son in seclusion, so that you could be close to your dark past, which you couldn't give up." They stopped as if to catch their breath, when, really, they were just waiting for their words to sink in.

"Another rumor they've been spreading is that Choice may not be Fate's son and that Fate didn't even want you to be the mother of his child once he had found out about your childhood encounters with the Archons. Some have even gone as far as to say that you were forced out of Demire by Fate when he knew you were pregnant with someone else's child; others are saying you separated the son from his father because you wanted revenge against Fate."

With that, they grew quiet and waited for Destiny to speak. She just sat there, her eyes wide, her mouth in a shocked O. She knew perfectly well that the Drazians were capable of spreading lies. They'd done it before, and they would do it again. She was also sure that Choice would never believe such things. Still, she could not resist asking Time and Space about his reaction.

They hesitated a moment.

"What you may not realize, Sweet Destiny," Time said, "is how much Choice has changed. He is not the same boy who left your home in Mimadamos. He is now a young man who has faced many challenges in the Forget Lands. In fact, he commands an army of many thousand Forgetters!" He and Space glanced at each other. When they looked back at Destiny, her eyes were filled with tears.

"Oh, don't cry," they said together, guilt rising like a tidal wave within them.

She shook her hand to silence them, then brought it up to wipe her tears. Time and Space just stood there, half-expecting her to start sobbing. When she raised her eyes to them again, they were brimming with confidence, even defiance.

It made Time and Space feel worse than ever, for they were about to say the cruelest thing of all. "The moment Choice realized who his father was, he headed for Demire, determined to meet him. Unfortunately, Fate did not feel the same; in fact, he shunned him."

"What?" Destiny exclaimed.

Fate would never abandon someone—certainly not his own child! But that was what Time and Space were claiming.

From the looks on their faces, they had more to say. "Fate has ordered Choice to come here and take revenge on you. Instead of giving your son access to Demire, he has given him access to Hope."

Destiny looked at them quizzically. "Hope?"

"She is a Drazian girl. Fate has taken her as a disciple and is planning to give his entire kingdom to her instead of Choice. The only way Choice would be considered is if he succeeded in avenging his father and removing you from his life and his home—and Mimadamos – altogether. He is marching here as we speak. Otherwise, Fate will never acknowledge him as his son."

Listening to this, Destiny's mind raced, and her heart clenched with fear. Time and Space had spoken convincingly, yet she still wasn't sure she believed it. None of it made sense. Then again, how much did she really know about Choice and Fate these days? She remembered when her son had left her for adventures in the world beyond Mimadamos. She hadn't believed that he would do that either, but he had, and he was only a boy then.

She felt her eyes filling with tears again, but then Fate's image flashed through her mind. *This is just gossip,* she told herself, and peace settled over her like a warm blanket.

Time and Space had other plans, no matter that these plans had been foisted on them by the Archons. They had a job to finish, and no amount of sympathy they felt for her changed that. They were nearly as powerless as Destiny—more, in fact. Once Destiny realized what they were up to, she would be free to fight it, but not Time and Space. They must continue to do the Archons' bidding until, by some miracle, they were released.

"There is only one thing for you to do," they said gravely. "You must leave Mimadamos before Choice gets here."

Destiny drew back. "Since when must a mother fear her own son?"

As they had no answer, they went general, talking about "darkness" and giving a vague scenario in which Choice could be in danger if she didn't do anything. This gave Destiny pause.

"You must run away from here," they advised again.

"But where would I go?" she asked. For the first time, they saw real fear in her eyes.

"Well, you could always go to the lake," Time said, fighting the sudden nausea rising within him, "since you have taken refuge there so many times before."

Destiny looked at them, aghast. Just the thought of the lake repulsed her.

CHAPTER 51

THE NIGHT HAD PASSED AND HALF THE DAY AS
well. Time and Space had left hours ago, but Destiny's mind was still ring-
ing with their words. The first time they had uttered them, their claims had
sounded outside the realm of possibility. However, the more she thought
about them, the closer they seemed to the truth.

If Destiny had learned anything over the years, it was that life was
unpredictable. Whenever she felt sure about a person or a situation, life
betrayed her. After a while, she had come to believe one thing: she could
not believe in anything.

The first shock had come when she failed to adjust herself to Fate's
reality. Her whole life, she had prepared for it, even joyfully anticipated
it. But when the time had come for her to take her place as the first lady
of Demire, she had found it was not at all what she had expected. Even
as she had packed her things and headed back to Mimadamos, she hadn't
believed the size of the gap between what she had desired and the reality
that had manifested.

Still, Destiny had not lost hope. She had built a magnificent home for
her son in Mimadamos, a safe, secure haven where he could learn and
grow. Yet once again, her hard work and heartfelt desires had crumbled
in the face of reality. Her darling Choice had left her to set out on his own.

Now with Time and Space's words, the seeds of uncertainty deep
inside her heart had begun to bear fruit in the form of disturbing thoughts.

No matter how well she thought she knew her son, the truth was that she had no idea what he was capable of.

Destiny was even more confused when it came to Fate. She knew that he was wise, and she knew that he loved her. Had she imagined that he still watched over and protected her? She had thought he did, but experience had taught her that one could never be completely sure about anything, including Fate.

She felt she was losing her mind. There was a nagging feeling of doubt that told her that what Space and Time had said could not be correct, yet that doubt was growing smaller with each passing moment. As her anxiety grew, Destiny's thoughts ran to the Drazians. Of all the things Time and Space had told her, there was one she had no problem believing: this condemned nation had poisoned her family against her. After all, it wouldn't be the first time. Many years ago, she had returned to Mimadamos expecting to find her family and friends waiting for her. Instead, she had found her old home empty with no word of where they had gone, and she had always suspected the Drazians had played a role in this. They had certainly made a dreadful situation worse.

They had spread lies about her, portraying her as a woman who would not only desert her husband but also run her family off. As a result, the people of Mimadamos and the Forget Lands saw her as an extremely selfish person who had constructed the great palace for her son just to be in the limelight. She didn't love Choice, they said. He was just another prop she used to make herself look important.

In the beginning, Destiny had been shocked to hear all that. She had been even more shocked to hear that people believed the Drazians' lies. In time, she learned how skilled the Drazians were at manipulating others. Now there was a good chance they'd done the same with her son. She could deal with almost anything, but the thought of losing his love filled her with despair.

As she sat on a divan by the window, Destiny pushed another thought from her mind; it was the ugliest of all. Although she'd left Fate for very different reasons than the Drazians claimed, she had, in fact, left him and had taken his only son with her. Time and Space's words unearthed this long-buried guilt and, with it, her greatest fear: she had deserved everything she got.

CHAPTER 52

CHOICE'S HEART HAD NEVER BEEN SO HEAVY; IN fact, until recently, he had never known a sad day. What was there to be sad about when everyone had the free will to do as they wished? But when the rumors about Destiny reached his ears, the strength of his feelings surprised him.

He had left Mimadamos without looking back. He had experienced the darkness of the Forget Lands without flinching. He had seen any manner of strange, even disturbing things in his travels, but none had shaken him as this one had. Every step he took felt heavy until he wondered if he could go on. The mere thought that his mother was not the person he had always thought her to be halted his feet. He had learned of his mother's past while traveling through the Forget Lands to reach Mimadamos. At first, he had believed it a lie, but the more he thought about it, the more it had started to make sense. Confusion and a long list of questions filled his mind and heart and brought him no end of anguish. What if everything his mother had told him—and taught him—had been a lie?

As Choice's mind became more confused, his body felt weaker and feverish. Still, he pushed on. He forced himself to walk toward his homeland even though his legs grew more fatigued with every step. But it was more than that; there was a strange feeling tugging at the back of his mind, weighing him down. Try as he might to decipher the feeling, he could not, for it was so unfamiliar, it was in complete disharmony with who he was. He had no way of knowing that this feeling was *doubt*.

The same cruel reality that had befallen Destiny was now hitting her son hard, both in his head and in his heart. As he tried to digest these new harsh realities, he remembered something. He recalled how Fate had visited his mind while he was suffering in the Forget Lands. That was when Fate had shown him that nothing was real except what Fate had remembered. With a shock, one great reality made its way to him. He realized that in the middle of his doubt, he would find clarity, but he would have to work for it. It was as if he had been tossed in the air and found himself hanging there, weightless. When and how hard he fell would depend on what he did while suspended. Fate had shown him that a thin shred of reality was present even in the dreamlike state through which he was passing. How he found it was up to him.

Choice now understood that there was but a thin line dividing reality from doubt. Still, he wondered: what was the composition of this line? Something inside him, he realized, determined it, and it was called intuition. Intuition was the heart's voice inside the mind and the ultimate tool that determined the difference between extreme doubt and extreme certainty. Certain truths, at the moment they dawned upon the mind, called for an immediate celebration prior to arousing any need for validation. Intuition determined who was stoning the Messiah and who was worshipping the Devil, even at moments when the Messiah appeared as a Devil and the Devil as a Messiah. Something inside Choice told him that it was necessary to make such a distinction. He needed to sharpen his mind's ear to the voice of intuition to reach any truth. He must cure his own sickness through discovering the true meaning of immunity, for immunity was not about fighting the disease as much as neutralizing its effects.

The confusion in his mind confused his body as well. He had no idea what was going on except that he had to do something to stop it. There were many other strange things happening, things of which he had no knowledge yet could control.

Choice was not just any other man. He was the son of two great forces, and he had great powers. Some of these powers, he had discovered already, but there were other hidden talents inside him too. The fact was that his feelings were influencing not only the dark world of the Archons but also the functional capacity of the Agents of Awakening. As translator of Fate's word, Choice resonated inside every creature. Those who were ignorant and defiant of Fate's will saw in him a great threat to their very existence, and those who were knowledgeable about and in harmony with Fate's will saw in him a Savior and one to follow.

Once, he had been able to conquer Time and Space singlehandedly and free Hope. All of this was because of his determination and belief in his capabilities. However, his doubts were rendering him weak. He was retreating to Mimadamos, yet it was not making sense to him. All his training in life had taught him to move forward; he was not prepared to move back.

What he did not know was that every time he lost belief in himself, an army of Dhumans under the Archons gained strength. The moment he felt he could overcome his sickness and felt better, Hope and the Agents of Awakening became strong enough to stand in the face of captivity and the opposing forces. Thus, the war in the Forget Lands was a direct translation of Choice's internal struggle, and the result depended solely on his willpower and perseverance. It was as if they were all puppets and he was directing them, except he was not aware of his own power. Something controlled the puppeteer, too.

CHAPTER 53

THERE WAS A RARE AIR OF HAPPINESS IN THE
Forget Lands; it played hide and seek with the frail branches of trees,
sending them to and fro. The air giggled when the leaves touched and
laughed when they missed. This festivity in the skies mirrored the celebrations on the ground below. The Forgetters were happy for a change, and
realizing that this was probably temporary, they partied as they never had
before. Even the Archons were dancing their hearts out, all except one.
Sonamrud, the hero behind this temporary victory, was standing somberly on the sidelines.

And the reason for this celebration? Choice's departure from the
Forget Lands. The Forgetters had been convinced that he posed a threat
to them and believed that he had taken their troubles with him. For the
Archons, however, the fact that Choice had left was proof that their plan
was working, and they owed it all to Sonamrud. His wisdom had, at least
temporarily, prevented the union of Fate, Destiny, and Choice.

But even the Archons were not aware that in hindering Choice's activities, they had also hindered Fate's. Not directly, of course; there was no
way to do that. However, the fact that Choice had retreated to Mimadamos
meant that Fate could not do anything, either. In Fate's world, nothing
could be hurried or slowed, and every event had to unfold on its own—he
would do nothing to alter its course. Then again, he didn't need to; he

knew everything would happen in its own perfect time and space and in service to a higher purpose.

In Destiny's world, there was no comfort to be taken in the present moment, for all odds appeared to be in the Archons' favor. Only Sonamrud knew that this was no time to rest on their oars; they needed to work now for the future. Sure, he allowed his friends to party; he even enjoyed a moment of victory in his own way. He put aside all thoughts of planning against Destiny and her family and turned instead to inner reflection.

Of late, Sonamrud had been pondering the nature of his role in the web of life around him. He had been instrumental in weaving the fabric of existence as he stitched his colors into it. He had never been an overly introspective sort, but these days, he found himself wanting to discern the exact shades of those colors and determine how they fit into the larger picture.

There was one thing he was sure of: all he had done had been in the name of survival. Defending himself and his kind was not considered evil, only natural. He had often thought that his only fault was to love life too dearly to make sacrifices. Although Sonamrud could not say it—not even to himself—he knew in his heart that the Archons were seeking Destiny for a reason. Behind all the disdain they claimed to have for her, all the times they called her loving nature "weak," they yearned to be close to it. Sonamrud believed that there were some elements so embedded in humans as to be part of their genetic code. No matter how far a person strayed, this universal code would draw him back to his roots, the same old desire for Destiny's energy.

Now as he stood under the shade of the tree, glancing around at his fellows, Sonamrud had an epiphany, albeit one he was reluctant to accept. While the Archons craved Destiny's love and approval, on some deep level, they did not consider themselves worthy of it. Being Archons, they had decided that instead of earning it, they would snatch it away.

The implications of such a thought startled him. Could things be different if they had learned to ask for the sunlight rather than cutting out all the shade? Sonamrud shook his head as if to clear it. No good could come of trying to classify the others' behavior or discern the reasons behind it. Such thoughts, if true, could lead a man on a dangerous path, one that could bring him to the infinite sea of madness. Truth, whether good or evil, had always been Dhumans' enemy.

Sonamrud sighed. If only life were as simple for them as it was for Fate. Of course, he realized with deep regret that Fate was white as snow, while the Archons were more the color of grey charcoal. No matter how hard they had tried to travel in a single train, their tracks had been different. They were not pure! Even as he tried to cease his musings, Sonamrud found that they disturbed him and stirred chaos in his soul but soothed him as well.

A glance at the army of Drazians brought him back to reality. He was not sure about the Archons' decision to allow them to lead, but bringing his concerns to Dhumanos had been futile. There was nothing Sonamrud hated more than being snubbed by Dhumanos. The two had always shared this love–hate relationship throughout the centuries. Sonamrud was worried that the Drazians would mess up eventually; truth be told, part of him even wanted it to happen just to prove Dhumanos wrong. However, he knew that would mean their demise, which Sonamrud did not want at all. These were the thoughts that kept him ensnared in such a vicious cycle.

* * *

Miles from the Forget Lands, past the Valley of Doubt, in his majestic castle in Demire, Fate was sitting on his throne like the splendid king he was. His eyes were full of stories from the past, moments of the present, and secrets of the future. It was true that he was not fully awakened, for how could he be when the Archons had prevented his power from being activated in the collective mind? Yet he knew that the time was not far when he would be. It all depended on when Choice awakened, for when he did, he would bring about the victory of light over darkness.

In the meantime, there was nothing Fate could do except send his light to his son. He had another plan as well: he would rewrite history and revise the various versions of the future. He went inside his giant factory, where he had constructed every bit of the reality that he knew and that, through him, the world also knew and believed. For him, everything had happened already, and he knew every part of it. Even the events that were the future for the Archons, Destiny, and even Choice were merely fragments of the past for Fate. He went inside his carefully constructed factory to re-examine every inch of it. He felt an urge to deconstruct certain parts and rebuild them. He knew that the world needed to experience chaos and unpredictability before it could re-emerge. It was necessary for the universe to be deconstructed before it could be resurrected, reformed, and reawakened.

Before Fate deconstructed certain parts of his factory, he visited the feeling of full awakening in his mind. He knew that the world was coming to death and rebirth, and he knew that the Dhumans would lose most of their earthly memory like thoughts thrown back into the black hole of unconsciousness. The event would render their dark powers dormant, yet he somehow wanted them to experience the least of the sublime feeling of awakening experienced by the Agents of Awakening.

When the Awakening came, Fate would manifest in his full light and power like a beaming sun at noon, and he would appear to the world in his pure form, the ultimate light. It was necessary for the world to know about it beforehand so that the people could sustain their reality when Destiny's protective filter was removed and they would behold it in its raw form. This memory of light would help even the Dhumans accept the new reality the world was about to face.

CHAPTER 54

UNAWARE OF THE DANGERS FACING HOPE AND
her followers, Choice continued moving toward Mimadamos. But even as
he placed one foot in front of the other, he lacked his usual sense of purpose. He had the vague sense that he had a role to play in the showdown
between the Dhumans and the Agents of Awakening; it seemed just out of
reach. His mind was plagued with doubt.

This opportunity was too good for the Drazians to pass up. Seeking
to prove their worth to the Archons, they cast a strong, dangerous spell of
doubt on the Forget Lands, crippling all its citizens. They suddenly found
themselves running in circles like a movie that is continually rewound
and fast forwarded.

Only Hope seemed immune, for she had always understood how to
advance in circular motion. Being chased by Space and Time had only
sharpened that ability. Under cover of darkness, she reached out to a few
of her followers and explained how they could harness the push and
pull of the spell to gain momentum toward emancipation. These followers spread this awareness to others, while the Drazians were completely
unaware of the glitch in their spell.

As was often the case, the Drazians leapt at the chance to show off their
powers without worrying about the complications. Whereas the Archons
combined their dark powers with intelligence and consulted with Time
and Space, the Drazians refused to exercise an ounce of discipline.

At first, it seemed to work: while the Drazians' spell kept the Forgetters in a time loop of sorts, the Archons forced things back to a past state. But something was not quite right, the Archons noticed. They did not yet realize that it was Hope's power, pushing in the opposite direction. Still, the Dhumans had an advantage over the Agents of Awakening, for they could summon strength from the memories of their historic conquests. They drew dark power from the Archons and the Drazians, which they used to wage war against the Agents of Awakening. This was not a battle for land or currency but a spiritual war for hearts and minds. So far, the Dhumans appeared to be winning.

There were moments when the spirits of Hope and her followers rose and gained the upper hand; these were the moments when Choice broke through the fog and focused his energies. The Agents of Awakening had one source of power: Fate. Although the light came from him, it was filtered by Destiny and channeled through Choice. Without Destiny to filter it, the light would clash with the earthly human energy and cause the body to crumble and get sick. Perhaps this was why Fate always spoke to the ill and weak—their physical infirmity weakened the ego and made them more receptive to his energy. In this way, sickness, while considered by most a punishment from God, always contained a hidden reward.

Contact with Fate could also bring on a dark night of the soul much more dangerous than any physical ailment. Fate was the ultimate source of time and history, and the moment anybody looked at him, they could see their entire life—past, present, and future—stretched before their eyes. It was like a drunkard who drinks to forget the miseries of life but only sees them more vividly. Nobody but Destiny had the strength to accept all their realities without going mad.

As for the Agents of Awakening, they were pure at heart and had the capacity to reflect much more light; they did not spend energy in absorbing any of the light's residue—the heat of the ego that accompanies it. As time passed, they acquired the capacity to reflect increasingly more light without being too aware of their power to harness an ego.

CHAPTER 55

THE GOLDEN CURTAIN ON THE WINDOW BLEW
inward as the air forced its way into the room. The sky outside the window
was black, and there was not even a single star to illuminate it. The darkness outside was nothing compared to the blackness residing in Destiny's
soul. Time and Space had not been to Mimadamos in some time, but they
had visited her mind with awful regularity, stoking the flames of her guilt
until she could not do anything without dwelling on it.

On some level, Destiny was aware that something—not Fate but
something dark and undesired—was influencing her. Her mind was
often cloudy, and the simplest tasks were overwhelming. Nights were the
worst; as soon as the sun went down, she'd have terrible nightmares in
which Choice and Fate confronted her. Sometimes she was back by the
lake, facing hordes of angry Archons. She would awaken from these horrible dreams, shrieking at the top of her voice, but there was no one to
console her.

The force that the Archons were exerting on Choice seemed to have
taken a toll on Destiny, even though she was miles away. That, coupled
with the Drazians' spell, succeeded in casting a shadow in Destiny's mind.
She would think about her past, particularly the moment when she had
left Fate and returned to Mimadamos. Even worse, she had robbed him
of his only child. Destiny had never thought much about how her actions
must have hurt him, yet now guilt plagued her as heavily as if she had

committed these crimes hours rather than years ago. According to Time and Space, Choice, furious with his mother for keeping him from Fate, was headed back to Mimadamos to destroy her. Although Destiny felt Choice had every right to his rage, the thought that her son hated her made her heart bleed.

However, she had finally decided that there was no point to hiding there in Mimadamos anymore. In fact, if Fate and Choice were truly seeking her to finish her off, she would go to them herself. There was no way she could let Choice hate her. As for Fate, she knew she deserved his judgment, even if it meant death at his hands. This was the only thing she wanted now. She could no longer stand to relive the old episodes of guilt from which she had once been purified. It was as if her life story were stuck within a soul-murdering loop. She longed for permanent freedom from guilt or from living altogether.

All of Destiny's demons had been shouting inside her head, directing her to go to the Forget Lake, where she had experienced a miracle. Either she would meet her end there, or she would meet a new beginning. Time and Space had also suggested several times that she seek shelter in the Forget Lands. Finally, she decided to accept their advice—not to hide from Choice and Fate but rather to make her way from the Forget Lands to Demire, where she would confront Fate and ask him to end her for the last time.

Sudden as it was, Destiny's desire to die at Fate's hand was no less genuine. For the first time, she no longer could bear the slightest possibility of falling once more into the schemes of Archons, and the only way she could imagine gaining such freedom was through death. She had no further desire to play the heroine inside war scripts between light and darkness. Her soul had been battered enough. Now all she wanted was redemption. If she had to die, so be it.

The one thing that had kept her from taking her own life was Choice. She could not bear the thought of departing the world with her image tarnished in his eyes. Yes, she decided, she wanted to meet Choice one last time before her death, clear up a few things, and apologize for some others.

Since Time and Space had given the Archons access to Destiny's brain, they could feel her emotions. Anger and panic arose in them as they felt her growing indifference to their world and their scripts. They knew that the moment Destiny decided to forget all about them, they would start to fade away like washed dye on an old piece of cloth. There was only one way to stop this, and that was to use her son. They could continue to remind her that Choice believed the worst of her; hopefully, she would want to stay alive long enough to explain herself to him. Another option was to raise her concerns over her son's security so she would stick around to protect him.

Destiny had finally understood her destiny. She knew she must fulfill her role; for now, all her obligations were for her son. She wanted to look impeccable in Choice's eyes.

The Archons could not quite fathom her logic. They could not understand her urgency, because they had never truly loved. They did not know that real love required sacrifice. Giving without the smallest desire to receive something was the reason humans were created. All the Archons could gather from the situation was their chance to manipulate Destiny using Choice. Without delving deep into matters of her heart, they focused on the information beneficial for their survival. This was how they were programmed to operate, their default way of seeing.

CHAPTER 56

THE SPIRITUAL ARM-WRESTLING BETWEEN THE
agents of two opposing forces was still going on. They were utilizing their
powers to gain victory, but somehow there did not seem to be any way to
determine who would win. The reason for this ambiguity was that both
agents had the same source, even though for one, it was direct, and for
the other, it was indirect. Yet the source was the same, and that was Fate!

Although it would have been quite a surprise for everybody if this
information had reached them, it did not. The fact was that while the
Dhumans were the thoughts of Dhumanos embodied in flesh and blood,
nobody knew that Dhumanos, in turn, had been created by Fate unknow-
ingly. It was a great historical secret that was buried too deep in Fate's
heart to be publicly known. Even Dhumanos did not know about his
own origin.

Fate was the ultimate manifestation of the only known desire of the
Creator. The rest of the world had somehow grown out of him. He was
the cause of all causes. He was not only the cause of the eternal salvation
of souls, but he was also the cause of the eternal damnation of souls. The
Creator had shaped magnificent things. He was the powerful God and the
sophisticated Master. The universe needed to glorify Him, and so He, in
all His glory, created a refined being to acknowledge His brilliance and
represent it. This had resulted in the creation of Fate by his Lord.

When Fate had come before his Creator and confronted the beauty of what he saw, there were a few thoughts in his mind. The creative force behind that moment turned all these thoughts into the humans. This had been the birth of the anointed ones.

Unfortunately, Fate had a weakness. When he beheld the extreme light and infinite knowledge of the Creator, his senses had been excited to the extent that, momentarily, he looked back at himself and lost sight of the Creator. This self-centered look was called the Moment of Blindness. It signified the birth of Dhumanos, the blind eye that was more about vanity than appreciating beauty.

Dhumanos was the pure product of this universal instant of egoism. While Fate and the humans of his mind were exposed to the Creator and received full light from Him, Dhumanos stood behind and was exposed only to Fate's view of his greatness. He viewed only Fate the Great rather than Fate the mirror of Greatness. He failed to receive even a small ray of the Creator's light; therefore, he had always found himself surrounded by darkness. He had seen the greatness of the Creator from an erroneous perspective that valued greatness over goodness, vanity over beauty, complexity over simplicity.

Hence, the fight was not simply between two forces, but it was indeed a competition between products of the same substrate. While the Agents of Awakening were Fate's thoughts, the Dhumans were the thoughts of Dhumanos, who was himself a product of Fate's moment of weakness. Their strength was not very different, but predicting the result of such a battle was not easy.

Despite their similar source and equality of strengths, the Agents of Awakening had an advantage over the Dhumans. They had been with Fate at his creation, and they had experienced the light of the Creator right before their eyes. Due to their position at the back, the Agents of Darkness couldn't absorb any of the rays emitted from the Creator's face.

Owing to this innate knowledge of the oneness of their Creator, the Agents of Awakening had certain qualities. They could not only identify but also modify and rewrite scripts. They crafted them as a dreamer would if he could recognize that he was in a dream. They could control the contents of their dreams. They could make changes to what was shown to them according to their own purposes. This was the reason they were the Agents of Awakening. Their purpose was to alter scripts to achieve the state of awakening. They would scheme to align every script into the next one to compose the grand script of Awakening, which would occur when all the dialogues melted into the biggest script the way a dream recedes into the dreamer.

Conversely, the Dhumans were poor, clueless creatures who had to experience everything to get any idea of what was going on around them. They had not witnessed the oneness of the Creator with abrupt exposure like the Agents of Awakening. Instead, they were left to find it out through the tedious empirical process of trial and error. This meant that they had to take many risks. Even then, by the time they understood what was happening, it was too late. Therefore, they could not benefit from their information. As such, they always found everything to be a surprise.

Their experience was almost akin to how people would find crucial and rather shocking information minutes before an apocalypse. They would learn important information at the end of a situation when it was too late to take any appropriate precautions. They thought that they had a karmic effect in their lives that caused them to find things only on the verge of their destruction. This was called a *burn-to-learn* operation. However, it was already too late when they finally learned anything. They had an animal-like instinct, which was activated only when they sensed something harmful nearby. When times were peaceful, they had little capacity to read the signs.

It was something of an extreme misfortune that they had not seen the face of the Creator, even though they were present. Somehow it was written in their fate to remain blind to the Light of Eternity forever. The fortunate ones, who had recognized the light of the father shining through Fate, had their souls eternally baptized and salvaged by that Eternal Moment. However, those unfortunate people who could only see Fate through the eyes of Dhumanos, the Devil, could never witness the light shining through Fate. They were eternally punished by the karma of that Blind Moment that prevented them from ever benefiting from the light reflected through Fate's selfhood.

This had made all of them blind to the significance of Fate in God's eyes as being the Door and the Way, without which any chance of ever seeing or knowing the Creator was impossible. Instead, they saw him only through the eyes of Dhumanos. They were victims to Dhumanos's erroneous image of Fate. Dhumanos saw in Fate only the importance of his savior's role. He could never see the love involved in the process. He valued the burning power of the sun over its agency of vision and light. Respectively, the Dhumans had always seen Fate as someone with powers. They did not know anything about the true nature of Fate, including his immense knowledge. For them, he was someone with great powers who would destroy them if he were awakened from his deep sleep of dreams. These theories were fed to them by the Archons, and they had no other option but to believe them.

Dhumanos and the Dhumans were also devoid of their own thinking and knowledge. They had acquired knowledge from Fate himself. However, they only mimicked him. Although they had told the world that Fate inspired their actions, they only copied his externalities. What the Dhumans were following was what he did in physical form in the realm constituted by Time and Space and defined by History. They did not know anything about his spiritual powers. In their attempts to copy him, they succeeded only in developing pseudo-intelligence. Due to their inherent wickedness and his acquired manners, they developed only the dark powers of their minds.

Using these limited sources of knowledge, they decided to build empires upon empires of deceit in which they would spiritually enslave all those whose souls had not been destined for salvation since the beginning of time. These were the Dhuman Adamics. In other words, these were Dhumanos's thoughts incarnate that described his original rebellion against God's choice to place his power in the Adamic mold.

CHAPTER 57

DHUMANOS SAT ON ONE OF THE HIGHEST branches of an apple tree—the same apple tree, in fact, that he had directed History to sow in Destiny's garden. This tree had always been special to him, for although he had planted many such trees throughout the world, especially in those places where he wanted to have easy access, this tree was the symbol of his first conscious act against his rival, the human Adamic.

Although he did not yet realize it, Dhumanos was powerless. The Creator had deprived him of the most basic form of energy, the light of Fate, when he had indulged in the first and foremost context of error.

Eons and eons ago, far beyond the world of mortal beings, Dhumanos rejected the command of God. He was defiant toward God's Adamic model of divinity and his choice to reveal his grand secret through a humble earthly form referred to as human. Dhumanos had overestimated his own powers of deduction and reasoning, which had misled him to believe that divinity was somehow superior to such a form and should express itself in something much grander and greater than Adam. Dhumanos protested God's decision. He had observed it for many years, and as he considered and calculated the capabilities of the Adamic sculpture, he decided that it was worthless. This was the moment he became the first Fallen Angel.

From then on, he behaved like a prisoner trapped inside the human Adamic form and built a philosophy of hate toward the body. Ironically, this was a similar philosophy that would later inspire many religions that also depicted spirituality as an escape from this earthly plane.

The secret that Fate was an incarnation of Adam was known by only a few. Dhumanos sensed it, but in his ignorance, he thought he could somehow meddle with Fate's reality by controlling Destiny's realm. He was trying to prevent awakening thoughts from happening inside Fate's mind by meddling with scripts and events on Destiny's grounds. It was like trying to affect the shape of an object by playing with its shadow. He worked carefully on a script that could extend his influence over the human mind and harness the dark powers of Space and Time to enforce them upon the human psyche. He thought that if he could prove through this script that the truth was an event that was promised to happen in the future and that history was needed for it to happen, he could control humanity. He called his script Armageddon and kept his nation busy in its preparation, all the while continually postponing it.

He was oblivious to the fact that the so-called Battle of Armageddon had already ended before it started. It had ended back in Genesis when Dhumanos was forced to enter the realm of translation—Destiny's realm—as a person possessing the very mortal form he so degraded. It had ended when his great mystery was subjected to human history and contained by it, unable to have a say in the world of history making. Dhumanos lost the battle against Fate before it had even started. He could decide only how his loss was to be translated, and he had decided to utilize the negative power of translation—lies and deceit—to depict a loss as a victory. Dhumanos's grand ego that defied the image of divinity in Adam was crucified inside the very Adamic form he so resented and defied. He was simply a prisoner singing with a loud voice; yet to many, his words were catchy and seductive.

He was in the tree today to observe Destiny, for her thoughts lately had disturbed him. He knew he would have to ask Sonamrud to deal with that, but first he wanted to reflect on the matter. Destiny was his ultimate weapon against Fate, and he had used her so many times before that he had eventually started to take her for granted. But somewhere along the way, she had begun to change, and Dhumanos now traced the origin of those changes to Choice's birth.

Yet Dhumanos was not one to give up so easily. He had increased the effort to con her. He wanted her to fall for their plans once more. The indifference emanating from her when they had tried to warn her about the forces gathering against her was indeed disappointing for him. He knew they did not have much time before Choice would finally realize that he had been tricked. Once he found that out, he would embark on his journey to meet Fate with so much zeal that it would become impossible for the Archons and all their forces combined to stop him from achieving his true purpose, which was to awaken the world into a new reality and shatter the Archons' realm—the only realm where they could retain memory and significance.

Dhumanos had his eyes fixed on one of the most beautiful buildings in the world—the house built by Destiny for her son, Choice. He had to admit that Destiny had done a great job with the place. He approved of every bit of it. Nothing had pleased him more than the moment Choice had left this place, although he hadn't planned it that way, and History had paid an expensive price for influencing Choice's departure without consulting them. Still, the fact that Choice's departure had broken Destiny's heart like nothing else pleased Dhumanos. His priority had always been to drown her in a sea of hopelessness and sadness in order to subdue her.

For the moment, there was no signal from her brain, as she was probably sleeping peacefully. Dhumanos knew that it was the doing of Time and Space. They harbored a soft spot for Destiny. Between their duties to serve him, they often attempted to provide her relief as well. He felt that their behavior was alarming and dangerous. Therefore, he had ordered his fellow Archons to keep an eye on them. The duo was unpredictable, and Dhumanos could not afford surprises. He had been waiting to receive any kind of signal from her mind, but now that he was sure there would be nothing for a while, he decided to give up. Besides, he had begun to feel sleepy as well. Finally, he was too tired of his solitude and decided to summon Sonamrud before catching some sleep. This way, Sonamrud could take over the watch on Destiny.

"Hello, Dhumanos," said Sonamrud the moment he appeared. He was standing at the base of the great apple tree on which Dhumanos was sitting.

Dhumanos beckoned him to come up.

Sonamrud hated physical exertion. He held his hands high and gestured that he could not climb such a tall tree.

Dhumanos knew that there was no way to convince Sonamrud to do otherwise, so he begrudgingly came down to talk to him. "I think we should administer another dose of hopelessness to Destiny. What do you say?" Dhumanos tended to be direct and blunt.

Sonamrud checked his watch and sighed. "You should take some rest. We could deal with it later."

"No, I am fine, Sonamrud," replied Dhumanos. "Besides, somebody needs to keep a constant check on Destiny's thoughts. In fact, I was about to order you for the next watch."

"Well, I'll be on it. You go get some sleep," was Sonamrud's reply.

"I need to discuss something with you before that. I need you to come up with a plan to infuse so much guilt and hopelessness into Destiny's heart that she will decide to leave everything behind her and accept herself as a sinful creature with no chance of repentance. She must leave everything, including Mimadamos, Fate, Choice, and every good memory of Demire," said Dhumanos.

Sonamrud could feel the waves of hatred Dhumanos was emitting for Destiny. He knew that Dhumanos's hatred for Fate was explainable, but he simply could not find the reason for his immense hatred for Destiny. Sonamrud had never hated her. He had only thought of her as a tool to reach and damage the real machine, which was Fate. Knowing Dhumanos's direct methods, Sonamrud thought this very strange. He knew there must be a reason behind it, but he decided to let it go for now.

He told Dhumanos that he would devise a plan to deal with Destiny and sent him off to sleep. Meanwhile, he took his position under the shade of the apple tree and rested his back against its wide trunk. Unexpectedly, an apple fell from the tree right into his lap. He smiled as he examined it but tossed it away. He was too wise to eat it.

CHAPTER 58

CHOICE COULDN'T SHAKE THE MALAISE THAT
had gripped him since leaving the Forget Lands, but he was more troubled by his emotions than anything physical. He had two major concerns,
both involving his mother. The first was her well-being, and the second
was her past. He could not believe that the great Destiny could fall so low
as to interact with the Archons. There were many questions arising in his
mind that confused him. Unbeknownst to him, this was the major reason
for his sickness: Choice wasn't supposed to have doubts. They were like
poison to him.

As Choice reached the edge of the Forget Forest, he was still preoccupied with concerns about his mother and her activities. He just could not
let go of the fact that his mother had betrayed him. The next moment, he
would check himself for thinking ill of his mother without even giving
her a chance to explain herself. She had always taught him to give other
people the benefit of the doubt. This thought would give him a little peace,
but then again, he would think that the problem was not about others
but his own mother. He would find himself drowning in the deep oceans
of gloom. The war between the agents of two opposing forces was still
going on. Choice's emotions were still controlling it. With these thoughts,
he entered the Forget Forest, the same place he had met the Demiurge. He
kept walking until he found himself in the middle of that woodland.

For the first time in many days, Choice forgot Destiny and her crimes. Instead, he took in the beautiful atmosphere. The canopy of trees had formed a roof over the forest, and not the smallest stretch of sky could be seen. Suddenly, he had a sense of déjà vu coupled with strong nostalgia. The moment he realized the significance of it all, he found that nature was replaying a scene from the past for him. He was in the exact place where the Demiurge had revealed himself. Before Choice knew it, he was experiencing everything again, but he knew everything already. It was a very complicated feeling. He knew that the light-made creature was about to show itself once again. The moment he was finished with the thought, the Demiurge was there.

It still had its ageless smile on its face and an expression that could soothe a person in an instant. Choice felt as if he had been waiting for this moment all his life. Although his mind was entirely empty, a single thought wriggled its way inside: the thought of his father.

Choice could not help but wonder if Fate had anything to do with the appearance of this creature. It seemed like it had been ages since the winds around him had signaled that everything happened with the will of his father. In fact, he had a hard time remembering what it felt like to receive such a sign. He half thought that those signs had been only inside in his head. Nevertheless, the Demiurge was standing there, shining like a sun.

Choice bowed before it, his smile widening instinctively. The creature's smile widened slightly in response. Choice could not control his urge to ask the first question that came into his mind.

"Has my father, Fate, sent you to guide me?" asked Choice.

The Demiurge nodded.

"Is there anything special my father wants me to know?"

Another nod from the Demiurge.

"Does he not want me to go to Mimadamos?" blurted Choice.

The Demiurge nodded yet again. This time, it added, "He does not want you to go anywhere but back to the Forget Lands, then on to Demire."

More doubts entered Choice's mind. Although this was what he had wanted to do all along, he had been expecting a different answer from the Demiurge. Fate most certainly knew about Destiny's misery in Mimadamos; therefore, he must also know that it was Choice's duty to go to his mother's rescue. Yet here was the Demiurge, telling him the opposite. Something was not right. Although he had never seen or met his father in his physical form, he had a spiritual sense of him and knew him to be a man of infinite patience and sympathy. Choice supposed that the Demiurge could be lying, but that seemed highly unlikely. There was no reason for the Demiurge to do something like that.

Choice was still busy with these thoughts when he suddenly looked up and found that the Demiurge was not there anymore. Once again, Choice was standing alone in the dark forest with no light to guide him. He was also at a crossroads. He could either retrace his steps to the Forget Lands—and to Demire—or make his way to Mimadamos. Somehow, he knew that much depended on his decision and that he would ultimately make the right decision. After all, he was named Choice for a reason!

⁎ ⁎ ⁎

Meanwhile in Mimadamos, Destiny was facing the same struggle as her son. She was not sure whether she should stay there and wait for some miracle to change the course of events or run away to find her son and explain herself to him. Time and Space had informed her that Choice was in the Forget Lands. She had no idea that they had said so to lure her there. It was Dhumanos's secret plan to tempt her somewhere near the lake. He thought that once she fell into this trap, memories of her painful past there would engulf her, and there would be no going back.

Sonamrud, conversely, had devised his own plan to deal with Destiny. Just like all the rest of his plans, this one required the help of Time and Space, and Sonamrud and Dhumanos were both somewhat reluctant to stretch Time and Space beyond their capacities. The duo had a soft spot for Destiny, and any more stress on her could be detrimental to their dimension.

Sonamrud informed Dhumanos about his plan. "I suggest that we create horrifying scenarios inside Destiny's head," Sonamrud said, "so that she'll forget all about confronting Choice."

"How do you suggest we do that?" asked Dhumanos.

Sonamrud waited for a few minutes before replying. He was standing with his face turned toward the sun, which was shining intensely. After contemplating a while, he finally said, "I think we have enough access to her mind to perform the task well. One of us can disguise himself as Choice and then fill her with negative thoughts. This way, she would be so upset that instead of waiting for Choice to come to her or running to him herself, she would just give up. Then finally, we can tell her to go to the lake and remain there indefinitely."

As Dhumanos kept listening to the plan, he realized its perfection. There were times when he could not help but feel jealous of Sonamrud's intelligence.

"But Destiny has seen almost all of us," he said. "If she recognized the person, our plan would fail. In fact, she might run to Fate, and then our world would end up in ashes. We should stick to meddling with her mind only." Dhumanos smirked, smug that he was pointing out this hole in Sonamrud's plan. "Revealing ourselves in physical form to her is a dangerous risk."

"You're right, but there is one of us who has never revealed himself to her." Sonamrud paused for a moment, then added, "Actually, there are two of us she has never met in person."

"I know you are talking about me, but you realize that I am out of the question, since it involves a lot of risks. I am Dhumanos, the Archon of Archons, the King of the Forget Lands. There is a great chance that she'd recognize me."

Dhumanos looked at Sonamrud suspiciously. He was not sure whether to trust Sonamrud enough to reveal his thoughts and admit that he had always felt that he was the fallen one. He guarded his flashes of memories of primeval events and happenings that connected him with Fate and Destiny. He knew that he and Destiny were connected on a level so deep that it might alarm her if she saw him and ruin the whole plan. Even worse, it could instigate a deeper awakening in Destiny to her ancient significance in a story that he felt he could not control.

Sonamrud heard the hesitancy in Dhumanos's voice but was wise enough not to remark on it.

The two stared at each other for a moment, then Dhumanos asked, "Who is the other one?"

"Me," Sonamrud replied.

"Really?" asked Dhumanos.

"Yes. I've always remained carefully in the background, even when I was behind the planning." Sonamrud sniffed as if offended. "I thought you would have at least noticed that."

Dhumanos rolled his eyes. "I have so many things to take care of that such minor details often fail to remain in my memory."

"There is a difference between 'minor details' and a great role in crafting new ideas."

Dhumanos refused to be drawn into one of Sonamrud's arguments. "Do you agree to take the risk of revealing yourself to her?"

"Yes," Sonamrud replied, "but only as Choice, and only in her dreams."

Dhumanos took a deep breath, then nodded, and the two shook hands under the shade of the apple tree in the exotic garden of Mimadamos.

CHAPTER 59

THE DARKNESS WAS BEGINNING TO TAKE ITS TOLL on Hope. Held in the underground headquarters of the Drazians, she felt the heavy weight of their torture. Sometimes they left bruises, but the mental anguish of having to bear their presence, knowing the extent of their evil and the role they'd played in separating the Agents of Awakening, was much worse. It was like being slowly suffocated.

She was on the verge of losing all hope when suddenly she heard voices. She was too frail to open her eyes, but her mind was becoming fully alert for the first time in a long time.

Something is going on, she thought, *and it has to do with Choice*. He had finally done something to rescue her.

Choice had seen a vision in which Hope was being tortured by the Drazians. He immediately realized that things were not going well in the war between the Agents of Awakening and the Dhumans. He decided to send help for Hope and communicated his message to the people in the Forget Lands who had been supporting her. He had found and befriended a rockbird that had appeared at the same time as the Demiurge but had remained after the Demiurge's disappearance. The bird had volunteered to take his message to the concerned people.

This message had alerted the people of the Forget Lands and the many Drazians who wanted Hope to lead them. Powered by Choice, they summoned an ancient art of fighting that utilized one's palms as weapons. By projecting a blue beam of light through their palms, they could throw anyone out of their way. The power also helped them force an entry anywhere they wished. Many Forgetters, haunted by such a unique phenomenon, joined the fight with the Agents of Awakening. For some, it wasn't so much about a commitment to Hope as it was a strike against the Archons for temporarily handing power of the Forget Lands to the Drazians.

This was how all these people had attacked the underground headquarters of the Drazians, where they were keeping Hope prisoner. A fight broke out, and many Drazians were injured, since the Forgetters who joined the fight broke into the armory and stole the latest weapons developed by the Archons, one of which allowed them to defy gravity and levitate, taking their enemy from angles unexpected. The backwardness of the Drazians had always been their downfall, but they were too reluctant to allow themselves to learn the newest methods. The fighting did not last long. Soon they were on their way back to the Forget Lands with two strong Drazians carrying Hope on their shoulders, since she was too weak to travel on foot.

The moment she was free from the shackles of the evil Drazians, Hope started to regain her strength. Her eyes half closed and her mind relaxed, she became aware of her surroundings. Suddenly, a vision came to her: she was running through a forest. Although she had never been to the side of the Forget Forest that surrounded Mimadamos, she knew that was where she was. The moment she thought about it, she heard a voice. It was Choice talking to her.

She was puzzled to hear him talk to her like that. His voice was not coming from any source, but she felt as if the whole of the forest was filled with his presence and every leaf was talking to her. It was like the way Fate used to talk to her. She wondered if Choice had inherited hidden powers of communication from his father. She tried to focus on what Choice was telling her instead of all these random thoughts and questions that were arising in her mind.

"Dear Hope," the voice was telling her, "I know that you are free. I am sending you this message from the Forget Forest on the outskirts of Mimadamos. I am not sure myself how exactly I can send this to you. Although I sent my agents to rescue you, they couldn't penetrate the shield of the Drazians securing you. You are my most precious, and I can't afford to lose you. In fact, from the moment you received your freedom,

I found much of the burden lifted from my shoulders. I want you to help me win this battle. There is an enormous number of people following you. They support you and believe in your leadership. I want you to use them to fight this war against the forces of darkness. Your freedom has given me much hope. I am sure you will deal with the war on your side diligently."

The voice was silent. Hope awoke from the trance to find herself running around looking for Choice, but he was nowhere to be seen. Hope fainted.

When she woke, she was lying on a bed made of grass softer than the most expensive sheets. She was in a small room with a domed roof, which was so low that she was sure of bumping into it if she stood up to her full height. Every single part of the roof and walls was made of mud. Despite her sharp eyes, she failed to see a small woman standing near her bunk. Hope only saw her when she smiled. She looked like a matryoshka doll separated from her set and camouflaged to escape detection. Both women examined each other with interest without even blinking.

Finally, the woman spoke in a croaky voice that somehow matched her appearance. "I am Domini, a Forgetter who migrated from the vast Forget Lands of Sophistication that fall on the outskirts of Demire on the opposite side of the Valley of Doubt."

Within that area was a tiny nation inhabited by the Divautos, she said. They were considered strange because of that area's forbidding nature and its proximity to the mysterious side of Demire where Fate's timeless factory was rumored to be. Fate was said to have trusted and employed members of that nation in his factory due to their combination of high intelligence and good character.

Domini explained that hers had not been a migration at will, as a Drazian had kidnapped her when she was on a traveling expedition on the outskirts of Demire toward the Drazian side. He had sold her in the Forget market, and a Dhuman had bought her and put her into his service.

"He takes great care of me," Domini said, her eyes full of passion. "In the beginning, I used to hate him for everything, even for what the Drazians had done to me, but I have come to discover that the Dhumans know what mercy is after all and are much more to be trusted than the Drazians."

She paused for a minute. "You know, my name means *grape*. With all my suffering, I thought I deserved a nobler name." She laughed. "This is my only regret in life."

"Well," Hope said, finally finding her voice, "from what I know, a noblewoman is also called a *domini*."

Domini smiled, which emphasized her resemblance to the doll even more. She said, "Then I have no regrets at all. This means I must find a new affliction."

Hope asked in surprise, "Why?"

"Compunction of the heart is the sister of sincere humility and patience," the doll uttered. "It is something my mother used to say. Like all daughters, I didn't believe her until life taught me a lesson. Now I have learned to love the sisters like my own. They give me strength."

Hope smiled at this profound insight into the life of a stranger. She thought about the war out there that she had to fight. At least now she knew she was not alone. There were noble people at her back. She decided to forget war and tactics and to live this simple moment with this compassionate stranger to the fullest. She was realizing more and more what Choice really was.

CHAPTER 60

WHAT IS THE DIFFERENCE BETWEEN A REALITY
and a dream?

This question had bothered Fate all his life. Even when everything in
the universe made sense to him, and God had whispered all His secrets
right into his ears, the one enigma he could not solve was the human need
to differentiate between what was real and what was a dream. Both were
interwoven in a way that was obvious to him, so it took him some effort
to understand why ordinary humans needed the distinction. Fate rarely
slept. When he did, his dreams were a continuation of his waking state.

Fate could control not only the fictions inside his mind but also the
reality around him. Everything outside him was like a shadow of what
was happening inside his mind. His concern over the human need to separate the two was heightening. However, since his nature didn't allow him
to linger long in the regions of consciousness below, he decided to wait
for answers through the language of Destiny. He always looked toward
Destiny for reassurance that he was real, as she always reflected a strong
need for him to be real, to be who he was—the sun of her universe and the
anchor of the regions of consciousness below.

Fate had once told Hope, when instructing her through a dream,
"Dreams are unique for every person. There are no rules and assump-
tions. The only confirmed difference is between the dreamer's states, for
there are two kinds of states. One is the ordinary state, and the other is

extraordinary. In the ordinary state, the dreamer never realizes that he is dreaming while he is in the dream. It is only after he wakes that he realizes it. If something bad happens in the dream and he opens his eyes, this leaves him with a bitter taste in his mouth and an uncomfortable feeling. His nightmare will affect his waking hours as well. The negativity of his dream will control his reality until it is thrown back into his subconscious. However, this stored negative energy will fuel his next nightmare. This is a cycle. In such situations, it becomes hard to know whether the reality controls the dreams or vice versa.

"In the extraordinary state, the dreamer possesses the power to control his dream. If he encounters a wicked plan in his nightmares, he is simply awakened inside the dream to the fact that he's only dreaming. At this point, he can make a conscious decision to diffuse the negativity and turn the dream events in his favor. However, this requires energy."

For Fate, that source of energy was Destiny and Choice. Destiny's presence in his world acted as an awakening agency to his self and a reminder of who he was. Choice's presence fueled the power in him to move toward an awakening. Those two people were the most significant in Fate's world. They anchored him to awakening while he was dreaming, and they encouraged him to dream while he was awake. On some level, he needed them as much as they needed him.

While he never focused on anything, Fate was aware of every change in the earthly realms. Consequently, he often felt like he was dreaming even when he was in a waking state. This, in turn, made Fate appear indifferent, even cold to those around him. In fact, nothing could have been further from the truth. Fate's love for Destiny harnessed in him a desire to purify her world, so it did matter to him that an awakening happened in her realm. However, he couldn't work intentionally to do that. He couldn't allow his consciousness to be dragged into the lower levels where the flow of meaning was slow and matter was not as vibrantly responsive to what preceded it on the spiritual level, as it was in his pristine reality.

Each time Choice made a correct decision, the Agents of Awakening succeeded, which moved Fate toward an awareness for the need of an Awakening inside the Forget Lands. This would elevate Destiny to a new reality closer to his. He felt an Awakening coming at times, but then there were other moments when he could not feel anything. He knew the situation was changing, but again, he didn't want to be involved intentionally.

The physical world was also changing shape. It was an exceedingly slow process, recognizable only to a few. The shifts inside Fate's head governed every aspect of the physical universe—this control had been a gift from the Lord, a reward for Fate's ability to renounce his ego. It was an extremely powerful task, and sometimes Fate ended up causing changes by simply contemplating them without complete intentionality. Those changes could be said to be God-willed. Sometimes the power to control was beyond the control of the controller.

He had spent much time contemplating Destiny's world, an activity driven by his love for her. As he did, he was not fully aware of the extent to which his contemplation played a direct role in breaking and remaking the structure of reality as humanity knew it. It was as if his thoughts were the beating heart of Destiny's dreamlike world—it kept it in check and connected it to awakening. There were rare moments when he did realize the role he played in shaping Destiny's world; he knew then that he desired to interfere in it.

The most painful of these times was when Choice appeared at his front door. His son had traveled all the way from Mimadamos through the Forget Lands to Demire, and Fate did nothing to stop him from being sent away by the fake news of his mother being in danger. This was how life had always been for him. There had been too many scripts without any ending. His cruel job was to let things happen on their own without his intentional direct interference, while being fully able to alter the whole course of events and happenings in the blink of an eye. It seemed cruel not only for the people involved in the script but also for him. He had to see a man suffer and not do anything magical to alleviate the suffering, even when he could.

Only rarely could he reveal to people what a miracle was in the language they could understand. Otherwise, the man suffering, to him, was a segment of a wholesome meaning that translated the man's destiny to the man himself. Without such a translation, the man would suffer even more by failing to know what choice was or to benefit from such knowledge. There was no power more torturous to the human ego than having the power to do something to immediately change a scene for the better but not doing it.

This was a power no one could endure but Fate—something that made him more divine than human. It was the power to be powerless for a greater good that he was both privileged and tortured to know. Yes, there was a certain solitude to being Fate when viewed from an earthly perspective. He had to be willing to give up any tendency to view himself from the eyes of an earthly spectator, lest he see how great he was or how misunderstood, misjudged, and cursed he was for such greatness.

Fate had a sacred connection with Destiny that was too strong to be broken by times and distances. She defined his presence in a unique manner. In each life, their souls intermingled on so many levels that what happened to either of them affected the other. She was his reference point. Since Fate's world was not defined by time and space, he was free from the physical constrictions that restricted everyone else around him. He knew no past, present, and future. For him, everything was a long scroll of paper extending from the beginning to the eternity. He needed a cursor to remind him of which point the story had reached. Destiny was his cursor, without which he could be a little lost.

He trusted Destiny with all his heart, as he knew that no matter what, she would make an appropriate choice in the end. However, it was her fate to go through many trials and tribulations beforehand, since her birth was preceded by the birth of Fate's spiritual opponent, Dhumanos, and the power of the ego. After all, a man only suffered to the extent that his ego bled.

Fate was not required to make any sacrifices to touch the highest point. He was the sun that shone simply because that was what the sun did. There was no need for him to make any kind of intentional effort to provide his light to the world. His light reached everyone equally. Just like the sun, he was universal.

Dhumanos could never understand this simple fact. It was the law of nature that the savior must not claim to be a savior. For whatever were the powers bestowed upon Fate, he knew that he was a mere human. He ate and slept like everyone else. Moreover, he was liable to die and be reincarnated. It was his utter surrender to and acceptance of the rules of nature that led him to rise above them. He was a savior not because of the great powers bestowed upon him or because of extra efforts he made. He was a savior because his mere form and meaning resonated with salvation on every level.

Dhumanos was foolish enough to fall for Fate's image of a savior, which was nothing but the product of his own imagination. He could not understand that the only reason Fate was the authentic savior was because he never considered himself one. He did what he did out of his love for Destiny, while Dhumanos had always been a power-hungry wolf who sought to devour the light of Fate. This, in turn, had given him such a thick skin that even when the light was directly beaming on him, he failed to benefit from it. There was little hope for the light to reach inside his heart, because he guarded it with the powers of the ego—the darkness that constituted that moment of blindness in which the great father of all was absent from Fate's imagined world. Dhumanos did not know what the word *humility* meant, which was the same virtue that had increased Fate's rank in the eyes of his Creator.

In a way, Fate was the representative of the Creator on Earth. He was the means through which everyone and everything in the universe could reach the Creator. It was the most basic requirement of anyone who crafted anything that they wanted to be recognized through their creation. It was exactly this desire that had made Destiny fall for the mirror gift presented to her by the Archons. She wanted to experience her creative powers through the eyes of someone other than herself. This desire had made her descend from her high throne of prestige into the imperfect world of the Dhumans as she fell for the temptation created by the Archons' scripts.

For Fate, these events had felt like a dream. Yet even in the dream, he had a physical presence governed by the laws of the universe. The truth was that for anyone to have existence, it was necessary to have a human form and be subjected to the rules of space and time before he could break those rules altogether. This was the ultimate wisdom of the Creator behind the creation of Adam and the Adamic experience on Earth.

What set Fate apart from all other humans was his supreme self-consciousness, which was a gift from the Lord to His first creation. Even in the deepest layers of his sleep, Fate could grasp his reality at any moment. The evil scripts could not control him, because he was the shining sun that lit those scripts. He was always fully aware of his power over those scripts, being the original scriptwriter of even the wickedest of script makers, Dhumanos, the king of scripts himself. Fate was the one who knew, and he was the object of all knowledge regardless of the disguises of the translation. He was a circle, and there was no corner inside him for the Dhumans' antagonism to occupy. Even when he was dormant, he had overflowing energy, which had a dual nature. While it could light the world, it could also burn those who tried to touch him.

❋ ❋ ❋

While Fate was deep asleep, miles away, Destiny was sitting on her bed in the house she had built for Choice in Mimadamos. Her mind was still playing tricks on her. For one moment, she would be serious about leaving Mimadamos for Demire. The next second, she would be planning to run away to Forget Lake. The shadows in her dreams, the voice inside her head, and the real forms of Time and Space had all been unanimous on that notion.

A new person had started meeting with her. Although she had not seen her son in years, she could not help but think that it was her Choice. He had said many things to her that she had found interesting and useful, but one sentence had particularly caught her attention. His language was crafty, and she could not remember the exact words, but it was something about everyone ultimately returning to their origins. She could not stop herself from translating it as her return to Forget Lake.

His profound words affected her in a way that the previous speakers advocating the same idea could not have. For the first time, she had lost all hope in waiting for her son or in returning to Demire. Somehow this man had succeeded in convincing her to revisit a closed chapter of her life, one that had been, by all measures, hellish. He had prepared her to walk toward the lake where she had spent her guilt years—to walk toward her doom with full consent. She was finally sure about what to do with the darkness of her mind. She needed to surrender to it instead of fighting. Strange as the idea was, she decided to go with it.

Her decision made, she gathered a few things. In the darkness of night, she ran, her deep red dress flowing behind her. The cool air of the night made her hair fly as well. Clutched tightly to her chest were the memories of her years raising Choice. She had no idea how her decision was making extreme changes in her environment. She also had no idea that every step she was taking toward that wretched lake was paralleled by a step of equal significance that Choice was taking toward Mimadamos.

The movements of mother and son were shaping the future of the world. They were living events of the grand story that Fate had composed many millennia ago. They were helping the world take a new shape. Both ran toward the places of their origin, oblivious to the plans of Fate and unaware that the Earth around them was shifting.

Even the Dhumans felt it, or might have if their faculties had not been occupied with the war. The Agents of Awakening knew that soon they would be victorious. They could feel it in their bones, as Choice had regained some of his power to think clearly. Although both armies knew that the purpose of their fighting had long gone, they were still engaged in fighting for the sake of translating a story already past in Fate's mind. This was the power of momentum. The past was past, yet it always had a hidden claim on the present that forced the mind to overlook the obvious and seek the unknown that was the future. After all, a star's light could be seen eons after it faded from the sky.

Danger was not there anymore, for Hope had escaped from the clutches of the Drazians. Many times, the Agents of Awakening mirrored Destiny's desire to surrender earthly force as she made her way to the lake—a desire that ironically made them twice as powerful on the battle-field, since they were no longer fighting their own private anger but rather challenging the righteous anger of the divine.

CHAPTER 61

IN THE LAND OF DEMIRE, THERE WAS A STORY
that every child knew by heart. Every night before they went to bed, they
would gather around their parents, grandparents and, in some cases,
elder siblings to hear the famous story. It was a warning to mischievous
children, especially the spiritually inclined ones.

On this night, an old grandfather sat in a rocking chair by the fire and
began the tale for the village children. "The most sacred and geometrically
accurate shape is a circle. When you move in a circle, you find the truth.
Not a single child in Demire has ever questioned the truth, because inside
themselves, they have experienced the significance of a circle."

He held a paper loop in the air and used the other hand to illustrate
his meaning. "A circle encompasses two major components, which are the
Knower and the Object of Knowledge. As long as these two things are
combined inside the circle, as they are inside Fate, everything is in a state
of perfect harmony."

The children loved the opening to the story and the way the circle led
to Fate, simply because Fate had always mesmerized them. They adored
and idolized him; even the naughty kids respected him. Surprisingly, even
at such young ages, they understood his importance and admired the awe
that his persona inspired in them. He was the ultimate hero in their stories
and their realities alike.

"Unfortunately," the old grandfather continued, "knowledge has a dual nature. It is both beautiful and terrible at the same time, and handling it requires a certain amount of humility. Every single person holds this circle of knowledge inside him or her, but as one component moves toward the other unevenly, the balance is broken. A terrible aspect of knowledge unleashes itself. The circle, as a result, will slowly but surely degrade into the lesser form of a triangle."

The storyteller mashed the sides of the circle inward to illustrate how it might change into a triangle. An older child stood to assist with two more hands, a role coveted by those who understood the analogy, until the triangle was more obvious.

"This was how the ancient angels fell from their high place with the Creator." He lowered the paper loop to his lap and gestured for the child to sit.

The old grandfather raised an apple in front of his audience and then a hand mirror. He hid the apple behind the mirror and began the tale. "Once there lived a woman who would gaze upon a mirror and see nothing but her reflection." He held the mirror to look into it and pretended to brush his hair.

The children giggled.

"This mirror was inside a circle, like so." He lowered the paper hoop around the hand mirror parallel to the floor so the mirror bisected the circle. "The woman was on the mirror side of the circle, and behind the mirror was the apple." He held the apple up to demonstrate how the children could not see it inside the mirror.

"One day, the woman wished to see what lay beyond the mirror. She set down her brush. She reached toward the glass—and through it! What do you think she found?"

The eager audience shouted, "The apple!"

"That's right. She grasped the apple and brought it back through the mirror. And she ate it."

Gasps of shock and disbelief at the audacity—albeit fake, as the children knew the story—swept the gathered listeners.

"She looked back at the mirror to see herself as an ugly beast. She dropped the bitten apple, but it was too late. She found herself trapped in a triangle with three sides of it mirrors."

Older children loved this participatory part of the story. Three leapt up to surround their grandfather with small mirrors in a rough triangle. The old man pretended to cower from the reflections. He gestured for them to sit again and recited the lesson of the story. Small bodies grew restless as he continued.

"The Lord had given the angels the fruit of knowledge to enjoy, but they were more interested in devouring more and more of it rather than relishing each bite. Their greed for more, without understanding what they already had, led the Knower to travel farther from the center of their circle of knowledge. With every passing day, they kept drifting from their focal point. They were losing the concepts of everything, because the translations were losing their meanings. The angels failed to perceive how far the translation had drifted from the happening."

He raised the paper hoop again, now with three crimped corners. "As it moved away from the core, it started forming corners. A triangle can be viewed as a deformed circle, as you see here. As its circumference develops corners, it also develops a linear aspect prone to error and wicked planning. Truth is unbeatable knowledge. There is a limit to how much translations can serve before they lose their power to translate. One must always be ready to give up on the translation at some point to savor its meaning.

"This is precisely why the clingy souls of the Dhumans always suffer at the end of the cycle of a given translation. The falsehood tends to expose the truth, albeit reluctantly. It is an undefeatable law of nature, proven true in the case of all these angels as well.

"These angels have developed the habit of misconstruing the meaning of truth. They practice the evil act of tampering with the true translation of the messages for their own egoistic benefits. Each time they do it, the two entities of knowledge—the Knower and the Object of Knowledge—separate until the Knower is transformed from an eye that witnesses into a mouth that devours. The Knower's presence in such an equation ultimately defeats the purpose of knowing.

"This was how the Fallen Angels lost their angelic glow. As punishment for their vile attitudes, the Lord left them to dwell in the sea of ugly darkness. This was how they came to be the Fallen Angels, as they fell from the status of their spiritual mystery into mundane human history, where their mystery grew increasingly diffused and their powers were entrapped by the laws of Space and Time. Each time Dhumanos and the

Archons revolt against the nature of their spiritual imprisonment—the physical realm they so love and hate—they descend farther and are forced to harness the dark powers of translation until it completely defeats its purpose and meaning and exposes itself as a useless language."

The children loved the story, but they did not like the philosophical fabric of the story that somehow always called for a lecture to accompany it at the end.

"You must consider how Destiny deviated from the will of Fate, how she broke the circle's balance into her own duality and developed a darker side, which robbed her of the light inside her. I caution you against this dark side, as all humans have it. It is necessary to keep it under control and not fall for the temptations created by Dhumanos and the Dhuman Adamics."

As the children were led away and tucked into bed, only a few of the wiser parents delved into the forbidden wisdom behind the story. The others either did not know much about it or thought that the children were too young to understand it.

All the children asked, "What is the concept of such wisdom?"

One wise mother explained it this way. "It has three aspects: unity, duality, and trinity. The first stage is the Creator, who is a divinity beyond people's capacity to understand. The second level is the highest state of self-conscious existence, which is Fate's realm. To reach the first level, a person is supposed to understand the second one. However, there is a third level, which rules every unconscious part of Fate's mind. It is Destiny's realm, where Fate lost his balance as an indifferent knower and drifted on a daydream in which he imagined the power he had in being such a Knower."

Although the children hated that part, it was only because of the morality induced in the end without any story to follow. However, they liked Destiny a great deal. She presented to them a different angle of the same story. No matter how much their parents had talked about her actions badly, she was the star of the story and the only one with whom the children could identify.

The wise mother further explained, "Every person is initially sur-rounded only by positive thoughts. When Destiny decided to preserve the realm of the Archons—that is, to contain and embrace the darkness and imperfection that resulted from Fate's moment of blindness—another realm formed. The original thoughts around the circle of self-conscious existence were polluted by another kind of thought. These were the thoughts of Dhumanos, which started moving around the circle to deform it out of his fear of its nature. This increased the tension between the two entities of knowledge; ultimately, it violated the sanctity of the circle. This is why every human now has two types of thoughts."

The children knew the struggle to resist evil almost as well as their parents. Yet while the parents were content to blame Destiny for their own failure to resist the temptations of Dhumanos, the children were wise enough to realize how difficult it would have been for Destiny to stand firm against these temptations.

The creation of this tension between knowledge and its object was responsible for reshaping the circle forever. The circle would mutate into a triangle because of this tension. Prior to this stress, there were no corners, but corners arose from it and were responsible for creating dimensions of separation between the Knower and the Object of Knowledge. This was how people fell from Eden, and the ultimate ego was put to the three-dimensional cross of Space and Time, which kept it in check and under control.

Although neither the children nor their parents knew this for certain, that was exactly the reason Dhumanos had presented Destiny with a mirror. A circle was free of corners, so there was no distance separating Destiny and Fate. Once a triangle took form inside the soul, the Forget Lands came to separate Mimadamos and Demire.

Giving Destiny the mirror was Dhumanos's attempt to make her aware of her lower self and break her unity of being. The mirror represented to her an outer imaginary world full of eyes looking back at her, acknowledging her beauty, and nourishing her ego. It was supposed to make her realize that there was a world out there full of admirers. It escorted her away from the circle of her selfhood into the corner best suited for a sided vision of the truth. Dhumanos's main purpose in bestowing a mirror upon her when she was a young girl was to awaken her numeric earthly ego and suppress her higher divine self.

This was the story of the Fallen Angels, now called the Archons. In Demire, every single child knew it, but it was not true for other parts of the world. For them, only a few members of society knew this secret. Not everyone knew the story of Dhumanos's fall. Therefore, they did not know his hatred for Fate, either.

The children of Demire knew many other things, but one reality was hidden from them—and from the rest of Demire for that matter. It was the truth about Time and Space.

These two partners in crime had been hanging around the universe for quite some time. Ever since humans opened their eyes in a world with physical dimensions, they somehow fell under the power and spell of these two. Space and Time were responsible for nourishing events with a logical sequential significance that gave birth to a view of reality built upon past, present, and future connections. They could create motions and forms to appear in a timely consequential mode as though they possessed a life of their own. They deformed the circle of the now ruled by Fate into the triangle of past, present, and future controlled by none but Dhumanos himself.

These two friends had been tampering with reality throughout their lives, because they had been given immense power over the human psyche. They were considered to have powers to color moments and connect events using patterns of those colorful impressions. This was why the Archons had used them since the dawn of time and on countless occasions for their own benefit. Time and Space were engaged in translating realities according to their own interpretations or as the Archons had directed them.

When Fate had come face to face with the Creator, his blind moment of ego had resulted in the creation of Dhumanos by translating the ego involved in that moment. However, the moment he realized what had resulted from him, he projected Destiny into presence as his lesser-self and helper in order to contain the damage. Ever since, she had been Fate's delegate in the dark realm—one who had allowed Fate to continue to focus on the original moment when only he and the Creator existed and thus preserve his place in his Father's vision.

Dhumanos, however, refused to accept Destiny as Fate's delegate and was quick to harness the dimensions of the dark world and the laws of Space and Time to weave scripts aimed at Fate through torturing his delegate, Destiny. Dhumanos had always thought that every plan to make Destiny fall was a successful way to harm Fate.

The reality that Dhumanos couldn't fathom was quite different. The fact was that nothing happened in any realm without the consent of Fate, even Destiny's suffering at the hands of the Archons. This was the eternal truth, but Dhumanos missed it, because his mind simply could not fathom it. Although Time and Space had warped the events of reality according to their wishes, all their tactics had been part of a bigger plan written by a higher scriptwriter. It was true that Destiny had fallen into Dhumanos's traps, but it was only a small part of the bigger picture that served knowledge, which was the only path for the dark world to be reclaimed by light. Fate himself directed that picture.

The evil and error of Dhumanos were ultimately the servants of knowledge and translation. They needed these things to exist. It was difficult to accept that error could enter the realm of knowledge. Even in a scenario where it was a possibility, the operating mechanism was quite different from what Dhumanos had been imagining. Whenever such an incident occurred, the error was transformed into an obedient servant of knowledge, for however deceptive the machinations of translation were, the ultimate truth was that they were controlled by a higher power no matter how many layers of pollution were collected along the way.

Following this trail of truth, the conclusion was simple – that Gnosis, the divine knowledge, was not about the thread of forms and motions depicted by Time and Space through the medium of light. Rather, it was about the attributes of light itself that made vision possible. Although they could blind their targets to the importance of the light, it was always temporary. Even when a person stepped outside and saw only the immediate object visible to him, deep down he still knew that the real source illuminating every single thing was the sun. The sunlight gave identity to major characteristics, such as color, shape, mass, and volume. This was the significance of true Knowledge.

When light was established as the true source of power, harnessing everything, the most fundamental question concerned the importance of Time and Space. This question had been asked many times but only between Time and Space. The only other person to ponder this enigma was Sonamrud. Even with his immense knowledge, he did not have the answer.

The only one who had the key to this lock was Fate. Only he knew that Time and Space were foolish human concepts. They were nothing but a manifestation of the human desire to have a reference point to anchor all their dreams and wishes. Had it not been for humans' feeble minds and weak wills, the laws of Time and Space would have been lifted, beginning a magical era. Time and Space would be exposed in such a world to be agents of imagination whenever reality failed meaning.

CHAPTER 62

THE WORLD OF DESTINY, CHOICE, AND FATE WAS
shaped by their activities. Although their souls occupied a higher seat in
the ancient pyramid of knowledge, the story still had to play out at a pace
that even the most ignorant and low of creatures could understand—even
if this meant that Destiny and Choice forgot, albeit temporarily, who they
were in the eyes of Fate and the Creator. They were the extraordinary
humans constituting the Kingdom of Heaven. Behind them, there were
many rows of forms and events. On one hand, there were the giant shapes
of a handful of planets, while on the other, there were also the unique
forms of microscopic animals. There were large animals and green plants
occupying every part of the world. There were different shades of skies,
extremes of weather, intensities of air, flows of waters, and strengths of
fire. Then there was the metaphysical world surrounding everything. It
included thoughts, feelings, and movements. Yet this assembly of so many
things represented one single entity.

The people of wisdom, who dwelled in the noble land of Demire,
knew the reality of Dhumanos. They'd held great gatherings to discuss
him; in fact, it was their favorite pastime. If Armageddon had already happened, and all the evil plans of Dhumanos could not have any effect on
the core, what was the purpose of living in this world? They knew there
had to be a purpose, for they staunchly believed that nothing ever happened without a reason. This led them to question Fate's logic in allowing

Dhumanos to work his evil and leave such deep marks on people's lives when Fate could have ended it all in the blink of an eye.

One day when the debate had reached a particularly heated pitch, an old man among them announced that he had the answer to their query. When he was young, he had apparently been quite close to Fate, though it was not always easy to be near Fate because of his enormous energy. As much as Fate had admired him, he'd had to let go of him, as he was not one to impose on the free will or realities of others. As the two had said goodbye, the man had made the mistake of looking into Fate's eyes. The light projected from those eyes struck him so hard that he lost many of his years; even so, it had proved to be a glorious moment, for many secrets were revealed to him. Among them was the reason behind Dhumanos's efforts.

"I am not actually old," the man announced to the shocked crowd. "I experienced scores of years in that brief glimpse into the eyes of the Wise One. That moment also revealed many secrets to me, so I would like to help you solve this mystery if you allow me."

He awaited their response. Many of them were young people who did not believe that he had spent time with Fate. However, others knew that he was telling the truth. Whatever they thought of him, all were interested to hear what he would say next.

"I listen to you good people arguing about the significance of Dhumanos's evil works. Believe me when I tell you that if not for seeing the truth in Fate's eyes, I never would have reached this conclusion on my own. I take no credit for the discovery; I just want to share it with you."

Many of the men rolled their eyes, for the man had always been one to go on about things. Indeed, it was common knowledge that once he started talking, there was no way to stop him until he completed his lengthy and difficult narration. However, he always asked for the listeners' permission before he started talking. He used to say that there was no way to impart knowledge without the consent of the audience. Many times, he had been denied the pleasure of talking when he asked, because they knew about his habit of long talks. Now, however, they were so hungry for the truth that they steeled themselves for a lengthy speech.

After several more moments of pontification, he finally came to the part they were all interested in. "The real reason that Fate allowed Dhumanos to continue with his futile efforts to sabotage man's reality was to draw a line between the blind and the seers who have been blessed with the power of vision. Dhumanos's acts of evil are, in fact, nothing but a tool to distinguish right from wrong and evil from the supreme good. Fate has always used him to bring out the truth, and poor Dhumanos has no idea about it."

The old man kept babbling all the secrets he had found in his one moment of glory, but the crowd was no longer listening. They had found a new and profound insight into their age-old question, and they were busy discussing it. This was the real flaw of human nature. They had always failed to reach their true potential and spiritual height, because they could not hold their thoughts and they failed to resist their temptation to talk. If they had listened to the poor old man a little more, all the mysteries of life might have been revealed to them.

Although there was no doubt that Destiny's pain was too severe to be taken lightly, Fate had blessed her with his light as compensation and as a sign of his love for her. He had given their son Choice his beloved Hope and had granted the Agents of Awakening unique powers. His light was a relief to them. Even when they were trapped in the deep problems of their lives, Fate's light was a source of salvation for them. It was their silver lining against the darkest clouds. He allowed them to live in the haven of his Selfhood, Mimadamos—the Soul of Adam.

While all the dwellers of their world had thought that Mimadamos was Destiny's abode by chance, the reality was quite different. It was a secure place provided to her by Fate. It was his gift to her. It allowed them to elevate above the mortal body of translation and glimpse reality from his conscious eye. They could charge their vision with his light, so that even while their bodies were caught in the net of the darkest earthly contexts and events such as extreme torture and illness, wars, and famine, their souls were always resting in peace inside the warmth of their ancient home inside Fate's vision.

This was Fate's way of providing protection to them all. He had given them the power to see things through his perspective. He had granted them the power to wake up inside the dream. He had elevated them to the level of his vision, where they could glimpse the Creator's day prior to drifting inside the Dark Night of the Soul, the daydream called his-tory (Dhumanos's story) that was scripted and directed by Dhumanos.

Fate's vision gave them access to the script of all scripts. It allowed them to see the reality before they were subjected to the fallen scripts of Dhumanos. They witnessed the *Statue of Be* before entering it, and they saw Dhumanos imprisoned inside its meaning. They could see the net of scripts set for them, meant to capture them inside the maze of his meaningless contexts. This evidence clearly showed the false notions generated by Dhumanos. It revealed his plans based on the thinking that by capturing their bodies and controlling their actions, he could alter the truth-in-finality and capture their souls.

Yet he had no idea that they were free souls who could not be subdued even by the strongest machinations of physical and psychological imprisonment, because freedom was a quality inherent to them, granted them by the true master. It not only resided in every feather of their large wings but also inside every corner of their hearts.

CHAPTER 63

THE SKY ABOVE THE FOREST HAD TURNED THE darkest shade of purple. Destiny looked up. There was neither moon nor star. She felt as if an eggplant had somehow stretched to cover the whole sky. She had no idea how long she had been traveling, but the road seemed never ending. Her throat was burning with a thirst that she had never experienced. Yet although it had been a difficult and painful journey, she harbored a hope that it might never end.

She was more afraid of what waited for her at the other side of her trip. If she was on the road, she was free of the torture she had to face at her destination. She had stopped many times on her journey to reflect on her decision to go to the Forget Lands. She was not sure if her cowardly choice could be of any use to anyone. Yet she continually resumed her journey, because she thought that it would at least end the torment she had to face in Mimadamos. However, as she moved farther from home, her thoughts had become clear. The influence of Dhumanos and his fellow Archons was weakening with every step she took away from their center point. Something inside her made her keep going.

The reality was that the guilt inside her heart for what she had done was so deep-rooted that she could not help blaming herself, even when she was away from the Archons and their evil tactics. Every atom of her being and every yard of the fabric of her soul were stained with the blemishes of despair that were now permanent residents in her being. This was indeed her biggest mistake, and it was even worse than when she had fallen into the traps of Archons and betrayed the trust that Fate had placed in her. There was no worse way to insult Fate and his virtue than to think of him as incapable of forgiving the one who had harmed him. The despondency had made a home too deeply inside her. In a way, she was not completely to be blamed, because this time, it was not really under her control to tame her feelings.

Besides, she still remembered how Fate had punished her by not signaling for her to come back when she was expecting Choice. In her mind, given the Archons' current influences, the punishment had meant that there was no way she could be forgiven. Afterward, she had found that when Choice had left her alone, it was also a punishment for her, because she had been foolish enough to trust History. In addition to all her miseries were the whisperings from Dhumanos and his minions, intended to keep her world full of darkness and completely devoid of light.

When Destiny could not think of even a single reason for her existence, she decided to follow the advice of Time and Space. She had no idea what the consequences of her actions would be. She felt as if centuries had passed since the time that she had been unmarried. She could not even think of the feelings that used to arouse her interest and curiosity in the little things of life. She had forgotten the time when she would think of nothing but Fate, to the extent that it was not even a part of her memory anymore. She could almost feel herself laughing as she tried to recall her excitement of the past, when she used to believe that all her problems would be solved the moment she found her savior, her Fate.

It was ironic to see the same Destiny, who once had the look of a queen and the pomp of a noblewoman, now completely lost in every sense of the word. She looked more battered than a beggar. Her robes were ripped in different areas, and her feet were full of sores and boils due to her long journey in the shadowy lands. The last time she had passed on these tracks, she'd had Fate's protection. Even when he was not alongside her, he had sent people to keep her safe. Yet now there was nobody to shelter her from the harsh weather and poisonous loneliness. She kept walking.

The lands had become even more dangerous than before. Destiny had fainted many times on her way, due to lack of nutrition. To make matters even worse for her already poor self, the tracks kept changing direction. There was a point in her journey when she kept walking for about a week only to realize at the end that she had been moving in circles. There were all kinds of animals to make things even worse for her. So many insects had bitten her, she had turned immune to their poison; her body had somehow succeeded in manufacturing an antidote against the venom. Several birds and animals had attacked her.

Even after all these hardships and cruelties of nature against her very presence, she somehow persisted. It was not her desire to reach the destination that had kept her going; it was simply her wish to endure so much pain. She had developed an idea that physical hurt would redeem her soul. This was the philosophy of Dhumanos. She was not sure why she was inflicting so much pain on herself, except that she felt that it was helping her forgive herself.

By the time she reached Forget Lake, she was completely exhausted and shaken. One look at the despicable abode of her guilty childhood, and her eyes welled up. When the first tear rolled down her cheek, she found herself in shock. It had been ages since she had cried. After facing so many hardships in her life, her eyes had dried up as if they could never shed a tear. Yet somehow, she found herself crying after so many years. One tear followed the other, and soon the flow increased. She had no idea how long she cried before falling to the ground. She lost consciousness in the physical sense of the word, but her self-conscious woke up.

The world of Destiny, Fate, and Choice was very strange. They did not know how to differentiate between dreams and reality. Destiny had not known that what she had been undergoing until now was nothing but a dream and that what she saw in her unconsciousness was indeed reality. It was all an illusion, a code that Destiny had failed to break.

Just as she fainted and her mind accessed the realm of reality, she saw images she could not decipher. She was standing in a stadium that she had never seen before, and there was a large screen before her. She turned to see the rest of the stadium, but she found herself covered with a screen from all sides. She knew there was a reason for this screen. She even knew what the reason was. There was something she needed to see.

Just as this thought entered her mind, the screen showed a single image: a map. Destiny knew it was the map of her world. She looked at it with boredom. She had seen it many times, and she had no idea why she was being shown it now. She felt uncomfortable and wanted to return to the world that she considered reality. She was fed up with all these games. They had been messing with her brain for too long.

Destiny looked hard at the screen. It was indeed the same map. At the center of the map was Mimadamos, surrounded by the Forget Forest. On top of it, beyond the Forget Forest, was Demire, represented by a narrow line. This stirred her thoughts. She was thinking that despite being so small, the land of her husband was quite beautiful and significant. There was also the thin Valley of Doubt between the Forget Forest and Demire. She was surprised to see that she had never noticed it before. Suddenly, she realized that it was meant to be hidden to generate doubt in the minds of the people seeing it. Surrounding the whole area were the undefined layers of the vast Forget Lands of Sophistication.

She kept looking at the map before deciding that she would wait for only a few seconds. Then if nothing changed, she would return to her reality. She had no idea how she would consciously return to her world, but she made up her mind anyway. She had thought that seeking an exit would be a much better option than just staring at something she had seen all her life. She was just about to move away from the screen when something happened that made it impossible for her to breathe because of excitement.

She witnessed the map of her world changing shape. She could not believe it, yet it was happening. She was not sure if she would remember this dream after waking, but she thought it would be a great loss if she forgot it. She gasped in surprise and shock as the little line that was Demire started enlarging. Her mouth was half open when she saw Mimadamos, the land of her birth, shifting to the right side of the map as Forget Lake also started moving, taking its place on the map's left. Suddenly, every part of the map was moving and adjusting, and Destiny found herself losing track of these amazing movements. Although she was not sure what to make of it, she knew that it had great significance. The world was shifting, and she had no idea why.

When the screen stopped moving and everything had shifted for the last time, Destiny was standing in the middle of the stadium with her eyes wide open. The circular world she was used to seeing had turned into a triangle. She looked around, realizing that the stadium had also changed shape. It was not circular anymore but a triangle with sharp corners.

She shrieked, and her eyes opened. She was back in her reality, which was nothing but a dream. Not a trace of what she had just seen was left in her memory. She was lying flat on the banks of the dark Forget Lake. The moment she realized where she was, all the bad memories of her past came rushing back to her. They were much more forceful now, as if water, which until then had been contained, had finally found an outlet. All the moments of guilt and shame were right before her eyes. She could almost touch those moments. She felt as if they were being played before her in slow motion.

The vivid pictures from the past were disturbing and haunting. She would give anything if she could only change the scripts of the moments and the reality of the events. She knew there was no way to undo what had already been done. The ghosts of her past scared her as one event after another revealed itself. Her heart ached, and her soul was disturbed and dissatisfied. All her senses were screaming, and she couldn't breathe. For a moment, she almost hoped for another round of unconsciousness, but no such relief came to her.

Although her dream eluded her, she suddenly felt a little optimistic. The feeling was fleeting, and she tried to jerk away from the image of herself snobbishly leaving Fate's mountainous residence in Demire for her home in Mimadamos. Every atom of her body was shouting to her with the pain that she had failed to feel at that moment in her memory. She did not know this, but it was how Fate had felt when she had left him. Even he'd had no idea that he could feel something so strongly, yet he had done what he was required to do at that time. As the Great Father required, he had let her go. She was feeling all these things simultaneously.

Destiny had no choice but to experience all this pain. She had resigned herself to this fate, but then something different happened. Until now, there had been no wind, and everything had been eerily still. It was as if she were standing in a vacuum and the turmoil was inside her, but now a strong wind blew in her direction. It touched not only every part of her body but also her soul. All the images dancing around her lost their significance. The pain subsided, and an emptiness of immense magnitude replaced it. The vacuum was now internal, not external.

The moment struck her too harshly, and she found herself rebelling. She refused to feel all the pain and guilt surrounding her. As the desperation caught her in its claws, she hit the images in a frenzy, trying to shatter them. She attacked each of them, one by one, using her hands to punch one, nails to scratch another, and even her legs to kick the rest.

The moment she had destroyed all of them, she stood there. She was breathing heavily, yet she was an empty well so deep that a single coin thrown in would take centuries to reach the bottom. Realizing her strange state, she did something even stranger: she laughed! The sound of her laughter reached every corner of the Forget Forest, yet nobody came to her. In fact, not even a bird so much as moved a wing.

Destiny was looking straight ahead. The whites of her eyes were turning red. She blinked, and her eyes fell on the deep lake, which was inviting her. She accepted the invitation with a smile, as it was so tempting. She was comforted by the idea that, if nothing else, she would still have the lake beside her no matter how tough things would be. She was oddly satisfied as she felt at home. This was the place of her origin, she thought, and it made sense to return to it in the end. The start was the stop, and everything was a circle. It was not a triangle with three defined corners symbolizing three stages of life. She recalled something she had learned as a child.

It was a theory that a circle could change into a triangle, depending on the events in a person's life. Both shapes represented life. However, she decided not to focus on the theory, because, as she recalled, these changes could be induced only by the activities of people who were significant in the eyes of their Creator. She was sure that she was not among them. Besides, it also required a great sacrifice to trigger the events, which could lead to ultimate changes in this geometry of life. She was sure that her era was not the one in which such a huge change was to take place, and there was no way that she could be a savior. For her, life would always be a circle—and not just any circle but a circle of fire. The only way she could be rid of it was to jump into the lake. What else could end fire but water?

She took a few steps toward the lake, which was full of ice-cold water, yet she was not afraid of it. She had only a few dirty rags left on her body as a pathetic excuse for clothes, but none of her skin was showing, because where clothes had failed, blood had succeeded in covering the flesh. Her feet were so bruised that every new step brought a different stroke of pain, yet she had somehow reached a level far above these small problems and minute scratches.

The wind had stopped blowing, and the atmosphere around the lake was even quieter than before. In this extreme silence, a splash sounded with the magnitude of a blast. Suddenly, the magical silence covering the whole area snapped. Birds started chirping, the wind started blowing, leaves were rustling, and all the natural elements of life resumed their singing in their usual sounds. The spell was broken. Although Destiny had not known this, a sacrifice had been made. She was the savior, though none knew it but the universe!

CHAPTER 64

AT THE EXACT SAME TIME DESTINY REACHED
Forget Lake, Choice reached Mimadamos. The moment Choice crossed
the gate of Mimadamos, he found an old, rather portly woman standing
there. She was stooping very low, and the only reason she had not fallen
on the floor was a stick upon which she had put all her weight. She was
wearing robes of mud-brown color, and a matching hood was covering
her head. Since she could not stand straight, she had to reply without even
looking at Choice, but her voice rang out loud and clear, startling him.

"Who are you, boy?"

"I am Choice. My mother's name is Destiny. Have you seen her?"

She started crying.

Choice was not sure what to do. "Please calm down."

The sobs kept coming. Resigned to this strange turn of events, he
decided to proceed and turned away, but the woman suddenly recovered
and called him back to her. "Wait. I once was acquainted with Destiny, and
I really liked her. She was my friend who used to console me in times of
distress, but I am afraid I failed to help her with her problems. I often felt
Destiny was sad, but I never tried to break her shell. Ultimately, she ran
away, poor girl."

The news felt like an arrow that pierced right through his heart. His
initial feelings were of sadness, because he felt that he had lost his mother.

Then a different feeling kicked in—guilt for leaving her behind and not being there for her when she most needed him.

"Do you know where she went?" he asked.

"I heard she was last seen heading up to Forget Lake—probably intent on drowning herself. Oh, preserve us."

Anger swallowed Choice's previous feelings. He could no longer stop himself from feeling disgusted with his mother as, in the back of his mind, he battled the terrifying thought of his mother drowning. All his previous emotions, which he had been suppressing, came bursting out. Upset by the new information, he decided to leave Mimadamos forever. He had turned away to retrace his steps back to the land of Demire when he decided to take one last look at his house. When he turned to ask about his home, the old woman had vanished.

Sonamrud chuckled as he straightened his posture from the stooped disguise as the old woman of Mimadamos. For a young man with such potential power, Choice was gullible. Granted, Sonamrud had told him the truth. Destiny had gone to Forget Lake, but her motivations were not as he'd said.

As Choice was busy making the decision about whether he should visit his home, his mother was drowning in Forget Lake. Her struggles against the vicious waves of dark water were of no use. The real reason behind her defeat was her lack of will to fight back. She was sinking into the depths of Forget Lake. It was ironic that she had once found a solution to her problems beside this same lake.

However, she did not remember any of that, since Time and Space had tampered with her memory. They had already done enough damage, not only to her soul but also to her mind. All her happy memories had been either tampered with or destroyed. They had left her with only bad memories and disturbing scenarios, and even those were highly exaggerated from their original versions. There was no hope left inside her, either. It was impossible for her to fight back, as anything minutely optimistic was taken away from her. The Archons and their allies had snatched away every ounce of her strength. She was empty of happiness and joy. She bore the heavy burden of guilt, failures, and bad luck, which was weighing her down in the depths of the water.

The dark water was engulfing her smoothly, and she was letting it do so without showing any reluctance. She was willingly sacrificing herself, even though she was not sure what her sacrifice would achieve. But things took a different turn when a disturbance made her open her eyes. As she looked around to see what was happening, she witnessed a giant monster moving toward her. Although she was already in too much pain, as the water was cutting into her skin and making it impossible to take another breath, looking at the monster felt like looking death straight in the eye.

Destiny started struggling against the waves to reach the surface of the water. She was scared out of her wits as she saw the huge monster advancing toward her. She knew that she did not want to die like this. She swam and swam until she broke the surface of the lake. She inhaled and exhaled fiercely, and oxygen entered her system, inflating her lungs. Her brain was not working except in a single direction. She had no thought but to escape the brutal fiend who waited for her deep in the lake.

She was relieved that she had escaped the brute, but she was mistaken. Just as she reached the bank of the lake and was about to get away from it, something grabbed her left leg. Although she could not see it, and the lake's surface was as calm as if nothing had happened, she knew exactly what creature was clutching her limb. For all the times she had wished for death, now that it was upon her, she was rigid with fear.

The purple sky above the lake calmly looked on as the deep blue blanket of water engulfed Destiny. It almost looked as if she were wrapping the blanket around her while deep in sleep. In reality, she was paralyzed because of the terror that surrounded her. In a last desperate attempt, she clenched whatever her hand could find on the shore. Unfortunately, it was nothing but dirt. The monster dragged her into the lake.

Once she was beneath the surface, she could feel her death inching its claws toward her. She knew she would die, but that was what she had wanted in the first place. Why was she so afraid of it now? She had no answer. Her mind had become energized, and she cursed it because now it meant that she could feel the pain of each blow in its entirety. This was exactly what happened when a giant claw hit her in the face and the water around her turned a little red. She was dazed. Before she could regain her composure, another punch in her stomach brought new pain.

Suddenly, she dived even deeper into the water. It was her way of escaping the monster. The gigantic, ugly green mass followed her. It was a shapeless thing with only a single limb protruding from the middle of its body. It was lined with sharp claws. The upper part of the body had a single eye and no mouth. Destiny did not have the chance to wonder how this thing ate.

She swam deeper and deeper. When the monster was nowhere to be seen, she started swimming upward to take a gulp of air. As her mouth emerged at the surface, she breathed deeply. She touched her face and felt blood. It was strange that, even though she was in the lake, the blood had not washed away. She took some water and washed her bruise. She attempted to escape the lake one more time, but she saw the monster's green body lurking near the bank. She inhaled deeply and dived back into the depths of the lake.

* * *

Choice had moved past the entrance gate of Mimadamos and was advancing toward his house. There was no way he could just move away from Mimadamos without having one last look at the place where he had learned so much and been so loved.

His anger toward his mother had subsided considerably. In fact, the more he thought of the old woman who had delivered the news, the more he realized that she was a rather suspicious character.

Choice was not sure about Destiny's betrayal. It was true that his mother had acted in a strange manner by associating herself with the infamous Archons, but Choice still had no proof. He had only heard rumors through third parties. He had never heard her side of the story at all. Even if she had faltered and caused the separation with Fate, was that not enough of a punishment for her?

He remembered that touch of sadness in her eyes. Since he had seen a few glimpses of her previous life when she had been mostly happy, he knew she had repented of her faults. He failed to feel hatred toward his own mother as he realized how much she had done for him. In fact, the main reason behind his desire to visit their home in Mimadamos was to reminiscence about his time with her.

With all these thoughts in his mind, he kept treading the familiar path that went to his home. The moment he crossed the threshold of Destiny's paradise, which had been her gift for her son, he felt a tremor pass through his body. He felt as if a battle had been triggered inside him. There were two opposing forces fighting for their own causes. While one of them told him to return to the Forget Lands and not go farther even if his life depended on it, the other force was encouraging him to keep going. His thoughts turned hazy, and he felt as if he was losing control over his thinking capacities as well as his actions.

Several times, he caught himself retreating to the gate of Mimadamos, walking backward. He had to pull himself together and struggle to move forward. It took him a long time to make progress toward the house, but before he could enter, something else caught his attention. The apple tree in all its magnificence was standing tall in the garden. He could still recall how History had planted it and how he used to take care of it.

Choice could not stop himself from moving toward the majestic tree. As he got closer and closer to it, a huge cloud of emotions engulfed him, and he realized that he could not control his feelings anymore. With a shaking hand, he wiped the tears rolling down his cheeks.

He looked up and saw the canopy of the apple tree. The green leaves were many in number, and their vividness hinted that a heavy rainfall had recently washed them. There was not a single fruit on the tree, but it was bent as if it were laden with many apples. Choice was moving as if in a trance. He kept moving toward the tree. He stopped only when he had finally reached the base of the trunk. Instinctively, he looked up and saw a strangely hanging red apple, almost unnoticeable, hanging from one of the branches.

Years of evolution, reconstruction of genetic codes, and exposure to different environmental situations had failed to teach the son of Adam how to resist temptation. Choice followed the path of his ancestors as if it were embedded deep inside his genetic makeup to do so. He took a step forward toward that branch, stretched out his hand, and plucked the apple. He examined it closely. It was the reddest, largest apple he had ever seen. It lay innocently in his palm until he decided to take a bite of it.

CHAPTER 65

DESTINY WAS SWIMMING IN THE DEPTHS OF Forget Lake. She was thinking of moving to its other side just to get away from the strange creature. As she turned her head to the other side, she began to remember a few things about her last stay near the lake. There had been a girl here who called herself Hope. Destiny recalled her to be an elegant child. Although her memory was foggy about what had happened afterward, she remembered the child. She had enjoyed her talk with the respectful little girl, who had sounded much more intelligent than her age.

Destiny had no idea why all these memories were coming to mind. As she sunk herself deeper toward the bottom of the lake, she saw numerous human skulls and bones piled. It didn't take her long to realize that these were the remnants of people hunted by the gruesome monster of the lake.

Destiny passed these half-decayed bones and kept swimming. Just as she decided to rise for a breath of oxygen, her eyes fell on something shiny. She swam to it and found that it was a bejeweled sword.

The moment she touched the sword, a charge shot through her hand, up her arm, and into her skull. A flash of insight connected her to her son as a deeper connection revealed itself to her: Adam eating the apple of the tree of knowledge in the Garden of Eden.

Many things happened in the universe simultaneously. She could not tell, since she was deep in the water, but the surface of the lake was not as calm as before.

Everything was happening just as Fate had known it would, for the moment she had touched the sword was the exact moment when Choice had bitten into the apple. The events were aligned in this manner to destroy the ruling power of Time and Space, which they had been abusing for too long. This one last, timely event would set it all right, for it triggered a series of events that could shift the reality of everything as it was now.

Reality had always been a very subjective thing. One person's reality could be a dream for another. The world was a hazy place, and things had a way of shifting. The world was dynamic, and it was not supposed to stay the same forever. The transformation was a key for the survival and success of everything. The only thing that could not be changed was how things were supposed to happen according to the plan of divinity. A human eye could never see beyond its vision. To perceive what was behind the veil required faith in the heart and divine knowledge. Not everyone was blessed with these gifts. Fate was the only one who knew the true nature of events, but the cost of knowledge was that he was not supposed to use it in his favor.

The Creator had given Fate the capacity to exercise patience that the rest of humanity did not have. Fate's reality was always different from everyone else's. He had known for centuries how things would turn out in the end, but for the rest of the world, it was a completely new experience. None of them would have ever imagined seeing their world shifting its shape. The duo of mother and son had stimulated a chain reaction that made many changes.

While Fate was in Demire, his place of origin, Destiny was at Forget Lake, her place of origin, since in the eyes of God, she had started to exist when Fate had touched her with his light of compassion, and Choice was where he was supposed to be. In fact, Choice was right where the story had begun—from Adam's choice to bite the apple.

Destiny's version of the Fall was destined to happen the way it had. God wanted her to descend along the path of sin and temptation so that she would know the true meaning of ascension and experience it to the fullest. For this purpose, it was necessary for her to penetrate Dhumanos's mind and experience all the despair in the world so that she could contain its damage. Yet with all the planning, she had somehow faced suffering and pain when it came to earthly equations, and there was still no stopping it. For unlike Fate, who lived the purpose behind suffering and falling in every breath of a second, she was often less aware of it. This had increased the impact of her suffering and her dependence on Fate to save her in her younger days.

A different energy entered Destiny at the moment she touched the sword. The idea of Choice choosing to bite the apple, choosing to engage in the sinful act, signified that sin itself was unreal in finality – but only real as much as it could serve the dream setting of historical existence. When Choice chose sin, he deactivated its code, and Destiny realized that her sin was unreal and that she could rid herself of it by simply telling herself that she was in a dream and she only needed to wake up to end it all.

The monster of Humanity's fear was sin, and it was all somehow symbolically associated with Adam biting that Apple. When Choice chose to bite the apple, he deactivated its code and defeated the monster. After all, the alleged Fall from heaven was in Fate's reality the code of rising. It was meant to be, and it served to help the soul understand and rejoice in the Eden of its finality.

For the first time in ages, Destiny felt empowered to fight back. The monster lurking on the banks of the lake was nothing but the manifestation of her own fears. In her own magnanimity, she had allowed her fears to grow, but as fears often do, they had turned monstrous. She knew that she had to conquer the beast of her own imagination. Therefore, she took the sword and swam toward the bank to face the monster of her fears.

She reached the bank, but there was no monster to be seen. She came out of the water, and still there was nothing to grasp her legs. Just as the monster had looked for her, now she was in search of it. She looked at the horizon of the lake, but there was still nothing.

Then she spotted the ugly, shapeless green figure of the monster swimming away in the opposite direction toward the bank. It looked as if it were trying to run away from her! Destiny took a deep breath and jumped back into the lake. She swam speedily and soon reached it. She looked straight into the monster's single, creepy eye before piercing it with the sharp tip of her sword. The monster made a horrible noise, but she was immune to it. She dragged it to the bank with the help of her sword and threw it there.

The monster looked dead. Destiny was about to leave it when it stirred, and she saw its head rising. She tightened her grip on the sword, ready to strike. The monster advanced, and so did Destiny. His clawed hand and her sharp sword touched in midair. Time seemed to stop as the sword shattered into a million pieces. But the sword had cut the monster's hand, which flew away from them. The moment its hand was detached from its body, the rest of the monster simply melted away.

Destiny did not know how it all happened, but she knew that she had finally been granted freedom. The fears inside her mind would not bother her decisions and her life anymore. All her memories, which Time and Space had tampered with, returned to her.

The events of her life were now playing once again in front of her eyes, but surprisingly, they were all the good moments. The memory that stood out the most was one she had forgotten. She saw herself sitting at the same spot where she was standing now as Fate removed the sin of spiritual prostitution from between her breasts. As she was freed from her fears, she found herself cleaner and purer than when Fate had cleansed her. This time, she was her own savior, which meant that she had not disappointed Fate after all.

Scene after scene, her life flashed before her eyes. As she saw Hope standing in one of the scenes, she realized something. She had promised Hope that she would return to her one day. Destiny was now sure that she must fulfill her promise.

She started moving toward the Forget Lands, oblivious that the land had shifted and changed. The lands had not only moved, but their size had also been altered.

✳ ✳ ✳

What exactly triggered these fateful changes could be found in reality as it was shown to Choice when he ate the apple. It was not any ordinary apple but an apple of knowledge. When Choice ate it, he was transported to another world. It was the world of reality, which no one could reach unless they were invited. The apple had acted as a portal for Choice.

All his confusions evaporated, and all his questions were answered. The events of the past flashed across his brain. He could see them as if he had been there when they had happened. It was like his lessons with History, except he could experience the events and not merely listen to a narration.

One moment, he could see the creation of Adam, and the next, he saw Eve coming right out of Adam's rib. He was in a hypnotic state in which every part of his body was paralyzed except his brain. On the contrary, every nerve of his brain had been charged with heavenly energy. He had entered a dimension that was timeless and did not follow the laws of space. The only currency acceptable was energy, and Choice had been given a lot of it. He could not only witness past events, but he had also been granted the power to interpret them quite fast. His neurons were working at the speed of light. This was why he comprehended that the story of Adam and Eve was, in fact, the tale of his parents as well. Adam was Fate, and Eve was Destiny. In fact, their story was the reality of all human beings in the world.

The picture in front of his eyes dissolved, and another scene emerged. The first thought that came to Choice's mind as he saw a pious angel busy worshipping a light was of respect. Yet he could feel that something was amiss. He could tell that things were not as they seemed. Still, he couldn't put his finger on the exact problem. His suspicion turned out to be authentic when the same pious spirit turned into an evil entity on seeing Fate and Destiny as they happily trod the exotic paths of Eden.

The scene dissolved, and another one replaced it. The dubious spirit disguised itself as an angel and started whispering in Eve's ear. Choice watched as the spirit lured Destiny into a small pond and pointed to her reflection in the water.

"Look at you," it whispered. "You're as beautiful and perfect as Adam, if not more so. Why should Adam be greater than you in God's eyes? Why should you follow him? Claim your own beauty; this garden was made for you."

At first, she refused to look at the water, for this practice was forbidden in Eden, but then she gave up and saw herself through its eyes. Ever since then, the pond had been her refuge, and staring at herself had been her greatest pastime.

The next scene was rather shocking for Choice. Sensing a change in Eve, Adam followed her to the pond one day and discovered her secret. From his hiding place, Adam heard an angry voice berating Eve for breaking the law of Eden. It was the voice of that same pious angel, yet Adam in his confusion mistook it for God's voice. When he heard the angel insist that Eve be punished for her wrongdoings, Adam rushed to the pond, intent on doing whatever she had done so that he could share her punishment. As Adam glanced at the waters, he saw a reflection of a big, red apple. He turned and saw that there was indeed one red, shiny apple hanging from a branch of the majestic tree. Choice watched as Adam did what he had just done himself: he ate the forbidden fruit. The moment the first drop of the nectar from the juicy apple touched his lips, the image of Eden shattered.

The trance that Choice had been in, for God knew how long, broke as well. The last thing he had heard before opening his eyes was the sound of ruthless laughter. He knew its source. He could see the truth of every single event that had ever occurred in his life. Nothing was a secret anymore. He had awoken from the dream.

As Choice took in his surroundings, he found himself lying on the grass underneath the apple tree; only it was not the same tree he had seen in his vision. The green leaves were burned, the bark was dried, and every part of it had shrunken. There was no way this tree would bear fruit, ever.

Deeply surprised, Choice thought at first that he had been transported to some other place. But no, he soon realized that he was still in Mimadamos at his mother's house, and it was indeed the same tree from which he had seen Adam take the apple.

After that, it did not take him much longer to solve the mystery. The apple tree was from heaven, and it had sacrificed its life to show Choice reality. This journey took energy, and the tree had used all its power in the process.

Suddenly, Choice smiled, for he understood that everything had happened exactly as Fate had wanted it to. During his stay in the Forget Lands, he had found out that the apple tree in the paradise of Mimadamos had been sown by the orders of Dhumanos. But as the seeds had originated in heaven, he knew that Dhumanos's plan had backfired.

Choice had also made the most important discovery of all—the Archons had been meddling with his mother's mind. They were behind all of Destiny's bad decisions and mistakes. The rage started to well up within him, but he quelled it. There was no point to being angry, for he had discovered his newfound faith in Fate and his plans. He did what he did best: make decisions!

CHAPTER 66

OF ALL THESE MAJOR CHANGES OCCURRING, NOT only in the structures of lands but also among their inhabitants, the most drastic change of all was happening in the lives of Time and Space. Although they had always known that their importance was, in fact, only an illusion, it was becoming clear that the truth was about to be revealed. After all, a fool's castle can crumble at any moment.

Still, they had one thing at their disposal, and that was the ability to access information unavailable to others. They used this power now to learn of an important event that was about to happen. It had different names and multiple consequences, the most important of which was that it would mark the end of their rule.

This event was marked with the revelation of certain historical secrets to Choice. The moment he found out the Truth of all truths, the secret of light was also revealed to him. He had found out much more than the story of his ancestors under the apple tree.

According to the myth started by Space and Time, if Choice reached the depth of every truth, Time and Space would be shattered along with the world itself. However, nothing could have been further from the truth. Time and Space did not control the universe as they had made the world believe; the only rules it followed were of the light. Thus, the only real consequence of the destruction of Space and Time was that truth prevailed.

They were not destroyed in the true sense of the word but were rather imprisoned for their meddling in Destiny's mind and the language of light and for taking the universal law into their hands.

Time and Space knew that this punishment was much less than they deserved. It was irrelevant that they often felt guilt for hurting Destiny or that the Archons had threatened them. All that mattered was that, one way or another, they were a part of every misshapen event.

Indeed, the repentance in their hearts was the only reason they were spared complete destruction—or perhaps their survival was part of the Creator's plan that remained a mystery. In any case, Time and Space were trapped inside a creek that resulted from the land shift. Their disappearance from the Earth's surface resulted in more problems for the Forgetters.

Their energy and power, along with those of the Drazians, were depleted. Their movements became slower, as if under water, and their actions chaotic, helpless, and meaningless. They grew more restless with each passing day. They awaited the return of the Archons, but the Archons were nowhere to be seen and sent no news of their activities. In the meantime, the Forgetters' hatred for the Drazians, who were still in charge of the Forget Lands, continued to grow.

Hope had recovered from the wounds inflicted upon her by the Drazians during her time as their hostage. For the first time in her life, her fellow human beings had given her a warm welcome. Before that, most of them had pretended that she did not exist. Even she did not remember her childhood, except for meeting a beautiful woman near Forget Lake. She did not know who the woman was or why either of them was in that spot. It was as if they had always been there.

There was no way Hope could have known that she, like every human on Earth, was a product of Destiny's mind. Of course, her physical birth was like that of all other vile creatures lurking in the Forget Lands, but there was one very important difference. Whereas the others were also products of the Archons, Hope was the embodiment of the hope that had dwelled in Destiny's heart before Fate cleansed her.

This was why people had not accepted her—they were not sure of her origin. They left her on her own to take care of her matters until Fate began teaching her to use the light of consciousness. Every lesson she received from her mentor turned her into a better person. After many such lessons and hard work, she was finally capable of taking care of herself. She did not need the help of anyone anymore. Since she had received light directly from Fate, she developed many unique qualities that had aided her in dodging Time and Space when they chased her all around the Forget Lands.

Yet despite her experience with Fate and, later, Choice, it was the Lady by the Lake who had most shaped her life. Hope could not forget the beauty and elegance of that lady, especially the soothing tone with which she had addressed Hope. In the woman's voice, Hope had heard the balance of leadership and obedience to the true leader, and it had inspired her to become who she was today. Although she didn't know the woman's identity, she often gave her thanks, and she looked forward to the day when they would meet again.

Now as the situation in the Forget Lands grew worse each day, Hope knew that it was almost time for her to become the leader the people were crying out for. Initially, she had been reluctant to take such a heavy responsibility, but then she dreamed about the light of Fate. He had sounded angry that she would not work for the welfare of her people. She took this as a sign.

The next day, Domini, the matryoshka doll lookalike, entered Hope's room along with her breakfast.

Hope sat up in bed and told her, "I plan to lead the coalition of moderate Forgetters and the rebellious Drazians against the atrocities perpetrated by the Drazians' ruling class."

Domini smiled. "I am very happy to hear that. A great many people want you to step up, not just me. I'm confident that you will be a good leader."

"We'll see," Hope said. "Preaching common sense and faith is one thing; leading an army is another. But someone must lead, and it might as well be me."

A sound like a heavy bureau being dropped upstairs shook the house, followed by the bed shaking, lamps swinging, house joints squeaking, and a rumble that rolled through the ground. Domini held onto the bedframe to stay on her feet.

By the time Hope realized that the very Earth was in flux, the shaking and rumbling had stopped. She turned large, frightened eyes to Domini, then ran for the door outside. People milled about, confused and frightened. They did not know what the tremor was, yet they were completely shaken out of their wits. The confusion only mounted, because the Drazians failed to find a suitable response to the chaotic outcries of the Forgetters. This wave of shock turned into a signal for the rebellion.

It was indeed the moment when, miles away, Choice tasted the forbidden fruit and the secrets of life unraveled before him.

It was the exact same moment when Destiny, the mother of all humanity, found in the depths of that wretched lake the weapon to fight and destroy the monster of her fears.

✳ ✳ ✳

The design of God had worked as it had always been designed to work. The moment of destruction had come and passed, but it had not destroyed those who by His will were to be saved. Fate, and by the extension of his light, Destiny, Choice, and Hope, had prevailed in every possible dimension.

Hope, the face of the rebellion, had decided to come out of her shell, which she had hidden in since she had started to dwell in the Forget Lands. She had borne the prejudices of her fellow Forgetters and the shameful hatred of the Drazians. A major part of her life had been spent running away from two of the most mischievous souls ever to roam the universe—Time and Space—yet this had done nothing to erase her natural leadership abilities. In fact, her troubles and her tutelage from Fate had only honed them. Although she and Choice had gone through very different experiences, their skills and sensibilities as leaders complemented each other.

Choice was as aware of Hope's importance as Fate had been of Destiny's. As such, Choice had taken it upon himself to take care of her in every way. It was a journey that started when he first rescued her from the hands of Time and Space. Since then, he had neglected her only once and only out of concern for his mother. The core of their hearts was the same—it was the light of Fate; therefore, when Choice was activated after tasting the forbidden fruit, Hope was activated as well.

Since Hope had been assured, through some mysterious way, of the role she was bound to play in shaping the future of the Forget Lands, she decided to walk in a war with the previous dwellers of the Valley of Doubt, the Drazians. They, in turn, had decided to remain her enemy, for they were mistaken to believe that, had it not been for her, their long-desired rule over the Forget Lands would have remained unchallenged. It was rather foolish on their part to think that things were fine among the Forgetters regarding their rule. They were quite mistaken in that supposition. The Forgetters somehow hated the Drazians even more than the Drazians themselves ever dared to hate Hope.

With this new strength of conviction, Hope, followed by a huge army, challenged the appalling rule of the evil Drazians. The results of such a war were far from anybody's guess!

CHAPTER 67

WHILE THE WHOLE OF THE FORGET LANDS AND
the surrounding Forbidding Forest were humming with the excited sound
of war, the Archons were traveling back to their permanent abode. It was
a happy trip, for they completely believed Destiny and Choice to be irre-
trievably lost. Even Sonamrud was in a celebratory mood, so convinced
was he that mother and son had been mortally wounded. It was very easy
for him to believe that the plan was perfect, since it had been his. Like
many brilliant people, Sonamrud often fell victim to his own vanity.

Oblivious to what had occurred after leaving Choice, he was uncon-
cerned about the consequences of Choice's discovery of the truth. Instead,
he moved on to other topics to ponder, particularly the topic of Dhumanos.

The truth was that he could not drop the single thought that had been
circling his mind ever since he had made a discovery about Dhumanos.
Sonamrud could not stop thinking that Dhumanos was indeed the First
Fallen Angel, the notorious one, the Devil!

At first, he was most upset that he could have been blind to a truth that
danced naked right in front of his eyes. Then another thought occurred to
him—if the true nature of Dhumanos was revealed to the Forgetters, they
would surely refuse to allow him to rule over them.

Sonamrud was preoccupied with these thoughts as the Archons traveled toward their destination. Even when Dhumanos tried to consult him
about what he assumed to be the situation in the Forget Lands, Sonamrud

failed to produce any satisfactory answer. He could not bring himself to board that train of thought when he had in his sight a path paved from much more promising and interesting notions.

Although Sonamrud's strange behavior greatly alarmed Dhumanos, he decided not to dwell on it too much. He had always known that Sonamrud was as eccentric as he was brilliant; besides, Dhumanos could not contemplate, not even for a second, that this faithful servant had figured out his deepest, darkest secret. What would have been even more absurd to Dhumanos was that Sonamrud was planning to overthrow him.

Sonamrud was aware that the Forgetters were planning an uprising against the Drazians. He had come to this conclusion partially from his own understanding and partially from Time and Space. Now he planned to use it against Dhumanos by telling the people that the war and all their misfortunes since the beginning of time were punishment for Dhumanos's disobedience of the Lord and for bearing the responsibility for the ancient Fall. Before making this announcement, however, Sonamrud wanted to consult Time and Space, but they were nowhere to be found. Like the rest of the Archons, he did not know that the two had been trapped in the creek.

Such was the plan of the Lord, and such were the pictures that Fate had the fortune to see. The enemies were drowned in their own ignorance. They were removed far from the truth of the matter, also by the designs of their Lord.

Everywhere Fate looked, miraculous things were happening. On the banks of Forget Lake, Destiny was standing triumphant after conquering the fears that had overpowered her all her life. In Mimadamos, Choice had finally found the truth and had simultaneously defeated Time and Space. In the Forget Lands, Hope and her supporters were preparing to face their enemy. The Archons were moving toward the Forget Lands, and Fate was sitting on his high chair in Demire, smiling and waiting for the process of Awakening, as triggered by Choice's actions, to be completed.

Although he was unencumbered by timetables, Fate knew that his life had always been moving toward the Awakening. He also knew that this event was crucial if he was to be reunited with Destiny. The Awakening would change many things and purge earth's darkest memories. He could not help smiling as a glimpse of the future kept presenting itself to him.

Fate was also pondering the inevitable changes to the geography of his home planet. The Awakening was bound to rouse the sleeping conscience of people; it would also be accompanied by the revival of the power of Trinity.

Long before the concepts of vice and virtue were developed, there existed a greater concept of Trinity, a three-cornered concept. It represented the concept of the Awakening. In fact, Trinity was the face of the Awakening. Fate knew that a few events still needed to transpire before the process could be completed, but he had no doubt that it had been stimulated. He was aware of the space formed that had trapped Time and Space. However, there was still some time in the formation of the desired triangle.

* * *

It took Choice quite some time to gain enough consciousness to make sound decisions concerning his next moves. The first thought that came to his mind was of his mother. He was not as alarmed as he was supposed to be, considering how he had once dreamed about her jumping into the same lake to which she had run away now. The reason behind his considerably calm demeanor was his superior knowledge.

On one hand, his comprehensive dream had allowed him to peek into the treasure of past knowledge, but on the other hand, the taste of the blessed fruit from the historic apple tree had bestowed on him mysterious intuitive powers. Therefore, his intuition had satisfied him that his mother was safe. In fact, he had reason to believe that she was a little more than safe, for he could picture her smiling.

However, he knew that she was still near the lake. Despite being safe for now, there was no guarantee that she would continue to remain so, especially since he knew that the Archons were returning to their abode. Thus, he decided to pursue his mother. He replenished his energy levels and hurried to meet her.

* * *

Refreshed by the taste of victory, Destiny was set to put an end to all the acts of cruelty that had been directed toward her. She was neither diffident nor vain, as once she had drowned deep in the two opposing emotions.

Rather, she was confident and a little furious to have been so ill used by the Archons and their deceiving partners in crime, Time and Space.

She decided to sit on a stone near the lake, which was not as silent as usual. Ripples were forming on its surface, perhaps because of the activities of beings beneath it. Destiny hugged herself tightly. Until that moment, she had not realized that the wind had turned into icy edges, which felt sharper than the sword she had used on the monster. The splinters of her broken sword were still scattered on the rocks nearby, and so were the disturbing remains of the monster itself.

Although she thought that the best option for her was to move away from the lake as soon as possible, something stopped her. She felt that remaining at her place would bring Choice back to her. Even though she was now free from the guilt concerning her family, which had been her continuous companion, there still resided in her bosom a desire to be united with the people who meant the world to her.

Undecided as she was about her future moves and warmed by the feeling of her loved ones, Destiny did not realize that she was losing her way from the conscious world to the palace of her dreams. It was her first dream after being liberated from the abominable influences of Time, Space, and the Archons.

Surprisingly, her dream was set exactly at the same time and place where she was lying as she slept. In her dream, she was not sleeping. She seemed to be waiting for someone, perhaps her son. Soon, a little figure emerged from behind the trees, and she knew that it was not Choice.

She strained to recognize the visitor and was surprised to see a little girl coming her way. She had almost made up her mind that she had never seen her when the girl spoke as if she had known her all her life. Destiny realized that she must have met her somewhere in this life or another; she was not sure, though.

The girl addressed her very respectfully and bestowed her with gracious praises that Destiny was not sure she deserved. The girl finally stated her reason for visiting: she wanted her help. This earnest request for assistance rather amazed Destiny for, according to the girl's account, there was a war going on. What amazed Destiny even more was that this little girl was the leader of one side! Destiny could not feel hopeful for her side, but as the girl spoke, she found her to be very sensible and sharp. She also possessed a great quality that Destiny had particularly found herself lacking: pure, bold hope. The girl was hopeful about the prospect of their winning. In fact, she sounded hopeful about every prospect of life.

Destiny envied the little girl's great virtue.

They ventured into a long debate, discussing the pros and cons of a rebellion. It was not exactly a war but an uprising, the girl explained. Destiny was more concerned about what her role could be and how she was supposed to make any difference in the present condition. After much reflection and debate, Destiny accepted the offer.

The Destiny in the dream was much more affected by the pleasant manners and sensible talk of the girl than she had been impressed by the cause the girl was advocating. In Destiny's eyes, both sides were full of flaws. Observing the little girl closely, Destiny remembered meeting her at the same spot where they were now talking. Although she was still not sure if it was real or a dream, she knew she had seen the girl's face. She also realized that just before meeting the girl, the worthiest of humankind had purified her of her sins.

At last, Destiny smiled at the little girl, and the dream ended. Even though she continued to sleep, a few miles away, the girl of her dream, who was now a young lady, woke up.

＊＊＊

Hope's body was chilled as if she had been sitting outdoors for an hour or two. She was extremely surprised. After reflecting on what had passed in her dream, she could not help but smile at the strange ways nature worked. She knew she had met her mentor. She also knew that Destiny, the greatest of all women, would be coming to meet her soon. The joy she felt surpassed every emotion she might have ever felt.

CHAPTER 68

WHEN DESTINY FINALLY WOKE, THE SUN WAS right overhead. She was unsure of how long she had been sleeping, even though the support of a surprisingly soft tree trunk had been as agreeable a resting place as anyone could hope for in such a situation as hers. She stood up, and the aches in her body revealed their presence.

Soon she was famished. She decided to enter the forest to find something to eat, but something startled her. It was a huge bird flying over her head. She looked up, and her shock at seeing such a huge bird turned into ecstatic delight. The bird was not a solitary one but held a rider: her own son, Choice!

He waved to her from above and glided to a landing in front of her. She couldn't believe her eyes that it was her Choice standing right before her. She cupped his face in her hands to make sure that what she was seeing was real and not another one of her dreams. She then pulled him toward her and they embraced tightly; next he smiled and pulled out some food. They ate in silence, since they were very hungry, but Destiny's eyes remained firmly on her son as though he might disappear again.

He found her looking and smiled at her, and Destiny was deeply relieved to find not even a hint of reproach. The two had much to catch up on, but there was no time to waste. Destiny told him about the dream she'd just had as the two flew toward the Forget Lands. They arrived to find that the fighting had already begun.

Her angel from the dream was fighting with the Forgetters and one faction of Drazians beside her, as Destiny had related in the dream, but Destiny also saw Archons fighting on the girl's side. It was all very strange, and she was amazed to see that all these forces were against the majority of Drazians, who seemed to be losing the battle. She confided in her son that there was no way they could fight for the Archons and related to him the extent of their villainy.

Choice was aware of the situation. Using his sharp eye, he singled out the little figure of Hope fighting three Drazians at a time.

He mounted his bird and asked his mother to wait for him. He flew above the fighters and stopped near Hope. "Get on," he ordered.

Hope scrambled onto the bird behind him and held on, and he carried her away from the fight.

Nobody noticed his action except a shrewd Archon gliding above the fighters; Sonamrud had evidently decided not to participate in the fighting.

Choice directed the bird to land near his mother. It was high time for the three of them to talk face to face about the events that had caused them so much distress.

The two of them, mother and son, faced the girl, two against one. Choice scowled in confusion. "Hope—how could you fight alongside Drazians and Archons? What is going on?"

Since it was too much for Hope's nerves, a tear or two of pure vexation escaped her.

Both Choice and Destiny looked at her tenderly. Choice felt a wave of guilt pass over him. "I'm sorry if I sounded harsh."

She waved it away. "The pressure on my nerves has done its trick finally."

Choice felt rather strange to see Hope looking hopeless. He could not help but remember his own time of agony when he could not make a sane choice. He also knew that many other people had suffered only because of a certain hesitancy on his part. He pulled her into a hug. This resulted in more tears and sobbing, furthering Choice's discomfort and guilt. Hope clung to him, leaning into his arms.

Destiny instructed, in a soothing, motherish tone, "Take a breath. That's right. Nice, deep breath in – and let it out. There. Do it again. You're all right, dear. We love you and want to hear your side of things. When you're ready."

It took Hope a few moments to regain her composure, but soon she was her normal, confident self. Her audience waited in anticipation of what she was about to relate.

Before narrating her side of the story, she needed to do one more thing. She stood and kissed Destiny's hands, which surprised the latter very much, but she did not object. Hope's eyes glimmered brighter than the most sparkling jewels Destiny had ever possessed. She knew that it was a very uncommon sight for a person's eyes to shine in such a manner just because of you, especially when the person happened to be a stranger. However, Destiny did not consider Hope to be a stranger; somehow, she found her to be as familiar as if she were a part of herself. All these thoughts were moving in Destiny's mind, but she decided not to bother with them. Instead, she smiled at the young lady sitting in front of her with a humble expression.

Encouraged by Choice's soft tones and Destiny's amiable conduct toward her, Hope began her story. She started it with a dream that she'd had only twenty-four hours before. She was astonished to think that so much had happened in such a short period. As she described the details of her dream, an exclamation of surprise escaped Destiny, as she realized that she'd had the same dream herself.

"Nature works in mysterious ways. I think it was all part of our fates," commented Choice on hearing the extraordinary coincidence.

Both women agreed, and Hope resumed her story. Right after she had the dream, Drazians who believed in her and Forgetters on her side told her to engage in a war against their oppressors. Although she was reluctant to do so immediately, since she was inclined to wait for Destiny's arrival, which she was sure would happen soon, the situation was not completely in her control anymore. She was almost forced to make the decision.

"How did the rebellion go?" asked Choice.

She replied that it had gone quite well until the Archons' arrival disturbed them.

"Have these beasts forced you to do things for them without your consent?" asked Destiny with feeling. These villains had stung her so deeply that it was impossible for her to utter a single word without thinking of the misfortunes she'd suffered at their hands.

"Not exactly," replied Hope.

This answer conjured up confused looks on the faces of her well-wishers, and she was inclined to explain further. She told them that at the Archons' arrival, the Drazians had become quite comfortable and confident, while the Forgetters felt guilty for defying the orders of their true leaders. More than half of the Archons who claimed allegiance to some man named Sonamrud decided to take the side of the rebels and considered their cause just. By the time the Forgetters informed her about this new development, she was so deeply involved in the fight that there was no chance for her to return.

"However, it turned out to be a severe blow for the Drazians, who lost their moral support. Their newfound spirits shattered so badly that there was no chance of their returning to the fight with strength equal to our side," added Hope.

"Does this mean that you'll be fighting on the Archons' side for now?" asked Choice, his mouth hanging open.

"Of course not!" exclaimed Hope furiously, her face turning a deep red. Attempting to regain her composure, she added, "I mean, I was aware of their evil since the start. In fact, I faced almost all my life's misfortunes because of them, even when, unlike the Drazians, they had no personal animosity toward me. The only reason I was still fighting was that I could not pull back safely from the battleground. Had it not been for you on that giant bird, there was no way I could get away from the fight without losing much of my physical vigor."

"Sorry for misunderstanding you again," Choice said as he hung his head, ashamed at addressing her in a harsh tone.

Hope acknowledged him but with a certain air of indifference. Choice felt a pang of disappointment at her behavior. He opened his mouth to reprimand her, but Destiny interrupted him.

"Do not bicker for no reason, children, as there is no way you can afford that." She asked, "How about we let the two evil forces fight on their own without interfering?"

"Sounds like a good idea to me," said Hope, who sagged on her feet, clearly tired of fighting.

Choice was not sure. He knew that it was not in the placid nature of his mother to sit still when there was an evil force to be defeated, and there was no question of it when there were two such forces. He wondered why she had advised this.

His curiosity was soon answered when his mother added, "Let one win over the other, and then we will take care of the victor."

Choice could not help but smile.

The audience of three kept watching the fight from a distance, only commenting once after several minutes. Then something happened that made all three breathless.

Suddenly, the good Drazians felt the absence of Hope and stopped fighting. Soon, the Forgetters followed suit; in a few minutes, the Archons secretly lead by Sonamrud realized that they were the only ones retaliating against the ordinary Drazians. Meanwhile, Sonamrud was still floating high above them, observing the developments keenly.

"Cease fire! Cease hostilities!" was called out across the remaining scuffles scattered at the edges of the field. The Archons asked their comrades, "Why this lack of participation?"

"There is no way for us to fight when our leader has abandoned us," the comrades replied.

Hope was amazed to hear their insolent answer to the Archons, whom they had considered their masters all their lives.

Dhumanos, who had just arrived few minutes earlier, puffed himself up and frowned, face red at hearing such words. For the first time in his life, instead of giving way to his anger, he decided to act coolly. "Your leader would never leave you, and I am always by your side. Who commanded you to fight this battle to begin with?"

His so-called comrades said, "Sonamrud did! But neither you nor he is our leader anymore. Our true leader is Hope, and it is impossible for us to function without any hope. Hope is the face of this rebellion, and it means betraying her if we listen to anyone except her."

Dhumanos couldn't hide his shock upon hearing Sonamrud's name. It was clear to any spectator that he had been hoping for a different answer than the one he had received. Without warning, he lost his temper. "Destroy them!" He pointed toward a few of the good Drazians. "Banish this rabble!" He waved at the Forgetters.

What he did not realize was that in his absence, he had lost authority over his people. They were no longer blindly obedient to him. Since Dhumanos had always been a dictator, he did not know how to take no for an answer. He took the hesitancy of his people in such a way that only aggravated the situation and resulted in a complete rebellion against him from their side as well. Despite the uprising from his subjects, there was still a chance that he would be forgiven at the end of the war if not for Sonamrud's intervention.

Before Dhumanos could make any further remarks about the disobedience he was being subjected to, Sonamrud yelled, *"Harath!"* in a voice so loud that it was carried across the entire battlefield.

Choice gasped. Among the many teachings of his tutors and History and the books he had consumed on his own in his library in Mimadamos was a listing of terms from dead languages, one of them the language Forgetters used to use when first they forgot and lost their way in the Forget Lands.

The word that had such a strong impact on Choice was Dhumanos's old name, his real name, his darkest secret, his title earned because of his single deed that had turned him into what he had now become: the First Fallen Angel.

Choice raised his voice to address the confused crowd. *"Harath,* derived from the word *Heerath,* meaning *doubt* and *confusion."* He then uttered a single word that blemished Dhumanos's name forever. "Among you Forgetters, *Harath* is the ancient name for the Devil."

There was no way to turn back time and undo what had been done. The second Choice uttered the word, a silence fell over the crowd; it was even eerier than the noise of battle. The accusatory finger pointing toward Dhumanos was somehow more damning than the words themselves. When another Archon, trusted by both Sonamrud and Dhumanos, hurled obscenities at their leader, the crowd erupted into anger.

It was apparent that, although most people considered Dhumanos evil, they had not known the extent of his wickedness. Even now, the people didn't know the weight of the accusation. They started moving away from the man they had once revered.

Although Dhumanos had manipulated the concept of original sin for centuries to give the idea that it had been the doing of Eve, or Destiny, legends still taught that the Devil, or Harath, was the one who had awakened the energy of sin in Eden and had caused all the diseases and misfortunes in the world since the beginning of time.

The Forgetters had always cursed Destiny for anything they found imperfect in the world and their lives, yet they found themselves often aware that it was Harath who had influenced the first act of sin. Eating the forbidden fruit was by no means the original sin. It was simply a manifestation of the plans of someone far more evil than this act. The original sin was the disobedience of the Lord that the Devil had committed by not accepting the choice of the Father of all Fathers in revealing himself through Adam and the frail Adamic mold. That was the first sin and the mother of all sins.

All sinners need someone to blame for their faults, and the Forgetters had been accustomed to blaming their sins on Destiny. As they studied the pedigrees of sinners, they concluded that the one who could be unanimously considered the originator of all vice was the First Fallen Angel, Harath.

Dhumanos stood there, watching everyone turn against him. He had often had nightmares about this moment when he would be exposed. He beheld the eyes of more people than he had ever seen in his life carrying hatred of such extreme intensity that he could not even imagine its magnitude.

Before he could think straight, a noise started echoing inside his head, "Head on to your eternal damnation! You are the fall that serves every rise unwillingly. No matter how much you try to manipulate destinations, cripple man's power to choose, and run away from Fate, in every action that you take to rise, a fall will be disguised for you."

He knew perfectly well that, in his attempts to ensure that Adam and his spouse eternal strayed from the truth, he had only paved complex paths leading to his own downfall. It was as if Genesis was the ending and all that came after was merely a translation of it. He had thought he was progressing away from that moment, when he had been regressing toward it like a translation tied by the original meaning. All his efforts had been intended to put the people of a straight path on his uneven path, but the only thing he had succeeded in was increasing the thorns lying in his way. With every scheme he had made, he had only sharpened the edges of those blades.

All the time, he had chosen to blame Fate and the Creator for his losses and defeat, but he was responsible for his own misfortunes. He had attempted to cast himself apart from the Edenic equation. He had tried to take revenge on Fate through Destiny, when he was dependent on her for his survival. In his attempts to gain control over the divine equation, he had distanced himself from it, but he had succeeded only in removing himself from the meaning in a behavioral sense while remaining there in the real sense, which he had no control over. He had become meaningless, trapped inside a translation. He had not only failed in his ambition to exclude himself from the Edenic equation, but he had also exhausted his true significance without even admitting to the disastrous consequences of his choices.

Like all other beings, Dhumanos had only performed the role God had chosen for him. It was God and not Dhumanos who had escorted Adam outside of Eden. Dhumanos's ego had led him to believe that he controlled the Fall and that he was responsible for it. There was not a grain of truth in the belief. He had only played the hero role inside the script of all scripts, which was written by no one but Fate. The ultimate truth was that the Lord wanted Fate to fall into Space and Time so that he could fully rejoice in the meaning of the gift He had granted him, which was rising to Eternity.

Dhumanos saw that even his faithful Archons were receding from him. He could not understand how Sonamrud had discovered his secret. Then he remembered his own foolishness, how he had been obsessed with the apple tree outside Destiny's house in Mimadamos. He knew that the exceptionally shrewd Sonamrud would have guessed it from his obsession. Besides, Dhumanos remembered that Sonamrud had been a learned scholar. The wretched genius must have grasped the striking resemblance between Dhumanos and the pictures of the Fallen Angel depicted in the ancient books of knowledge.

Dhumanos had no other option but to curse himself for the ego that had blinded him, leading him to believe that his code was unbreakable. He looked around to find at least one person who would be holding him with awe in his eyes, but there was no such person. Each man in the crowd was looking at him with extreme hatred. Their fear of him was also subsiding with every passing minute, and Dhumanos was not dumb enough to think that they would spare him.

He thought, *They have no idea about my hidden powers*. Yet, of course, there was no way he could overpower so many people on his own. He envisioned Destiny and focused on her eyes as he decided to muster whatever he could from the power left in him and vanish from there. He glanced at Sonamrud for the last time to see if he could reach him before departing, but there was no way it was possible, since Sonamrud was high above him. Dhumanos knew that Sonamrud had planned the moment, and it was not a coincidence that he was stationed at an unreachable place. He gritted his teeth, cursed Sonamrud, and threw a flash of energy around, taking down about a hundred people as he vanished from the surface of the Forget Lands.

As Dhumanos vanished, a vacuum effect took place that caused Sonamrud to fatally crash to the ground. A large snap rent the air, and the other Archons looked around helplessly. It was not clear to them what had happened to Sonamrud; all they knew was that he was lying motionless. Clearly, Dhumanos had projected his nefarious power upon them. Panic ensued.

Chaos and turmoil spread in every direction after Dhumanos's disappearance. People were running here and there, cursing each other. Apparently, there was no war anymore since there were not two distinct sides. Dhumanos had equally damaged both sides, and the mutual pain of the two nations had turned animosity into unity.

Destiny, Hope, and Choice had witnessed every second of the ghastly scene in front of them with great curiosity. Destiny finally signaled Hope to venture out and help her people. She went to do that.

Destiny looked at her son, who seemed extremely angry. "Son, what is the reason behind your anger?"

"I'm going to follow Dhumanos and destroy him for good," said Choice.

Destiny was extremely puzzled by the answer. She looked at him in surprise. "You have tasted the forbidden fruit, and you know a lot of the secret. If this is the case, there is no way you can say something so foolish."

Choice realized that she was right. He had known that there was no need for him to do much anymore except to find Fate. His last steps were supposed to take him on a journey of union with both his parents. He clenched his fists in impotent rage. "I'm sorry. You are right, Mother."

They both knew that his impulsive reaction had flared because of his nature. He was the one who took action, and accepting the course of fate was somehow difficult for Choice.

Both mother and son stood there, witnessing the remains of the great war dying on its own with only minimal help but enormous sympathy and kind words from Hope. She was taking care of the damages of the war. She was doing what she was best at doing: being optimistic and helping others do so, too.

CHAPTER 69

FAR FROM THE VIOLENCE, FATE WITNESSED THE war with his usual indifference. The war, he knew, was but a minor part of something big that was about to happen.

The ultimate meaning of existence shone like sunlight through Fate's realm. Each numeric Object of Knowledge, be it physical or mental, be it an apple or a thought, that people encountered on a perceptual or a conceptual level, was brightly reflecting the one and only Selfhood that truly existed. The unity of Fate's Selfhood was expressed through the deceptive multiplicity of the many identities encountered and experienced in Destiny's realm. The numeric possibility that constituted the prospect of perceptual multiplicity was only a translation of the machination of this one higher Self that now appeared more vibrantly than ever. It was Fate's story at the end of the day. It was his way of making himself known to himself, and the nature of such knowledge entailed that there must exist a world of translation under: Destiny's world.

All the exhibitions of the multiplicity, no matter how authentic and true they were made out to be, were nothing more than a mere translation of a higher reality. All its forms depended on the core and originated to translate it. All its shades revealed nothing about itself but the one true color. The world, which was the realm of translation, however real it may have seemed was but a dream compared to Fate's reality. It was just a passing stage, but most dreamers had taken it to be a permanent abode.

All the laws of logic pointed toward one fact: the core was the important part, not any translation of it. Giving priority to scripts over code was often a major reason for the people's misfortunes. There would be no sense in attempting to maintain sight of the core if one was lost inside the machinations of the translation. Rather, the right way to reach the underlying truth was through identifying and negating the multiple deceptive facets of the translation. It was a difficult task, and only a few people could break this code, but it was the only way to recognize reality in the realm of Fate.

In the noisy humdrum of war and sensational activities on the part of the Archons, nobody heard the loud sound of the land shifting. The part of Forget Lake where Destiny had found and lost many things and where she had stayed more than once during her life had already started moving backward. It was merely giving space to Mimadamos so that it could move forward toward Demire. The Valley of Doubt had also started squeezing toward the crack where Time and Space were trapped. If viewed from above, it would be apparent that the geography of their land was converting into a triangle. For now, though, the transition was by no means complete. All that could be seen from above was an incomplete triangle with three corners: Demire, Mimadamos, and Destiny's Forget Lake.

There was one significant change in the very place they all had been fighting. Unbeknownst to the Archons and the Forgetters, the Forget Lands were slowly being trapped inside these three sides. The Valley of Doubt, which was the home of Drazians, was right in front of the secret creek of Time and Space.

Fate saw all of it clearly, almost as if he were watching a movie. He sighed deeply, knowing that he had to be patient and wait for the time when he would play his part. It was becoming difficult for him to wait for his reunion with Destiny and Choice, for they were the two missing pieces of the puzzle of his life. He remained persistent and allowed the light of the Father to travel at its own speed.

Destiny and Choice were positioned on an elevated area; from there, they were observing the scenes of the waning battle. Just as the Drazians lost their claim to the throne in the Forget Lands, an army of light was liberated that, until now, had been trapped inside their prisons. They were the Agents of Awakening! Destiny was extremely happy to see her beloved army. They were Fate's gift to her, and she could now feel him near her.

Chadi B. Ghaith

While she was admiring the Agents of Awakening, Choice was busy contemplating another scenario. As the war had reached its climax, the Forgetters and the Drazians were acting in a rather civil manner to each other, but someone had started talking about leadership. Choice had known the moment Dhumanos had flown away that this problem would eventually arise. However, as he had witnessed people's loyalty to Hope, he had been sure that they would choose her to be their leader. The situation turned out to be completely different. Domini, who had encouraged Hope to escape her imprisonment, was asked to rule the Forgetters and was supported by one of the Archons who had helped Sonamrud expose Dhumanos. Apparently, Domini had stolen energy from Hope, and somehow, her shine was noticeable among the dead crowd.

Choice wanted to avoid such an ending, but then he saw how happy Hope looked. He went to her. "You are the source of the power they are admiring. You should claim the leadership. Listen to them: they are calling upon your energy, not hers."

"I never wanted to be a leader, Choice." She crossed her arms. "You, of all people, should have known that. Do you not remember me being chased by Time and Space as if I were a damsel in distress?"

"It is all about perspective," he said, "for what I saw was a strong woman evading mischievous acts and remaining hopeful. Besides, the way I saw you killing three opponents in one attack, I am ready to accept you as my leader." He reached for her hands and held them after she uncurled her arms.

"Thank you very much for your excessive praise. I haven't forgotten how you helped me by sending forces to rescue me from the evil Drazians." She squeezed his fingers and looked up at him. "Yet, despite all your arguments, I think Domini deserves it much more, simply because she is as willing to do it as a machine is about to be turned on. Who would be a better leader, one who is reluctant or one who is ready?"

Choice had to drop the argument, since she was making sense. He simply replied, "All I know is that the one who deserves a charge never asks for it. If it makes you happy, let her be the Queen of the Forget Lands."

Hope only smiled in answer. She was happy to see her people liberated from the tyrannical rule of the Archons. She was still smiling when a loyal Drazian from her army approached her. He was looking distressed, which she found rather odd, for they had just won a war. He asked for permission to speak. Upon receiving it, he told her that she was required to be present urgently on the battlefield.

Mildly surprised—what could be so important?—she asked Choice for his leave and went with the Drazian.

As Choice was left to ponder, he absentmindedly fixed his eyes on the woman claiming to be the Queen of the Forget Lands. She was wearing a long robe, and Choice could not help noticing that it was too long for her rather short figure. Looking thus, he suddenly felt that the woman looked strangely familiar. He started walking toward her to have a better look, since he was unable to place her face, but her movements certainly reminded Choice of someone.

As he strode toward her, the woman suddenly looked in his direction. Their eyes met. The moment Choice looked into the eyes of Domini, a very recent memory flashed across his mind. He knew who this person was!

Domini realized that Choice had recognized her. Her face started fading, and the face of a man started emerging, a face Choice had wanted to see for so long. Yes, it was indeed none but Fate staring back at him. "Do you see me now, my son?"

Choice was mustering every bit of power to remain on his feet. He could not determine whether this moment was a dream or a reality.

Fate turned to the crowd and addressed them with a voice like thunder. "To whom belongs the kingdom today and every day?"

The crowd replied in one voice as if in a trance. "To you, our Lord."

Not quite able to believe what he was seeing, Choice approached Fate and tentatively reached out to touch him. As he did, he saw himself back in the garden of Mimadamos, standing beneath the apple tree. His hand was stretched toward the one mystical red apple hanging from the branch.

As he touched it, he looked around in astonishment and saw the tree was no longer in the garden of his childhood, but in the middle of the battlefield! Wide-eyed, he turned to his father and saw Fate grinning at him with something like amusement.

Of course, he's smiling, Choice thought, *he knows the ending. For me, it is a whole new beginning, a new world I helped create.*

✒ **END** ✒

Made in the USA
Coppell, TX
20 April 2020

19624151R00194